I0761881

THUNDER'S KEEPER

A NOVEL

ADAM SMITH

LINVILLE PRESS

Linville Press, LLC
Birmingham, AL

This book is a work of fiction. Names, characters, places, and incidents either are products of the author's imagination or are used fictitiously. Any resemblance to actual events or locales or persons, living or dead, is entirely coincidental.

communications@linvillepress.com

www.linvillepress.com

First Linville Press hardcover edition 2015

Jacket Design: Linville Press, LLC
Interior Layout and Design: Linville Press, LLC

Manufactured in the United States of America

ISBN 978-0-9963300-0-8

Thunder's Keeper

To my wife Shellie
For believing in me even before I did.
Always.

Thoughts Before We Get Started...

This book began as most do, I suppose, as a few sentences scribbled in the back of a spiral notebook back in 2001. At that time I was working on an equity trading desk handling stock and bond orders and cranking out a paragraph or two as time allowed.

I distinctly remember being midway into chapter three on September 11, 2001 when I looked up at the TV screen to see the second plane hit The World Trade Center. It was hard for me to write anything after that for quite a while – writing a fictional story with an evil character in it did not appeal to me at all after I had witnessed true evil play out on live TV. I didn't pick the story up again until two years later at the urging of my friend, Bobby Morris.

It became something fun – something to pass the time as I wrote and got immediate feedback from the guys (and gal) on the desk. It was finished a few months later, and I was content with that. It sat in a binder on my shelf for over a decade gathering dust until my wife Shellie urged me to get it published. A new journey began.

Rewriting a novel is not the glamorous experience some may think it is. It's exhausting, frustrating, and downright tedious. But support from family and friends goes a long, long way. That said, I want to say "thank you" to some special people who helped me along the way, be it with encouragement, critical feedback, editing, or just plain patience. You guys helped me make this happen.

And, Shellie ... Book's done. I'm coming to bed now.

Special Thanks:

Bobby Morris
Joe Kervin Wendy
Knight Christopher
Brooks

CHAPTER ONE

-1-

The terror had returned. Just as it had each night for weeks. Only hours before, when Brig Bailey laid his head upon his pillow, part of him knew it would come again – *the bad thing* – the thing that had plagued his subconscious for so many years – the thing that, despite his attempts to escape, kept sucking him back in. Back there. Back to Jones Chapel.

It was a small Kentucky town, back-dropped by a canvas of rolling hills. A wide spot on the highway leading to Mammoth Cave, it was a town where people still left their doors unlocked at night, the occasional stranger was greeted with suspicion, and town gossip was the preferred news source.

Sleepy rural towns have secrets, and country folks know how to keep them better than most. The summer of 1978 was no exception as the body count had been disproportionately high that year. But just as the townsfolk had always done, they gathered, they prayed, and they buried their dead along with their secrets so that life could continue on for better or for worse.

It was here – *then* – that Brig returned night after night to relive his mind's version of a tragedy he was incapable of changing. Brig's nightmare had been recurring with escalating frequency, despite the twenty-two years that had passed since his brother Jacob's death. The gradual passage of time had done little to erode the memory of skipping rocks across the surface of Barren Lake that stifling summer day.

Brig was twelve that summer and filled with all the energy and stamina twelve-year-olds possess. His brother Jacob was the age he would forever be; he had died when he was only nine years old. The two boys stood on the banks of the lake laughing, skipping rocks, and counting each skip together in cadence. Each took a turn trying to outdo the other.

Just as he had done so many times before, and helpless to alter the course of events, Brig left his brother waiting on the bank while he searched for more rocks. Walking back a few minutes later, a strange sense of déjà vu twisted in his stomach. Foul fumes of dread hung in the air, pungent and palpable. That's when it came. Brig, powerless to scream, looked towards a heavy *whooshing* sound high above as a strange scaled creature swooped from the sky. Jacob stood alone on the bank, unaware and vulnerable. Brig opened his mouth, but no words came – they never did and tonight was to be no different.

The creature plunged from above, snatching Jacob in its talons. Brig raced along the rocky shoreline, straining his voice as he screamed his brother's name. Jacob's little body writhed and twisted in the creature's grasp. His desperate cries for help fell upon Brig's ears, who could only stand and watch as unspeakable horror consumed his brother.

Brig sat up with a gasp. Thinking himself awake, he rubbed his face only to remove his hands and find himself on a flat expanse of swirling desert sand. Three pock-marked moons hung in a gloomy purple sky as a fourth set on the far horizon. Silhouetted in the light of the setting moon was the unmistakable shape of a cross with a body hanging on it.

This part of the dream was new, and Brig's mind zoomed in for a closer look. Whistles of wind whipped by, seemingly amplified in the absence of any other sound. Closer now, Brig saw the male body was naked, save a ragged, purple cloth wrapped around its waist flapping in the hot, fetid breeze. Orange moonlight washed over the figure, making him appear almost alien.

Brig moved closer still, desperately wanting – *needing* – to look upon the man's face, obscured in somber black shadows. The sounds of the wind were joined by creaking wood fibers and the steady *flap flap flap* of the cloth. Two ravens lighted on the horizontal cross piece and began pecking at the body before a thunderclap tore across the sky, sending the birds on their way cawing their complaints.

Startled, Brig jumped back as the man lifted his head to reveal a face bruised and bloody from what must have been a merciless beating. His eyes were puffy and red with hair clumped and matted in crusty scabs across his forehead. Brig's hand went to his mouth to stifle a scream as he realized the man on the cross was himself.

The crucified Brig spoke in a parched and raspy voice: *"Malocere ..."*

-2-

The telephone rang, jolting Brig into the waking world. Buster, his brown Labrador retriever, lay at the foot of the bed, raising one ear and cocking his head with an impatient whine. Brig covered his head with a pillow, shielding his eyes from a sea of painful sunlight. On the nightstand beside him sat a clock that told him it was only 7:20.

He reached for the receiver, knocking over a large bottle of ibuprofen and a cup of water he had used to chase down four tablets the night before. The cup hit the carpet with a thud and a splash just as he managed to get the handset to his ear.

"This had better be good..."

The voice on the other end belonged to his ex-wife, Erin. "Good morning to you, too ..."

Brig set the cup upright and used a dirty sock that had been lying on the floor to soak up what he could. "Mornin', babe. How are you?"

"I told you to stop calling me that," Erin said in a low voice.

Brig laughed, tossing the sock away without looking. Buster watched it move through the air, but made no attempt to fetch. It was too early in the morning to fight. The hangover Brig had awoken to was enough and it throbbed behind his eyes. "I know," he said, "old habits die hard, right? What's up?"

After a brief pause, Erin continued. "I don't mean to be short. Kaitlyn has had me up since four a.m. I'm tired. I'm cranky. I just want to go back to sleep."

"Is she sick?"

"No, she had another one of those dreams about your mother last night, and she's been hounding me to call you all morning. I waited as long as I could. I know you sleep late."

A year had passed since his and Erin's divorce was finalized. It had been a difficult time for all of them. Until recently, Kaitlyn seemed to have been taking the adjustment well. Far better than Brig.

Erin had gotten remarried only a few months after the divorce - a union Brig still vehemently opposed. He hated the thought of another man raising his daughter. It made him feel impotent and insecure. He'd badgered Erin a great deal with regard to her motives, accusing her of making a desperate move while she was on the rebound. His insinuation only steeled her resolve.

Kaitlyn now lived in Havens Fork, Kentucky with her mother where Erin and Brig had first met as college students. Brig made the drive to pick his daughter up when there were no other options, but he preferred to make the handoff in Nashville. Havens Fork was only thirty miles south of Jones Chapel, and the familiar sights brought back too many painful memories - not to mention the anxiety attacks.

Brig had been back home only once since he'd moved to New York in 1987, and that had been for his mother's funeral a year ago. Those were sad times. He knew the right thing to do was to stay with his father and help him through the grief, but in the end, Brig had left after only three days and hadn't been back since. He still spoke with his father quite often by phone, and there was an unspoken understanding between them with respect to the visits.

In the background, Brig heard Kaitlyn jumping up and down insisting, *"I wanna talk to Daddy!"*

Erin told him, "I'm going to put Kaitlyn on, okay?"

"Absolutely." Brig said, "Put her on."

A loud bang followed as the receiver hit Erin's kitchen floor. Muffled breathing followed as Kaitlyn put the telephone to her face. Erin prodded her - "Go on, talk to daddy!"

A small voice broke the silence: "Hello? Daddy?" Across the span of miles, Brig heard the faint shuffle of pajama-clad feet, and he pictured her standing there in her favorite pajamas with blonde hair standing on end.

"Hey!" he said. "How's my Kait-Kait?"

"Fine, fine. Kait's fine," she said. "How are you?"

"Daddy's fine, but Mommy tells me you had a dream. Do you want to tell me what it was about?"

Without hesitation, Kaitlyn blurted out, "Nanna came to see me!"

Brig's heart sank in his chest. The day his mother had died, he and Erin broke the news to Kaitlyn by telling her that her Nanna had "Gone to heaven." It came as no real surprise when the then-five-year-old hadn't understood, so they opted for "Nanna went to sleep," as an alternative explanation. Looking back, it probably wasn't the best choice. They both had failed at communicating the finality of death.

Although he and Erin had never spoken of the subject at any great length, they were on the same page in that they both believed Kaitlyn's frequent dreams were her mind's way of dealing with the loss of a loved one. We all deal with things in different ways, and he saw no harm in indulging her fantasies if they brought her a peace he had yet to find.

"She came to see you?" he asked. "That's special, Kait. She loves you a lot."

"Uh-huh," Kaitlyn confirmed. "She came down from heaven to see me!"

"Well, what did she say?"

"She said she loves me and misses me! She told me it's my turn to take care of *you*, daddy."

Brig laughed and said, "Yeah, somebody needs to take care of ole dad." He sat up in bed and swung his legs over the side, smacking his big toe on the nightstand mid-way through the motion, gritting his teeth just as he set his foot down on the patch of soggy carpet, soaking his socks to the skin.

He shouted, "Son-of-a-*BITCH*!"

To his horror, Kaitlyn giggled and parroted his words: "Sumbitch!"

Erin's voice boomed, "Kaitlyn Bailey!!! What did you say???"

"Daddy said 'Sumbitch!'" the little girl replied in a 'thank-you-very-much' tone.

Life as a bachelor allowed for precious little time to develop a good filter, and Brig had grown far too accustomed to saying whatever came to mind. In no mood for another one of Erin's lectures for cursing around his daughter, he tried his hand at a little damage control. "Tell Mommy I'm sorry."

Kaitlyn relayed the message: "Daddy said he's sorry!" She paused briefly before speaking again. "Daddy, Nanna said a bad man wants to hurt us. She said he's 'bad news!'"

Brig's response was weak: "It was just a dream."

Kaitlyn silently debated this. "Are you sure?" she asked.

With a great deal more conviction, Brig said, "Of course! Your daddy would never let anyone hurt you!" More than anything else, he wanted his daughter to believe in him. He wanted her to believe that so long as he was alive, she needn't fear the monsters that prowled among the dark corners of her room after the lights went out at night.

She seemed content with his answer. "I love you, daddy," she said. Her soft voice washed over him. She was his world, and he missed her so much it hurt.

"Daddy?" Kaitlyn said as she tried to recapture his attention. "Daddy are you there?"

"Yeah, honey. I'm here."

"How's Busser?"

"Buster's fine," he said. The dog stood up at the sound of his name, but lay back down with apparent indifference. "Fat and lazy as ever!"

The little girl giggled and said, "Busser's a lazy ol' dog!"

"Yeah, he sure is. A Bailey to the bone!"

They talked a while longer, the flow of dialogue changing direction several times. These conversations had no structure whatsoever, which was one thing Brig loved about talking with his daughter most. Trying to have an intelligent conversation with a near-six-year-old was about as useless as it was entertaining.

Erin's voice rose once again, "Tell daddy bye-bye!"

Kaitlyn tried to resist, but soon resigned with the understanding that she wasn't going to win. She blew a kiss into the receiver and said, "Love you, daddy! Bye-bye."

Brig blew a kiss in return. "I love you too, Kaitlyn!" Lonesome dead air followed the click on the other end. He sat on the edge of the bed a while longer, holding the receiver and thinking about his dream – trying desperately to recall elements of the new addition that were quickly fading from memory. Without trying, his thoughts drifted back to the summer of 1978.

-3-

It was the summer following Jacob's third year of grammar school. Brig had just completed the fifth grade, and the two were inseparable. There wasn't much to do in Jones Chapel back then, but the boys had managed to keep themselves occupied on the family's farm. They spent many afternoons exploring and fishing in several small ponds dotting the property.

Jacob Bailey was a good kid – cute as a button, with blue eyes and sandy blonde hair. As long as Brig could remember, there had always been something different about his brother, though. It was something with the way he stared off into space as though he were looking into a world no one else could see. Their mother had often said he was "an old soul."

A month before his death, Jacob's nightmares had begun to haunt him. Many mornings, Brig awoke to find his brother in bed with him. At first the whole thing seemed silly, and Brig complained as all kid's do when a sibling invades their personal space. But as time drew on and the nightmares increased in both frequency and severity, Brig's irritation turned to concern and his protective nature emerged.

The night before Jacob's death, Brig was roused from a deep sleep as his brother dove into bed with him and hid beneath the covers, trembling. Brig yanked the blanket back and asked, "What's wrong?!" Jacob was on the verge of tears; he stuttered, trying his best to describe something his limited vocabulary just wouldn't allow.

He finally got his breathing under control and said, "It's back! The thing in my room..." as he pointed across the hallway. "It tried to get me!" His hands had made exaggerated gestures as he spoke. Jacob huddled back under the covers, pulling them over his nose, exposing only his eyes. "I'm scared!" he said.

Brig attempted to comfort him in much the same way he would try and comfort Kaitlyn years later. "It's okay," he said. "I'm here, Jake. It was just a dream."

Jacob gritted his teeth and said, "NO! It was *real*! You've never believed me. I'm telling you, something's in my room!" He held out his arm, displaying three scratches across his bicep. "Is *this* my imagination, too?"

Brig touched the scratches and Jacob withdrew, hissing at the sting. "Jake," he said. "We have to show mom."

"No." Jacob said. "Mom can't know. I shouldn't have told you." From across the hall came a sound, and in the darkness, something moved. Jacob then found what passed as strength and he turned to Brig with tears in his eyes. "He only wants me."

Jacob cried himself to sleep that night, but Brig stayed awake – unable to decide if he had actually seen what he thought he had seen across the hallway. In the end, he decided he hadn't and by morning, Jacob's scratches were gone.

At the breakfast table, their father discussed the day's chores. Brig's help was needed, and the boy dutifully agreed. Though he was a kind father, defying Gabe Bailey was ill-advised. The boys knew this, so a simple "Yessir" from Brig brought an abrupt end to the conversation.

"What about me, dad?" Jacob asked. "What can I do?"

Gabe stood and moved to the sink, placing his plate beside it. His son's nightmares were no secret, and Jacob's face was the picture of sleep deprivation. Gabe mussed up the hair on the boy's head and assured him there were jobs for him to do, but not today. "I think your mamma has plans for you, young man."

Their mother Rose, offered to take Jacob to nearby Barren Lake for a day of swimming. The boy jumped at the chance if for no other opportunity than to get out of the house. Rose would later recount the hours that followed with obsessive repetition for the remainder of her life as though re-telling the story might somehow bring her absolution.

According to her, they'd arrived at the lake an hour later. She and Jacob swam a bit and had attempted to make a sandcastle with questionable success. That day was a steamy one, and she soon tired from heat and activity. No sooner had she lay down on the sand to gather her strength than Jacob came running up the beach, clapping his hands to get her attention.

"Mommy!" he shouted, "Can I play on the float?" He hopped up and down, pointing to an old inner tube sitting on the nearby shore.

They were in a section of the lake which was clear of boat traffic, and since it was a weekday, there weren't any other swimmers in the area. Rose saw no harm in it; after all, Jacob was an excellent swimmer, thanks in no small part to his brother's coaching – something for which she was grateful. As a child, she had been terrified of the water and hadn't wanted her children to suffer from similar phobias.

She lay back on her blanket – the same one she would use to cover her son's body later that evening – and watched the clouds go by, blissfully unaware of the tragedy to come. Sleep crept upon her, and when she awoke a couple hours later, Jacob was nowhere in sight. The faint hope that he had wandered off on one of his impromptu exploration expeditions gradually faded as the tortuous minutes of searching passed.

She called the sheriff from a pay phone at the beach house, and the department responded with surprising speed. Hours later, a young, rookie deputy tried fruitlessly to calm her down. It was then a call came in from dispatch, reporting a boy's body had been found by a local fisherman. Strangely, the location given was five miles from where Jacob had last been seen.

The deputy helped Rose to the squad car and the two of them headed off toward their destination. It was the longest five miles the deputy would ever know. He drove on, patiently listening as Rose Bailey tried to convince herself that the body they were enroute to see was not her son's as she peered out the car window for any sign of him.

The police cruiser pulled into the address relayed by the dispatcher. Both the deputy and Rose saw the shape of a boy's body on the bank. The angler who had discovered it sat with his back turned, unable to look at it. Rose began screaming hysterically at the sight of the boy's blonde hair, now dry and blowing about in the cool, twilight breeze. She burst through the car door and ran over to Jacob's body. She wrapped him in her blanket, held him close, and cried.

That night, an unimaginable sense of loss hung over the Bailey house. Wails and sobs floated up to Brig's ears from the living room below. His attempts to block them out by covering his head with a pillow proved futile. He lay there, staring across the hall, just as he had the night before, into a door Jacob would never walk through again. The tender age of twelve is far too young to face mortality, but face it he had, and he started to cry.

The days leading up to the funeral were a blur as hundreds of people had come by the house to offer their condolences. In small southern towns, death brings with it a duty on others to descend upon the living bearing casseroles. Jacob Bailey's death was to be no exception. The kitchen table accumulated them one by one, but no one ate. Despite the generous abundance, Jacob's chair sat empty – a reminder of a void that could never again be filled.

The day of the funeral arrived, and Brig wore a dark suit, matching the one his brother wore inside the casket. The service was a particularly long one as the priest droned on and on about God working in mysterious ways, and that something good would come from this... the standard company line. For the first time in his life, Brig felt true contempt for God.

Back home that night, he climbed the stairs and went into Jacob's room. He sat in there for hours, sifting through his brother's toys. He tried to cry. He needed to cry. But the tears just didn't come.

Something happened after he'd fallen asleep on his brother's bed. Even now, twenty plus years later, he was unsure if it had all been a dream or not, but when he awoke, he'd forgotten for one blessed second that his brother was actually dead. He heard hollow footsteps coming up the stairs and lifted his head, fully expecting to see Jacob in the doorway, but his little brother never appeared.

No sooner had Brig rested his head back upon the pillow when something seized his ankle and yanked him to the floor. Eyes wide in the darkness, Brig struggled, but whatever had grabbed him pressed his face into the carpet, muffling his screams. The grip on his head was tremendous and he was certain his skull would crack.

Just as quickly as it had begun, Brig found himself free of the clutches that had bound him. He got up, and ran from the room, making a quick right as he started down the stairs where he slipped on a puddle of water, which sent him tumbling down the narrow staircase only to hit the floor at the bottom in a crumpled heap.

Attempting to stand, he howled with pain. His parents, fearing his ankle was broken, rushed him to the emergency room at nearby Wicklow Memorial Hospital. In the end, it was just a nasty sprain, but when they returned a few hours later, Brig examined the stairs and found them dry.

Brig never spoke to his parents of the incident in Jacob's room. Try as he did to convince himself he had imagined it, that night was the last time he ever entered his brother's bedroom. Some things lurk in the corners of our minds. Others lurk among the shadows of this world. Too often, the distinction is a difficult one to make, but it's better to not tempt fate.

-4-

Brig placed the receiver back onto its cradle. He stepped on the soggy patch of carpet a second time when he stood up and kicked the cup under the bed as he stumbled into the bathroom. Sharp blades of morning sun pierced his eyes while he winced and waited for his vision to adjust with his hands on the vanity for balance.

He peered into the mirror, studying every detail of his face. He feared he might be starting to show his age. The carefree days of his early twenties were far in the rearview mirror, and the thought of his upcoming thirty-fourth birthday bothered him more than he was willing to admit. The years were ticking by – faster and faster – soon he would be forty, fifty in a blink, and then …

His hair was his greatest source of discontent. Now, gray intermingled with brown and he had begun to obsess over it. Each day he looked into the mirror, a new wave of despair washed over him. He'd considered biting the bullet and going to a salon, but days passed and the gray just kept on coming. In his mind, making that move was somehow admitting the problem existed, and he wasn't willing to do so just yet.

He couldn't blame his busy schedule for his procrastination. Nowadays, he had more time on his hands than he knew what to do with. A retired investment banker at the age of thirty-four, he was the envy of all his friends. He'd made a small fortune in the tech boom of the mid-1990's, but unlike his colleagues, he'd had the sense to get out before the bubble burst with the turn of the new century.

The price of his stocks had spiked in late '95 and he'd sold out. Then, in what his friends dubbed a pure stroke of genius, he short sold a sizeable amount of internet stock before the market went south. It was a monstrous gamble, but it had paid off – *big*.

He leaned into the shower stall and turned the valve; a blast of cold water struck his back, giving him a start. Obscenities echoed against the bathroom tile. He stepped back, snatched a towel off the rack, and dried his head. It wasn't long before the room filled with steam, and his thoughts turned to Erin as he stepped beneath the warm shower spray.

-5-

He and Erin had met while they were freshmen in college. One day as Brig sat through a particularly boring philosophy lecture, someone tapped him on the shoulder. He turned around and the person in the desk behind him handed over a folded slip of paper. Brig opened it and saw two words: CALL ME!
A telephone number was written below that. His eyes searched the room for who had sent it. That's when his eyes first met Erin's.

At the time, they were midway into the fall semester. The weather was unseasonably warm, and the classroom windows hung halfway open. A balmy breeze moved about the room, shifting Erin's bangs playfully. Brig smiled at her and she smiled back, pointing towards the door as she mouthed, "Wait for me after class."

Brig did just that. Seconds seemed like hours as he waited for her to filter out of the classroom, all the while wondering what her voice would sound like and imagining the scent of her perfume up close. Eventually she emerged, and they talked as they walked up the hill to their next class. There was chemistry between them. There was no denying it, and before they parted, Brig promised to give her a call later that night.

By nine o'clock, he must have tried to dial her number a dozen times. Self-confidence was not a problem for Brig, but oddly, this call was proving difficult. Disinterested in his situation, the clock on the wall ticked on. With every passing minute, Brig grew more and more aware of the late hour. He found the courage and dialed the number without hanging up. Erin answered, and they talked until two in the morning. She agreed to go out with him that weekend after Brig suggested they drive to Nashville for dinner in an open air restaurant inside the Cascade Ballroom of the Opryland Hotel.

He picked her up that Saturday night at her dorm. An hour and a half later, they pulled into the hotel's parking lot. The building was a sprawling structure - more palatial than your standard hotel. Lights were everywhere, but Brig only saw the ones reflected in Erin's eyes. He'd fallen for her – fallen for her hard – and she knew it.

Shortly after dinner, the two strolled along the winding garden paths past fountains, over bridges and along pools filled with koi. Erin took his hand and Brig relaxed, lifting hers to his lips for a quick kiss. He bumped her with his shoulder. "I'm glad you came tonight," he told her.

Erin squeezed his hand. "Me too. This place is beautiful, Brig. Is there where you bring all the girls?" she asked with a sideways smile.

Brig laughed and interlaced his fingers with hers. "No," he said as he shook his head. "My parents used to bring me here when I was a kid. Back before they tore down the theme park." He nodded, agreeing with no one in particular. "Good memories here. Good ones."

Erin put her other hand on his, shrugged her shoulders and inhaled deeply. "The Wabash Cannonball. God I loved that coaster."

The two walked on down the path until they found themselves alone with only the sound of a nearby waterfall. Brig took her face in his hands and kissed her. More importantly, Erin kissed him back. Try as he did to control it, his hands moved over her body until she took them back into her own. In the distance, a clock chimed midnight.

Erin looked up at him and said, "Listen," brushing a shy wisp of hair from her eyes, "it's getting late."

Brig gently stroked her arm. "I'm sorry. That was too soon, wasn't it? C'mon, let's get you home."

Erin was quick to cut him off: "No, that's not what I meant at all. I'm having a great time – I don't want to go home *now*! What I was trying to say is that it's getting late, and it's a long drive back to Havens Fork." She tilted her head and once more gave him that sly, sideways smile. "Why don't we just, you know ... stay here?"

Brig didn't blink.

Erin waited a bit longer for a response before saying, "Well, if you don't want to ..."

Brig blurted, "Sure, I do. I mean ... yes, definitely!" He wasn't accustomed to his dates making the first move. That sort of thing simply wasn't done in Jones Chapel.

Erin pulled him close and hugged him. His unease was unmistakable, and part of her wondered if this would be his first time. After a quick kiss on the cheek, she whispered into his ear, "Don't worry, I'll be gentle."

To Brig's delight, he'd brought along enough money to pay for a room. After a simple matter of a registration card and one very convincing fake I.D., the clerk handed him a key. Brig turned to Erin with a wink, and once clear of the front desk, the two of them were off and running to their room, giggling like schoolchildren.

When they reached their door, Brig slid the key into the lock, praying it would work. He had convinced himself that if he was to go back to the desk, the clerk would ask questions. In the end, all that worrying had been for naught. The key *worked.*

In contrast to the brightly lit hallway, rinsed clean of shadows, the room was dark. Brig felt along the wall for a switch, but found Erin's hand instead. Unable to see her in the darkness, he felt her warm breath on his ear. She whispered, "The lights stay off," and pushed him against the door. She pressed her lips against his neck and scraped his skin with her teeth. Erin grabbed his shirt and threw him onto the bed. In that moment, he understood she was going to be anything but gentle.

-6-

Despite the financial difficulties associated with such things, the two of them married a year later. Sheer stubborn will and mutual sacrifice saw them through the last two years of college at which time Brig graduated with a degree in business, Erin a degree in journalism. Brig was the first to get a job offer. It was at a high-profile brokerage firm in New York City. After much discussion and a mutual desire to spread their wings, Erin supported the move. She knew it would be good for his career, and perhaps more selfishly, she knew her own prospects were much greater in Manhattan. They wasted no time beginning the arduous task of packing, and within a month, they were in the Big Apple.

The move proved quite an adjustment for them. Compared to Kentucky, New York was a foreign land. Still, they took to it well and in short time they had begun running in a large social circle. Long hours and relentless ambition yielded success as their careers progressed. In the years that followed, they adapted to city life and even managed to shed their southern accents. Conformity was the order of the day, and somewhere amid the glare of city lights, they found a palatable distinction between selling out and fitting in.

The tough times in life – the ones that hit you blindside and right between the eyes – so rarely come with a warning. And so it was for Brig that one random Tuesday, Erin came home to their small apartment and told Brig there was something she needed to discuss with him as she placed her keys on the kitchen counter. She went on to describe a promising position she'd been offered with CNN in Atlanta and how badly she wanted to take it. At first, Brig opposed the idea. A transfer to Atlanta was out of the question; his firm had no office there. Besides, if he wanted to be in the securities industry, New York was the place to be. This was where they had built their life together, and this was where he wanted to stay. Nevertheless, he ended up letting Erin go ahead without him, understanding how important the job was to her. He was naïve enough to believe their relationship could withstand the distance.

His mother had often told him that when in a moment of doubt, to trust his gut. It was difficult advice to follow as denial is a seductive mistress. Still, as time drew out following her move to Atlanta, Brig became increasingly suspicious that Erin was having an affair. On several occasions, he'd called her late at night. Sometimes she answered, sometimes she didn't, and too often her explanations for her whereabouts were weak at best. Over beers on many occasions in a smoky bar in lower Manhattan, Brig often remarked to his friends that his wife was good at a great many things, but she was a piss-poor liar.

It wasn't until his windfall in the stock market that the rotten wood beneath the surface of the relationship started to show itself. Brig took a part-time consulting position in Atlanta, thinking his marriage was still salvageable. They say time heals all wounds, but the cruel reality is that time produces more fatal wounds than it heals. A field untended goes fallow and becomes ever more difficult to tend. In short, his relocation to Atlanta proved to be the death knell for their marriage.

By the time the first boxes were placed on the moving truck, Brig and Erin had lived apart for going on three years and had become entirely too set in their ways. Brig had hoped for a steamy reunion upon his arrival, but what he found was far colder. The sex between them was virtually non-existent, and only grew worse. Ironically enough, the frustration over the lack of bedroom activity had caused him to consider having an affair many times. But even in the weakest times, the loneliest times, the nights plagued by the nausea of uncertainty as to Erin's fidelity, he held onto hope. So when those moments came as he sat on a stool in his favorite haunt just off of Peachtree Plaza and a young woman slipped him her phone number, he thanked her. Flattered but unwilling to break a much older promise, he always tipped the bartender and left the folded slip of paper on the bar.

Things started looking up in the spring of 1997. Erin began spending more time at home, and their sex life had improved. The next "hit you between the eyes" day came on a Thursday when Erin emerged from the bathroom holding a test strip and told Brig that she was pregnant. The emotion that came over him was a strange sense of relief. A child was not in the cards – hadn't even been discussed at any length between the two of them, but his capacity for naivety knew few bounds and that dumb blind hope resurfaced, convincing him a child would solidify their relationship.

Once Kaitlyn was born, stale apathy returned to the marriage and quickly ushered it to its ultimate demise. Brig's lifestyle did little to slow the decay – quite the contrary. Erin's insistence that his drinking had been a prime factor in the breakdown of their marriage was a truth he had still not come to fully accept. His demons aside, he had always been true to her. His conscience was clear on that.

The divorce was a cold one, but not uncivil. A strange ballet of events ensues once the words "I want a divorce" are uttered. Soon enough, the lawyers take over, and barring any major disagreements, the whole thing becomes rather clinical. When all was done, the two of them simply divided their assets and parted ways. For Brig, the most painful part of the whole situation had been making the decision to forfeit custody of Kaitlyn.

His mother had impressed upon him that a man wasn't meant to raise a little girl all by himself. She'd gone on to say that there would be certain things his daughter would need, and he wouldn't always be able to give them to her the way a mother could. He stood in the driveway that cold January morning and watched as Erin's SUV disappeared in the distance, loaded down with suitcases and escorted by a large moving van. A lump formed in his throat as he watched Kaitlyn in the rear window, waving goodbye.

-7-

Brig finished his shower with a quick rinse of his hair after which he stepped out onto a ratty blue towel he used as a bath mat. Décor was not a specialty of his, that had been Erin's department and left to his own devices, the situation had only gotten worse. "Make it do or do without," his mother had always said, and Brig took the advice to heart if for no reason other than the typical laissez faire attitude men adopt when living alone.

Passing the vanity mirror on the way out of the bathroom, Brig caught a glimpse of himself from the side. He was noticeably thinner – no doubt a result of poor eating habits resulting from an unshakable blue feeling that hung over him like a cloud since the divorce. He'd heard it called 'the divorce diet' and it had made quick work of almost twenty pounds.

He dried off and slipped into a white T-shirt and a pair of jogging shorts. As he passed the bed, he knelt to sop up what water he could from the soggy carpet. Buster, just waking from a nap, hung his head over the side of the bed. Brig scratched the dog's head and said, "C'mon boy, let's get us some eats." Buster hopped up, excited at the prospect. If there was one thing that got the dog moving in the mornings, it was eats. Buster bolted towards the kitchen, out front with a comfortable lead. He turned and barked back at Brig, anxiously shuffling beside his food dish.

Once there, Brig opened the pantry and pulled out a twenty-pound bag of dog food and poured some into a red dish on the floor; "BUSSER" had been painted on the side in large, yellow-block letters. Kaitlyn had given the dish to Buster as a birthday gift a couple of years prior and her childish pronunciation of his name stuck. She liked him, and Buster liked her, too, but seemed somewhat unsure of how to behave around such a small, energetic person. The dog started eating before Brig had even finished pouring. Food pellets showered over his snout and scattered across the linoleum floor.

Brig opened the fridge. Inside, there sat a lonely Mountain Dew bottle on the top rack of an otherwise empty refrigerator – empty that is save a lone bottle of ketchup and a packet of lunchmeat, which had started to grow a crop of furry, gray mold. He reached in, grabbed the soda, and headed back to the pantry from which he removed a box of fruit-filled Pop Tarts. He removed the last foil package and put the empty box back inside the pantry without thinking.

A twist of the cap on the soda bottle and it started to hiss. The sound elicited a bark from Buster, who soon settled down and resumed eating once his opinion had been voiced. Brig shook a Xanax tablet from an amber prescription bottle and washed it down. His doctor had prescribed the pills shortly after the divorce when Brig had gone to the hospital suspecting that he might be having a heart attack. The doctor assured him his heart was fine and went on to say that what Brig had experienced was known as a panic attack. Apparently, retirement and divorce are two of the most stressful things a person can experience short of the death of a parent. Little did Brig know that he would be experiencing the latter in less than two months. Depending on the pills bothered him, but they did help.

If anxiety wasn't enough, the doctor had added insult to injury when he'd diagnosed Brig as teetering on the depressed side, as well. He'd written a script for Prozac with a year's worth of refills. Brig had it filled once, but he'd forgotten to consistently take his daily dose and before long, decided it wasn't worth the effort. Rum and Xanax, however, proved to be quite a decent concoction, indeed. Brig poured five or six ounces of the alcohol into a plastic cup. The ice inside popped and cracked as it bathed in it. Brig topped it off with Mountain Dew and took a swig. The familiar warm sensation snaked its way through him, bringing a smile to his face.

Buster had finished eating and scratched at the door wanting outside. "Alright, Buddy," Brig said, "let's go outside." He opened the door, and Buster burst through. The dog's toenails clicked across the deck boards as he raced for the steps on his way to a line of hedges where he liked to do his business.

The morning sun had just crested above the roofline of the house. Shadows crept across the deck in long, black fingers attempting to push back the early morning light. Brig settled into a chair beneath a blue and white striped umbrella. Southern summers were notoriously cruel, but this was springtime and for humidity to be this thick at such and early hour was simply oppressive. Erin had always said the air felt like syrup in her lungs, and in the concrete jungle of Atlanta, there was little escape.

After their divorce, Brig had bought a lake house on the outskirts of Birmingham. It was now spring break, and with the warm weather came a virtual wave of scantily clad college girls on wave runners and water skis. The main boating channel ran behind his house, and he had already spent a fair amount of time that week sitting on his deck in hopes that a sexy coed might lose her top on the way by. On que, a ski boat roared past full of kids with dark tans and a load of beer. An inner tube was tied behind the boat, and it skipped violently upon the surface of the water. Its occupant held on for dear life as the captain of the boat, a stocky, dark-haired boy in neon Bermuda shorts, hammered the throttle down.

Brig was overcome by a sudden urge to call his father. Inside the house, he grabbed the cordless phone from the kitchen counter and went back onto the deck. By this time, the sun had cleared the top of the house, and the temperature was steadily rising. He put his sunglasses on and sat back down as he dialed the number. After ten rings and no answer, he hung up. It was par for the course. Ever since he was a child, Brig remembered his father waking at dawn if for no other reason than to get out on the farm and work while he watched the sun rise.

So long ago . . .

The last time Brig had been home, he was shocked at the radical change in his father's appearance. When he had left for New York, his father was a muscular man in his early fifties, but the stress of watching his wife slowly die of cancer had taken its toll. Gabe Bailey was roughly ninety pounds lighter and had gone completely gray. Lonely eyes sagged inside a face creased with countless, hard-earned wrinkles.

Brig often worried about his father being alone on the farm. One night while they were talking, Brig had suggested that his father move down south to live with him. Gabe had responded with a "Thanks, but no thanks." He'd gone on to stress that the farm was his home. His wife and youngest son were buried there, and it was where he wanted to live out his days. Brig had said that he understood, and they'd left it at that.

Gabe was a strong man, emotionally speaking. He'd been the glue that had held the family together following Jacob's death. By the time Rose passed away, he had logged a good bit of time and experience in the grief department. On top of it all, he was quite astute at covering up his emotions. Nonetheless, Brig had always been able to see through the façade his father erected for the family's benefit, and he'd known how bad the man was hurting. Still, he knew better than to call undue attention to it. It was best to let his father believe the illusion had worked.

The sun beat down on the back of Brig's neck, and he decided to take a swim to cool off. He tipped up his cup, polished off the rest of his drink and went inside to change. The trunks he put on were a pair that he had bought while on a trip he'd taken with Erin to the Cayman Islands just five years before. The color had long since faded, but they were comfortable, and that was all that mattered. Outside, Buster bounded up the stairs, panting wildly. "You wanna go swimming boy?" Buster responded with an affirmative yelp, and the two hurried down the boardwalk where they jumped from the edge of the dock. Brig went under like a stone, but resurfaced soon after as Buster paddled around him.

The lake water was cool, but it had a fishy odor to it he didn't care for and Brig didn't linger long. Soon after, he swam towards the bank until he was able to touch bottom and then walked the rest of the way. His face drew up in a sneer as soft lake mud squirted between his toes. The sensation brought with it memories of childhood, memories of Jacob and unwanted memories of Jones Chapel. Those memories were becoming more frequent, more vivid, and harder to avoid.

Buster emerged from the water soon after looking like a drowned rat. Brig laughed out loud at the sight as the dog shook himself dry. Without warning, the dog's ears perked up, and he turned towards the house before bolting towards the deck – something he only did when he heard the telephone ring. The dog bounded up the stairs and barked at the door about the time Brig reached the first step. Buster rose on his hind legs and glanced back. Brig said, "I know, I know! I'm coming!" He reached the door and hurried inside, still dripping wet from his swim. The phone rang once more and quit.

The name on the handset said, H PALMER. H PALMER was actually Harvey Palmer, his father's hired hand – Mr. Palmer to the kids in town, Harv to just about everyone else. Harv had worked for Gabe for going on thirty years; so long that he was practically a member of the family.

Brig pressed redial, and Harv picked up on the second ring.

"Hello?" The old man's southern drawl made the salutation sound more like 'yellow.'

"Harv?"

"Yep, this is Harv"

"This is Brig. I saw that you called."

"Well, hey, Brig!" He took the phone away from his mouth long enough to blow his nose into his handkerchief. He cleared his throat and said, "What's new with you, son?"

"Not a lot, just staying warm." Brig understood that you had to engage in small talk with the folks back in Jones Chapel. That kind of idle banter hadn't been necessary in New York, and it had taken Brig a while to get out of the habit, but when you spoke with the folks back home, you talked about the weather, crops, and whatever else was on their mind at the time. Anything less was considered rude.

"Yep," Harv agreed, "this year's shapin' up to be a hot one, that's for sure."

"So what can I do for you?" Brig asked. The tension rose noticeably as soon as the words fell from his lips. Perhaps it was Harv's hesitation to respond, maybe it was something else, but nonetheless, Brig's stomach tightened with nervous distress. He knew something was wrong.

"Now, I don't want you to get all excited," Harv said, "but I've got some bad news. Brig, it's about your daddy ..."

"Dad? What's wrong with him?"

"Don't know. But you really shouldn't worry ... you know your daddy; he's tough as a bull. He just got a little sick is all. He hasn't been feeling too good lately, and last night he started complaining about his stomach. I figured it must have been somethin' he ate – you know, heartburn or somethin' like that. Truth is, your daddy hasn't been eatin' so good since your momma passed on. Don't suppose you knew that."

Brig knew alright, but he hadn't said anything to his father about it. Thirty-five years in the Bailey clan had taught him a thing or two about the fundamentals of interpersonal dynamics. When it came to Gabe Bailey, it didn't pay to be proactive. Brig had learned never to imply that his father was incapable of taking care of himself.

"Yeah," he said. "I've been worried about that. I even offered to let him move down here and stay with me, but he wouldn't hear of it."

"Well, hell no!" Harv scoffed. "I'm not surprised! That'd be like the blind leadin' the blind, now wouldn't it? Nope, I don't see your daddy ever leaving that farm. The land is in his blood – yours too, you know. It's been in your family for generations."

"I know," Brig said. "I figured it was probably a long shot, but I thought I'd try, anyway."

"Yep, you're a good one, kiddo. Now listen, your daddy would never tell you what I'm about to – *not in a million years* – but I think you should know. He's been stayin' with me the past couple of weeks. When he asked me if I minded, it struck me as a tad odd, but I said, 'sure.' Didn't ask no more questions."

Harv continued, "I ran him up to the hospital yesterday. You know, no sense in taking chances: 'don't tempt fate' and all of that. I called you partly because I knew you'd want to give him a call."

Brig said, "Yeah, I would, and thanks for taking care of him. The old goat appreciates it, even though he'd never admit it."

"I know. Your daddy's a hard-ass, that's for sure. But he'd have done the same for me. Hold on just a second, I'll get the number for you."

While he waited for Harv to get back on the phone, Brig wondered why his father had chosen to stay somewhere other than his own house. It occurred to him that it was getting close to his parents' anniversary, and he thought he might have his answer – the memories were creeping back.

Brig knew all too well the emotional devastation that memories were capable of. Just when you think they're gone, just when you breathe deep, because you can no longer smell their foul pollution hanging in the air, they jump out from behind the door to torment you some more. They never tire. They never sleep. They come in the dead of night and sit beside you on your bed, whispering soft whispers that permeate your dreams, ensuring that you will never, ever forget what once was.

After a few minutes, Harv picked up the receiver again. "Brig? Brig, you still there?" Brig confirmed that he was, and Harv went on to read Gabe's phone number off of the small dinner napkin on which he'd written it. Brig scratched the number onto a yellow legal pad, and retraced it with his pen, making the numbers dark. He then drew a box around the numbers for no reason at all.

"I'll call him right now," he said. "Thanks again."

"You bet, you tell your daddy I said, 'hi,' ya hear?"

-8-

Brig dialed the number, but the voice that answered sounded nothing at all like his father's. Despite the effects of the Xanax, twinges of anxiety had built up inside of him. He knew his father would never tell him the full story if he were, indeed, sick – Harv was right about that. Gabe Bailey was not one to jockey for attention. In his eyes, illness was a sign of weakness, and weakness was not in him. He would play it off until the end.

"Dad? Dad, is that you?"

"Brig? How are you, boy?"

"How are *you*? I just got off the phone with Harv and he said you weren't feeling well."

"Ah hell, you know Harv. He can make a mountain out of a molehill better than anyone can. There's nothing to be worried about. I just got to feeling a little queasy is all. I'll be fine, don't you worry about your daddy."

The comforting warmth of denial wrapped around Brig like an old blanket. It was good to hear his father's voice again. The two of them had always shared a good relationship, and his father had always been there for him. Brig felt a bit guilty for not having done the same for him. Still, he knew his father would never take the opportunity to confide in him - even if it was offered. Gabe was a problem solver, not one to cause those close to him any excess worry.

"Dad, Harv tells me that you've been staying with *him* the past couple of weeks. Is there something going on that I should know about?"

Gabe's voice broke through thirty seconds of uncomfortable dead air: "Well, son. I don't suppose it's anything to get worked up over, but ever since your momma died, things just haven't been the same around the house."

Brig thought he understood. For weeks after his divorce, he'd haunted the house like some kind of specter - little more than a shadow on the wall. Nighttime was always the hardest. It seemed that everything got worse once the sun went down. There had been no one there to talk to, no one to confide in, and no one to hold. The latter was probably the worst of it; he'd never realized how much he'd relied on Erin until she was gone.

Even now, Brig lamented the loss of his and Erin's relationship. Not so much as it had been just prior to their breakup, but rather the earlier days of their marriage when things were new and exciting. Life had been good then. They'd shared so much, laughed so much; it was the greatest time of his life. At night, while the world slept, those tormenting memories would return to remind him that the divorce had been the death of all of that.

"I think I understand, dad. It can be lonely at times. I'm sure the house seems pretty empty."

"No, I don't think you *do* understand, son. I could handle 'empty.' Death is just a part of living. It hurts, sure, but your momma and I were always church going folks. We were raised to believe that you'd see your loved ones again." Gabe trailed off. "I just never thought . . ."

"Dad, there's something you're not telling me. Have the doctor's given you some bad news?"

Typically, Gabe would say something to defuse the situation whenever he sensed Brig getting worked up, but this time, he didn't offer to change the subject. "Son, I wish I could tell you what's wrong," he said. "I really do. I just don't know how to phrase it. Hell, *I* don't even know what it is."

Brig's voice took on a determined tone and he said, "I'm packing my bags and coming up. I'm not going to sit down here and worry while you're lying up there in some hospital room. I'm just not going to do it."

"Now, Brig ..."

"No dad, I'm serious. I can be up there tonight. I'll check things out at the house and take care of whatever needs to be done. You need to rest. Harv and I can handle it." He waited for another rebuttal, but none came. Instead, Gabe blurted out:

"About the house ..."

"What about it?"

"Well, you're right, after your momma died, things *did* seem pretty empty. It was sad; I won't lie to you about that. But here lately, things don't seem quite so empty anymore. I've been thinking a lot about Jacob and your momma, too – some of the things I haven't thought about in *years*."

Brig tried once more. "That's perfectly natural," he said. "I went through the same thing with Erin . . ."

Gabe was quick to shut him down. His tone changed and he said, "No, it's not the same thing at all. Listen Brig, over the years, a house can absorb a lot of memories. Some of them good – some bad. It only makes sense that sooner or later something has to give."

"I don't follow."

"You'll understand when you come up. I promise. I don't want to talk about it now, but I do need to talk with you about your brother."

"What about him?"

"Can't talk now. People are going to think I'm a loon if they hear me talking about it. It's something I should have told you a long time ago. I learned some things after Jacob died – things I just couldn't talk about while your momma was alive. She loved your brother so much, you know."

Brig thought back to the heartbroken sound of his mother's sobs and said, "I know she did. His death was pretty hard on her, wasn't it?"

"Damn near killed her!" Gabe insisted. "You don't know the half of it; she never would have let you see her that way." He continued, "A day or two after your brother's funeral, I was about to go crazy myself. I couldn't get my mind off of Jacob. Sitting around the house wasn't doing any good, so I figured I might as well try to get some work done, you know, to take my mind off of things."

"I went on down to Shorty's to grab me a can of pop before I headed into town. That's when this man comes up to me, a really tall fella. He was an Indian - well, you can't say that anymore, they're Native Americans now. His name was John, John Blackwind. He said he wanted to talk to me about Jacob. He told me that there were some things I should know. Things the cops didn't tell us."

Brig asked him to go on, but Gabe refused. "I'll tell you the rest of the story when you come up. I want you here in front of me. You need to see that I'm serious and not some crazy old man."

"I know you're not crazy ... Do you want me to stay at the house while I'm up there?" Brig asked, desperately hoping for anything other than an affirmative answer.

"Yessir, I do. It's still your home. Besides, I think you *need* to stay there. You know where the spare key is, don't you?"

"Yes."

"When did you say you'd be up?"

"I'll leave in a few hours. I can be there tonight. Think you can hang on till then?"

"Well, hell yes! I told you, I'm not sick! I've only been sick once in the past ten years! I don't know why everybody's making such a fuss over me. The way these doctors and nurses come in and out of this room, you'd think I was on death's door! Don't you worry. Drive careful now, understand?"

The two of them said their goodbyes, and Brig hung up. There was a lot to be done before he left for Kentucky, but he decided to call Erin first. She had always been close to his father, and there would be hell to pay if he failed to pass along the news.

An unsettling thought crept in as he started to dial, and it filled him with unease. If the worst came to pass, how would Kaitlyn react to the news of her grandfather dying so soon after her grandmother? *Is she old enough to understand?*

-9-

Erin picked up the phone, but her voice was groggy. Brig feared that he had woken her. He was married to her long enough to know that was never a good thing. She tended to get cranky when her sleep was interrupted. True to form, she snapped at him:

"What do you want?" She asked. "I told you we have been up since four in the morning! I just managed to convince Kaitlyn to take a nap – you know how difficult that is at her age! I laid her down an hour ago, and this is the first chance I've had to get some rest! So help me, God, if you woke her up ..."

"Erin, dad's sick."

Her tone abruptly changed. "What's wrong?"

"I don't know. He wouldn't tell me very much. I spoke with Harv, and all he would tell me was that dad hadn't been feeling well and that he'd taken him to the hospital. Dad sounded pretty rough when I spoke with him a minute ago. I'm worried about him."

"C'mon Brig, it could be anything. Why do you have to assume the worst?"

"I don't know. It's just a feeling, I guess, but something isn't right. I'm headed up that way tonight. I have to wrap some things up here, and then I'll be on my way ... Oh, one other thing – he said he wanted to talk with me about Jacob. Any idea what that might be about?"

Through the phone, Brig heard Erin clicking her fingernail against her front teeth. It was one of her more annoying habits, one he'd found endearing when they'd first started dating. It was something she always did whenever she was lost in her thoughts; he supposed it helped her concentrate.

"I don't know," she said. You're dad has never really talked with me about Jacob. I had always assumed it was a sore subject. I didn't want to dredge up old pain – salt in the wound and all of that – so I never asked. What do you think?"

"I don't know," he said, "I guess I'll find out when I get up there. I just wanted to let you know what was going on in case."

"Don't talk like that!" she said. "Nothing is going to happen to your dad. It's going to be something minor. I'm sure he's feeling a little bit lonely. You know how it is... You're doing the right thing by coming up, though. It'll do you both a lot of good. Will you have time to stop in and see Kaitlyn while you're here?"

"I'd love to, thank you." He was glad that she'd been the one to bring it up. Even though she had never denied him of any opportunity to see his daughter, the idea of having to ask for permission didn't sit well with him. He doubted it ever would. Moreover, he resented Erin's new husband, Tom. The man had moved in and taken over Brig's life, which had always consisted of his wife and daughter – there wasn't much left to take.

"She's really worried about you," Erin said. "I don't know why, but she keeps insisting that you're in some sort of danger. She doesn't put it in those terms, but I know what she means." She waited for Brig to respond, hoping he might offer some token of insight.

"Don't worry," he said. "She probably just misses her daddy, that's all. It's been a while since I've seen her, and I'm sure that hasn't helped matters any."

"You're probably right," she said. "But you really should call once you've made it up, just to make her feel better."

"I will," he said. "Listen, I'm going to be staying at the farmhouse, do you remember the number?"

"C'mon, I've talked with your dad more in the past six months than you have. Of course I do."

"I know. You've been awfully good to dad, and I appreciate it. It helps to know that you're so close if anything should happen."

Erin and Gabe had always shared a good relationship. Even through the divorce, Gabe had managed to hold a neutral stance. He liked Erin, and Brig believed that deep down, his father still blamed him for letting the marriage go sour. Not that all of it was Brig's fault, but blame has a funny way of finding its way home, fair or not.

"He means a lot to me," she said. "You get up here and take care of him. Keep me informed."

"You bet. Thanks." He hung up, and Buster crawled out from beneath the coffee table where he'd been napping. He laid his head in Brig's lap, and looked at him through what looked like concerned eyes. Brig patted his head and told him, "It's gonna be alright boy. We're going on a little trip."

Brig grabbed a notebook and a ballpoint pen from the coffee table and started a packing list. When he finished, he went back to the bedroom, opened the closet door, and pushed a bunch of hanging shirts aside, revealing his suitcase. He opened it, and a painfully familiar smell hit him – Erin's perfume. The first time he'd smelled it was the night of their first date. After he'd taken her home the next day, he realized his shirt still smelled like her. Although he would never admit it, it had been quite some time before he'd been able to bring himself to wash it.

A more reasonable man would buy new luggage, but Brig simply loaded the suitcase and took a final look into the closet. With a deep sigh, he reached for his black suit – just in case – and loaded up his hanging bag. With that done, he changed into a pair of blue jeans and a button-down shirt, leaving the latter untucked. He slipped his feet into a pair of sneakers and grabbed his keys.

A small wooden cross dangled from the key chain, and he traced his thumb over its surface. It had been a gift from his mother when he left for college. The marred piece of wood reminded him of his dream earlier that morning. He saw himself beaten and bloody, hanging on the cross like wall art, but just as quickly as the memory surfaced, he chased it away.

He headed out to the garage with Buster hot on his heels. Once in the garage, Brig loaded his luggage and various other items into the back of his SUV. Buster hopped in and worked his way toward the front of the truck, assuming his usual spot in the passenger's seat. The two of them pulled out of the driveway and began a trip both of them had taken many times before.

CHAPTER TWO

-1-

Brig crossed the state line into Kentucky, and pulled off at a rest stop to allow Buster the opportunity to run off some energy. The trip this time seemed unusually long. Back when he and Erin were together, they had made the drive at least five times each year. Now, making the trip alone with only bad music and his thoughts to keep him company, the minutes ticked by like hours.

Brig sat at a concrete picnic table watching his dog explore the new surroundings. He took a swig from the water bottle in his hand and took in the scenery with a toothpick parked in the corner of his mouth. The geography looked familiar again. Alabama's spindly pines had given way to broadleaf maples and beneath his feet was that familiar bluegrass.

It was a shame that it had taken a medical emergency to get him back home. He had allowed his fears to control him for far too long, something he wished he could deny, but control him they had. He was older now, presumably wiser, and he hoped more in control. His father needed him. Brig knew that, and was not about to let him down.

Brig called to Buster who came running. The two made their way to the truck as Brig tossed his water bottle into a nearby trash can. The dog hopped in through the open passenger door and soon, the two were on the road again. The sun had already sunk below the western horizon, adorning the sky with inky purple brush strokes. A few more miles of interstate later and the day was swallowed by the night.

Not long after, the truck's headlights splashed against a reflective, green sign on the side of the road, which read: "Havens Fork - Next Three Exits." He thought back to when the town was much smaller with only one interstate exit and about as many traffic lights. Things had certainly changed since then. Brig found himself in a three-mile stretch of road construction where the interstate was being widened from two lanes to four, and as he passed her exit, blew Kaitlyn a kiss. He was anxious to see her. It had really been too long.

Further up the road, the artificial glow cast by the metallic forest of towering interstate streetlamps grew dimmer and dimmer in his rearview mirror. There was little between Havens Fork and Jones Chapel aside from 31 miles of winding interstate and the odd shimmer of road reflectors. This allowed Brig more time with his thoughts than he cared to have. Again, he struggled with ghosts of the past, memories and nothing more – old things long forgotten by most that could never harm him unless he let them.

Brig looked beyond the range of his headlights and surveyed the darkness. The absence of traffic seemed strange. Just above the tree line, a fuzzy light appeared in the distance. It was the glowing, orange "76" ball perched atop Shorty's filling station. It had been there for as long as Brig could remember, and it was hard to imagine Jones Chapel without it.

In high school, the filling station was the place to meet up, talk and sneak a beer when no one was looking. Relationships were born and relationships died in that parking lot as the complicated game of teenage chess played out. It was the nexus of Jones Chapel – the proving ground where fights were waged, gossip shared, and hearts broken. Every town has one though they often take different forms.

Brig gently applied the brakes as he approached the exit ramp, flipping on his blinker out of habit despite being the only car in sight. Buster slid forward on the leather seat before stabilizing himself again. "We're here, fella!" Brig told him. The truck slowed to a stop at the end of the ramp. A left turn would have taken them out to the farm, but Brig turned right and headed towards Shorty's, instead. He pulled up to the gas pumps and told Buster, "You stay here. I'll just be a minute." The dog responded with a bark.

After filling the tank, he went inside the store, which had been improved a great deal since his last visit. It was clear that Shorty had done some remodeling. The lights were brighter, the floors clean and tiled. A new Slurpee machine claimed a corner of the store where before there had been only mops and a broken vending machine. Brig looked into the beverage refrigerators craving a beer, but in a dry county, a coke would have to do. He had the local Baptists to thank for that.

"How are ya?" a female voice asked. Brig turned to see an older woman standing behind the counter. She was smiling, proudly displaying the large gap between her front teeth. Her nametag read: Irene. She was a short, pudgy woman, who looked to be in her mid-sixties. Her hair was heavily sprayed and it had been dyed jet-black.

"Fine," he said. "You?"

The watchful narrowing of Irene's eyes was something Brig had grown accustomed to. His demeanor must have seemed far too casual for someone who had just pulled off the interstate, but at the same time, she couldn't quite place him. It was something everyone in town had always done - a quick, non-verbal, almost subconscious assessment: *Are you one of us or aren't you? Are you in or are you out?*

"Doin' fine," she said as she took her eyes off of Brig while she fiddled with a roll of scratch off lottery tickets, trying her best to feed them into their dispenser. "You don't look familiar. Guessing you ain't from 'round here? Don't reckon I've seen ya before."

Brig took a Coke bottle from the cooler and spoke as he walked towards the checkout counter. "I used to live here several years ago. I'm Gabe Bailey's son."

Irene's face lit up. "Well, I'll be," she said. In New York that sentence would have been spiced with *'a sonovabitch,'* but in Jones Chapel, *'I'll be'* was all you got.

Brig nodded, confident in the knowledge Irene had made her assessment and he was *'in'*. Setting the bottle on the counter, he continued, "I went to high school with Shorty. I don't suppose he's around here, is he?"

Irene craned her neck, trying to look into the back storeroom. "I'm sure he's around here someplace," she said. "Let me go find him. I'm sure he'll be tickled to see ya!" She left the register and disappeared through the back doorway. While he waited, Brig spied the magazine rack and reached for Field and Stream. He flipped to the middle, half-heartedly reading an ad for a new fishing rod to pass the time when, from behind him, a familiar voice called out.

"Well will ya look at this! I knew somethin' had blown into town. Familiar stench!"

Brig smiled when he saw Shorty in the doorway wearing a pair of coveralls that were unzipped to mid-chest, revealing a stained undershirt. It had been at least five years since Brig had last seen his old friend. It looked as though he'd put on about fifty pounds.

Brig extended his hand offering a shake. "Hey, bud! How are you?" Shorty slapped it away and pulled him in for a bear hug.

"A shake? That's how you greet an old friend?" He slapped Brig on the back. "C'mon outside, let's talk!"

Brig removed his wallet and motioned with it towards the cash register. "Let me settle up with Irene here and I'll be right out." He presented his credit card, but saw Shorty making a 'no-

no' motion in the reflection of Irene's glasses. She was quick to draw her hands back and shrug her shoulders as if to say, *What do you want* me *to do? He's the boss.*

Shorty grabbed Brig by the arm and said, "This tank's on me, buddy."

Brig objected. "C'mon now, don't do that."

"I just did. Now get your ass outside, I need a smoke."

Placing his wallet back in his pocket, Brig waved to Irene and thanked her. Outside next to the ice chest Shorty was attempting to light a cigarette with a hand cupped around the flame. His face soon glowed with reddish-orange cigarette light. After a quick drag, he blew out a lungful of smoke.

"You know those things are gonna kill you." Brig told him.

Shorty flicked his ashes and took another drag. "Somethin's gonna get ya," he said. Nodding towards Brig's vehicle sporting Alabama plates, he asked, "You up here by yourself?"

"No, I brought Buster with me."

"Buster? Friend of yours?"

Brig laughed. "I don't think you've met," he said. "Hang on, I'll get him." He walked back to the truck and opened the passenger door. Buster jumped out and followed Brig back to the ice chest, wagging his tail.

"Well, hey there, fella!" Shorty bent down to pat the dog on the head and paused. He looked up at Brig and asked, "Friendly?" Brig nodded, so Shorty ruffed up the fur on the dog's head. "Good lookin' Lab, Brig. How old is he?"

"Two. I got him just before Erin and I split up."

Shorty shook his head. "Yeah, I heard about that. Damn shame. I thought you two were a good match – shows how much I know, huh?" Another drag and a change of subject: "By the way, I'm sorry to hear about your dad, how's he doin'?"

"I really don't know," Brig replied. "I spoke with him earlier today, but you know dad... He won't tell me anything. He's still as stubborn as ever. How'd you hear about it? Gossip mill still in operation?"

"Hell, Brig. Not much has changed since you left. People on the other side of town know what color your shit is before you flush it! Sometimes I get the feeling people in this town live for this kind of stuff."

Brig smiled. "Yeah, home sweet home..." He kicked a small rock against the curb. "Dad's never been into the gossip mill. He always told me he leaves that up to the women." He motioned towards the filling station. "Looks like you've really cleaned up this old joint."

"Had to," Shorty said. "They put that new RaceTrac up across the street, and I wasn't getting any traffic. Cost me a mint to do it, though. I'm too much like my daddy – my ass puckered up like a snare drum when I wrote that check, let me tell ya." He pointed to signs a little further up the road. "Got some new restaurants since the last time you were here, too."

"Growing like crazy, huh?"

Shorty flicked his cigarette into the parking lot, making sure to aim clear of the gasoline pumps. "Yeah. Regular fuckin' boomtown." He reached into his pocket and pulled out another one. "You were up here for your momma's funeral, but you blew out of town pretty fast. Damn shame. 'Bout your momma, I mean." Shorty shifted his weight to his right leg and shook his head to stress to the point.

And there it was. Memories and deeds never die in Jones Chapel. They hang around like fog, blinding people to the present through a sticky haze of the past. The inability of the people here to let things go did little but breed an ever-present climate of animosity and distrust that had plagued the town for far longer than either of the two men standing here had laid witness to.

Brig politely nodded his agreement and said, "I don't want to be rude, but I just got into town and I'm pretty tired. I'm going out to dad's, but I'll be in town for a couple of weeks. What do you say we get together one night and have us a beer? You know, catch up." No sooner had the words left his lips than his keys were jingling in his hand.

Shorty stuffed his hands in his pockets. "Hey, listen," he said. "I'm sorry if I said anything that..."

Brig waved the comment off. "No, it's nothing like that, promise. Tell ya what, since you bought the gas, I'll buy the beer. That should square us up."

Shorty grinned, clearly relieved. He patted his stomach and said, "Well, I guess that'd be alright, but I'd hate to cheat ya. I can really toss 'em down."

Brig thanked him again and climbed into the truck. He opened the passenger door and called to Buster. After the dog had jumped in, they pulled out of the station, giving the horn a quick, customary tap. Shorty responded with a wave.

-2-

Brig crossed over the interstate and smiled when he saw the sign for Hillbilly Hill. It was a small amusement park that had been around since he was a kid. At this time of night, most of the park was cloaked in darkness, but from what Brig could see, it didn't look as though much had changed.

The focal point of the park was a black and green, two-story, Victorian house adorned with two large, bloodshot eyes. Below the eyes, the parlor windows danced with flickering strobe lights. Inside was an animatronic ghost named *Charmin' Charlie* playing the piano just as he had every night for as long as Brig could remember. "HAUNTED HOUSE" was painted in large letters across the front, just beneath the eyes.

While empty now, the park would pack out in a few months when the summer tourist traffic rolled into town. That was the time Jones Chapel came alive. There was little major industry in the area. The overall society was primarily agrarian, but was known for its tremendous and complicated cave system, which offered a certain adventurous allure that attracted weekend warriors with pockets full of cash, desperately wanting a piece of it before parole was up and they had to reclaim their desks at work.

Gabe's blue mailbox appeared in the distance, and Brig slowed down before turning into the drive as he waited for a pickup truck to pass. The familiar sound of gravel crunched beneath the tires, welcoming him home. His Explorer rocked along the uneven road, an oddity considering his father was near compulsive in keeping it graded and well-maintained.

The truck's headlights bounced up and down on the side of the tobacco barn, which sat to the left of the drive further ahead. Brig pulled alongside the barn and killed the engine. The haunting whine of cicadas in the trees and the chirps of crickets in the grass were all that interrupted the thick, rural silence. He missed those sounds; they had always comforted him – the sounds of home. Once out of the truck, he bent over and picked up a chunk of gravel. Chalky, white dust rubbed off onto his fingers, and he pitched the rock into the hayfield.

He had once clocked the distance from the house to the highway - two trips to the highway and two trips back equaled one-mile. The summer before his sixteenth birthday, he'd spent a lot of time running up and down that drive, chasing his goal of making the track team at school. In the end, his effort had paid off. He'd made the team and came in first place in all but one track meet that year. He remembered fondly how it had felt to be in such good physical shape. But that was years ago.

Brig stretched his hand wrist-deep into the gap between two wooden barn doors and lifted the latch that held them closed. He went inside and his nose filled with the smells of fresh cut hay, sacks of grain and the stale, dusty air kicked up from the dirt floor. Soft shafts of moonlight cut through the wall slats, giving the appearance of white prison bars.

From his pocket, Brig removed a small flashlight and panned the beam around the room, catching the retinal reflection of a trio of rats who quickly dispersed with typical rat-like urgency. He followed the thin beam to the back of the barn where he lifted the lid of a small wooden box nailed to a barn pole and felt along the back of the box as spider webs stuck to his hand. His index finger found the spare house key hanging on a rusty brad nail. He pulled it off and snatched his hand from the box, wiping the spider webs off onto his jeans as he went back outside and latched the doors behind him.

Buster sat up inside the truck and stared down the drive towards the house with both ears erect. When he saw Brig, he dropped his head and let out a little whine.

"What's wrong, boy?" Brig asked. "We're here – trip's over!"

Buster hopped into the backseat and hid on the floorboard beneath the shadows. Brig climbed in and drove on towards the outline of the farmhouse. A window illuminated in one of the back rooms, which startled him enough to step on the brakes, causing the truck to lurch to a halt. That's when he remembered his father had put some of the interior lights on timers – the kind that was supposed to make would-be burglars think someone was home. Two more windows simultaneously illuminated on opposite sides of the house, verifying his suspicions. He drove on with a sigh of relief, pulling up to the house and parking at the end of the sidewalk.

Buster hopped out from the back passenger door, uncharacteristically nervous. "It's okay boy," Brig told him. "This is where I grew up. Go on, check the place out!" Buster sniffed around the front yard with reluctance as Brig leaned against the front fender of his Explorer and stared at his childhood home. The house stared back with a disinterested expression.

The house had stood there for nearly two centuries, sheltering many generations of Baileys. It had endured several renovations in that time. The original structure was a two-story, shaker-style house, which still served as the main living area. It had been remodeled further after Brig left for college. To Brig, it no longer felt like home. He looked at the upstairs bedroom windows and remembered the night he'd sprained his ankle.

A house can absorb a lot of memories...

Brig popped the truck's hatch and rummaged through his suitcase until he found his bottle of Xanax. The house loomed in his peripheral vision, and it was as though all those memories started to whisper at once. He popped the pill and tipped up a bottle of water, thinking: *It's just a house.*

-3-

Buster pressed himself against Brig's leg as they entered the house. The air inside was hot, stagnant, and stale. It was pitch black save a thin shaft of light emanating from the back office and the faint glow of lamps upstairs. Beyond the foyer, a steep and narrow flight of wooden stairs rose to the second floor – the same flight of stairs Brig had fallen down so many years before. Brig reached out and ran his hand along the railing just as Buster backed out of the doorway with a frightened sound.

Brig turned to reassure the dog, but he continued to back away and only stopped when he'd reached the edge of the porch, his eyes seemingly fixed on something at the top of the stairs. Brig felt eyes upon him, but he was sure it was his imagination. Still, the whole scene – the expression on Buster's face, the stale air and the tense feeling they were not alone unsettled Brig to his core. At that moment, he wanted to be anywhere but where he was.

He turned his head, half-fearing what he might see, but there was nothing there. The door to Jacob's room appeared to have opened a bit wider, allowing more light into the hallway, but Brig dismissed it. *You're letting your imagination get the best of you*, he thought. *There's nothing here but shadows.* He felt along the wall for the light switch and flipped it on. Buster relaxed a bit, more at ease with the unfamiliar setting once the lights were on. He nosed his way back into the house, eventually lying on a rug at the foot of the stairs.

Through squinted eyes, Brig read the thermostat set on 85. He shook his head and set it to a more reasonable temperature, knowing it would take several hours for the house to cool off. After propping the storm door open to allow in some fresh air, Brig plopped down in his father's recliner and surveyed the room. There was a smaller chair to his left. It was his mother's – undisturbed since her death – where she had spent hours reading beneath the glow of a floor lamp.

The chairs faced a bank of bookshelves cluttered with family pictures which told a story of joy and love. A story of happy times. Kodak moments. Smiles, vacations and Christmas sweaters. But the flip side of every happy memory is an untold truth. An inescapable reality rooted in the same storyline. They don't take pictures of those moments. Amongst the collection of frames there were no coffins, nor were there pictures of his father comforting his sobbing wife through hollow eyes, sagging heavy with grief. Sadly those were the memories Brig recalled most. They were the memories that had kept him away for so long. And now, they had brought him back.

Brig cleared away some envelopes from a table littered with unopened mail only to find the empty base where the cordless phone should have been. A brief search of the house led him to the handset on the desk in his father's office. Remembering his promise to call Kaitlyn, Brig started to dial Erin's number, but hung up, deciding he should try to reach his father first. After dialing the number scribbled on a folded piece of yellow paper removed from his back pocket, Gabe's voice came on the line.

"Dad, it's me," he said. "I made it up okay."

Sounding relived, Gabe said, "Good. I was beginning to worry. It's a long damn way. Did you have any trouble?"

"No, uh-uh. Things went fine. How are you feeling?" Brig asked. "Any better?" Somewhere in the distance he heard faint beeps and whirs. Remembering the times spent in the hospital with his mother, the sounds of the machines were a familiar and unsettling symphony.

"To tell you the truth, not so good. They've been doing tests all day. Every time the doc comes in, he scribbles something on my chart and starts pressing on my chest. I've been jabbed with more needles today than I care to tell ya. I don't like it one bit."

"I'm sorry to hear that," Brig said, not knowing what else to say. "Do you want me to come on up there and see you tonight?"

"No," came the reply. "You need your rest. We can talk tomorrow. This place is crawling with folks until about lunch. Why don't you come on up around noon. We can talk then. By the way, I'm sorry about the house. It's a mess, I know."

"It's fine dad, really."

Then there was a minute of silence. A strange pause in the conversation that wasn't unusual for Gabe, but something about it was uneasy and unfamiliar. Finally he spoke up with a slight shakiness in his voice that Brig interpreted as exhaustion. "Everything okay there?"

"Everything's fine. Buster's taking a while getting used to the new surroundings, but he'll adjust."

"Good," Gabe said. "You've got Harv's number if you need anything?"

"Sure do, but I can take care of myself, don't worry. You get some sleep and I'll see you around lunch tomorrow, alright?"

"Okay, son."

Brig was about to say goodbye when his father broke in one more time and said, "I love you, son. You're a good boy. You make your daddy proud, you know that, right?"

This was a sort of tenderness his father rarely displayed, and Brig was taken off guard. He choked back unexpected emotion and said, "I know. I love you, too."

-4-

Brig hung up the phone and pondered the conversation alone in uncertain silence with only the tick tock of the clock on the mantle to cut through the fog. He lost himself in his thoughts, resting on one arm and tapping the phone against his cheek before glancing up at the clock to see Kaitlyn's 9:00 bedtime was quickly approaching. From outside, the sounds of crickets drifted in the through the open door, carried aloft by the cool evening breeze.

"Erin? It's me," Brig said after dialing the number. "I just wanted to call and let Kaitlyn know that I made it in alright."

"Good, I'm glad you called," came the reply. "She's been asking about you." Brig assumed the silence that followed was the typical pause before Erin handed Kaitlyn the phone, but instead Erin spoke again, this time in a much lower voice. "Brig, I'm concerned."

"I don't understand."

"Kaitlyn won't stop talking about this dream of hers, and the details are getting more and more bizarre. I don't know if she's making them up as she goes along or what, but I remember her psychologist said..." Erin stopped mid-sentence, realizing that she'd let a little secret slip.

"Wait, a psychologist? What psychologist? Why would Kaitlyn need a psychologist?" He was angry. Forgetting to tell him about something trivial was one thing, but to intentionally hide the fact that Kaitlyn had been to see a shrink was another matter entirely. The realization he had been kept in the dark only underscored the disconnect he'd been struggling with. Times like these made it abundantly clear he had become a weekend dad, and that did not sit well with him.

Erin's tone grew defensive. "Brig, don't get all upset," she said. "I just thought that she might be having problems dealing with your mom's death, not to mention the divorce, that's all. She's been having a lot of these kinds of dreams here lately. We weren't exactly honest with her when your mom died. I know you've been having a hard time, and I just didn't see the need to worry you unnecessarily."

Brig paused. He knew himself, and he knew it was better to avoid saying something he would regret and be unable to take back. As for Erin's professed concern for him, he had his doubts, but this was about Kaitlyn, not him. "So she's been having dreams," he said. "What's the big deal? We've been through this before and it always passes."

"This one is nothing like the others," Erin told him. "I wouldn't be this concerned if it was." She moved from the kitchen to an area of her house with a bit more privacy. She continued, "My initial concern was that she didn't understand the reason your mother wasn't coming to see her anymore. I feared she might begin to develop some behavioral problems. She might think she's been... well... abandoned. But that's the funny thing. It seems she does understand. I tell you it's creepy. These dreams of hers – she thinks they're real!"

"Erin, she's five. Almost six. Kids have imaginations, and she's a really bright child. I really don't think a few vivid dreams are anything to get into a fuss over."

Kaitlyn shuffled into the room with the all-too-familiar sound of little feet slapping on tile. She called out for her mother with typical childish insistence. It was story time, and the little girl was not taking 'no' for an answer. Erin spoke up, "Listen, let me let you talk to her and you can decide for yourself, okay? I'm not trying to sway your opinion one way or the other. I just want what's best for her, don't you?"

"Of course I do."

"Here she is," Erin said. "I'm glad you made it in alright."

"Daddy?" The little voice said. "Daddy is that you?"

"Yeah sweetie, it's me! Whatcha doin'?"

"Nothin'," she said. "When are you gonna come see me? I miss you, Daddy!"

Brig stood up to move around the room, pressing the phone between his ear and his shoulder. "Daddy's gonna come and see you soon. I'm up here at paw-paw's right now. I have to take care of some things first."

"You're taking care of paw-paw?" She asked. "He's sick ya know."

Brig clenched his jaw. Erin knew better than to share that kind of thing with Kaitlyn. *What was she thinking?* "Paw-paw's gonna be *fine*, sweetheart. Don't you worry. He's tough." Empty promises were soothing at times like these for everyone concerned. In uncertain circumstances, they are handed out recklessly, and this was one of those times. Brig wondered to himself if he was making this assurance to ease his daughter's mind or his own.

"That's not what Nanna says," Kaitlyn countered. "Nanna says it's *time*. She says I shouldn't be sad for paw-paw." A chill washed over Brig then and it became clear Erin might be onto something. This time was not like the others. Nothing at all like the others. Kaitlyn lowered her voice to a whisper, seemingly conveying a secret to him and only him. "Nanna says, 'Don't worry.' She says, 'Welcome home.'"

Brig stood in the middle of the kitchen silent, doing his best to process all of this. *It's time? Time for what?* Erin told Kaitlyn to give her the phone. His daughter told him "Bye," but passed the phone to her mother without waiting for a response.

Erin got back on the line and said, "Brig? Brig, are you there?"

"What the hell was that all about?!"

"*That's* what I'm talking about! Is that not the creepiest stuff you've ever heard? And from a five-year-old, no less!"

"Did you tell her about dad?" Brig demanded. "I specifically asked you not to say anything!"

"NO! That's just it, how could she have known??"

Brig struggled to make sense of this, but couldn't. He paused with his hand on his forehead. It was too much for one day, and the morning's headache seemed to have followed him to Kentucky. Truth told, there were probably a dozen different ways Kaitlyn could have heard the news about his father, and that was probably the answer. The simplest explanation tends to be the right one, isn't that what they say?

Erin broke the silence. "Are you alright?"

"Yeah, yeah. I'm fine. She just caught me off guard that's all."

"Promise to call me when you find something out about your dad?"

"Yes. I will. I promise."

"Alright, I'm gonna go and tuck her in. I'll give her a kiss for you. Try and get some sleep, Brig. You sound tired."

"You're right," he said. "I'm beat. Goodnight." He hung up and set the receiver on the kitchen table when he was startled by an unfamiliar sound – Buster growling. Brig peered around the corner and saw the dog crouched in a defensive posture with eyes fixated on the stairwell again before turning them to Brig as he moved down the narrow hallway leading to the living room.

No sooner had the words, "What is it, boy?" left his mouth than Brig heard the sound of footsteps running up the staircase, and that's when he remembered he'd left the front door wide open. Buster barked in protest, but didn't budge from the rug he'd been lying on.

Again the house fell silent, but Brig feared that someone had slipped in while he was on the phone, so he eased up the stairs, fists clenched, to investigate. The area upstairs was bathed in soft lamplight, and the walls were accented with dark, angular shadows. There were far too many places for someone to hide, so Brig flipped on the overhead lights and chased the shadows from the rooms. After a careful inspection satisfied him that he and Buster were alone, he was still puzzled and a bit shaken.

He walked back down the stairs and sat on the bottom step while he struggled to gather his thoughts. *What's going on*, he thought, *Am I losing my mind?* In his head, he replayed his conversation with Kaitlyn and ended up getting stuck, again and again, on one comment that she'd made. She'd said that his mother had given her a message to pass along to him: 'Welcome Home.'

He lifted his eyes in time to see Buster retreat outside under the truck and hide behind one of the tires. He called out, but the dog wasn't about to budge. That's when Brig looked up and saw a small, cross-stitched sign hanging over the front door, which read:

WELCOME HOME

Brig had always prided himself on being a rational person, and he was sure there was an explanation for all of this, but finding it would have to wait until tomorrow. He needed some sleep. After calling for Buster once more and getting no response, he closed and locked the door. The dog would be fine spending the night beneath the truck, which was probably better anyway. His father had never liked having animals in the house.

He plopped back down in the recliner, and retreated into his thoughts. Soon, the clock on the wall chimed ten. His eyes grew heavy – a sure sign that sleep was near, but he knew what would come once sleep was upon him, and tonight he longed for a dreamless sleep. From his suitcase he removed a prescription bottle and shook a small, white Ambien tablet into his hand. His doctor had cautioned him about mixing medications when it had been prescribed to him, but after today's events, Brig was willing to take that chance.

Patiently, he waited for the pill to kick in. All the while, the air conditioner hummed away, filling the house with pleasant, white noise. The pills worked in a curious way. Just before they turned out the lights, they relax the muscles and fog the mind often projecting the imagination upon reality – a sort of waking dream. At least that was the explanation Brig would try to sell himself on the next morning...

From the fog, he began to hear giggles, like a child's laughter. He also heard bits and pieces of conversations he'd had that day.

"A house can absorb a lot of memories . . ."

Next, Kaitlyn spoke up: *"Welcome Home."*

There was more giggling from behind him, and the sound of someone telling the child to *shush*. His father's voice broke through again: *"It's about the house... Things don't seem quite so empty anymore."*

Brig's eyes closed, but not before catching movement in the mirror over the fireplace – a smooth motion, almost a glide but whatever had made it had no form. He opened his eyes again to see a woman dressed in flowing, white robes. She stood in the hallway, watching him.

His father spoke again: *"We was raised to believe that you'd see your loved one's again. I just didn't think..."*

The woman in white floated towards Brig - she was solid and transparent at the same time. His pulse quickened. He wanted to run out of there, but found himself paralyzed, near helpless as he fought The Sandman back. Each time he opened his eyes, the woman in white was closer. She reached out as she knelt beside him just as the timer on the living room lights clicked off. The room was consumed in darkness, and his mind screamed. The woman whispered in his ear, speaking in an ethereal voice, *"S-L-E-E-P."*

Kaitlyn's voice was the last familiar sound he heard:

*"Nanna says it's **time**."*

CHAPTER THREE

-1-

Brig woke, wincing at sunlight pouring into the room. He stood and stretched before going into the kitchen to brew some coffee, knowing he would find it there. Coffee had been an essential staple in the Bailey household for as long as Brig remembered and without fail, he found it in a cabinet over the maker. Thinking back to the events of the night before, his memory was fogged with the hazy amnesia so prevalent in the moments after waking as dreams slip further and further out of reach – *but was it a dream?*

Two teaspoons of sugar soon swirled in his coffee mug as Brig reached for the cordless handset sitting on the kitchen table. Its rapid chirp told him the battery was dead. From the comfort of the recliner, he saw Buster sleeping beneath the truck as he had been the night before. It didn't appear as though the dog had moved at all and had no immediate intentions of doing so. Brig set the phone back on its charging station and sipped his mug. Unable to recall last night's events, he dismissed them and thought instead about his father.

I'm a shitty son, he thought as he took another sip. Thinking back to all the time lost to the void, never to be regained. It all seemed such a waste. But that was in the past, and as his father would be quick to tell him, that's where it belonged.

He stepped out onto the porch; Buster crawled from beneath the truck and ran up to him. "*There* you are," Brig said with a laugh. "My great protector!" He opened the rear hatch of the Explorer and rummaged around, taking the rest of his luggage out and setting it on the ground. An old tennis ball rolled out as well, barely bouncing when it hit the gravel.

Brig held the ball above his head, and Buster rose on his hind legs, barking with excitement. Brig threw the ball up the drive, and the dog ran after it. A calm came over him as he waited for the return. Amazing how such a simple thing can bring such peace, but mindless as it was, that's what the game had always done for him. Already well on their way, with every toss the events of the night before drifted further and further away.

A quick check of his watch told Brig he had precious little time to take a shower and grab something to eat before he was supposed to be at the hospital. He called to Buster, who obediently trotted up to him. Brig grabbed the bag of dog food from the truck and walked over to a small, chain-link pen beside the garage where he opened the gate and motioned for Buster to go inside. The dog looked confused, with a peculiarly human expression – Buster was a house dog, so pens were something of a novelty to him.

"It's alright, boy, go on in there. I've got some stuff to do – can't take ya with me today and I can't have you wandering off."

He motioned as before, and the dog eventually obeyed. Brig reached into the bag and pulled out the red food dish, filling it to the top. He noticed the second "S" in "BUSSER" had begun to chip, and knew it was a problem Kaitlyn would be more than happy to fix when she came to visit.

Once inside the house again with his luggage in hand, he tossed his bags onto the couch and unzipped the duffle. He grabbed his shaving kit and headed down the hall to the guest bathroom for a much-needed shower. He was anxious to make it to Wicklow – anxious to see his father and to finally get answers to the questions burning in his mind.

-2-

In town, traffic was light, but it was a weekday so that was nothing unusual. Brig pulled off of the highway and into the McDonald's parking lot. The clock on the dash said that it was 11:00, which meant breakfast was no longer being served. More specifically, it meant no sausage biscuits. He stopped at the drive-thru to place his order. A disembodied voice crackled over the speaker, giving him his total. He pulled up to the window where a pimple-faced teenager handed him a paper sack and a soda.

Thirty minutes later, he arrived in the parking deck at Wicklow Memorial. After brushing his hair in the rearview mirror, he got out and headed towards the entrance where the automatic doors opened with a swoosh. Ahead, was the receptionist's desk. Behind it sat a large woman admiring her fingernails while talking to someone on the telephone about plans for the evening, the receiver cradled between her ear and her shoulder. Brig cleared his throat the woman finally acknowledged him.

"May I help you?" she asked, cupping her hand over the mouthpiece.

"Do you know which room Gabe Bailey's in?" he asked curtly.

She set the receiver down and turned to face her computer. The monitor's light reflected in her eyes making them big and blue. She typed in rapid spurts with a good deal of force. Then she paused.

"Oh..." she faced Brig again, and he thought she sounded much more timid than before.

"Your name, sir?"

"Brig. Brig Bailey. I'm his son."

"Could you wait here for a second?" she asked. "I need to check something on another computer." She got out of her chair and hurried away.

Brig rested his elbow on the corner of the desk as he scanned the room. It seemed larger than he remembered, and it had since been painted – he was sure of that. The walls were once a wretched pea-green color. That had been replaced with a less-offensive earth tone. His eyes continued to move across the room until they settled on a corner near the vending machines where he and his father had made the decision to pull the plug on his mother after the doctors had assured them all hope was lost. Brig wondered how many other families had made that same gut-wrenching decision within these walls and all the sorrow they had absorbed.

Five minutes passed and the receptionist still hadn't returned. Her behavior seemed odd to him, but it was dismissed easily enough about the time he glimpsed a familiar face coming up the hallway. It was Harv. He was wearing a black pair of slacks and a white button-down shirt, an ensemble which was far more formal than usual. Brig held his hand up in an effort to catch the old man's attention, and he called out him in an elevated voice from across the crowded waiting room. At first, everyone *but* Harv looked up, but the old man finally raised his eyes and saw Brig standing beside the receptionist's desk. His shoulders sagged, and he walked over to Brig, giving him a hug before speaking a word.

"It's good to see you, son," he said. "I guess you made it up last night?"

Brig agreed that he had. "I got in late, but I was able to talk with dad before he turned in."

Harv produced a handkerchief from his pocket and wiped his nose. "That's good." He looked up at Brig and said, "You're holdin' up pretty good."

"Well, yeah. Why wouldn't I be?" Harv put his hand on Brig's shoulder and opened his mouth to speak just as a figure in a white coat appeared.

"Mr. Bailey?" The doctor asked. No sooner had Brig turned around than the doctor launched into what Brig knew was a well-rehearsed speech – the kind doctor's must learn to recite robotically to keep from losing their minds. "Mr. Bailey, I'm Dr. Michaels, your father's cardiologist."

"Cardiologist?" Brig asked, turning to Harv. "Dad has heart problems?"

Harv dropped his head with guilt. He hadn't exactly been straightforward with Brig about his father's condition. Harv was an honest man, but hadn't wanted Brig to worry. Gabe had requested that he keep quiet about the severity of his medical condition, and Harv had willingly obliged.

Dr. Michaels continued. "Yes, sir, he did." The doctor was speaking in past tense, but that had yet to register with Brig. With one arm, the doctor motioned to a nearby sofa. "Would you sit down, there are some things I need to discuss with you." Brig sat in one of the nearest chairs instead. Harv sat beside him on the sofa with his arms crossed over his chest.

"Mr. Bailey," the doctor continued. "I want you to know how very sorry I am about your father. I knew him well. He was a very good man, and I want you know we did everything we could when he coded around midnight, but we were simply unable to resuscitate."

Brig stood up immediately and pointed one finger towards the doctor whose eyes widened with surprise. "Wait!" Brig interrupted. "Wait one goddamned minute. What happened?!"

His head turned back and forth, looking for reassurance from Harv. "Is dad alright?"

The doctor, clearly confused, turned to Harv who had a small tear running down the side of his face. "He doesn't know?" Harv shook his head, and the doctor sighed. "Mr. Bailey, I'm sorry to be the one to have to tell you this, but your father passed away last night from a massive heart attack."

Brig stepped back. "No!" he shouted. "I just talked with him last night! He was fine!"

"I'm sorry, sir."

Harv interrupted, "I tried to call you last night at the farmhouse and your home phone, but didn't get an answer at either one. The nurses tried, too. We just couldn't get a hold of you. With you living down in Birmingham, your daddy had me down as the emergency contact. I just figured you hadn't made it up here yet, but I was on my way out there to check when you stopped me." He buried his face in his hands and started to sob. The muscles in Brig's legs went limp, and he fell back into the chair.

The doctor scribbled something on a pad of paper. He tore off a small page and handed it to Brig. "Here's my number," he said. "I know you'll have questions in the coming days. Please call me, and I'll answer them as best I can." He stood up and turned to walk away, but looked back at the two men in the lobby chairs. "I'm truly sorry for your loss, gentlemen."

Brig waved the doctor off. He and Harv sat, not speaking, for about ten minutes as the shock settled in good and deep. His mind swirled with thoughts, brief flashes of moments far in the past before cratering into the reality that both his parents were now gone. Brig wiped a tear from his eye – the first of many. This type of soul-sucking grief was an emotion one never really gets used to – familiar, maybe, but never hardened to.

After suggesting the two of them make their way to Gabe's hospital room, Harv led the way down the long, tiled corridor. The hospital staff swarmed about like ants, but Brig paid them no mind. The two stopped in front of room 412. Brig stared into the room where his father had breathed his last less than twelve hours before. The machines in the room were eerily silent. Brig cautiously approached the bed that had been stripped of its sheets, giving it a cold, clinical look.

From behind him, Harv said, "You okay, son?" Brig nodded that he was. "Doesn't seem real, does it? This time yesterday, I was sittin' right here talkin' with him. He seemed fine to me, too, 'course I ain't no doctor." Brig shook his head. He wanted to keep from speaking as long as he could, knowing full well silence was all that was holding back a flood of tears.

A cool breeze crept into the room through a window which had been left partially open, barely detectable, but strong enough to lift a slip of paper from the nightstand. It floated to the floor, landing at Brig's feet. He leaned over and picked it up. On it was written "John B." and what looked to be a telephone number. Brig stuffed it in the hip pocket of his pants, then in a tone cold enough to surprise even himself, he said, "I guess we need to go ahead and make arrangements."

Harv shook his head. "No, your daddy didn't want you to have to worry about that nonsense. He already took care of it after your momma died. He said he'd been through enough funerals to know you ought not to be worried about plannin' at a time like this."

Brig stared at the empty bed and asked, "So what do we do now?"

Harv cleared his throat, "Start callin' folks I s'pose. Won't take long for word to get around. People in town thought a lot of your daddy. News'll travel fast. I reckon we'll just need to call the preacher and a couple others."

"Priest."

"Oh yeah, sorry. Your daddy never did talk about religion much. Guess in my head he's always been a Baptist."

Brig dreaded the first call he'd have to make. Erin was going to be devastated, and Kaitlyn... With a bit of difficulty, he recalled speaking with her the night before.

*"Nana says it's **time**. She says I shouldn't be sad for paw-paw."*

For a moment he even entertained the idea that she had known what was going to happen beforehand in the same way she seemed to know about him being ill without anyone having told her. He quickly dismissed the notion and focused, instead, on what he was going to say to her. He promised himself he wasn't going to sugar coat it the way he had the last time – especially if the way he and Erin had broken the news of his mother's death was really causing Kaitlyn problems. No matter what he chose to do, he knew it wasn't going to be easy.

He turned back to Harv and said, "Listen. I'm sorry. I don't mean to act so damn heartless. I guess I'm just in shock. I haven't even asked you how you're holding up."

"I know, son," Harv assured him, placing a calloused hand firmly upon his shoulder. "It's hard - hard as hell. We'll get through this, though. Your daddy would have kicked us in the ass for mopin' around this long, you know that?" The old man was doing his best to lighten the mood in spite of crushing sorrow weighing upon him. "You go and do what you gotta do," he said. "Go take care of that little girl. Your daddy loved her... Loved her like she was the greatest thing on two legs. I reckon that's exactly what he thought, don't you?"

"Yeah," Brig agreed. "I think he did." He pictured Gabe beaming with pride the day he and Erin had placed the newborn infant in his arms. Brig's mouth turned up at the corners.

The two shook hands and then exchanged a hug. Harv headed home, and Brig headed back to the farm. Halfway there, he pulled to the side of the road as the shock wore off and the pain hit with full, unrelenting force. As he sat sobbing, it occurred to him once more that he was alone. Both of his parents were gone and his wife had remarried; he was truly alone.

Soon after, Brig was on the interstate headed southbound in the direction of Havens Fork. It had been more than twenty-four hours since he'd had a drink, and he needed one badly. The next wet county was Warren, about 30 miles south. Havens Fork was mere minutes from the county line, and Brig considered stopping by Erin's to break the news in person. After a short debate with himself, he decided that he'd rather not do that. Instead, he chose to wait and call them when he got back to Jones Chapel, even though he knew that wasn't the right thing to do.

One by one, the miles flew by, and Brig was consumed with thoughts of his father – thoughts of happy times, thoughts of not so happy times, feelings of regret, and feelings of guilt – so much more of the latter. His exit appeared in the distance, and he pulled off the interstate and turned into the parking lot of County Line Liquors. An electric door chime heralded his presence when he walked inside. "Afternoon," the clerk said. Brig answered in kind and grabbed two bottles from the shelf.

The trip home was a quick one. Storm clouds had started to gather in the west, threatening what had started as a sunny day. Brig found it appropriate. Once in the farm's driveway, he stopped just past the tobacco barn when an animal limped in front of his truck. It looked like a coyote, or some other kind of wild dog. Nothing unusual for this part of Kentucky, but whatever it was, it was trailing blood and looked to be badly hurt. Brig assumed a car had hit it on the highway and doubted it had long to live. He'd seen that kind of thing too many times in the past. Most likely, the animal was looking for a good place to die. He watched it a while longer until it disappeared into a low valley.

Back at the house, he got out of the truck holding a bottle in each hand. The air was muggy outside as it always seemed to be just before a good thunderstorm. Rumbles in the distance had grown more frequent as the front moved closer. Brig let Buster out of the pen and went to the front porch where he sat down in the swing. Buster hopped up beside him, and Brig said, "Looks like it's just you and me, fella." Another round of tears followed, but Brig managed to get control of himself and went inside. Inside the house it was cold by comparison. Brig examined the thermometer, which read 50 degrees even though the thermostat had been set no lower than 70.

The phone rang, diverting his attention and a quick glance at the handset told him it was Erin. He had hoped for more time to prepare, but it didn't look as though that was going to happen. She must have detected something was amiss. The apprehensive tone in her voice suggested that she feared the worst. "Brig? How's your dad?"

And there it was. The question was on the table, warts and all. He tried to think of a way to break the news gently, but the more time he wasted thinking, the thicker the tension became. "Erin," he said. "I have some bad news. Dad passed away last night." His voice cracked in mid-sentence as he fought to keep from crying again. By Gabe Bailey's standards, he'd cried too much already, but it was out now – the Band-Aid ripped off quick and clean, leaving nothing more than the sting.

"Oh Jesus, no. No, Brig. *No, no, NO!*" It sounded like Erin had cupped her hand over the phone. Her muffled sobs were punctuated with an occasional, harsh sniff. "When did it happen?"

"I'm not exactly sure, but I think it was around midnight. The doctor told me dad suffered a massive heart attack. Erin, I didn't even know he had heart trouble, did you?"

"No," she said. "He'd mentioned going to the doctor several times, but I didn't think anything about it. Guys his age..." She was unable to finish the sentence before her hand went back over the mouthpiece again.

"Do you want me to tell Kaitlyn?" he asked, hoping Erin might offer to drop the bad news herself.

"She already knows! She woke me up at two o'clock this morning to tell me her paw-paw had 'gone to Heaven.' After that, she just went back to sleep as if it was no big deal. I didn't believe her... I told you, those dreams!"

Brig didn't want to hear any more about the dreams; frankly the whole thing was spooking the hell out of him. He changed the subject as quickly as he could. "Harv told me that dad had already made funeral arrangements. I feel so goddamned helpless! I just want to wake up. Tell me this is all a nightmare and that I'll wake up." He picked his coke bottle off of the table and took a sip. It was hot, but it was the only thing he'd had to drink since earlier that morning, so he gulped half of it down. He drank too quickly, and the carbonation burned in his throat long after the liquid had gone down. In frustration, he smacked a coaster onto the floor.

"I wish I could, honey. Really, I do." It was the first time she had called him 'honey' since their divorce, and he appreciated the tenderness in the gesture. Erin exhaled and said, "Kaitlyn and I are coming up."

"Thank you," he said. It never occurred to him to argue. Something inside him wanted them to come. It wasn't simply a desire to have someone there in this difficult time. It wasn't the fact that he missed Kaitlyn so deeply. It was more than that – an indescribable urge to have them near him. "When will you be up?"

"We can be there in a couple of hours. Are you going to stay put?"

"Yeah, I'll be here," he said. "But please drive careful. You guys are all I have now." The words had left his lips and there was no pulling them back. He half-expected an awkward silence, but none came. Erin's reply was immediate.

"Just stay calm and we'll see you around four."

Brig agreed, ending the call with a simple "Goodbye." He went into the bathroom and shook another Xanax tablet from the bottle. On his way to the kitchen, he grabbed his liquor bottles, placing one of them beneath the sink and opening the other only to pour a generous amount into his cup before placing the bottle inside the fridge next to the expired jug of milk.

As he walked back into the living room, intending to top the concoction off with what coke he had left, he froze, seeing that the bottle was sitting on its coaster again... the same one he'd knocked onto the floor only moments before. He told himself that he was just stressed out... that he was seeing things, maybe even forgetting things he'd done – things like picking up coasters and putting them back on tables, but deep down he knew better.

-3-

He had a good buzz going by the time Erin and Kaitlyn arrived an hour and a half later. He made a beeline for the bathroom, gargling with mouthwash in an attempt to get the smell of liquor off of his breath. The last thing he wanted was for his daughter to smell it on him.

Erin pulled into the small stretch of gravel connecting the garage to the drive. Brig watched from the living room window as she unbuckled her seat belt and did the same for Kaitlyn. His mood had lifted just knowing that they'd made the trip safely. He'd assumed the two of them were only coming up for the afternoon, so he was surprised to see Erin pop the trunk and take out three bags.

When he stepped out to meet them, Erin looked up, but her smile quickly faded. She set her duffle bag onto the ground and walked towards him with her arms open, wrapping them around his waist and giving him a squeeze. "Hey, there. How ya holding up?" She rubbed her hand across his shoulder in a consoling gesture.

"I'm fine, I guess. About as good as can be expected." He slurred the last word a bit, causing Erin to cast a suspicious glance back at him. They had been apart for a while, but she knew him well enough to suspect that his pleasant demeanor was most likely chemically induced.

He turned his eyes to her bags, and Erin's hands went to her mouth as though she were ashamed. "Oh, I guess I should have asked," she said. "I kind of assumed you'd want us to stay – I mean, I wanted to. I didn't think you'd mind. Is it alright?"

Of course it was alright. Brig was relieved to know he wouldn't have to go through the next few days alone. Of course Harv would be there for him, and his father's friends would be stopping by with the customary casseroles and pies, but at the end of the day, it would be him, an empty house and time to think. A dangerous mix indeed. Still, he wondered about Erin's new husband, Tom. There's no way he would be okay with this – what man in his right mind would be? When asked, Erin laughed.

"Well, to tell you the truth," she said. "He wasn't very happy about the idea. But I told him I was coming and that was that. He left the house in a huff about an hour before we did. It doesn't matter, though. He'll get over it. The important thing is that we're here for *you*. I'm going through this too, you know. Besides, I think Kaitlyn needs us both."

Brig nodded his agreement. "Where is she, anyway?"

Erin yelled, "KAITLYN BAILEY?!"

A small voice spoke up from behind the garage. "Comin' Mommy!" The little girl came running around the corner, with Buster close behind. When she saw Brig standing beside the car, her face lit up. She broke into a full sprint, her little, white dress flaring around her legs as she ran. Brig worried that she might fall on the gravel and bust her knee open, so he ran towards her in hopes that he could get to the edge of the drive before she did.

The two of them met next to Buster's dog pen. He scooped her into his arms and spun her around in the air before pulling her close and squeezing her hard enough to make her grunt. "Hey, sweetie!" He said. "How's my girl?"

Kaitlyn used both hands to push away and look him in the eyes. "Fine," she said. "How are you? You sad?"

"Yeah, Daddy's sad," Brig admitted. "He misses paw-paw."

"It's okay," Kaitlyn told him. "Paw-paw's not sick anymore!"

Her sentences were getting longer. Brig suspected that before long, she would be rid of her cute, childish phrases. He didn't want that; he wanted her to stay his little girl forever. He was missing out on so much, already. She had grown a good bit since the last time he'd seen her. Her hair was longer, and Erin had pulled it back into a set of unbraided pigtails. There was a crumb of what looked to be Oreo cookie on her cheek that Brig wiped off before kissing her on the forehead.

"You're right," he said, trying to be strong. "He's not sick anymore."

Kaitlyn took his face into her little hands and rubbed his cheeks. Her nose wrinkled up and she giggled. "Daddy needs a shave!"

The wind gusts had grown stronger, and the rumbles of thunder were much closer now. Brig looked up, but the canopy of trees blocked the sky's western exposure. He turned to Erin and said, "Looks like a storm's rolling in. We'd better get inside. He put Kaitlyn down and grabbed Erin's luggage as the four of them, Buster included, stepped into the house.

Erin stopped at the foot of the stairs and asked, "Which room do you want us to sleep in?"

"I guess you can sleep upstairs," Brig said. The rooms only have twin beds, so you can take my old room, and Kaitlyn can sleep in the other one." With that settled, he carried the bags upstairs with Erin two steps behind him. It was obvious to her that he'd lost some weight since the divorce. Still, she had always liked the way he looked in khakis, probably because it was such a rarity to see him in them.

She stood at the top of the stairs, holding onto the newel post as Brig put her bags at the foot of his old bed. She followed him into Jacob's room where he set Kaitlyn's bag on the floor. Her little suitcase was purple, and it rolled just like the big ones did. The Flintstones were on the front; Fred was driving the car, and Dino's head was sticking up through the roof.

Brig's mother had redecorated Jacob's room a year after he'd died, largely on Gabe's insistence. He'd said it wasn't healthy for her to keep torturing herself by keeping his room as some sort of shrine. The task was understandably hard on her, but she'd gotten it done. Most of Jacob's things had been given to a local charity, save two boxes of toys and various knickknacks she had been unable bring herself to get rid of. The room was then converted into a guest bedroom complete with a rocking chair and a desk. His mom had always loved rocking chairs, and each room in the house contained at least one.

Brig suggested to Erin that she might be more comfortable if she went ahead and unpacked. Erin agreed, but took a moment to look at the quilt on the bed. "This is beautiful!" She said.

"Yeah, mom made that some time ago. She was pretty good at sewing and quilts were her specialty, I guess. She made quite a few over the years. After she died, dad made sure to give one to each of her friends. I've got one back home. Come to think of it, dad saved a couple for you and Kaitlyn, too. I'll have to look for them."

"Don't worry about that now," she said as she ran her hands over the fabric, further admiring the detail. When her hands reached the center of the bed, she jerked away.

"What's wrong?" He asked.

Erin tested the area again and said, "This quilt is *wet*!"

Brig felt it, too and it was sopping. He looked up at the ceiling, but saw no water stains that would indicate a leak in the roof. "That's strange," he said. "I found some water on the steps yesterday. It has to be coming in from somewhere. Tell ya what, I'll get some more sheets, and we'll dry the quilt. Help me move the bed. If water's coming in through the ceiling, Kaitlyn will wake up in a puddle with this storm coming in."

Together, the two of them managed to move the bed over to the window. Deep indentions in the carpet marked the spot where the bed had sat for many years. Still, the area was curiously free of dust bunnies. Erin bent down to pick up a long, metal box that had been hidden beneath the bed. "What's this?" She asked, fiddling with the latch on the front. "It's locked."

Before Brig could answer, Kaitlyn burst into laughter after something crashed to the floor downstairs. He and Erin hurried downstairs to find that one of the living room lamps had fallen over. Kaitlyn covered her mouth with her hands, attempting to stifle another burst of giggles. Buster had hidden on the far side of the couch, but his tail stuck out, giving him away. Brig saw a yellow tennis ball a few feet from the lamp, and he quickly put two and two together.

"Busser can fetch!!" Kaitlyn said, pointing to the dog.

Brig growled and set the lamp upright. "Yeah, Buster can fetch pretty well, but we don't play in the house, okay?" Kaitlyn's lower lip puffed out in a pout. Brig immediately felt guilty and went to pick her up. He had never been a very good disciplinarian where Kaitlyn was concerned. He'd always left punishment up to her mother.

"It's alright sweetie," he said. "You didn't know."

"She does, too!" Erin protested. "I've told her at least a hundred times!" Brig put his finger over his lips and shook his head as if to say that now wasn't the time.

Erin said, "Alright. Enough rough housing. I think it's time someone went upstairs and did some coloring."

Kaitlyn buried her face against Brig's neck. "I think that's a good idea," he said. "You play upstairs for a while, and Buster will be here when you get up, okay?" Kaitlyn reluctantly agreed, and he handed her off to Erin who took her upstairs amid a flurry of cajoling over the wonderful pictures she'd drawn the past few days.

When Erin came back down, she held the quilt and an armful of sheets. "I guess I'll go ahead and put these in the washer," she said. "You don't want them to mildew. You'll never get the smell out." Brig watched her disappear into the laundry room and thought how much more alive the house had become in the short time the two of them had been there.

Once the load was going, Brig sat at the kitchen table staring off into space with his mind focused on thoughts of his father. Erin opened the fridge and looked back at him. "What's this?" She asked, holding up the bottle of rum he'd placed inside hours before.

To Brig's eyes, the letters on the label were large and bold. He read the words out loud without thinking: "It's *poison,*" he said matter-of-factly.

Erin laughed and said, "Well, it's not health food, I'll give you that, but I think 'poison' might be taking it a bit far."

He blinked and his mind returned from wherever it had been. Still, he knew he had seen "Poison." Brig got out of his chair and went over to the fridge. Erin saw a strange look in his eyes, and moved out of his way. He opened the refrigerator door and grabbed the bottle inside – all it said was 'Bacardi.'

"Are you alright?" She asked.

He didn't want to sound crazy, although he thought he might just be. Something was wrong with him; he was seeing things, and the hallucinations had progressed well beyond anything that stress could induce. A feeling came to him like an itch, and he couldn't shake the notion that someone was trying to tell him something – *but who? – Why?* He put the bottle back in the fridge and closed the door.

"Oh yeah," he said. "Everything's fine."

"I'm not judging," Erin told him. "Just try to watch it while Kaitlyn's here, okay?" Erin looked in the freezer next, finding it every bit as bare as the fridge had been. "Why don't I make a run to the store and get us some groceries to hold us over for a while?"

"We can take care of that tomorrow," Brig said. "Tonight, I'll just bring something back from town. Will you be alright while I'm gone? Anything in particular that you want?"

She waved him off and said, "Yes, yes, I'll be fine. I don't care where you go. I could eat anything at this point. Just be sure to pick Kaitlyn up a happy meal. She'll pitch a fit if you get her anything else, and be sure to get the girl toy."

-4-

Before leaving the house, Brig called in an order for a pizza. Delivery drivers didn't come out as far as the farm, which was in the sticks even by Jones Chapel standards. The sky outside had darkened considerably and the wind was growing stronger. The storm was going to bring a downpour.

Alone in his truck, he thought about Erin and Tom and the way she'd described his reaction to her coming up to stay with him. While, Brig understood Tom's response, something about the way Erin had told the story made him wonder if there might be more serious problems with the relationship. It was a tone he'd heard in her voice – almost ambivalence, but he set those thoughts aside for now.

Sadness crept back in on him as his mind replayed the conversation he'd had with his father the night before. Even though he hadn't gotten the chance to see his father before he'd died, Brig took solace in the fact that the two of them had parted on good terms. Still, Brig knew he should have been there; he should have been at his father's side when the time came. He tried to imagine what dying might be like. He'd read many books on the subject, and had managed to develop a host of preconceived notions that were probably influenced more by pop-culture than they should have been. Notwithstanding, he wondered if his father had seen the light, or if all that had met him at the end was an eternal void – life's final cruelty.

The Haunted House loomed on the hill ahead of him – another grim reminder of a life forever lost. The dark clouds rolling in from the west cloaked the house in an ominous shroud. Brig thought back to the summer day a month or two before Jacob died, when the two of them had spent the greater part of three hours inside that house. Their mother had turned them loose one afternoon after enduring a considerable amount of begging from both of them. It had taken them an hour to walk up to Hillbilly Hill from the farmhouse, but the boys had been more than willing to do it.

It was a day of fun and laughter, chair lift rides and enough cotton candy to make a grown man stagger. The two of them had eventually found their way into the Fun House, as it was called then, and made it all the way through in about twenty minutes. Jacob and Brig then turned around and went back inside where they'd split up, attempting to scare the bejesus out of one another. The majority of their time was spent in the mirror maze, and after about an hour, they'd mapped the place out pretty well. Even now, more than twenty years later, Brig believed he could find his way through.

A few minutes later, with pizza and Happy Meal in hand, he pulled up to the farmhouse. Light shone through the upstairs bedroom window, and Brig saw Erin's body silhouetted against the drapes. He killed the engine and watched her until she slipped on a shirt that obscured the outline. A wave of guilt came over him and he looked away. He shouldn't have those thoughts, and certainly not at a time like this.

But if truth be told, his father would have laughed. Gabe had always loved Erin, having told Brig on many occasions that he was an idiot for letting such a fine woman get away. Despite

Brig's vehement assertions that the two of them had suffered from "irreconcilable differences," it was an excuse Gabe had never bought into. He knew his own son, and though he loved him, understood there were two sides to every story.

Still absorbed in thought, Brig failed to notice the front door open. Erin emerged wearing a pair of blue and white, checkered flannel pajamas. She smiled when she saw the pizza box, and clapped her hands. "Great! I was hoping you'd go to the Hut." Brig laughed at her reaction and followed her back inside. He set the box on the kitchen table and held up the happy meal bag. "What should I do with this?" he asked.

"Just put it in the fridge." she said. "Kaitlyn's sleeping pretty hard. I don't think she's going to get up until morning, and I don't want to wake her. She's had a restless couple of nights, you know. Let's just let her sleep."

Brig agreed and placed the bag on the top shelf as Erin gestured with one of the glasses she'd taken from the cabinet. "Do you have anything besides water to drink?" she asked.

"Dad usually keeps a pretty good supply of drinks out in the garage."

Erin went into the garage and found a bottle of store brand cola. She went back into the kitchen and said, "Looks like all we have is generic."

"Hey, don't knock it," he said. "I grew up on that. It's pretty good stuff." He filled the glasses with ice and set them on the counter. To his surprise, Erin opened the fridge and took out the bottle of Bacardi.

She shrugged her shoulders and said, "Rough day." going on to pour about six ounces into each glass before topping them off with cola.

Back in the living room, Erin set her plate and glass on top of the coffee table. Brig bit into his slice; it was greasy and good.

"Harv called while you were out," she said. "He wants you to call him when you get a chance."

"How did he sound?" Brig asked.

"Tired. He seemed surprised to hear my voice, though."

Brig reached for his glass and took a swig; it was strong. "Did he say anything about the funeral plans?"

Erin detected a hint of worry in his voice and said, "No, uh-uh." She knew about Brig's anxiety attacks, and thought, *This must be killing him.* She also knew he was too much like his father to ever admit it. He had too much pride for that.

Together they finished off half of the pizza before Erin reminded him to call Harv again. Brig hadn't forgotten; he just didn't want to make the call. Erin's visit was a welcome distraction, a distraction that would come to a screeching halt the moment he dialed those digits.

Eventually, he picked up the phone, but instead of dialing Harv's number, he dialed the number to his father's hospital room. He wasn't sure why he'd done it; perhaps he thought there was some remote chance that his father would answer - one of those silly things you do in the grip of grief. Maybe he thought his desire was strong enough to break the bonds of death if only he believed that it could. In the end, his faith was found to be lacking when the voice of an old woman answered. Brig hung up and walked to the foyer, resting his head against the doorframe.

From where she sat, Erin was unable to see his face, but she saw his shoulders shake up and down, and she knew he was crying. She got up and went to him, wrapped her arms around his waist, and laid her head against his back. "I know," she said. "I know." It was good that he was grieving. He needed to. "Let it out, honey," she said. "It's gonna be okay, I promise."

Brig turned around and looked at her through red and puffy eyes. The tears that had built up in them spilled over his bottom lids. She pulled him close, wanting to say some magic words that would make things better, but she knew no such words.

"I want him back, Erin," he said. "Why? Why did this happen?"

"God works in mysterious ways ..."

Something in her comment struck a chord and Brig drew back, eyes narrowed. "God? What the hell does God have to do with it? Let me tell you something about God, Erin. He doesn't give a shit – not about you, not about me – *nobody!*"

Her mouth dropped open. She tried to tell herself it was the grief talking. "Come on, Brig, you don't mean that."

"*The hell I don't!* He took my brother. He took my mother. Now he's taken my dad!"

"People die, Brig. You can't blame God! That's just the way it is."

"Fuck that!" He shouted.

Erin drew her hand back and slapped him across the cheek. She shoved him against the door hard enough to knock a picture off the wall. Brig's eyes widened, and it felt like his cheek was on fire. He realized what he'd said and he immediately tried to apologize.

"Erin, I..."

"Don't you ever, *EVER* talk to me like that again!" She shouted. "I understand what you're going through, but that's no excuse. I'm in this with you, dammit! You don't think I'm hurting? You don't think I'm a little angry, too?"

"Of course you are," he said. "I'm sorry. I never should have said that."

Erin walked back to the coffee table and lifted her glass to her lips, taking a drink. She cut Brig a look that told him he'd picked a fight with the wrong person, and he knew it to be true.

He went over to her and motioned for her to sit down, which she did. Her expression morphed back to concern when he got down on his knees to look her in the eyes.

"I need you here, Erin," he said. "I can't do this alone. I don't have it in me."

She patted her lap and gently pushed on the back of his neck. He laid his head down, and she stoked his hair. "*Shhh*," she whispered. "It's okay." She jiggled her glass against her lips until an ice cube slid into her mouth. She took it out and rubbed it against his cheek in an attempt to soothe the sting.

-5-

Half an hour later, Brig found the strength to give Harv a call. Erin was right, he sounded exhausted. Brig wondered how long it had been since the old man had slept. Brig asked how he was doing, expecting the standard response.

"I s'pose I could lie to ya, but I won't," Harv said. "I've been better. Once you get my age, things just ain't the way you thought they'd be." He sighed. "They call 'em your golden years. I hear you're supposed to enjoy 'em, but it's kinda hard when you read the obituaries every day, looking for the names of folks ya know. Your daddy and me was good friends since before you were born. Friends like that don't come around every day."

Brig tried to console Harv, but found it difficult. He asked about the funeral plans, knowing full-well that the only uncertainties were likely small specifics. There was only one funeral home in town, so there was little question as to who would be handling things.

Harv went on to tell Brig that he had spoken with the funeral director earlier that day. "He seemed pretty upset, too," Harv said. "Gabe had a lot of friends, ya know. He said your daddy wanted a church funeral, said he's got everything planned out, right down to the songs we'll be singin'."

"Is there anything I need to do?" Brig asked.

"Nope. The wake is tomorrow, five o'clock. The funeral is the following day at ten in the mornin'."

Brig had always been amazed at how the folks in Jones Chapel wasted no time where death was concerned. They planted you in the ground before the shock wore off and the casseroles got cold. He'd never understood the rush, but that was how it had always been done: *Ashes to ashes, dust to dust... and save me a piece of that pumpkin pie.*

"I guess dad planned to have the service at St. John's Cathedral, right?"

"Lemme see," Harv trailed off as he riffled through his notes, searching for the information. "Uh, yep. That's right, St. John's. That's in Wicklow, isn't it?"

"Yes, it is."

Harv paused, not sure how to bring up the next issue. "I reckon the funeral home boys'll be out sometime tomorrow to open up the grave. I thought you might want a little warnin', you know, in case you wanted to make yourself scarce and all."

Brig was surprised he'd overlooked that detail, and he hoped he wouldn't have to see the deed done. The small family cemetery was just at the far end of a large hay field within sight of the farmhouse. Three generations of his family were buried there. It only made sense Gabe would want to be there too beside his wife and son.

Harv continued. "Are you gonna be alright tonight?"

"Yeah, I'll be fine. Don't worry about me. Erin and Kaitlyn are here. They'll be a lot of help."

"I'm glad to hear it," Harv said. "You need folks around ya at times like this." When he spoke again, he sounded unsure of himself and through all of the condolences and well wishes, there was that familiar stink of Jones Chapel gossip mill. "I thought you two was split up ..."

Brig hesitated and said, "Hang on, Harv." He cupped his hand over the receiver and whispered to Erin, asking her to please fix him another drink. She took his glass into the kitchen, and when the coast was clear, he continued: "Yeah, we are. We're still pretty close, though. It's better that way – for Kaitlyn, I mean."

Erin overheard the last part, and she frowned, knowing they were talking about her. She went back into the living room and put Brig's glass on the table beside him. His lips formed the words, "*Thank You,*" without making a sound, and his eyes cut to the clock as it chimed 9:00.

"That your clock?" Harv asked.

"Yeah, it's nine."

"Well, I guess it's gettin' pretty late. I should probably be turning in. We've got a long day tomorrow." It was a graceful exit, and Brig appreciated the tactfulness. "You best be gettin' yourself some sleep, too," Harv told him. "I want you to listen to me: if you need anything, you call me, ya hear?"

"I'll do that – same goes for you. Say 'hello' to the wife for me." Brig hung up and leaned back in his chair. Erin waited for him to say something, but he wasn't volunteering.

After a few tense minutes, she broke the silence. "How's he doing?" she asked.

"Alright, I think. He's having a tough time, too. The real litmus test will be tomorrow."

"What time's the wake?"

"Five. The funeral will be the day after tomorrow at St. John's... then we'll come back here for the burial."

Erin nodded. "That's how it should be," she said. "Your dad loved this place. It's part of your family and probably always will be. I can't imagine he'd want anything else."

Brig stood up and stretched. It felt as if the walls were closing in on him, and he needed some fresh air. "Hey," he said. "Would you mind if we stepped out onto the front porch for a bit? I need to get out of the house."

Outside, the sound of thunder faded in the distance, overshadowed by the – *plink, plink* – sound of rain hitting the barn's tin roof. Brig sat down in the swing and looked over to Erin who was leaning against one of the posts, staring up into the starless sky. "C'mon," he said, patting the seat beside him. "I won't bite."

She smiled and sat down next to him. Buster, who had been curled up on the other side of the porch got up and stumbled towards them. He hopped up, placing one paw on Brig's leg, the other on Erin's. They both petted him for a minute or two, but the dog soon hopped back down.

For a brief bubble in time, it was as though the past two years hadn't happened at all. Erin lost herself in the moment and rested her head against Brig's shoulder. He interlaced his arm with hers and gave her a kiss on top of her head. They sat, swinging in peaceful silence, as they listened to the rain moving eastward. After the thunder died, a symphony of crickets filled the void with harmonic, mournful chirps.

When the clock struck again, Erin sat upright, unaware that she had drifted off to sleep almost forty minutes before. She rubbed her eyes and asked, "What time is it?" Brig told her that it was ten o'clock. She stretched and spoke through a silent yawn: "Guess we'd better turn in, huh?"

"Yeah, I guess so," he said. "But first, I'm going to go upstairs and check on Kaitlyn." He went inside and climbed the stairs where he stopped in the doorway. Kaitlyn was sleeping soundly, and when she let out a little snore, Brig laughed to himself. He walked into the room and picked up her teddy bear, which had fallen out of bed. It was a talking teddy bear she had named Charlie. In the days before Kaitlyn had acquired the skill to pronounce her "L's", it had sounded as if the bear's name was Charry. Brig tucked it back under her arm. He froze when she started to stir, afraid that he'd woken her, but he relaxed again when her head sank back into the pillow. He kissed his finger and placed it on her cheek. Back downstairs, Erin was waiting for him. "How is she?" she asked.

"Sleepin' like a rock."

Erin glanced up the flight of stairs and said, "I just remembered something; we didn't put the sheets back on the guest bed."

"Oh, don't worry about that now," he said. "it's too late. You can sleep in dad's room. I'll be fine. I spent last night in the recliner, anyway. It's actually pretty comfortable."

Erin shrugged her shoulders, and said, "Well, if you're sure."

She opened the door to the master bedroom and started to walk inside when Brig said, "Erin?"

"Yeah?"

"I'm really glad you're here. Thank you for coming. I'm sorry about what I said before." She smiled that familiar smile. It made Brig think of their first date all over again.

"I'm glad I came, too," she said. "Goodnight."

CHAPTER FOUR

-1-

By 4:30 the next afternoon, a steady stream of cars lined the highway between Jones Chapel and Wicklow as Gabe's friends and neighbors made their way to the funeral home. Death was a big deal in Jones Chapel, common though it was, and Brig, Erin, and Kaitlyn arrived thirty minutes beforehand to take care of any last minute details and to prepare themselves for the three hours that were to follow.

Upon arriving, Erin took Kaitlyn into the restroom. Brig followed the arrows on the signs which read: 'Gabriel Bailey' until he stood in the doorway of a large room filled with cushioned, folding chairs. A cherry wood casket lay at the front of the room illuminated by seven overhead lights. The top half of the lid was open, but from the doorway, Brig couldn't see his father's body.

Erin's hand touched his shoulder, startling him. "Are you alright?" She asked. "Are you ready for this?"

He turned his back to the casket. "I don't know. I'm not sure I can do this." He had told himself to be strong – for Erin and Kaitlyn – but he didn't feel strong. He felt weak and ashamed and turned his head away, unable to look her in the eyes.

Erin placed her hand on the side of his face and gently turned it towards hers. "That's why we're here," she said. "This isn't going to be easy, but it's something you have to do. Pretty soon, a lot of people are going to be coming... let's get this over with." She nodded her head towards the casket, directing him.

Brig drew in a deep breath and said, "Okay, let's do it."

They entered the room, and Erin sat Kaitlyn down in the back row. "You stay here and color with your crayons," she told her after producing a coloring book and a box of Crayolas from her purse. "Mommy and daddy will be right up there." Erin pointed towards the casket, but Kaitlyn couldn't see over the back of the chair in front of her, so she stretched her neck to see what her mother was talking about.

"Is paw-paw up there?" She asked.

Erin wasn't sure how to answer. The decision to tell the truth had been an easy one while Gabe was alive; but now, in the face of the situation at hand, she started to doubt her convictions. "Yes," she said. "He is."

Kaitlyn shook her head. "He can't be."

"What do you mean, honey?"

Kaitlyn pointed to the ceiling, "Nanna says Paw-paw's in Heaven now."

Tears swelled in Erin's eyes, and she thought how easy it would be if death were that simple and she could view it all through the innocent eyes of a child. She had been raised as a Baptist. She believed in God; she believed in Heaven; she believed in Hell, but she still struggled with the uncertainty of it all. It occurred to her then that her faith might be better described as something else – hope. After all, that's what it boiled down to, plain and simple.

"Yes, honey, he's in Heaven... at least his spirit is." Brig listened with interest when he overheard his daughter getting her first lesson in death.

"Spirit?" Kaitlyn asked.

"I'll explain when you get a little older, Katie." Erin patted her daughter's knee and stood up, hoping Brig wouldn't see the tears in the corners of her eyes.

Kaitlyn's face twisted with confusion. "Is Nanna a spirit?" she asked.

Erin looked back at her then and saw an expression that underscored a genuine desire to understand. Even more important, this seemed to be the opportunity to set the record straight, clumsy though it was. "Yes, honey, she is."

Kaitlyn's eyebrows lifted, and it looked as though the mental puzzle pieces had come together at last. Erin waited for another question, but none came. Instead, the little girl simply nodded and proceeded to sort through the crayons in her lap as she silently considered the information that had just been put to her. Erin took Brig's arm and led the way to the front of the room. The two of them were well out of earshot and unable to hear her when Kaitlyn softly spoke out loud to no one in particular: "There's spirits at Daddy's house..."

-2-

As they neared the casket, Gabe came into view. The body had been dressed in a black suit with a red tie, which contrasted sharply against a white shirt, hands folded in the standard way at his waist. Brig and Erin stopped three feet from the casket, after Brig told her he couldn't go any further. He looked down at the body and tightened his jaw, fighting back the tears. His father looked thinner than he remembered; his hair was completely gray and neatly combed to one side. Beside the body was a pillow in the shape of a heart which bore the embroidered names: Brig, Jacob, and Kaitlyn.

Erin pointed at the pillow and said, "That's nice. Did you tell them to do that?"

"No, uh-uh," Brig answered.

A voice came from behind them. "I did." Both turned and saw Harv walking up the center aisle. "Wanted to do somethin' special. The wife sewed the names on last night. Hope you don't mind." He was dressed in a blue, pinstriped suit with a white shirt. His tie was yellow, but too short. The tip didn't make it past the center of his stomach, and the knot was too thick.

"No, not at all." Brig said. "I think it's great. Where is Judy? I'd like to thank her."

"She'll be along," Harv said. "She had to run to the beauty parlor. You know how these women are." He tipped an imaginary hat towards Erin. "No offense to *you*, ma'am."

She laughed at the courteous gesture. "None taken."

Brig's eyes cut to the back of the room where Kaitlyn had sprawled out over four chairs in the back row. "Do you think she's okay?" He asked.

"Yes. She's fine. She'll color all night long if we let her."

"Got a little artist on your hands, do ya?" Harv asked as he walked toward the casket and looked down at Gabe's body. The old man shook his head from side to side at the sight of his lifelong friend - neatly dressed and packaged up in a pretty wooden box for all eternity. "Damn shame," Harv said. "Good fella your daddy was."

Brig thanked him in the tone of voice he'd rehearsed especially for that night. "He looks good, don't you think?"

Harv nodded and scratched the back of his head. "Yep. Sure does. Looks like he's sleepin'. People's gonna tell you that he looks 'peaceful.' Ev'rybody says the same thing, 'peaceful.'" The statement was almost prophetic: Before the night was over, those very words were spoken repeatedly.

Kaitlyn ran up the aisle holding a piece of paper. Brig and Erin positioned themselves shoulder-to-shoulder in front of Gabe's casket to block her view.

"Daddy," she said. "Daddy, I made you a picture." She held it out, and Brig took it from her. In it, he saw a white house surrounded by a green lawn. Above it was a pastel-blue sky complete with puffy clouds and a yellow square that he assumed was the sun. What caught his attention the most was in the center of the page: a man and a woman were holding hands, wearing huge grins on their faces. The corners of his mouth turned up when he realized that he was the man. Kaitlyn had drawn him as a stick figure wearing a black suit. His head was enormous, and she had even gone so far as to add in little black specks where his cheeks should have been. He assumed they were beard stubble.

The woman in the picture was clearly Erin. She had been drawn as a slightly shorter stick figure with long, brown hair. Brig examined the picture closer, and his mood darkened again, understanding what must have been going through her mind when she'd drawn it. The answer was simple; she wanted her mommy and daddy together again.

He glanced up and watched Erin lead her to the back row again. Something inside him wanted that, too. He thought about the divorce and the part he had played in it. At that moment, he wished he could turn back time and change the decision he'd made – that one and so many like it.

-3-

To Brig's relief, the night finally ended. Kaitlyn had fallen asleep an hour before, and Brig carried her in his arms to the truck where he laid her down in the backseat. On the way home, he reflected on the evening's events, taking solace in the comforting things people had said. The outpouring of support had surprised him. There was strange consolation hearing first-hand how his father had touched the lives of so many. The reunions, distractions, and anecdotes had helped ease the pain. He felt stronger because of them, but he knew too well his strength was due in large part to Erin. She had been strong enough for all of them.

He remembered one instance in particular when a friend of his father's, a lady named Thelma Morris, had come up and offered her sympathies. Brig thanked her, and the old woman had gone on to remark about how much he'd grown since she last saw him. Thelma looked at Erin and said, "This must be your wife. My, what a pretty little thing." Brig had expected Erin to correct her, but she played along instead. Thelma continued on despite the line of people behind her. "Brig looks good," she said. "You have certainly taken good care of him." Erin waved off the praise assuring her that Brig pretty much took care of himself, but Thelma chuckled and leaned forward as though she were about to whisper a secret, softly patting Erin on the arm. "You just let him keep thinking that, dear. We know who the boss is, don't we?"

Erin wrapped her arm around Brig's back and given him a little squeeze. "Yes, ma'am," she said. "We certainly do."

Brig parked his truck in the driveway, behind Erin's car. He opened the back door and slid his hands beneath Kaitlyn's limp body. "Careful," Erin whispered, "don't wake her up." Kaitlyn hugged her teddy bear close to her body and made an irritated sound when her father lifted her.

"Shhh," he said. "We're home, now."

Brig handed his keys to Erin, who unlocked the front door. Once inside, she put down the items she was carrying and held her arms out. "I'll take her upstairs," she said. Brig gave his daughter a soft kiss on the forehead before handing her off. He flipped on the stairwell light and watched as the two of them disappeared through the doorway. The ordeal was halfway done. All that remained was the funeral in the morning and things would begin to settle down enough for him to make sense of it all.

He removed his suit coat, laying it across the back of his mother's chair before thinking better of it and going into the laundry room for a hanger. Erin was back in the living room when he returned. "You did really well tonight," she said. "I'm proud of you."

"Thanks, I couldn't have done it without you." He loosened his tie, undid the top shirt button, and scratched his neck.

She laughed at his obvious discomfort and said, "I thought you'd be used to wearing a suit by now."

"Guess I've gotten out of the habit," he said. "Can't say I ever really liked them to begin with." His eyes drifted to the pictures on the bookcase, and he went to look at them. Erin followed and rested the side of her head against his shoulder. Brig rubbed her hand as she wrapped her arm around his waist and said, "They're all gone now. You know that?"

She squeezed him a little tighter. "I know, hon. It's gotta be hard on you. But I'm still here."

He turned to face her, and looked deep into her eyes. There was warmth in them, and in the soft living room light, her pupils were large and rimmed in light blue. Something came over him, and he put his hands on the sides of her face. He waited for her to stop him. When she didn't, he leaned in and kissed her on the lips. Part of him expected her to pull away, but instead she pulled him closer.

The moment soon passed, and both of them felt embarrassed by what they had done. To her embarrassment, Erin added guilt. She thought about her husband, probably still fuming back home. Tom had hinted that something like this might happen. But it was a simple thing - a kiss - nothing in the grand scheme. A slight indiscretion, really. Rationalization is easy when you try, and Erin did her best until regret yielded to excitement. It was an emotion she allowed herself even though she knew better.

Brig stroked her arm and said goodnight before turning for the master bedroom and disappearing through the door, closing it quietly behind him. Erin rounded the railing and headed upstairs, gentle with her footsteps so as not to disturb the little one. She changed into a white nightgown and sat in front of the dresser mirror, brushing her hair. She stopped and set the brush down, unable to shake the tender moment from her mind – part of which told her the kiss had been a mistake, but her heart told her it hadn't been.

Was it possible a spark still existed? Something smoldering in the recesses of her mind – in Brig's mind – something she just hadn't allowed herself to see? Things were different now. Brig was different now. It was no great leap to allow herself to consider the possibility, but the conflict within her was fierce. She tapped the nail of her index finger against her front teeth and thought, *He's vulnerable now. I'd be taking advantage of him. I can't believe I'm even* considering *this!*

Brig had long since settled into bed and pulled a pillow to his chest. The events of the day were heavy in his thoughts, but he was thankful to have gotten through them. From the bathroom could be heard the steady drip of a faucet which grew fainter and fainter as it was gradually replaced by the familiar tune *Amazing Grace* softly hummed by a chorus of disembodied voices.

He turned and saw his father's casket perched above an open grave. It appeared the graveside service was complete, and all of the mourners had left, leaving only himself, Erin and Kaitlyn. He took their hands into his own as the casket was lowered into the earth. He approached the grave with both of them in tow just as the humming stopped, and Brig looked back down at his hands only to find them empty. He was alone beside the grave, just he and his father's body in a vacuum of silence if not for the gentle breeze moving across the fields.

The casket lid flung open and Brig stifled a scream as his father's eyes fixated upon him, milky and white. Brig's pulse quickened, his feet anchored in place preventing him from running away. Gabe struggled to speak and once the words finally came, they were dry and dusty.

"Protect her..."

Brig was pushed from behind - ever so gently nudged - and he fought to regain his balance before falling into the grave atop the casket with a hollow thump. Gabe's arm reached out for him, but Brig backed away, not wanting to feel the cold touch of the corpse. He retreated as far as he could before his back struck the clammy grave walls. Gabe sat up in the casket and extended a finger to point at Brig, *"It's up to you."*

Brig screamed and found the strength to climb, fearing with every foothold that he would feel a grip on his ankle. The humming resumed as he struggled out of the grave. A quick glace back into the hole revealed the lid to his father's casket was closed. He drew in a breath and stood up just as a muffled voice came from inside the wooden box:

"He's coming. Just like before."

Brig jerked awake, his heart pounding and his forehead damp with sweat. He opened his eyes to see a white figure silhouetted in the doorway. His memory flashed to the night before and he remembered the lady in white through the amnesia haze. He feared she had come for him again, so his fingers franticly searched for the bedside lamp as the figure moved towards him, slow and with purpose. In his mad frenzy, he knocked the clock radio from the nightstand before his finger found the lamp switch. A soft, golden light filled the room.

Erin stood at the foot of the bed in silence. Her satin gown clung to her hips, and there was a softness in her eyes he hadn't seen in years. He studied her face for some explanation, but found none. She climbed onto the bed and slipped beneath the covers, spooning up beside him with her arm across his chest, pulling him closer before planting a gentle kiss on the back of his neck. Brig reached out and flipped off the lamp, taking her hand into his own. Words were unnecessary, so none were spoken. The moment was as tender as it was unexpected, and he found comfort in her embrace.

-4-

Around 6:00 the next morning, Brig awoke to the smell of bacon and eggs. In a sleepy daze, he stretched his hand over to the side of the bed where Erin had been sleeping, finding only empty space. He opened his eyes to see the impression her head had left on the pillow. Her presence had been soothing and for that, he was thankful. Remembering what lay before him today, he threw on a robe and made his way to the kitchen where he found Erin busy making breakfast.

She greeted him as he stepped in from the hallway, and Brig kissed her on the cheek. "Morning, what's all this?"

"Oh, I woke up early, so I thought I'd make us something to eat. Are you hungry?"

"Yeah," he said. "Starving." He made his way to the coffee pot and poured a cup, rubbing his eyes with his spare hand. Never one to be a conversationalist so early in the morning, his words were few.

Brig heard footsteps on the stairs and went into the living room in search of the source. Kaitlyn was awake, and she made her way downstairs with her little hand holding the railing; Charlie the bear was held tightly in the other arm. Her hair was awry, and her eyes were puffy. One footie of her pajama footies was stretched out too far, and it flopped beside her as she walked.

"Hey, Katie!" He said.

"Mornin' Daddy."

"You hungry?"

She raised her hands above her head and made what looked like bear claws with them. "Uh-huh," she said. "My tummy's goin' *grrrrrrrrrr.*"

Brig scooped her up. "Well, come on, then! Mommy's makin' us some breakfast."

"Fruity Pebbles?"

"No, not Fruity Pebbles. Bacon and eggs." Brig set her down in one of the kitchen chairs and scooted her to the table. She proved a little too small for the chair, so he went and got a phone book for her to sit on.

Erin put a plate in front of her and another in front of Brig. "You eat it all, Katie," she said. "Did you sleep well last night?"

"Nope."

"Why not?"

Kaitlyn took a big bite of her eggs and chewed with her mouth open. She stared up at the ceiling as if she were trying to remember something and said, "They wouldn't leave me 'lone."

Erin narrowed her eyes in Brig's direction, concerned they were about to hear about another one of her dreams. Erin waited a while longer before asking, "Who wouldn't leave you alone?"

"The Spirits."

It was a standard response, certainly nothing out of the ordinary as Kaitlyn had said things like that many times before. Typically a bit more prodding was needed before the information could start flowing. Erin was used to this. Brig, not so much, and he coughed after a bit of his eggs went down the wrong way. Erin shrugged her shoulders as if to say, '*I told you so.*'

"Nanna again?"

Kaitlyn answered with a shake of her head and Erin suspected her daughter must have simply had a nightmare about their discussion the night before at the funeral home. She dismissed it as such, and went to the stove to prepare her own plate.

Five minutes later, Kaitlyn dropped her fork, announcing to the room that she was done. Brig clapped his hands and held one up for a high five. "Good job!"

Erin took the little girl's plate and put it in the sink. "You sure are!" She said. "Mommy's gonna run your bath now, okay? We have to start getting ready."

Brig was already busy clearing the table. He assured Erin he would take care of the rest and thanked her for making breakfast. He finished loading the dishwasher and stepped onto the back deck for some fresh air. To the east, a small group of men were erecting a large, green tent inside the family cemetery, about a thousand yards from where he stood. Two of the men fought against the breeze using a tarp to cover a mound of dirt from the freshly excavated grave.

In an adjacent field, cattle grazed seemingly oblivious to the activity going on around them. A small flock of turkeys walked about, and deer could be seen just beyond the tobacco barn. For them, life went on just as it did for the men erecting the tent and as it would for so many of the people attending the funeral today once they had said their goodbyes and returned to their lives. In that moment, it all seemed so futile - living and dying - and part of him wondered, as it always had, if there really was something after it all - something beyond the pain and the heartache - something that made it all worthwhile.

Brig had his reservations. He'd never voiced them out of respect for his mother, but the constraints of their religion had always been a little too much for him - far too intellectually confining. He often wondered if it all ended with a whisper, a coffin, and a cold hole in the ground - a cruel joke with no one there to get the punchline.

-5-

The three of them arrived in the church parking lot well ahead of the service in time to see the hearse pull up to the curb. Four stocky men in blue jeans and dirty t-shirts climbed out of a beat-up Chevy pickup that was behind it. They opened the back of the hearse and pulled Gabe's casket out. Brig's anger swelled as he watched them carry it into the sanctuary. They handled it with about as much care as airport ground crews handle luggage. His brow furrowed, and he started towards them when Erin grabbed his arm.

"No, Brig," she pleaded. "Don't. Not in front of Kaitlyn."

He looked down at his daughter who was wearing a frightened expression. The little girl was gripping her mother's leg with her right arm, her teddy bear in her left. When he knelt down beside her, she hid her face. Brig looked up at Erin and asked, "What's wrong with her?"

"She doesn't like to see you angry. It scares her."

He reached out and touched Kaitlyn's arm, but she jerked away. "Katie?" he asked. "What's wrong?"

From behind Erin came a little sniffle. Kaitlyn showed her face again, and through the tears said, "Daddy's mad. Don't hurt mommy. I'll be good, I promise."

Confused, Brig looked up at Erin again; she had a small tear forming in her eye. "What the hell is she talking about?" He demanded to know.

"I don't know. She just gets scared of men sometimes."

Brig bent down and picked Kaitlyn up. He gave her a kiss on the cheek and said, "Don't worry, sweetie, no one's gonna hurt mommy." He pointed at the hearse. "Daddy just got upset with those guys over there, that's all."

Kaitlyn scratched her nose and wrapped her arms around his neck. "Promise?" she asked.

"Promise."

He gave her another kiss and put her back on the ground. Kaitlyn hugged her mom's leg again and when she did, Erin's dress lifted, exposing her upper calf. Erin pulled it back down, but not before Brig caught a glimpse of a nasty bruise. An expression of concern must have flashed across his face, because Erin was quick and dismissive.

"Don't be silly. I know what you're thinking. Tom would never… I mean, Tom didn't…"

Brig pulled her close to him, her ear next to his lips so that Kaitlyn couldn't hear what was said. "Really?" he whispered. "Where'd the bruise come from, Erin?" He crossed his arms waiting for an answer, but she hesitated a bit too long.

"That's what I thought," he told her, pulling her close again. "That son-of-a-bitch! So help me God, Erin if he has laid so much as a hand on Kaitlyn…"

Erin was fighting back the tears now, carefully wiping her eyes to preserve her mascara. "Now, don't overreact – please. Tom has never laid a hand on Kaitlyn, I swear."

"And what about you?" No answer came, and the fire in his eyes cooled to pity and concern. With his rekindled feelings for Erin, Brig found himself in a strange place, unsure what to do next. Though the fire in his eyes was gone, his stare was hard and he was not looking away.

"Listen," Erin said. "We'll talk about this later. This is hardly the time," she urged pointing at the cathedral. "This is your dad's funeral for Christ's sake!"

"Alright," he said, "but we *ARE* going to talk about this. You best be honest with me when we do, and if I find out he's put so much as a finger on my little girl, God help him Erin, he'll answer to me."

"Yes, yes," she said. "Let's just focus on this right now, okay? One thing at a time."

Brig knelt down and stroked the back of Kaitlyn's head before kissing her on the cheek. The little girl held her teddy bear tighter when he took her hand and the three of them walked towards the church where the priest stood in the doorway, offering handshakes to the mourners as they came in.

"Brig Bailey?" He said. "Remember me? I'm Father O'Connor. How are you?"

Brig shook his hand. "Yes, of course. I'm fine, Father. Thank you." He motioned to Erin. "You remember this lovely lady, I'm sure." The priest assured him he did with the typical pleasantries before Brig introduced him to Kaitlyn. Father O'Connor looked down in time to see the little girl duck behind her mother.

"Bashful?" he asked.

"I'm afraid so."

The priest turned to Brig and said, "I'm terribly sorry for your loss. You can take comfort that your father is with God now." Brig smiled politely, but said nothing. Just then, another couple stepped up and diverted the priest's attention long enough for the three of them to slip into the sanctuary and take a seat in the front row, which had been reserved for family.

Within fifteen minutes, the church had filled with people; some of which Brig knew, but most were nameless faces in the crowd. He felt a tap on his shoulder and turned to see Harv standing with his wife Judy. Brig stood up and hugged both of them.

"How ya holdin' up, boy?" Harv asked.

"I'm fine. You?"

"Hangin' in there, I s'pose. Do you mind if we sit here with ya? I know this spot's for family. I don't mean to intrude."

Brig waved the comment off as unnecessary courtesy and motioned for them to sit. "You know we've always considered you both members of the family."

Harv's smile was genuine. "I appreciate that," he said. The old man was dressed much better than he had been the night before, and Brig suspected that Judy had a lot to do with that. He gave her another hug and thanked her for the pillow.

"Oh, I was happy to do it," she said. "It was the least I could do. Your daddy meant a lot to us, Brig." She turned to look at the casket, but turned away. "It's just hard to believe he's gone."

Brig nodded and said, "I know."

Father O'Conner approached the altar as the organ music began. Kaitlyn was consumed with her coloring, lifting her gaze only momentarily when the low roar of voices in the church muted to silence.

The service that followed was long, and Brig felt renewed grief when the priest made mention that Gabe had gone on to be with his wife and youngest son who had died before him, causing him to shift uncomfortably in his seat. Erin took his hand and gave it three quick squeezes. It was a code his mother had come up with to say that she loved him once Brig had reached the age that saying, 'I love you,' in front of his friends was no longer cool. He wished he had the chance to say it now.

He realized how many chances he had missed to say what was on his mind, chances he would never have again. There was nothing he could do about the past; however, he resolved right then and there that his past need not dictate his future. He turned to Erin and said, "I love you. I want you to know that. I've never stopped loving you."

He didn't expect her to respond, but she took his hand and said, "I love you, too."

A while later, the organ music died out, and Father O'Connor took the podium again. He said, "We've come to the end of our service. At this time, we'd like for all of Gabe's friends to come and pay their respects, after which, the family will be given some time alone. We ask that you wait outside and join in the procession to the gravesite where there will be a short service." He concluded with a blessing of benediction and stepped down from the podium.

One by one, each person in the church filed past the casket and then to the family where they offered condolences and well wishes. Once the church had emptied, Harv stood up and said, "Well, I guess it's our turn."

Brig held up his hand and said, "Please, stay here with us." At Erin's direction, Kaitlyn stayed behind on the pew while the four of them approached the casket. Brig filled with nervous unease, remembering his dream from the night before. The proper respect and solace of the moment was lost amid a strange sense of dread. He took his hand from his pocket, wanting to run his finger along the casket's edge, but he stopped himself.

Kaitlyn shuffled up behind them and held out her teddy bear. Brig knelt down and tucked her blonde hair behind her ear as she told him, "Daddy, I wanna give Charlie to paw-paw."

Brig smiled a tight smile. "You want to give paw-paw your teddy bear? But why?

"So he'll remember me," came the reply.

Brig was trying his best to convince her otherwise. "You love Charlie. He protects you. Didn't you tell me that?"

Kaitlyn shrugged and said, "I don't need Charlie anymore." She held the bear out again and Brig hugged her tightly, wiping away a tear. Erin knelt down and embraced them both. In that moment, it seemed as if they were a family again. Erin took the bear at Kaitlyn's insistence and placed it in the casket. The little girl blew a kiss from the palm of her hand and said, "Love you paw-paw."

-6-

A little over half of the people who had attended the funeral were present at the graveside service. The after party is never as well-attended as the main event – something funeral homes know based upon the number of chairs placed beside the grave. Brig listened to the prayers as a warm spring breeze blew through the crowd, causing the green awning to clap and pop. He was struck by how much had transpired since he'd left Birmingham only four days before. His life had been turned upside down by the events of a single day.

Erin tugged against his arm, and that's when he noticed all eyes were upon him. She held three roses in her hand, one of which she gave to Kaitlyn, the other she held out to Brig. The three of them approached the casket and set the roses on its lid one by one. Brig placed his on top of the other two and said, "Goodbye, Dad. I love you." Without looking up, he turned and walked away, not waiting for the service to conclude.

Twenty minutes later, the house had filled with people. Brig was soon overcome with the familiar scents he had come to associate with death: carnations, roses, cheap perfume, and hairspray. The air was heavy with the thick, fragrant brew, and he stepped onto the back deck to get away from it all.

Harv followed him outside and said, "Nice service."

"Yeah," Brig agreed. "It was." He glanced across the field and saw the same crew of men he had seen earlier that morning. Two of them were disassembling the awning while the other two shoveled dirt. He averted his eyes and said, "Thank God, that's over with."

"I wish I could tell ya that you're through the rough patch," Harv said. "Truth is, the hardest part's still comin'."

"How's that?"

Harv sat down and blew his nose into his handkerchief. "Well, up 'til now, you've been able to kinda lean on everybody." He gestured towards the house with his thumb. "But pretty soon, they'll all be goin' back home. That's when it hits ya... That's when it *really* hurts. You're gonna be sittin' in the house, minding your own business, and the memories are just gonna rush in. They're like ghosts, Brig. They haunt ya."

Brig sat silent, staring at the deck boards. He knew a thing or two about the memories... *God, did he know about the memories.* He glimpsed up at Harv, wondering if Harv was haunted by the same misty specters of regret or if he had lived his life in such a way as to insulate himself from them. The creases on the old man's forehead told a different story, though, and Brig suspected Harv knew the sounds of the whispers quite well, indeed.

"I heard what ya said to Erin back in the church. 'Course it ain't none of my business, but I think your daddy would want me to set ya straight."

Brig looked him in the eyes and said, "You're right. It's none of your business, Harv."

"Now simmer down, son. I know you're a big boy, and you can handle your own messes, but I'm your friend and I'm worried that you're not thinkin' straight. You two split up, and she got herself another husband. It's a shit stinkin' mess, that's for sure, but you can't piss on another man's shoes for too long before he kicks ya in the ass. You get what I'm tryin' to say?"

"I think so."

"You have to be thinkin' about that little girl," Harv told him. "She's your family now." He paused when Brig started cracking his knuckles with obvious impatience. "You're probably madder than a hornet right now, but you're too much like your daddy to ever let it show. I just want ya to know I'm not pokin' around in your business for the hell of it. I'm just tryin' to look out for ya."

Brig looked out across the expanse of farmland and said, "I know, Harv. I appreciate your concern." He changed the subject before it had a chance to go any further. He said, "I could sure use you around here, Harv. I want you to know that you have a job as long as you want it."

"Thanks. Truth told, I was kinda wonderin' about that, but I didn't figure this was a good time to bring it up. Reckon you'll be keepin' the place?"

Brig nodded as much. It had been in his family for far too long to let it go. Until now, he hadn't given it much thought, but he turned to Harv and said, "Well, I'll need to know how you and dad handled things, but I guess we can go over all of that tomorrow, huh?"

Harv said, "Yeah, we can do it then. No rush."

Erin opened the door and leaned out. "Hey, I don't mean to interrupt you boys," she said. "But folks are starting to leave, I thought you might want to say goodbye."

Brig had already said all the good-byes he wanted to say for quite a while, but events such as these enslaved him to etiquette. He stood up and shook Harv's hand. "The ghosts are coming, huh?"

Harv nodded and said, "Yep, they sure are. Best get ready for 'em."

-7-

The crowd quickly filtered out, and the evening hours came. Erin put Kaitlyn to bed around 8:00 and came back downstairs to help Brig straighten up. She knew what he wanted to ask – she could see it in his eyes – but she also knew he would wait for an opportunity, which was one thing she was determined not to give him.

"So what were you and Harv talking about?" She asked.

Brig squirted a glob of detergent into the dishwasher and closed the door. "Oh, nothing, really. You know Harv, he was just rambling on."

"Yeah, right," she said with a laugh. "I saw the look on your face. The only time you look that way is when someone is telling you something you don't want to hear. C'mon now, tell me. What was it?"

Brig turned to Erin, his expression hardened and stern. "Let's go into the living room," he said. "We need to talk." The color drained from her face. She sensed she'd given him the very opportunity she'd been trying to avoid, after all. Like a child about to be scolded, she followed him into the living room and took a seat on the couch.

"I want to know about the bruise."

She considered blowing the whole thing off, but knew better. She put her foot on the coffee table and lifted her skirt to show the bruise to him. "There," she said. "See? It's not that bad."

Brig got up and examined it. It was the shape of a football, dark purple with splotches of red, yellow, and green. He looked closer and was able to make out shapes that looked like fingers. He sat back in his chair and crossed his arms. "Did he do that to you?" he asked. Erin looked away and mumbled something, but he cut her off and said, "Tell me the truth!"

"Yes."

In his heart, he'd known, but the truth hit him hard. His mind conjured up images of how it might have happened – none gave Tom the benefit of the doubt. "Erin," he said, "this is very important. You have to tell me everything. Has this happened before?"

"No."

"Honest?"

"*Yes*, I'm telling you the truth. He just got a little angry when I told him that Kaitlyn and I were coming up to stay with you for a couple of days, that's all. I was sitting on the bed when I told him. He demanded that we talk about it. I said there was nothing to talk about, and got up to leave. That's when he grabbed my leg. Honestly, I didn't think he'd grabbed it that hard, though."

"Has he ever hurt Kaitlyn?" It was less of a question and more of a demand.

Erin pointed a finger at him and said, "No! I would never lie to you about that. You know me too well to think I'd ever put up with that kind of thing."

"Alright," he said. "Now back to you – You say this has never happened before?"

"No, it hasn't."

"Do you think it might happen again?"

"No, it was an accident. That's all. I don't think he *meant* to hurt me. It just happened." She said, "I've told you the truth, Mr. Interrogator, let's turn the tables, shall we? What were you and Harv talking about?"

Brig had hoped to get around the question entirely. He feared that Erin might find some wisdom in Harv's warning. The last thing he wanted was for her to second-guess herself. It was a selfish thought, and he was aware of that, but he wanted her back, and the last thing he needed was for Harv's insights to muddy up the water. He said, "Harv heard what I said to you at the funeral. You know, when I told you I loved you."

"So?"

"Well, he told me...how did he put it? That I was pissing on another man's shoes."

Erin broke out in laughter. "I guess that's one way to put it!" she said. "But why would Harv care?"

"He said that I should respect the fact that we aren't together anymore and that you're with Tom now."

"And what do you think?" she asked.

"I don't know," he said. "I'm all mixed up, I guess. I want us to be together again, but not if it's going to stir up a shit storm for you. The past couple of days have been great – which is saying something considering the circumstances."

Erin thought for a minute and said, "Yeah, I agree. What if your feelings aren't real, though?"

"How do you mean?"

"Well, you said it yourself, '*...under the circumstances.*' Maybe you're just looking for someone to hold onto."

"C'mon, Erin, don't cheapen it!"

"No, I'm not, believe me I'm not. I'm really glad that I could be here for you. If that's all this was, I'm fine with it, but we have a little girl to think about. Unfortunately, we don't have the luxury of following our hearts, anymore. The carefree college days are gone."

"Don't do that!" he said. "Don't lecture me like I'm a child. You know I hate that! C'mon, seriously, what are we going to do?"

"Well, I think we both need time to think. We've been knee-deep in emotions the past couple of days, and I don't think that either one of us are in a position to make any snap judgments. I'll go back to my normal routine, you go back to yours, and we'll just see where we end up."

Brig said, "You mean you're going home. But what about Tom? I don't want anything to happen to you."

"*Nothing will*," she said. "Tom doesn't have to know anything. That is, unless we decide that we really do want to be together. If that happens, we'll deal with it then."

Brig told her he didn't want her to go, but Erin was equally adamant that she needed to. Her concern was clearly with Brig, repeatedly asking him for assurance that he was going to be alright. Finally, he gave in with nod. The larger question for him was what was next.

"Are you headed back to Alabama?" she asked.

He hadn't considered his options before now, but recent events had caused him to lean towards staying in Jones Chapel a while longer. Besides, there was something his father had wanted to tell him – something about Jacob – and Brig's curiosity needed satisfaction. "No," he said. "I don't think so. My schedule's pretty open. There are a few things I want to iron out before I head back home."

Erin excused herself and went into the kitchen for a glass of water. She turned around as Brig was leaning against the door frame with his hands stuffed in his pockets. "You're not going home tonight, are you?" he asked.

She hugged him and said, "No," not bothering to qualify the statement. Instead, she kissed him on the lips and said, "That is, if you think it'd be alright with Harv."

Brig laughed. "What he doesn't know won't hurt him."

Erin took his hand and hooked her index finger onto his. She led him down the hall toward the bedroom, which was dimly illuminated by a solitary night light plugged into an outlet on the far wall. Brig closed the door behind him and locked it before Erin turned to face him, her facial features defined by streaks of light and shadow. It had been many months since he had felt a woman's touch. In this moment, he wanted her more than he had realized. The past few days had been heavy with emotions, and reasonable people know better than to behave so irresponsibly at times such as these. As her fingers stroked his chest, however, he knew reason wasn't with him.

He leaned in to kiss her as she wrapped her arms around his neck. Her lips were soft, but the tenderness that had been in last night's kiss was gone, replaced by something else – something far more seductive. The two made their way towards the bed removing clothing piece by piece in a trail of small, crumpled heaps. Brig's hands moved across her body until she lifted her gaze to meet his. There was a look in her eyes he hadn't seen in years – a craving – and Brig was lost inside them. He whispered her name, but she placed a finger on his lips and shook her head 'no.' He understood this game. He'd played it many times before.

Her bare leg slid over his as she moved to straddle him. She was gorgeous hovering above him, soft light dancing on her skin. She felt amazing, a sensation he never would have thought he could forget, but clearly two years had been ample time for him to misplace the memory. He took her hair into his fist and kissed her as she whispered, "I want you." into his ear, her lower lip trembling.

Erin lowered her body onto his, slowly rocking back and forth until he took control and rolled on top of her. Her chest heaved and fell as his hands clenched around her wrists holding them firmly against the mattress. Erin had never been one to be submissive, and she struggled though her strength was no match for his. Finally she locked eyes with him and demanded he let her go, but it was too late and Brig called out her name.

She lay there, breathing heavily as their bodies relaxed, and her thoughts turned to what might have been, choices made, promises broken, and a sea of internal regret. Somewhere in the afterglow and silence, she heard her demons calling to her. They whispered, but she knew better than to listen to their lies. The two of them ended up falling asleep with bodies intertwined. Brig awoke sometime in the middle of the night and found himself making love to her again. He told her that he loved her and that he didn't want her to go. She didn't respond, and though unspoken, he knew she didn't want to leave.

CHAPTER FIVE

-1-

Brig's heart was heavy as he loaded the suitcases into Erin's trunk the next morning. Kaitlyn threw her arms around his neck and squeezed as he buckled her into the backseat. Wiping away a tear with a quick flick of his thumb, he kissed her on the cheek and asked her to wait in the car while he went inside to make sure nothing had been forgotten.

Inside, Erin embraced him and asked, "Are you sure you're going to be alright by yourself?"

Brig assured her that he would as he patted Buster's head. There was much to be done – all those gritty details that remain following a death, and they had to be dealt with. Those things would consume his time, sure enough, but he was quite certain there had been wisdom in Harv's words, warning him of what lay in wait when the silent hours descended.

"Take this," Brig began as he handed Erin a small black phone he removed from his back pocket. "It's one of those 'use it and toss it' cell phones." He held up his hand to block Erin's objection. "I want you to give me a call when you get back home, you know, to let me know everything's alright. I don't want you using your own phone any more than you always have. It's probably better if my number shows up on your bill as few times as possible. You don't want to change your behavior very much. If you do, Tom is going to suspect something."

The expression on Erin's face said she hadn't thought that far ahead. "Right. Good idea." She shot him a suspicious glance while tucking the phone into her purse and said, "You sure seem to know a lot about this kind of thing. Are you sure you haven't done this before?"

Brig said, "Nope. Let's just say I'm paranoid – it comes naturally. You're gonna call me, right? You need to call dad's landline. I have zero bars out here."

She gave him another hug and said, "Yes, I will. I promise. Listen, Tom is going out of town in a week or two. If you're planning on staying up here for a while, I thought we could get together. You know, like a date or something.

Brig smiled as he led her to the doorway with his hand resting on the small of her back. "I think I could handle that," he said. "But let's just focus on getting you home safe right now, okay?"

"*Don't worry,* I'll be fine. I'll call you tonight. Kaitlyn will want to talk with you anyway." She gave him a final kiss and stepped onto the porch. Brig followed and watched as she climbed into her car and backed up with a quick goodbye wave before heading home. Watching the car make its way along the narrow drive, Brig frowned, not at all happy to see them leave, but knowing full-well that for the time being there were no other options.

He stepped back into the cool shadows of the living room. Images of the past three days blinked in his mind. In retrospect, it seemed to have all happened so fast that even now there was a certain veneer of unreality to it. But here now, alone with no one but Buster, there was something he wanted to do and he thought he had best get to it – better now than later.

In a drawer beside the recliner, Brig found a set of keys to his father's old pickup and he walked out into the garage where it was parked. Gabe had owned the truck since Brig was ten. The white paint had dulled with oxidation and age, but true to form, everything inside the cab was neatly in its place. Gabe had never been much of a housekeeper, but his truck had always been spotless.

Brig ran his finger across the wooden rifle stock hanging on a rack in the truck's rear window. He remembered the hunting trips he had taken with his father all those years ago. During his teenage years, Brig had become quite a good shot, capable of hitting a coke can at two hundred yards. Gabe wasn't one to shower praise, but Brig's marksmanship was one of a few exceptions.

The truck's engine roared to life with a turn of the key and Brig backed out, anxious to get this particular errand over with as soon as possible. It was a partly cloudy day – partly sunny if you were one of those 'glass is half full' kind of folks – and the clouds drifting in the sky cast shadows onto the fields below that moved like giant sharks prowling a stretch of shoreline.

Brig turned off of the drive about twenty yards from the tobacco barn, and headed into an open field, which led out to the family cemetery. A family of rabbits scampered from beneath the safety of high weeds along a nearby fence row. Further ahead were the somber shapes of tombstones enclosed inside a black, wrought iron fence, and the telltale mound of freshly turned earth marking his father's grave.

Beside the grave, Brig saw the dog – or whatever it was – he'd seen on his way back from Havens Fork two days before – the one looking for a place to die. It was standing over Jacob's grave with its leg hiked; a distinct yellow stream shot out and splattered against the tombstone. Brig pulled up and slammed on the brakes. They screeched, but the dog didn't seem to notice and honking the horn won him no response. Finally he climbed from the truck, clapping his hands as he got closer.

"Hey! Hey, you little bastard!" he shouted.

That's when the dog looked up, and Brig got a good look. It was no dog. It was a coyote – nasty, opportunistic creatures notorious for infesting the surrounding areas, preying on anything unlucky enough to find itself in their path. The animal snarled and bared its teeth, which were white in places, but stained pink in others. Foam dripped from its mouth as it folded its ears back against its head.

Brig stopped mid-stride. *Oh shit,* he thought. *The damn thing is rabid.* He didn't want to make any more sudden moves that might provoke an attack, so he moved back to the truck and hopped inside to grab the rifle. Upon examination, he found the gun's chamber empty, but a box of cartridges was nestled in the glove compartment and Brig chambered a round.

Stepping back out of the cab, he shouldered the gun. It had been at least ten years since he'd fired a shot, but the feel of the stock against his body was as natural as it had always been. The magnified view through the scope was disorienting, and the gun's muzzle moved swiftly from side to side as Brig tried to locate the coyote. Eventually, it came into focus, and he centered the crosshairs between its front legs, aiming for the heart and what he hoped would be a clean kill. His aim steadied, and seconds later, a shot rang out.

The gun's recoil was impressive, but Brig managed to hold it. A puff of dirt rose from the ground on the coyote's right side as the bullet missed its target. An entire covey of birds took flight from an adjacent field. Before he could fire another shot, the dog took off running towards the woods. Brig started the truck's engine, intending to give chase.

The truck lurched forward as it accelerated, bouncing up and down over the rough terrain. Brig followed the animal until it crawled under a fence line at which point he was forced to proceed on foot. The animal shuffled under the barbed wire fence, tearing a long gash in its back in the process and leaving bits of fur and blood behind.

The blood trail made tracking easy enough, and Brig finally cornered it against a cliff-face some fifty yards from where the tree line began. The coyote bared its teeth, unable to retreat any further. Undaunted, Brig raised his rifle and fired, but once more his shot missed, ricocheting off the rock wall with a *zinging* sound after which it buried itself in the target's rear hip. The animal cried out in pain and staggered into a cave opening, which lay in the side of the cliff.

Brig watched with interest. Despite the many years he had wandered this property, the cave opening was something he had never seen before. Moving closer, the cave exhaled air cold, damp, and foul. A feeling came over Brig as he stood there. It bubbled up from inside him, and while he didn't precisely know why, he was sure he didn't want to go inside. His gut told him something else was in there, something other than a rabid coyote.

-2-

Once Brig had made it back to the gravesite, he looked towards the woods to make sure nothing had followed him. Satisfied nothing had, he returned the rifle to its rack and went to kneel beside the grave, covered in parched flowers, withering in the sun. He looked at the tombstone, one side of which bore his mother's name – the other side, his father's. It read:

GABRIEL C. BAILEY

1935 –

The date of death had yet to be engraved. How many times had his father looked upon that date and that hanging hyphen of uncertainty? How many times had he looked upon it and wondered what the final year might be? There were still many unused grave plots surrounding the tombstones, and Brig wondered if at some distant time in the future, he would be buried there, too. It was an unsettling thought and one he had never really considered, but he quickly chased it away. He sat down and crossed his legs as he lost himself in thought, slowing plucking petals from a wilted carnation. Just to his right was Jacob's headstone, weathered but otherwise in very good shape. The trail of coyote piss had already dried. It was then he began to feel uneasy. His stomach rolled with a sort of vertigo and his vision blurred as a deep bass sound pulsed from all directions like a heartbeat. Brig rose to his knees and leaned forward on one hand, prepared to vomit, but all that came was a stiff dry heave. In no time, another wave hit and through the tears welling in his eyes, he read his brother's tombstone just as his stomach erupted onto the ground in front of him:

JACOB M. BAILEY

BORN: 1969 MURDERED: 1978

Brig wiped his mouth on his shirt sleeve and looked again. *Murdered? What the hell?* He reached out and touched the surface of the stone which rippled like water after a stone has been cast into it. His heart fluttered in his chest, part of him fearing this was a heart attack and that his future grave wasn't as far in the future as he might have thought. Cold sweat broke across his brow and he thought, *this is where they'll find my body.*

He collapsed onto his side with eyes fixed on a nearby pear tree. The figure of a small boy peaked around the other side of its trunk just long enough for Brig to catch a glimpse before it ducked back out of view. No longer able to trust them, Brig shut his eyes, but opened them again to the sound of footsteps in the hayfield, growing closer. *It can't be,* he thought, realizing the figure crawling towards him on all fours looked just like his brother. With a hand on the tombstone, he attempted to lift himself up as the bass-like pulse intensified.

Murder...

The word throbbed in his mind as he fell back into the grass, which had been tall the day before, but had been trampled down by so many footfalls at the graveside service. Five feet from him, the figure lunged and Brig audibly screamed. All sensations passed as quickly as they had come as in midair Jacob transformed into Buster who tackled him and licked his face.

Brig pulled the dog close and held onto him, glancing back at the tombstone to see the word 'murdered' wasn't there at all. He buried his face into the dog's fur and thought, *my god… I really* am *losing my mind.* Rising to his knees, he grabbed a fistful of dirt and spoke to the grave beneath him. "What are you trying to tell me?!?" No answer came, and after five minutes in the hot sun, he concluded that whoever - or whatever - was toying with his mind had nothing more to say to him.

Back at the house, he planted himself in the recliner and turned on the television where a weatherman crouched next to a map with shirt sleeves rolled up in cuffs at the elbows using a dry erase marker in his hand to point to a strong line of storms which would be moving into the area later in the week. Sometime after the five day forecast and the looping radar feed, the news anchor arranged a stack of paper on the desk and turned to face the camera wearing a solemn expression. Lines of static snaked across the screen as the picture grew grainy.

"A tragic day today in Jones Chapel," the anchor began. Brig leaned forward to see footage of body bags being rolled away on stretchers towards waiting ambulances amid rotating strobes perched atop haphazardly parked police cars. The anchor continued as the scene cut to a single body bag lying beside a highway, "as five bodies have been recovered in various locations. Sherriff officials refuse to release any details pending notification of next of kin."

The footage cut to another location with a single Sherriff's department car parked beside a black hearse-like station wagon with no official markings. Another body was being loaded into the back as a woman lay weeping atop it. The woman lifted her head and Brig dropped his remote, realizing it was his mother. *It can't be,* he thought, standing to move closer to the television. *There wasn't any footage of that day.* The anchor faced the camera as the footage continued on in a smaller window just over her right shoulder. In it, Brig watched a young Sherriff pushing back the reporters and their cameras with one hand, a billy club raised in the other, clearly enraged. The static disappeared and the screen resolution returned to normal as the newscast continued with news from around the country.

Remembering the lockbox Erin had found beneath the bed in Jacob's room the night she and Kaitlyn had arrived, he hurried upstairs into Jacob's room and picked it up from the dresser where it had been sitting. He tried to open the latch again with no luck. After several minutes of rummaging through drawers in search of the key, Brig remembered seeing a small silver one on his dad's keychain which was now in his pants pocket. He reached in and removed the ring, taking the one smaller than the rest between his fingers and placing it into the lock. It fit perfectly. The overhead lights flickered when he turned the key, and the temperature in the room began to fall.

He lifted the lid and reached inside to remove a stack of documents sealed inside individual, plastic sleeves. The top document was Jacob's death certificate. Beneath it was a police report bearing the date: 6-24-1978. Repeatedly scrawled across the police report in bold, red letters was the word:

LIES

My God, he thought, *is that it? Is* that *what dad wanted to tell me*? He thought about the tombstone and how it had read *MURDERED* instead of *DIED*. The missing footage on the newscast. And the documents... the documents were... *Lies*. The overhead lights flickered again, seeming to confirm his revelation.

Brig's mind itched with questions - so many new questions. One step at a time, he walked down the stairs, the weight of his body heavy on weak knees. He stopped halfway when he heard a child's giggle. From behind him came the shuffle of rapid footsteps running across the hall from Jacob's bedroom into the other one. The phantom child giggled once more, forcing Brig to turn in the direction it had come from.

"Jacob? Is that you?" Brig asked, forcing his legs to walk up the stairs despite every desire to turn and run. His father had been right about one thing - the house certainly didn't feel empty. Of that he was sure, but the rational side of him - the part of him he liked to believe was in control for the most part - was coming up short on explanations for all of this. Upon reaching the landing, he panned his eyes around, unable to find anything that might explain the sounds he'd heard.

"Is anyone there?" He asked. "I saw the news, Jacob. Was it you doing that?" Just then, a shrill, high-pitched voice cried out: '*Mom-mee loves you!*' Brig snapped his head in that direction and slowly moved into his old bedroom where he found one of Kaitlyn's dolls lying on the bed.

It was an ordinary baby doll, the kind with a soft, plush body, supporting a hard, plastic head with big blue eyes that blinked above an unchanging, creepy grin. He picked it up and pulled the drawstring dangling from its back. The voice chirped '*Mom-mee loves you!*' again.

Having found the source of the voice did little to alleviate his unease. There was still the question of who had pulled the string. He was certain it hadn't pulled itself. "Who's there?" He asked, half-expecting an answer. From a direction he couldn't ascertain, he heard a whisper followed by a harsh *'shhh'* sound. Well-hidden memories of his first night back in Jones Chapel returned, and in his mind he saw the woman in white once more.

He shook his head 'no.' *It was a dream,* he thought. *Just a stupid dream...* He remembered Kaitlyn saying the 'spirits' wouldn't leave her alone, and he wondered if he and Erin had been too quick to dismiss her assertions as fantasy just as the house filled with that low bass rumble, pulsing in time with his heartbeat.

"What do you want from me??" he shouted.

Gabe's dry, death voice spoke up and said, *"Protect her!"*

Another voice cried, *"FIGHT!!"*

Brig covered his ears when the bass turned to the shrill screech of a woman crying 'MURDER!!!' What followed was a terrified scream – the sound of which went through his head like a lance, his hands over his ears unable to muffle the sound. Above it all, he still heard the voices in his head, and soon realized the scream had been his own.

-3-

An hour later, Brig pulled into the parking lot of the Electronics Barn, the only store of its kind in Wicklow. He had come in search of a camcorder, which he found on a display rack in the middle of the store. It wasn't fancy by any means, but it looked like it might serve his purposes. It was the digital kind, capable of hours of storage.

He made the purchase and headed back to the farmhouse, where he pushed aside his father's mail in order to plug the charger into the wall. Part of him hoped he could catch some of what he had been experiencing on camera if for no other reason than to prove to himself he wasn't insane - a prospect he was very much beginning to question.

The telephone rang, and he was thankful to hear a familiar voice on the other end. "Brig? This is Harv. How ya holdin' up?"

"I'm fine. How are you?"

"Can't complain, I s'pose. I'm calling because you said you wanted to get together today and talk. Are ya still feelin' up to it? I thought I might run over there for a bit. I'll bring some beer if ya want."

Indeed, beer sounded like a fine idea. More importantly, Brig wondered if Harv might be able to shed some light on the day's events, but decided it was probably best to keep his mouth shut until he knew a little more. No one was immune from the Jones Chapel gossip mill - living or dead - and the last thing Brig needed was a rumor starting. "Yeah," he said. "That'll be fine. C'mon over."

After they hung up, Brig heard the metallic sound of chain link. He went outside to find Buster hopping up and down in his pen. Brig opened the gate, and the dog knocked him to the ground with apparent excitement. Brig laughed and assured Buster that he was happy to see him as well. The shaded grass beneath the large maple tree was cool, and Brig lay there for a minute or two just as he had done on summer days as a child. Buster ran into the back yard and returned with his tennis ball in his mouth. He dropped it onto Brig's chest; slobber splattered onto his lower lip.

"Damn, Buster!" He said, tossing the ball further out into the front yard. "That's disgusting!" Buster watched it, calculating the trajectory as only dogs can. When he figured out where it would land, he took off after it, but stopped halfway and raised his ears before releasing a series of wild barks just as Harv's truck appeared around the bend trailing a cloud of gravel dust behind him.

The truck came to a stop, and the old man climbed out wearing a pair of faded jeans caked with stains from God-knew-what, and a short-sleeved denim shirt – much more Harv-like attire than the suits from days prior. The ensemble was topped off with a gray cap, which read: *'No Time For Sleepin', I'll Rest When I'm Dead.'* In his right hand, Harv held a half-case of off-brand beer. He must have seen Brig's expression, because he shrugged his shoulders and said, "You know me, I can drink just about anything."

The two of them went into the house and out onto the back deck where Harv tore the top off of the box and handed Brig a can. "So, where's Erin?" He asked.

"She went home this morning."

"Did ya tell her what we were talkin' about?"

Harv was being a bit more forward than normal, but Brig decided to let it slide. "Yeah, we talked last night. We both agreed the whole thing was just a shitty set of circumstances, if you know what I mean."

"Yep, I do. Good thing you talked it out, though. I'd hoped you weren't mad nor nothin', I just didn't want to see you get hurt. You know, a jealous husband can lay a whoopin' on ya. That's true enough, but there's nothing he can do to you that a pretty little lady can't top. Women seem to enjoy chewin' ya up and spittin' ya back out. I remember how bad off you were when the two of you split up the first time. It was hard for your daddy to watch you go through that, ya know. I just figured he'd want me to set ya straight is all."

The conversation gradually turned to Harv's duties on the farm, and the old man went on to explain the ins and outs of his daily routine in a little more detail than Brig had hoped for.

Fifteen minutes and three beers later, Harv said, "Well, that's about it, I guess. Never really thought about listin' all the stuff I did each day, guess I'm pretty busy."

"Sounds like it," Brig agreed. "I know you don't come here for the scenery, though. How much did dad pay you?"

Harv squared his shoulders and said, "'Bout a thousand a month." The tone in his voice suggested pride, and that wasn't something Brig was about to deny him even though the figure seemed ridiculously low. Still, combined with social security and Harv's military pension – not to mention the overall low cost of living in Jones Chapel – perhaps that was enough.

"A thousand a month," Brig repeated.

"Yessir," Harv agreed. "Is that gonna strap you?"

Brig drew on his beer and shook his head. "No, I don't think so. In fact, I tell ya what – I doubt I'll be up here very often. The place is going to need a little extra TLC from you, if you know what I mean. If a thousand a month is what dad paid you, that's not going to be a problem, but I was thinking more along the lines of some sort of partnership. You keep the place up and any profit we split fifty-fifty."

Harv was in the middle of swallowing a fairly large gulp of beer, and he choked when it went down the wrong way. He coughed and spat out what he could. "Fifty-fifty?? Are you outta your mind?"

Brig held up a hand. "It's alright Harv, I insist."

"Well, my momma didn't raise no idiots, so I don't guess I'll argue with you."

"Good, then it's settled."

The two of them sat in silence, the kind only men can truly appreciate, sipping their beers as they gazed out across open fields. Brig finally spoke up. "I went out to the cemetery today – ran into a coyote while I was out there, too. It was sick. Rabies, I think. I took a shot at it, but it's been a long time since I've fired a gun, and my aim's a little rusty. Needless to say, I missed and had to hunt the thing down."

Harv nodded and said, "Yep. Those things are a damn nuisance. Bad time of the year for rabies, too. When I was a youngster, I had a dog that came down with it after he got in a fight with a raccoon. Good dog, but my daddy put him down behind the barn so I wouldn't have to watch. Sometimes I can still hear the shot. I guess by the time ya get to be my age, there's plenty of things like that ya just as soon not have rattlin' around upstairs. That's one of 'em."

Brig stood up and looked toward the tree line as he reached into the box at Harv's feet and pulled out another can, gently patting Buster who lay at his feet. The heat had been quick to take the chill off of the beer. The cans were still cool, but sweating.

"Harv, you know a lot about this farm," Brig said, pointing at a thick grove of trees on a distant hill. "When I was chasing that thing, I saw something up in those trees I haven't ever seen before."

"Really? What was it?"

"There's a cave up there. I would have thought that as much time as Jacob and I spent in those woods, surely I would have run across it at one time or another."

Harv set his can on the deck and shook a finger at Brig. "You ain't got no business goin' up there, ya hear?"

The tone of the old man's voice gave Brig a start. Had he been a child, the warning might have had the intended effect, but it served only to stir his curiosity. "What do you mean?" He asked.

"Look, I've lived in this town my whole life. It's just understood no one goes up there. Your daddy knew it – probably the reason you never went up there. I ain't never been - never had reason to."

Brig sat back down and shrugged. "But why? Surely you've heard *something* in all this time."

Harv ran a hand through gray hair. "Oh sure - everybody's heard a story at bedtime or sittin' around a campfire. Can't put much stock in that kinda nonsense, though. Some folks say the place is haunted. Don't reckon I believe that, but I've lived here long enough to know things happen here that don't happen nowheres else. Bad stuff, and everybody seems pretty sure that cave is the reason. Maybe it is, maybe it ain't, but in all my years I can only remember a handful of boys dumb enough to try, and ev'ry one of 'em ended up dead." Harv sipped on his beer. "They ain't tellin' no stories, that's for sure."

"That mess happened the day your brother died. Made all the papers as far south as Nashville. Bloodbath. Me and your daddy got the story straight from one of the Indians that used to live around here Not long after the funeral. I can't remember the fella's name, though."

"Blackwind," Brig interrupted. "John Blackwind."

Harv thought for a minute and said, "Yep. That was it! How'd you know?"

Brig leaned forward in his seat, thankful the story might not have been buried along with his father after all. He lowered his voice even though the two of them were alone. "Dad wanted to tell me something this guy had told him. Do you know what it was?"

Harv nodded and took another swig off of his can. "I reckon I might... at least some of it. I didn't stay the whole time, and your daddy never told me what the two of them had talked about after I left. 'Fraid I can't fill in that piece of the puzzle for ya, but I'll tell ya what I know. Do you remember hearing about the massacre back during the Civil War?"

Indeed it was something every kid was taught in school – a truly nasty affair worthy of the Jones Chapel brand. Sixty men lost their lives that day deep in the caves while mining for saltpeter. Historians had long speculated the reason the north won the war was Mammoth Cave's strategic location and its inexhaustible supply of the mineral, a key component in the production of gunpowder. Without the efforts of the miners, the tide of the war might well have shifted in favor of the Confederacy.

Brig acknowledged his memory of the story, and Harv leaned back in his chair feeling slightly vindicated, holding up his index finger. "Only one man made it out of there that day," he said. "One man. Covered in blood from head to toe. No one knows what happened down there. Some say that fella killed 'em all. Others say it was some sort of accident. He never talked. Story goes he just wandered around babblin' nonsense for days 'til he tried to have his way with a little girl what lived over yonder while she sat outside playing in the front yard. Sheriff had him swingin' from the end of a rope the next day. The law was quicker back then."

Harv trailed off, his gaze focused on that distant tree line. Even in the sunlight, his skin looked ashen, and he continued to stare off as he spoke. "Then there's others... there's others who said them miners found somethin' in there. Found somethin' in a place they had no business bein'." He turned back and pointed to Brig. "That's your cave, son. Ain't nothin' in there but nightmares. Leave it be."

CHAPTER SIX

-1-

Four weeks earlier in Jones Chapel, Brent Usher and Sammi Pridmore had decided to spend a late afternoon at Barren Lake just outside of town. It was a quiet place – just far enough away to be out of sight. They drove, windows down, saying little to each other as the car made its way along the winding ribbon of asphalt.

Sammi held her hand out to feel the wind between her fingers. She turned to Brent and said, "Can you believe it?"

Brent took his eyes off of the road just as he shifted into fifth gear. "Believe what?"

"Six months," she said. "We've been dating six months."

Brent pushed his sunglasses further up the bridge of his nose and smiled at her. "I know. And to think, you almost said 'no'."

Her mouth hung agape and she gave him a shove. "I most certainly did not!"

Brent trained his eyes on the road ahead, one hand on the steering wheel. "Oh but you did," he laughed.

The two were both in high school, Sammi a junior and Brent in the homestretch of his senior year. Their relationship had begun shortly after school had started the fall prior. Brent first noticed Sammi two weeks into the school year while she was in gym class playing a game of volleyball. Unlike many of her fellow classmates, she was a late bloomer. Up until her junior year, she had been a little on the chubby side with glasses and braces, to boot.

Small town or not, kids were kids, and kids were cruel; Sammi had always been an easy target. Her story was not unlike that of most awkward teens subjected to bullying and ridicule. A sixteen year old girl's self-esteem is a fragile thing, and Sammi's was damaged.

Things changed over that summer. She lost the braces, replaced her glasses with contact lenses, and had one vicious growth spurt. By the time school started back, her skin was tanned, her hair bright blonde. Despite it all, she still failed to see herself as anything other than that awkward girl.

For the most part, Sammi was shy. She continued to keep a low profile, still hung out with her "B-list" friends, and had managed to get that far in high school without a single date – a fact that suited her mother just fine. Mrs. Pridmore no longer trusted men, reasonably so seeing as how her husband had run off to live with his mistress several years prior, and she had often told Sammi that she was better off without them. In spite of her mother's venom, Sammi's curiosities persisted with burning, adolescent unrest.

Like Sammi, Brent was an only child. His mother had died of brain cancer just a few years back. He'd been born while his mother was in her mid-twenties and supposedly infertile. That being the case, she had always considered him something of a miracle and had smothered him with attention. Her death hit Brent hard, and it had taken quite some time for him to come to terms with her loss.

Brent's father, A.J., had been the county's sheriff for the greater part of twenty-five years. His administration had been accused of all sorts of misdeeds across that span of time. One of the biggest scandals had occurred when A.J.'s younger brother Max was killed by a subordinate deputy the same day Jacob Bailey drowned – the same "tragic day in Jones Chapel" the news anchor had reported about on Brig's TV set. The deputy had later shot himself – or so it was reported. Even though suicide was the official story, only a handful of people in Jones Chapel actually believed it.

Two of Max's friends were also killed that day, bringing the body count to five. While it was never proven, most believed all five deaths were somehow related. Speculation and accusations had run amuck. The townspeople demanded answers, but A.J. Usher was not one to be ordered around. Within a matter of days, the collective cries for justice had all been silenced in one way or another.

Ahead, Brent saw a gravel drive partially hidden behind some bushes. He had been here many times after his mother's death, but never with anyone else. It was a special place – one where his soul exhaled. Just as he turned onto the road leading back into the woods, Sammi turned to him and asked, "Tell me again, what was it that got you interested in me."

Brent downshifted into second gear. "Your legs."

Sammi threw her head back and laughed. When she'd finished, she smiled at him and said, "You say the sweetest things."

Unsure if this was sarcasm, Brent asked, "What do you mean?"

"All my life people have teased me about the way I looked. It's just been this past year that things have started to change for me." She reached over and took his hand. "They changed because of you." Sammi shrugged her shoulders. "It just feels good to hear that kind of thing, that's all."

Brent shook his head. "I swear to God, I will never understand women. I thought you all liked to hear sensitive stuff; you know, feelings and all that."

She looked down at their hands again. "Yeah, I suppose girls who hear compliments all the time probably get tired of it. But not me."

Brent's Mustang pitched from side to side. The road was rough, better suited for trucks than sports cars, but ten minutes later, they emerged from the woods into a clearing high atop a cliff overlooking the lake. The sun hovered just above the tree line; it cast reddish hues on the water below.

"Oh!" Sammi exclaimed. "This is *beautiful!*"

"Told ya I knew a good place!" He said. "C'mon, let me show you the view!" Both of them climbed out of the car, and Sammi followed him to the edge of the cliff. A panoramic view spread out before them – the lake, a mirror so far below that it no longer appeared real.

"This is incredible," she said.

Brent wrapped his arms around her from behind and whispered, "The last six months have been incredible." He placed his cheek against hers and then gave it a peck before sitting down in a patch of grass and leaning back on his elbows. Sammi sat down beside him and laced her fingers in his. They sat in silence for a time – no words needed to be spoken – and watched the sun creep closer and closer to the horizon.

Brent turned to her and took her face in his hands. He leaned in to kiss her lips and gradually laid her back on the ground. As he kissed along her neck, his hand slipped beneath her shirt, quickly working its way upward. This was as far as Sammi had ever let him get. It wasn't for his lack of trying. Charming though he was, teenage boys crave one thing above all else and Brent was nothing if not persistent. Sammi had rebuffed his attempts many times. She knew it frustrated him. She feared that if she continued to do so, she would only drive him away, and that was the last thing she wanted.

Brent knew nothing of the internal struggle Sammi had been dealing with through all of this. In his mind, her rejection of his advances was symptomatic of her mother's religious programming. He had no conception of the well of pent-up sexual tension churning behind Sammi's Sunday school exterior. Nor did he understand her urgency to rid herself of it.

True to form, Brent tried again to push the boundaries just a bit further. His hand moved from her breast to the button of her jeans and tugged. This time Sammi didn't stop him.

A cool breeze whistled past them, and Sammi's bangs blew into her eyes. She brushed them back and lifted her gaze to meet Brent's. Far below, they heard the steady drone of outboard boat motors and the melodic chirps of nesting songbirds.

"Are you sure?" he whispered.

Sammi nodded. She had grown weary of being the good girl who was always in church on Sunday morning. She desperately wanted something to ask forgiveness *for*. Her heart raced in her chest. She knew this was what she wanted, but at the same time she was terrified. Her friends had told her the first time really hurt. As Brent worked the waistline of her jeans down over her hips she said, "Wait..."

Brent sighed.

Sammi looked at him then and that burning urgency returned. She looked toward the west. The sun was halfway below the horizon. Brent took notice of the faraway look in her eyes, and asked, "Are you okay?"

She looked up and said, "Just tell me you love me."

Brent kissed her again. "I love you." She lay back on the grass. Piece by piece, they undressed one another, and soon, Sammi knew there was no turning back.

She enjoyed the feel of his body on top of hers, but something about the act of intercourse struck her as rather anticlimactic. It felt okay once she had gotten past the initial pain, but it was nothing at all like her friends had described. She told herself it was the whole "first time thing," and hoped the fireworks would fly for her the second time.

Brent's arms clamped around her. She felt him push himself deep inside and then a strange sensation. She didn't realize what had just happened, but she liked the feeling of the intense pressure and bathing warmth. Brent's arms gave out, and he lay down on top of her. She rolled him to one side and kissed him on the lips.

"Was that... was that okay?" She asked.

He nodded and said, "Uh-huh," between heavy breaths.

Sammi lay back and stared at the clouds floating above her. They were stained pink and orange with the light from the setting sun. She kind of liked being naked, lying there in the open for all eyes to see. There was something wonderfully taboo about it. She looked at her body and saw her skin tinted the same hues as the clouds. She closed her eyes and concentrated on the sensation of warmth brought by the dying sunlight to parts of her body upon which it had never fallen. A fundamental part of her felt complete – she'd finally done it, and she smiled, knowing that no one, not even her mother, could ever take that away.

-2-

The trip home was a quiet one – neither of them sure what to say to the other. Awkward silence filled the car as both listened to the radio, Sammi shifting restlessly in her seat attempting to find relief from the stinging pain between her legs. The song ended before either spoke another word. In a defusing gesture, Sammi reached out and took Brent's hand as they pulled into her driveway. The look in his eyes made her a bit uncomfortable; it was almost as if he was looking *through* her rather that *at* her.

Brent put the car in park and said, "I still want to see you Saturday night." She agreed, and they set a time. After a kiss, Sammi climbed out of the car and went inside.

The house was empty; her mother had not yet made it home. Looking around, she thought the place looked different somehow. On top of the TV was a ceramic sculpture of a Bible, opened to the center. What would have been the left-hand page bore the twenty-third Psalm painted in gold lettering. On the right-hand page, a picture of Jesus dressed in flowing blue and white robes besieged her with self-righteous, knowing looks, which came from beneath a halo of golden light encircling His head.

She descended the stairs to her room, which was little more than a section of the completed basement. When she walked through the doorway, the first thing she saw was a shelf full of various stuffed animals collected over the years. In the corner of the room was a silver baton with white plastic caps on either end, pink and purple streamers hung from them. Not far from that was the hoola hoop she'd spent the greater part of her sixth grade year trying to master. These, and so many other remains of a childhood lost, seemed to breathe the sweet breath of innocence – the very innocence she'd lost less than an hour ago.

Sammi felt a guilty lump forming in her throat. She took another step forward as pain throbbed between her legs. Her hand went to it, and that's when she realized how very sore she was down there. A tear beaded in her eye, and she wanted to run to her mother. She knew she couldn't do that, and her despair deepened. She felt unclean, inside and out. All she wanted was to take a shower.

Once inside the bathroom upstairs, she undressed with her back to the mirror. She didn't want to see herself; the person who would stare back from the other side of the mirror would not be the same person she'd seen before leaving for school that morning.

She stepped into the bathtub, closed the curtain, and stood beneath the spray. She scrubbed and scrubbed with her washcloth, but the filth remained. She opened her legs and tried to clean between them, but winced. She spun around with her back towards the spray, attempting to shield herself from the liquid knives. She held onto the towel bar for balance while she waited for the pain to cease.

Somewhere down the hall a door opened, and she knew her mother must be home. She scrambled out of the shower and locked the bathroom door. After drying off, she wrapped the towel around her body, high on her chest. Sammi looked into the mirror, and to her horror, she saw a dark hickey at the base of her neck. She didn't dare wonder what her mother would do to her if she saw it, so she draped another towel over it.

From the back bedroom could be heard the off-key sound of her mother's voice singing gospel hymns. Sammi opened the bathroom door and checked to be sure the coast was clear. She shuffled through the living room and retreated to the relative safety of the basement.

That night, in the deafening silence of her bedroom, Sammi slept a fitful sleep. She woke at three in the morning, clammy with sweat, her mind buzzing from the nightmare she'd had. The dream had seemed more like reality – a seemingly prophetic reality that terrified her.

She broke into tears, fearing the weight of the world was now upon her. She curled into a fetal position, pulling a pillow close and squeezing it tightly. She wondered how she was going to be able to behave normally around her mother in the coming days. This thing that she had done... this thing she had wanted more than anything – *her very own private sin* – had returned to haunt her, and she knew she had to face it – *alone.*

-3-

Twilight came the Saturday night after their trip to the lake, and Sammi stood in front of the bathroom mirror blow-drying her hair. Truth told, she didn't want to go on this date anymore. In fact, she had intended to call the whole thing off, but couldn't muster up the courage to do so. Brent had called around two o'clock that afternoon to see how she was doing and if they were still on for the night and she'd agreed before giving herself the opportunity to back out. She knew he'd want it again. *Hell,* she thought, *he's probably expecting it.*

The soreness between her legs was gone. She was happy about that, but the mere thought of sex turned her stomach. She wished she could take back what she'd already done, but she knew that was impossible, so she was determined not to make the same mistake twice – even if it meant being an outcast for the remainder of her high school life.

Sammi had prayed about it – something her mother had always instructed her to do in difficult times, but it seemed God was no longer listening. Even the comforting feeling of benevolence upon which she had relied so much in the past was absent. After taking one last look in the mirror, she opened the bathroom door and walked into the living room.

"You look wonderful." Her mother told her.

Sammi said, "Thank you," and hoped that the scent of guilt wasn't leaking from her pores. The clothes she wore were conservative, having decided it best to keep things simple. In her mind, the less skin shown, the better. The little red dress she had bought a month or so ago for just such a night still hung in her closet. Instead, she had chosen to wear a pair of blue jeans, black ankle boots, and a white T-shirt.

Her mother ran one hand over Sammi's arm and said, "My little girl's dating. I still can't get used to it. I'd hoped I'd never see this day – you're growing up so fast." She pointed to a series of nicks on the coffee table. "It seems like yesterday you were teething. You gnawed and gnawed on this table. Your daddy and I didn't think those teeth would ever come in." Her voice broke on the last sentence, and she covered her mouth with her hand. After a brief pause, she continued, "I wish he was here to see you tonight."

Sammi hung her head and said, "I know, mom. I do, too."

In the six months the two of them had been dating, Sammi had made a concerted effort to downplay the seriousness of the relationship with Brent and keep him from meeting her mother at all costs. It was doubtful she would be able to keep it up much longer. She'd already achieved a remarkable feat in a small town. Her mother had heard rumors, but there were always rumors. You pick and choose the ones to believe.

She looked into her daughter's eyes. "This Brent – is he a *nice* boy?"

Sammi's eyes went to the floor. Her mother had always been good at reading her expressions, and Sammi wanted to be absolutely sure that she believed her when she said, "Yes, he is."

"Well, I hope so." Her mother replied. "His daddy and yours used to go out drinking quite a bit. Brent's father might be the sheriff, but he isn't exactly a *saint*, you know. I just want to be sure you're going to be safe. You know what they say... like father, like son."

"I know, mom. I'll be fine – really."

Her mother took her hand and looked into Sammi's eyes and said, "You keep your cell phone in your pocket. If that boy makes you feel the least bit uncomfortable, you call me and I'll come get you, understand?"

Sammi nodded just as Brent turned into the driveway. Headlights splashed into the foyer, and the engine roared. He tapped the horn twice, and Sammi's mother said, "Young lady, it's probably a good thing your daddy *isn't* here. If there is one thing he hates, it's a person who lacks the manners to come to the door."

"I have to go, mom."

"I know dear, you go on, but be careful."

"I will."

With that, Sammi walked out the door. Brent's car sat idling, and to her surprise, he got out and opened the passenger door for her. He gave her a kiss on the cheek and said, "You look great." Just like that, his charms started to work on her, and Sammi had a fleeting feeling she might be overreacting about all of this. A quick glance back at the house revealed her mother peering out though the sidelight window.

Once he'd climbed into the car, Brent suggested dinner and a movie. Nothing special, not that Sammi had expected any more than that. She tried to think of what might be playing – something the two of them would both enjoy, but she kept coming up empty. "What are you in the mood for?" she asked.

Brent put the car in reverse and said, "I'm not sure. I thought I'd let you pick when we got there."

She wanted to talk to him. She wanted to tell him she was scared and that what had happened between them wasn't going to happen again, but it didn't seem like the right time. She decided to wait, trusting that when and if the time came, she'd have the strength to say 'no.'

Twenty minutes later, they were sitting in a corner booth at the Jones Chapel Dairy Queen sipping milkshakes and enjoying casual conversation. It surprised Brent how comfortable he was around her, and as he looked into her eyes, he believed he could tell her anything. For the longest time, his cardinal rule had been to keep most of his life to himself. It seemed that every time one of his relationships had gone south, secrets that had been told in confidence had always come back to bite him in the ass.

Sammi asked him if there were any new developments with his scholarship, which in recent weeks had been in all the papers and was the subject of much discussion locally. It was something about which he was very proud, and he didn't mind talking about it at all. It was an opportunity to avoid the elephant in the room, so to speak, and Sammi seized it. The two of them had discussed the scholarship several times since it had become official. Unlike others in town, Sammi seemed to take it in stride – almost as if it was no big deal, and a part of him liked that about her.

"Well," he said. "I'm pretty excited about it, even though I won't be playing much the first couple of years. To tell you the truth, I'm a little scared about the whole thing. They have a pretty big football program at UK, and I guess I'm used to being the big fish, if you know what I mean."

Sammi laughed and said, "I can understand that, I guess. I bet your daddy is pretty excited for you, huh?"

Brent spun his key ring on the table with his index finger and said, "Yeah, he is. I think he's more excited than *I am*.. I don't wanna let him down, ya know. I'm afraid I'll get up there and screw up."

"You'll be great! What are you talking about?"

"I s'pose so," Brent dismissed with a wave. "What about you? I know it's a ways off, but what are you planning on doing? With college, I mean. I'm guessing you'll be going to Harvard or some other tough school, huh? Lord knows you have the grades for it." The words slipped past his lips and he couldn't pull them back. He half-hoped Sammi might say she was going to join him in Lexington, but the response he got was something different.

"Nah, I don't think so. You're giving me too much credit. I'll probably just stick around here – go to Western, you know, do the commuter thing."

Brent sat back in the booth and looked at her with partially sincere shock, and he said, "You're kidding me, right? You're gonna stick around Jones Chapel? Don't you want to get out of this place?"

"Maybe one day," she said, "I might even move to Havens Fork my sophomore year and live on campus. I guess it's different for girls. I don't want to be that far from home."

Brent checked his watch and pushed his cup aside. It was nearing 8:30, and they needed to get going if they wanted to catch the movie. He didn't say much on the way there, but that didn't bother Sammi; she was used to it. He rarely, if ever, talked while he was driving. Silence was something to which she'd grown accustomed, and there was a strange comfort about it. She thought about what was happening between them, and she realized that no matter how things turned out – good or bad – Brent would be leaving in a matter of months, and she would be back to life as usual.

He reached across the center console and took her hand, interlacing his fingers with hers and giving her hand a squeeze. "I've really been looking forward to tonight." The comment hit her as sincere. There didn't appear to be any hidden expectation in it, and the past three days of tension faded further. She returned his squeeze with one of her own and said, "Me, too. I'm having a great time."

-4-

When they arrived at the theater, Sammi suggested a love story, and Brent went along willingly, just as he'd promised he would. The movie ended around 10:30, and on the way home, Brent slowed down and turned onto an unmarked dirt road that disappeared into wooded darkness. Sammi turned her face towards him, hoping for some indication of his intention, but found none. Perhaps she was wrong and there *had been* expectations all along, but she was just too naïve to detect them. Her stomach tensed, hoping she'd have the courage to stick with her prior decision, and as her head flooded with the horror stories her mother had told her about what boys did to girls on back country roads, she hoped he would understand that *'no'* meant *'no.'*

The car came to a stop, and before she could say anything, Brent hopped out. She watched him circle around the front of the car and open her door, saying "C'mon out. You're about to see something pretty special!" He checked his watch and then looked up at the sky. Sammi stayed put in her seat until Brent extended his hand and said, "Trust me."

When she finally climbed out of the car, he scooped her off her feet, and set her down on the hood, soon climbing up beside her with a pair of binoculars in hand, which he'd removed from the hatchback that still hung open behind them. Sammi was confused, fully expecting him to make his move, but he lifted the binoculars and stared at the sky with curious contentment.

Sammi looked up. It was a black, moonless sky, and away from the streetlights and interstate signs, the stars beamed bright and numerous. She started to speak, but Brent put his finger over his lips and said, "*Shhh,* I want you to see something." He handed her the binoculars, and extended his finger upward. She looked to where he was pointing.

"Do you see those three stars – the bright ones that look like they're in a straight line?"

Sammi nodded her head. "Uh huh. Orion's belt."

He smiled and said, "That's right." He moved his finger a few degrees to the left and said, "Now, how about that little group of stars – the one that looks like a white smudge? Do you know what that is?"

"Nope."

"That's Pleiades. They call it 'The Seven Sisters.' They're all bunched together really close, but if you look closely, there's seven of 'em." He checked his watch again. "Now, keep looking between those two for the next couple of minutes."

Sammi did as she was told, and about five minutes later, a bright fire-trail tore across the sky. Another soon followed. "Shooting stars!" she exclaimed.

"Uh huh. It's a meteor shower. It was supposed to be tonight. You better make a wish!"

Sammi closed her eyes and crossed her fingers. "Okay," she said, turning to him with a laugh, "Did you make one?"

"Didn't have to," he said. "You're already here." It came out sounding like a line, just smooth enough to pass as sincerity.

Sammi turned to face him. "I didn't know you were into this kinda stuff," she said.

"Yeah, I guess you could call it a hobby. I've always been interested in it. Before my mom died, she used to tell me stories about Halley's Comet. She said it came by in 1986 when I was two. She showed me pictures in an astronomy book once. I've been hooked ever since."

"So are you planning to major in astronomy?"

Brent frowned and said, "No, I don't think so. I'd like to, don't get me wrong, but football is gonna take up most of my time.

Besides, dad says I have a better chance with pro ball. I suppose he's right; I'm better on the field than I am with books."

Sammi rolled onto her side and put her arm around him. She knew his scholarship was a huge opportunity, but she started to think his heart might not be in it. Brent looked down at her and said, "Is anything wrong? You've been awfully quiet tonight."

Her first instinct was to say, '*no*,' but she went ahead and told him anyway. "It's about the other day..."

"Yeah, I thought that's what it was. I guess I let myself get a little carried away, huh?"

"No, I mean, it's not your fault – I was there, too. I've just been really worried for the past couple of days."

"Worried? About what?"

"Well, that night, I had a dream – a nightmare, really. I dreamed I got pregnant." She buried her face into his chest. The words left a sour taste in her mouth that she didn't care for. No sooner had the words left her mouth, she felt foolish for saying them.

Brent stroked the hair on the back of her head, and said, "Why didn't you call me? We could have talked about it."

"I was scared. I didn't know what you'd say."

"Are you scared of me now?" He asked. The question was one she hadn't considered, and she gave it some thought before answering. The truth was... she felt safe with him – always had. There was more to him than she'd ever dared to guess, and she had found it all wonderful.

"No, I'm not."

"Good. I'm not a monster, Sammi. We've been together for a long time. You can talk to me – I want you to talk to me. I can understand why you're scared."

"You can?"

"Sure. That was your first time, wasn't it?" He felt her nod against his shoulder and he said, "Then cheer up, you've got nothing to worry about."

"I don't?"

"No – everybody knows you can't get pregnant your first time." It was a bad piece of information, but one he believed. After all, that's what he'd been told. To call the sex-ed program at Jones Chapel High sub-par would be an understatement, but Sammi didn't know any better, and so her mood lifted.

Brent squeezed her tight and said, "We'll just have to be more careful next time, that's all."

"Next time?"

"Yeah, well, I mean, if you want there to be a next time. I don't want to push you."

Sammi propped herself up on one arm and looked him in the eyes; he looked back without blinking. She searched his face for some indication that he was lying to her, but saw only sincerity. Brent couldn't believe that he'd said what he had, either. Only one other time had he allowed himself to get this emotionally caught up in a relationship and that one ended horribly. Sammi was different though – or at least that's what he wanted to believe. His feelings for her frightened him a little, mostly because of how badly he'd been hurt before and how he'd vowed never to let it happen again.

Sammi was quiet, and ran one hand along the side of his face before leaning forward and placing her lips on his. It was a tender kiss, and when she pulled away, he said, "I'd better be getting you home. It's getting late and your mother is gonna have my head on a pole if you miss curfew."

He hopped to the ground and held his hands out; Sammi took them as he pulled her forward. She slid easily over the hood, and together they walked towards the back of the car. A small light bulb on the open hatchback illuminated the area around them. Brent zipped the binoculars into their case just as Sammi hugged his arm.

"Thank you," she said.

"For what?"

"For what you said. I feel much better."

Her hand went to his back pocket, and he felt her fingers searching for something. He laughed a cautious laugh and asked, "What are you doing?"

Her head remained against his chest, but he heard her clearly when she asked, "Do you have anything with you?"

His heart jumped; he knew what she meant by *'anything.'* Truth told, this move of hers came unexpected. Not that he ever considered the encounter at the lake to be a 'once and done' kind of thing. Certainly he thought that once he was able to get Sammi to stop rejecting his advances, she would be increasingly more receptive towards them. Still, her initiation caught him by surprise. He pulled his wallet from his pocket and searched inside until he found a small, square packet of purple foil.

Sammi climbed into the hatchback and struggled to fold the seats down. Brent was quick to help her with them, just as he was with the removal of her shirt. The sounds of the night were all around them, and a cool breeze whistled its way across the field causing leathery tobacco leaves to creak and slap against one another. The two of them made love as the sky above them fell.

-5-

Twenty minutes later, they both lay on their sides facing one another. Brent ran his hand down the side of Sammi's body and pulled her bare leg on top of his. For Sammi, her expectations for the second time had proven true – the fireworks *had* flown.

Brent lifted his arm, and his watch shifted forward. The luminescent hands glowed back at him, saying it was nearing midnight – already a full hour past curfew. At Sammi's request, he had pulled the hatch closed several minutes before. He rolled onto his back in time to see ghostly circles of headlights appear on the hatch's rear glass, which was heavily fogged.

The lights grew steadily brighter along with the approaching sound of gravel crunching beneath tires and the eventual squeak of brakes. Brent hurried to pull his underwear on and step into his shoes. Before Sammi knew what was happening, he said, "Quick, cover your face! If anyone finds out it's you in here, your mom will kill us both!" With that, he jumped into the front seat and threw open the driver's side door.

A faint cloud of dust hung in front of the car that had pulled up behind them, making the bold lines of the headlight beams stand out clearly. Brent stood mere feet away from a dark silhouette shining a flashlight into the rear window of his car.

"Hey!" he yelled. "What the hell do you think you're doing?"

The flashlight's beam snapped in his direction and landed squarely on his face. He shielded his eyes, trying to make out who the figure was, unaware of how ridiculous he looked standing in the middle of a tobacco field wearing nothing but boxers and a pair of tennis shoes.

The figure drew closer, and Brent caught a glimmer of gold on its chest. He knew immediately that it was a badge, and he started to panic thinking it might be a state trooper. To his relief, he saw the figure's shirt; it wasn't state-trooper-gray, but rather sheriff-department-brown.

"Brent?" The figure said.

Finally stepping out of the shadows was Perry Sizemore, one of Brent's father's oldest deputies. Perry was a hulk of a man, standing at nearly six feet - six inches tall. His hair was solid white, and his voice was like sandpaper to the ears. Brent wasn't sure what had taken place between his father and Perry, but two years ago, the old guy had been passed up for promotion and switched to the graveyard shift - a move his father reserved solely for punishment.

"Brent, is that you?" Perry repeated.

"Yeah, Perry, it's me."

The deputy switched off the flashlight beam, and holstered it in his belt. "What the hell are you doing out here?" He asked. "Does your father know where you are? And what the hell are you doing in your underwear, boy?" The question was rhetorical; Perry knew damn well what Brent was doing. He pressed his face against cupped hands, trying to peer inside the car. "Who ya got in there?" He asked.

"No one you'd know, Perry. Dad doesn't know I'm out here, either, and he'd *better not* find out."

Perry stood up and tucked his thumbs beneath his belt, puffing out his chest. "You'd better get that tone outta your voice, boy. *I'll* decide what your father does and doesn't need to know."

Inside the car, Sammi lay with Brent's T-shirt over her face, listening to the conversation outside and trying to imagine how she could ever explain this to her mother. The air inside the car was hot - even hotter beneath the shirt, but she didn't dare remove it. Careful not to make a movement that would cause the car to rock, she slipped into her panties and then her blue jeans. She blindly put her bra on as well, hooking it behind her back with one hand.

Outside, Brent walked over to the deputy and said, "Really, Perry? Ya see, I think I'd keep quiet if I were you. It'd be a shame if dad were to find out about those drinks you like to have right around two in the morning, now wouldn't it? *Tsk, tsk, tsk.*

Drinkin' on the job. Nope, I doubt dad would like that very much at all."

Perry frowned and cut his eyes back to the Mustang. Inside Sammi lay motionless, her face still covered with the t-shirt. "Is she alright?" He asked.

"She's fine. Now do we have a deal or don't we? I'll keep your little secret if you keep mine. How 'bout it?"

"Alright, Alright," Perry replied waving his hands in the air. "I won't say anything."

Brent offered a handshake, which the deputy took. He climbed back inside his cruiser and executed a three-point turn before heading off in the opposite direction. Brent watched the car's taillights dim in the distance before he opened the car door. Sammi had moved into the passenger's seat. She held his shirt and pants out to him. Brent took them, and as he slid his left leg into his jeans, he said, "Sorry about that."

"You handled it pretty well," she said. "I was lying in here in a full-on panic!"

"Yeah, well don't be too impressed. Perry's a pushover. We're just lucky it wasn't one of the other guys. They would have hung my butt out to dry!" He bent down and looked into the car. "I must like you. I just played my only ace, you know that?"

Sammi smiled and said, "Don't worry, I'll make it up to you."

He buttoned his pants and zipped his fly. Plopping down into the driver's seat, he kissed her on the cheek and said, "You damn well better!" Checking his watch again, he shook his head. "We'd better get you home. Do you think your mother's still up?"

"What time is it?"

"About twelve-thirty."

"No. She went to bed hours ago. I'll just be really quiet when I go in. It'll be fine. Don't pull into the driveway, though. That'll wake her up for sure."

Brent nodded and turned left onto the paved road leading back to Jones Chapel. Sammi managed to pull her sweater on and fix her hair. Peering into the small vanity mirror, her makeup was a mess. She fixed it as best she could, hoping like hell she was right and her mother was down for the night.

Fifty yards from the house, Brent switched his headlights off and coasted to a stop at the end of her driveway. The two said their goodbyes, and Sammi snuck inside. Halfway down the basement stairs, a step creaked; Sammi froze and waited to see if she had woken her mother. Once she was satisfied that she hadn't, she slowly worked her way down the dark stairwell and flipped on the light switch at the bottom.

Safely in her room, she removed her clothes and laid them over the back of a white rocking chair before crawling into bed. Her thoughts consumed her, but they were different than those the time before. She lay awake replaying the night's events in her mind, hugging her pillow tightly and soon, dreams came upon her.

CHAPTER SEVEN

-1-

The kitchen phone rang at the Bailey house, interrupting Brig who was absorbed in his latest project – a mound of paperwork recently acquired courtesy of the county Sheriff's Department. He jumped up from the dining room table where he had decided to set up shop, and in so doing, smacked his knee on the a rail just beneath the table top. He cursed under his breath and limped to the kitchen to grab the receiver seconds before the fourth ring.

The sound he heard was one he hadn't heard in years, but one he knew all-too-well. The sobbing on the other end caused his mind to race with possibilities... *There's been a wreck... someone's hurt... Oh, God, Katie!*

Erin cried out, "Brig? Brig are you there?!"

"Yes, yes, I'm here. *Erin*? Erin, what's wrong? Are you in the car?" He was able to make out the sound of Kaitlyn crying in the backseat, faint and muffled the way a child sounds with their face buried into a blanket. His mind continued to race.

"Yes...We're on our way up there. That's okay, isn't it? We had to get out! I had to get Kaitlyn out! I don't know what happened, Brig. He just snapped! How did he know? How could he have *known?*"

Brig's jaw tensed, and he gripped the receiver tightly. "What did he do, Erin? What did that motherfucker *DO?!*"

"Wait until I get up there, okay? We're five miles from the exit now. I'll be there in ten minutes. I don't want to talk about this in front of her, Brig. Damn it, she's been through enough." Through the telephone came the sound of a horn from a passing

18-wheeler, which was followed by screeching tires and a loud shriek.

"What was that?" he asked. "Are you okay?"

Erin's spoke up, her voice shaken. "Yeah, yeah, we're fine. Let me get off of this damn thing. I can't talk and drive at the same time. I'll see you when I get there."

Brig hung up, and in a fit of frustration, spun around and pounded his fist into the casing that surrounded the kitchen doorway. The wood split, as did the skin covering the large, middle knuckle on his right hand. A large patch of blood was smeared across the white paint. Had he not been as infuriated as he was, he might have realized what he had done to his hand, but adrenaline kept his mind focused elsewhere and numb for the time being.

It wasn't until he looked down and saw the trickle of red dripping from his finger tips that he became aware of the pain. Examining his hand, he hissed as the pain became all-too-real. Snatching a dishtowel from the sink, he wrapped it around his hand in a sort of makeshift bandage. He turned to leave and noticed what looked to be words scrawled inside his blood smear. He leaned in closer and saw:

Mor to come

It's playing with me again, he thought, remembering the hallucinations from days before and unsure who or what 'it' was. He tried to speak, but all that came out was a strained croaking sound before finally managing a whisper. "Dad? Dad, please tell me it's you. Tell me you're the one doing this."

Upstairs, a door slammed shut, and the tingle that had been concentrated in the nape of his neck trickled down his back. For Brig, it was confirmation enough. By that time, he had been awake for many, many hours, pouring over yellowing police records pulled from musty boxes far back in a forgotten store room. He was tired; he was frustrated, and now he was scared - not just freaked out - *scared*.

He thought about Harv again and the conversation they'd had a couple of days prior. Something about it just hadn't felt right. Brig couldn't quite put his finger on it, but he knew it to be so. The knowledge was almost like an itch that wouldn't go away. He knew the answer to all of this was in the house - somewhere - and he was determined to find it.

He took one more look at the message scrawled on the doorframe and wiped it clean. For now, he intended on keeping all of this to himself - at least he would try. It sounded as though the news Erin was about to deliver would be enough for all of them; the last thing she needed was the ramblings of some fool chasing shadows around the house.

He hurried into the master bedroom and combed through the random piles of ATM receipts and McDonald's straw wrappers scattered across the dresser until he found what he was looking for - the small slip of paper he'd picked up off the floor of his father's hospital room. He looked at it closely. He knew in his heart that this John Blackwind was a huge piece to the puzzle. Fully intending to call him as soon as the coming dust storm settled, Brig slipped the piece of paper into his pocket and went to the front door when he heard the sound of a car engine roaring towards the house.

He stepped out onto the porch in time to see Erin's car rocketing down the drive at excessive speed. She negotiated the hard right turn just past the tobacco barn with surprising agility, steering into the resulting skid and fish-tailing once more before straightening the car out. Brig ran up the walkway, relived to see them arriving in one piece.

The car came to a screeching stop in the driveway. Through a large plume of gravel dust, the driver's side door burst open and Erin flew from behind it like a cannonball, sprinting in Brig's direction. Stunned, he opened his arms and Erin leapt into them, wrapping her arms around his neck before she broke into a full volley of sobs.

Before she buried her face into his shoulder, he caught a glimpse of Tom's handy-work. Her left eye was swollen and red – not yet a bruise, but well on its way. The underside of her right forearm was scratched and purple, something Brig instantly attributed to a defensive injury. What sent him over the edge was the condition of her lower lip – it was split down the middle, a wide cut which had scabbed, but looked puffy, misshapen, and no doubt hurt like hell. Losing whatever composure he'd managed to muster. He peeled her body away from his and asked, "What HAPPENED?"

Erin lifted her gaze to meet his, and burst into tears again. Her voice was unsteady, but just as she started to answer his question, Kaitlyn came running around the back of the car yelling, "Daddy, Daddy!" She ran up to him and wrapped her arms around his leg. Just as her mother had, Kaitlyn burst into tears.

"Daddy, Tom hurt mommy! Mommy's hurt!" she cried.

Brig led them to the porch and sat them down in the porch swing. Both looked scared, and he knew that it would be impossible to get the facts out of Erin knowing Kaitlyn was within earshot, so he did his best to think of some way to keep the little girl occupied. Over his shoulder he saw the nearby field full of daisies and wildflowers. He bent down and whispered into Kaitlyn's ear. "Why don't you run over there and pick some flowers for mommy? I bet that would make her feel better."

A smile broke across Kaitlyn's face. "Can Busser come?" Brig nodded and she sprung out of the swing running for the kennel to let the dog out before the two of them ran off into the field together. Erin hardly noticed, staring off into space no doubt with the horrors of the day replaying in her mind. Brig touched her cheek and received no response. Eventually she turned towards him.

"Are you okay?" He asked. Erin shook her head that she was, and he helped her to her feet. She was unsteady at first, but managed to follow him into the house where he helped her into one of the recliners. In the most compassionate voice he could muster, he asked her what had happened, and waited patiently for the reply.

Her story started to unfold with a great deal of gesturing and periods of vacant stares. Between the time when Erin had left the farmhouse and arrived at home, Tom had put two and two together – come to find out the "two and two" were actually a fifth of Jack Daniels and a fierce dose of jealousy. Neither of which ever lead to positive things, but in combination are rarely anything but explosive.

He confronted her immediately upon her arrival, and despite all of her attempts to deny that anything had happened, Tom called her a whore and proceeded to beat her in front of Kaitlyn until Erin was able to snatch the girl and run terrified in their bedroom until Tom had drunk enough to pass out. Once he had, she gathered what little clothing and various things she could before she and Kaitlyn escaped and headed north.

Brig was doing his best to control his anger and assure her that she had done the right thing. Had she stayed, there was no telling what Tom would have done next. He promised her she was safe, and that no harm would come to her while she was there. Erin looked up at him when he said this, and he saw gratefulness in her eyes. Gratefulness and total trust.

He stood up and began to cuff his sleeves. "But I'm headed down there and I'm going to kill that son of a bitch."

Erin took his arm. "No Brig. Don't. I beg you. He has a gun. He'll kill you." The tears had returned. They pooled in her eyes. Brig realized then she needed him to stay. She needed to be protected and not avenged. The time for that would come – of that he was sure. Domestic violence rarely dies a quiet death, and he decided then to wait.

About that time, Kaitlyn ran inside with a fistful of wildflowers - some of which still had the roots attached. Buster was close behind, tail wagging with excitement. She held the flowers out to her mother, and Erin took them. The first hint of smile crept onto her face.

Kaitlyn curled her finger back and forth in a 'come here' motion. Brig bent down and she ask if she and Buster could go exploring. Ordinarily, he would have agreed, but his gut told him no. He recalled the night before, when he'd had a nightmare about the coyote in the woods, the one that had pissed on Jacob's tombstone. Only this time, it wasn't the same animal. In his mind's eye, Brig remembered seeing the animal crouched, ready to attack. It was a hellish creature with bright, red eyes. It looked part dragon, part canine, and it had an almost human face.

Brig told Kaitlyn it was a bad idea – wrong time – and suggested she and Buster head upstairs to play while he and her mother talked. Kaitlyn dutifully obeyed with her lip poked out in a pout.

"C'mon Busser," she said, patting the side of her leg the way she had seen her father do a hundred times. "Let's go upstairs." Kaitlyn began to ascend the staircase, but the dog stayed back and stared up the stairs with a whine. Kaitlyn patted harder. "COME ON, BUSSER!"

Just then, Erin jumped at the sound of a vehicle coming up the driveway towards the house. Brig walked over to the front door to investigate. With a shaky voice, she asked who it was, and

Brig said, "Harv, I think..." He squinted against the glare and gave a thumbs-up sign to confirm. "Uh-huh, that's who it is."

Erin bolted upstairs. Brig didn't have to ask why. Kaitlyn on the other hand threw open the storm door and rushed outside where she jumped up into Harv's arms. Harv hugged her back and cut Brig a suspicious look.

"Did you come to see *me?*" She asked.

"No, I didn't even know you were here. I came to see your daddy, but I'm glad I got to see ya!" He set the little girl back on the ground, and Brig motioned for her to come to him. When she did, he whispered in her ear, telling her to run upstairs and check on her mom. She obeyed, leaving the two men alone in the front yard.

Brig said, "You're not going to believe this."

Harv crossed his arms across his chest. The expression on his face dripped of disapproval, but Brig paid it no mind. Harv had made no secret of his feelings regarding any sort of rekindled relationship between himself and Erin, but Brig could not have cared less. Ignoring the old man's judgmental body language, Brig continued.

"Erin is upstairs right now with a split lip and a black eye the size of my fist, and I'll give you one guess as to who put it there."

Harv hung his head. "I was afraid it was somethin' like that. They say women are the ones who can smell a lie on ya, but the truth is men are just as good. Reckon that husband of hers wasn't as dumb as you'd hoped he'd be?"

"I'm in no mood for 'I told you so's'"

Harv slapped him on the back and put his arms around his shoulders. "Didn't come here for that. 'Course this does make it easier to say what I did come here for. Since we're airing dirty laundry and all, I heard through the grapevine that you've been diggin' around in all that mess about your brother. Is that true?"

"Yeah, why?"

"Brig, listen to me. You can only dig around in a barrel full of rattlesnakes so long before you get bitten. The past is the past, son, *let it die*. Let your brother rest in peace." He pointed in the direction of the upper bedrooms. "You got the futures of three living people to worry about now. Don't be wastin' your time sifting through the past of one dead one."

Brig turned to face him, slapping away the hand that still rested on his shoulder. "What's got you so spooked, Harv? You know, I've been suspecting that you've been keeping something from me. I think you know more than you're letting on. What aren't you telling me?"

Harv shifted uncomfortably, and he spat on the ground. When his eyes met Brig's again, they were stern and serious. "I'll say it again... Jacob's dead. Let the past die with him. Ain't nothin' good gonna come of this."

"How could you know that unless there was something that you weren't telling me?" Brig pressed again without waiting for an answer. "Now listen to me. Dad wanted me to come up here so he could tell me something, and I don't think he was the only one who knew. I don't believe that the official story surrounding Jacob's death is the real one, and I have reason to believe he was murdered. If that's the case, you owe it to me – to dad – to come clean. I want to know who did it and why. They can't get away with this!"

Harv's face twisted with offense and rage. "And what if you found out that it wasn't some*one*, but some*thing*? What would you do then?"

"What are you talking about, old man?"

"You've been gone a long time, boy. You tucked tail and ran before you had time to learn about this town. That cave you found? It's just the beginning. I promised your daddy I'd protect you, and that's it. I don't know what it was that he wanted to tell you, and I don't appreciate you bowin' up and sayin' otherwise. I tell ya what, though... you're as hard-headed as he ever was." He stepped forward and pointed a finger in Brig's face and said, "You go down this road, and I can't protect you no more."

Brig laughed off the warning. "I can take care of myself."

Harv huffed and leaned back against the truck, stuffing his hands into his pocket as his shoulders relaxed. "Bull-headed enough to stand up to the devil, huh? Well, you might just get your chance... You're right, though; I don't think your brother's death was an accident."

Brig threw an angry punch at thin air. "I knew it!! WHO? WHO DID IT?"

"The *who* isn't important. The *what* is." Moving away from the truck and close enough to Brig for him to hear the whisper, Harv said, "Listen to me, I wish I could tell you everything you want to know, Brig. If that'd put your mind at ease, I'd do it. But, I don't know the answers you're lookin' for. All I know is that five people died that day: the sheriff's brother as well as yours, a deputy, and two other kids from town."

"How your brother fits in, I don't rightly know. All anyone ever heard was rumors – hell, all anyone ever hears around this goddam place is rumors. People said it was the Usher boy, but I'm not so sure – that boy was mean, but he was no *killer*. You won't ever get the sheriff to admit it was his own brother, either, so you might as well forget that shit. You'll just get yourself in a lot more trouble than you bargained for. He's one bad apple that won't think twice about takin' a bite outta your ass."

"So what are you saying?"

"What killed Jacob came outta that cave, Brig! No man killed your brother, whatever is in there did!"

"You're crazy, old man!"

Harv leaned in again, brow furrowed but eyes wide. "Am I? *Am I really?* Let me ask ya somethin', how have you been sleepin'? Been having *nightmares?*" Brig drew in a hard swallow and nodded his head. "You think you're the only one? I've been havin' 'em, too. So has Judy. So has damn near everybody else in town. I can't shake the feeling that somethin' bad is comin', but believe me when I tell ya that's all I know."

Brig's better judgment overruled his irrational impulse, and he decided to trust him – there was certainly no reason not to. He reached into his pocket and pulled out the slip of paper with Blackwind's telephone number on it. Brig held up the slip of paper and said, "You may not know the answers, but I bet I know someone who does. Remember that Indian? I've got his number right here."

Harv held out an open palm. "Think about what you're doin', son. You don't know how big of a shitstorm you're gonna stir up if you go pokin' your nose where it don't belong!"

Brig shook his head. "Be that as it may, this is something I have to do. I have to know."

Harv opened the door to his truck and climbed inside. He slammed the door closed using one hand through the open window. "Then you're on your own, Brig. I can't be a part of this." The engine roared and soon, the truck disappeared around the bend. When it was out of sight, Brig looked down at the creased slip of paper in his hand, understanding the time had come to make the call.

A high-pitched scream rose from inside the house. Brig ran towards it and opened the door in time to see Erin running down the steps as quickly as she could with Kaitlyn casually following along behind her. Erin pushed by him and continued until she was out in the yard. Her face was pale, and she was shaking.

Kaitlyn passed her father in the same slow, steady manner with a casual "Hi there Daddy." Brig looked at her and then back at Erin, confused at the differences in their emotional states.

"What's wrong?" He asked.

Erin pointed in the direction of Brig's bedroom window. "*WHAT THE HELL WAS* THAT???" She hugged Kaitlyn close in a desperate attempt to find comfort.

Brig looked to Kaitlyn in hopes of an explanation. The little girl shrugged her shoulders and said, "Mommy met my friend." She sat down on the ground and used a stick to draw circles in the dirt for no apparent reason.

"Your friend?"

She continued to draw and spoke without looking up. "Uh-huh," she said. "He's nice. He used to live in the room across from mine, but he got hurt... hurt bad." She completed a third circle and then a fourth. She had laid them out in a diamond-shaped pattern and went on to connect all four with sloping lines.

"Hurt bad, huh?" Brig asked, kneeling down to her level. "Let me ask you something, Katie. What's your friend look like?" His suspicion was deeper than that, though. He added, "What's his name?

"I don't know his name," Kaitlyn replied. "He doesn't talk much – I don't think I've ever heard him talk. He's bigger than me, though... I mean older. He's got hair the same color as mine, too."

Brig turned to Erin and said, "It's Jacob."

Erin held her hand against her forehead, another on her chest. The expression on her face said that she couldn't believe what she'd experienced any more than she could believe that Brig was encouraging his daughter with this line of questioning. "Your brother? You can't be serious."

"I'm afraid so. I haven't said anything to you, but ever since I came up here, some weird stuff has been going on. I suppose I could explain it all away. I could call it a cold draft – a wild imagination – but I'm telling you, I've felt him, Erin. I *know* he's here." He paused before he continued his thought. He didn't want to sound crazy, but he eventually concluded that there was no way around it. "Erin, the house is haunted."

"Haunted?!"

"Yes. I think they're all here. Mom, Dad, Jacob... But I think my brother might be the most restless. He wants to tell me something; I'm sure of it." Brig lowered his voice to a whisper. "I think he was murdered. I think I can prove it, too! I just need more time."

Erin held up a hand. "Wait... wait... wait." she protested. "You're trying to tell me that what just happened up there – the stuff moving around on the dresser, the doors opening by themselves – that was Jacob?"

"Or one of the others, yes!"

"And you expect me to believe this?"

Brig motioned to his daughter. "You heard Kaitlyn! Her friend was hurt. He lived across the hall from my bedroom once. Erin, it's him!"

Kaitlyn raised her hand like she had been taught in school, trying to get her parents attention. When she had it, she said, "The little boy doesn't talk much, but the others do."

Anxious to prove his point, Brig asked, "How many others are there?"

Kaitlyn ran to the passenger side of Erin's car and returned with a picture that she had drawn on the drive up from Havens

Fork. She handed it to her father and he saw three white figures surrounding a little girl sitting up on the edge of a bed.

"Who's the little girl?" Brig asked.

"That's me!"

"And the white people?"

Kaitlyn pointed to each one: "This one is Nanna. This one is Paw-paw. And this one's the little boy. He's funny, but he seems scared sometimes."

"Scared of what?"

"Of *him*." Kaitlyn pointed to a winged figure in the corner of the room that she had drawn black with large, red eyes. Brig thought back to the night before Jacob died and what he'd said was in his room that night – what had tried to get him.

"And who *is* that?" Brig asked her.

Kaitlyn looked up at him; her eyes cold and grim. "That's the one that Nanna says wants to hurt us," she said. "That's the one that hurt my friend. He plays with my hair at night... That's the bad man."

The three of them went back inside and Brig sat Kaitlyn down on the couch. He knelt beside her and said, "Katie, your friend's name is Jacob. I'm sure of it. I need to know what Nanna and Paw-paw have told you about him. Have they told you how he got hurt?"

"No," came the reply. "I think they tried to tell me a couple of times, but when they tried, the bad man ran 'em off. He's not very nice. I don't like him."

Erin spoke up and said, "This is nuts. I don't know what just happened up there, but ghosts? C'mon."

Brig remembered the camcorder he'd bought a few days prior. He'd set it up in his old bedroom that morning and let it run. *Video doesn't lie,* he thought. *If anything is going to make Erin believe, it's going to be the video!* He raced up the stairs and ran back down a few seconds holding the camera in his hand.

"What's that?" She asked.

"Proof, I hope." He spun the television around and fumbled with the wires in an attempt to hook the camera into one of the various inputs. With that done, he picked up and the remote and began sorting through the menu of inputs until a picture appeared on the screen.

The picture was of Brig's room from the vantage point of the dresser. The bed was to the right of the screen, neatly made; the '*mommy loves you*' baby doll lay haphazardly in the middle of the mattress. Brig and Erin watched the tape for about fifteen minutes before Brig grew impatient and pressed the fast forward button on the remote. Lines wiggled across the screen.

Brig grew frustrated. He fully expected the proof to be there, but no such luck. He set the remote down on the table and looked at Erin. "I don't know what to tell you. I'm not making this up. I didn't want to believe it at first either, but it just makes sense. It's the only explanation I can..."

The video's vacant hiss was suddenly replaced with something less electronic – something more this world. It was the sound of creaking wicker. The sound was coming from the rocking chair in the corner of the room. They both looked at the television screen; to Erin's horror and Brig's utter delight, the chair was rocking ever so slowly back and forth with no one in it.

The wicker cried a paper-thin cry, and the long-forgotten wood groaned and popped with the motion. Brig jumped out of his chair, nearly spilling Erin onto the floor. "Listen!" He said. "Do you hear it?"

"Hear what?" she asked.

"The song! Can't you hear the song?" He rewound the feed a bit and cranked the volume full-blast. He watched the color drain from Erin's face as a soft, phantom voice sang the words:

'Hush little baby, don't say a word. Momma's gonna buy you a mocking bird...'

Erin moved closer to the speakers. "What *is* that?" She asked. "Where's it coming from?"

"Someone's in the chair!" He said. "Do you believe me now? We're not alone!"

Erin backed away from the set with her hand over her mouth. Brig wasn't sure if she wanted to scream or to cry. He was pretty sure that either one would be an appropriate response.

Kaitlyn sat on the couch and pointed at the television set. "That's Nanna," she said. "She sings to me sometimes."

Just before the video cut out a final chorus was heard from the singer who wasn't there at all... *'and if that mocking bird don't sing. Mommy's gonna buy you a diamond ring...'*

CHAPTER EIGHT

-1-

Early Saturday morning, about six weeks after the night of the meteor shower, Sammi stepped out of her house. Her friend Sarah was waiting in the driveway, just as they had planned. As far as Sammi's mother was concerned, the girls were headed to Havens Fork to go shopping. It wasn't a lie, the girls were indeed going shopping, but it wasn't for a new pair of blue jeans.

Sarah smiled a wary smile and handed Sammi a folded stack of cash she had removed from her babysitting piggy bank. No debit cards were being used today. No paper trail meant no need to answer uncomfortable questions once the monthly statement arrived in the mail. As they backed out of the driveway, Sammi buried her face in her hands and started to cry. Sarah patted her hand and assured her that everything was going to turn out alright.

Thirty minutes later, the two girls walked into a drug store in downtown Havens Fork, within sight of the college campus. They had both agreed the trip south was the best choice given the circumstances. The last thing they wanted was to start a rumor back home. The hens in Jones Chapel already had enough to cluck about for the time being and Sammi had no intention of being added to their list.

The drug store was a small one, so it didn't take long before they found the item they had come for. It had been hard enough for Sammi to overcome crippling anxiety and make the trip in the first place. She stood still as a statue in the aisle staring at the assortment of boxes. Sarah reached out and took a box off of the shelf, placing it in Sammi's hand before the two went to the checkout counter where the clerk rang up the purchase, announcing the total with blatant disinterest for the situation she was in. On the other side of the counter, the weight of the moment weighed heavy on Sammi's shoulders. She wondered if the clerk realized – or cared – that the box that he held in his hand, the one he placed into a thin paper bag was going to determine her future.

The two girls got back into Sarah's car and drove to a grimy, out-of-the-way service station on a dusty back road. Sammi tore the cellophane wrapper off of the box and looked with a combination of disgust and embarrassment at the pregnancy test in her hand. The cruel gravity of the fact that the culmination of the past few weeks had come down to the simple matter of peeing on a stick was not lost on her.

She removed the test stick and read the instructions. Her eyes rose to meet Sarah's, who once again assured her that everything was going to be alright. Sammi nodded just before she climbed out of the car and walked into a tiny public bathroom behind a metal door. She was two weeks late with her period. Until this moment, she had chalked it up to stress. It happens. After all, just as Brent had told her, you couldn't get pregnant your first time and each time thereafter, they had been careful.

Brent knew nothing of this trip or even the eeking uncertainty that had prompted it. Sammi had kept it from him on purpose, fearing he would bolt as soon as he heard the words come out of her mouth. Sarah was the only one who knew, and god-willing, the only one who ever would.

Prior to this moment, Sammi had never thought of herself as a woman, but she understood the problem she was facing was certainly not one doled out to a child. She flipped on the light switch and closed the door behind her. The overhead fluorescent lights flickered and hummed before springing to life and bathing the room with a clinical shade of blue. Sammi had always heard that women's bathrooms were much cleaner than the men's were, but as she moved toward the toilet, she wondered how that could be. The bathroom was filthy, the floor sticky, and it smelled like a combination of urine and Mexican food.

Sanitation conditions were the last thing on her mind, however. There were much bigger problems on her plate. Her anxiety attack was in full swing and she was beginning to feel dizzy. Looking into the mirror, her face was flushed and her nostrils were flaring. Small beads of sweat had formed on her forehead. She took the test stick in her hand and whispered the sexually active teenager's mantra over and over again: "*Please, God! Oh please, oh please, oh please, oh please.*"

She wanted to believe that all of this was simply a product of paranoia. She wanted to believe the reason her period was two weeks late was stress. She wanted to believe the queasy feeling in her stomach was nothing at all.

But Sammi knew better.

She drew in a deep breath, paying no mind to the thick urine smell. She squatted over the toilet seat and peed on the stick. This was it. It had come to this – pissing on a stick in a filthy gas station bathroom. Suddenly the romance at the lake didn't seem so glamorous, and the 'private sin' she had so longed for had come back to bite her.

She stood up, leaned against the wall, and closed her eyes. She thought about the Christmas holidays that had only been a few months before, but seemed a lifetime away. She remembered the atmosphere and the love, the laughter and the smiles. She knew that if her worst fear became a reality, those would have been the last of the good times. There was no reason to kid herself on the issue.

She checked her watch, avoiding eye contact with the test strip. One minute left. She tried to think of something she could do to settle her nerves. Nothing came to mind, so she waited for the last thirty seconds until the second hand on her watch passed the number twelve. Her three minutes were up.

Sammi closed her eyes and raised the stick in front of her face. Her heart pounded in her chest and her throat tightened. *I can do this,* she told herself. *All I have to do is look at it and this will all be over. There'll only be one line... One line... Negative.*

Another deep breath and Sammi opened her eyes to see two lines boldly glaring back at her. Her legs were no longer able to support her. She slid down the cinderblock wall and sat on the wet, sticky floor, staining the seat of the white pants she was wearing with rank, yellow urine. She pulled her knees to her chest and cried. She was pregnant, after all.

Sarah rushed to her side when Sammi fainted onto the concrete sidewalk once she emerged from the bathroom. Sarah didn't have to ask what the results had been. The absence of blood in Sammi's face and the pale color that absence had caused was evidence enough.

"Oh, Jesus!" she said. "It's okay, Sammi. It's going to be okay." Sarah helped her into the passenger's seat where Sammi burst into tears again. Sarah climbed into the driver's side and reached out to hold her hand. It was trembling uncontrollably. "I know you're scared. We'll figure something out. There has to be a way to fix this. There just has to be."

"How am I going to tell him?" Sammi asked. "How do I tell Brent?"

Sarah sighed. "You're just going to have to. It's not like you're the first person this has happened to, Sammi. I know you think you are, but this isn't the end of the world!"

Sammi wiped a tear from her eye, and she stared at the floorboard. She thought about all of the dreams she'd hoped to accomplish in the coming years. They all seemed like a distant memory now. She was positive Brent would be furious – he would hate her and tell her she was on her own. Her mother would probably kick her out of the house. Her father would never talk to her again, either. As far as Sammi Pridmore was concerned, her life was over.

-2-

The trip back to Jones Chapel took much longer than the trip down had taken. Sarah had pulled to the side of the road a couple of times and held Sammi's hair back as she threw up. When they finally made it back into town, they drove past the Baptist Church to make sure Sammi's mother was still at choir practice. Thankfully, she was. That made sneaking back into the house unnecessary.

Sammi collapsed onto the bed and buried her face into her pillow. Sarah wasn't sure what to say, but she knew what needed to be done. She also knew Sammi would never be able to call Brent herself. She gently patted Sammi on the back and told her she was going to go upstairs to get some water. She asked if there was anything she could bring back down, but Sammi declined.

Upstairs, Sarah filled a glass with water from the sink and leaned against the countertop. She couldn't believe any of this was happening, but despite their friendship, she was thankful it wasn't happening to *her*. Unbeknownst to Sammi, it had at one time, but Sarah had parents willing and able to pay for an abortion. The father never found out, nor did the hens in Jones Chapel. The little secret was buried in the family closet and never spoken of again.

Sarah sat down on the living room couch and picked up the telephone. She took a folded slip of paper out of her pocket and dialed the seven digits scribbled on it. The phone rang twice and Brent answered. Sarah told him the news and waited patiently for his endless stream of "*HolyshitsweetJesusNO's*" to come to an end. When he'd settled down a bit more, she tried her best to comfort him in the same way she had tried to comfort Sammi. The results were about the same.

In the end, the two of them agreed that he and Sammi needed to meet as soon as possible. Brent suggested Sammi meet him someplace where they could talk without being interrupted and more importantly – *overheard.* The first place that came to mind was an old barn on the backside of his father's farm. Brent knew his father had to work late that night, so he told Sarah to have Sammi meet him at the barn around nine o'clock. He paused when he heard a click on the line, thinking Sarah had hung up. She assured him she hadn't and the two wrapped up the call.

Brent's father, A.J., set the receiver back onto its cradle and rubbed his temples. He couldn't believe what he had just heard. Brent had gone and knocked up his girlfriend. The boy's dreams were shot. To add further gravity to the situation, A.J.'s dreams crumbled right along with his son's. He wouldn't have the opportunity to sit in the stands and root for his son, the All-American. There would be no Heisman trophy celebrations, no NFL draft parties – that is, unless he did something about *this*.

A.J. knew the time and place Brent and Sammi intended to meet. He also knew his son would do anything to keep him from finding out about it. Brent just needed to be late for that meeting and all of this mess could be straightened out.

He rose from the couch and poured himself a glass of whiskey. He sipped it slowly as he formulated his plan. Regrettably, an accomplice would be necessary. Brent was sure to be a problem – an unknown variable that had to be contended with. He tried to think of the right person – someone he held in his back pocket – *someone with dark secrets of their own.*

Perry came to mind almost immediately. A.J. knew he had Perry's balls in the palm of his hand. He'd helped him cover up a small matter of a drunken driving fatality a few years ago. Perry had been itching to square the account with his boss ever since – he'd jump at the chance. A.J. downed what was left in his glass and headed to the office.

Sarah went back downstairs. She wasn't surprised to see that Sammi had passed out from the mental exhaustion. God only knew the hell her predicament had put her through in recent days or the amount of sleep she had lost. Sarah hated to do it, but she shook her until she woke up.

"What's going on?" Sammi asked.

"You're going to be angry with me," Sarah told her, "but I don't care. I did what had to be done because I knew you would probably never be able to bring yourself to do it."

"You didn't!"

"I'm afraid I did. I called Brent. I told him everything."

"Sarah! How could you?!"

"You may be angry with me now, but you'll thank me. He wants to meet with you – tonight. You two have a lot to talk about."

"What did he say?"

"Well, I won't lie to you. He wasn't thrilled, but he cares a lot about you, Sammi. He wants to take care of you."

"He said that?"

"Yes." Sarah went over the specifics with Sammi and told her where she was supposed to meet him. The two of them plotted how they would get Sammi out of the house without her mother knowing. It wasn't going to be easy, but for the first time in three hours, a ray of hope had cut through the darkness.

-3-

Both Brent and Sammi spent the next five hours being tossed about in their own personal hells. The maelstrom of emotions proved difficult to contend with. At one point, Brent had stood in his father's bathroom, his arm submerged in a scalding basin of water, a razor poised at a slight angle to his wrist. He had never contemplated suicide before, but it seemed far better than the alternative reality that lay before him.

Eventually Brent decided he wasn't ready to die... not just yet, anyway. He had come to terms with the fact that his future was most likely shot. There was no telling what his father would do to him, but consequences notwithstanding, Brent had a solid grasp on the concept of responsibility – a virtue instilled in him by his mother; noble virtues seldom flowed through his paternal line. It was this that caused him to put the razor down, despite the soothing release it promised him.

Sammi's strict religion offered her no such hope of escape. She lay on her bed staring at the ceiling, but she couldn't shake the sensation of vertigo and the accompanying nausea. She rolled over onto her side and pulled an oversized teddy bear close to her. She tried to imagine what Brent was going to say to her that night. *Would he blame her? Was he going to tell her that all of this was her fault?* She could keep this from her parents for now, but how much longer? Eventually she'd have to tell them, and then...

She shook the thought away. It was too much to deal with for now. From deep within herself, anger swelled. She thought about how many times she had watched daytime TV shows and listened to the woe and heartache of married couples unable to have a child. *Those people had tried and tried*, she thought. *They had fought for* years *and* nothing*! A couple of teenagers share a moment at the lake and BAM!!!* She told herself that this was a punishment. Her mother's voice spoke up in her head, *'All things happen for a reason.'*

She gritted her teeth and told her god just what she thought about Him and His 'greater plan.' It felt good to do. This anger had been building up inside her since she was ten years old. She was tired of listening to the fire-and-brimstone, holier-than-thou bags of hot air that pounded the pulpit each and every Sunday. She knew she wasn't a bad person. She knew that sometimes shit just happens. Sometimes people just screw up! And if God really gave a shit about her, why hadn't He protected her? For seventeen years she'd done exactly what they'd told her to with no questions. *I've never slipped before...* NOT ONCE... *and* THIS *is how I'm repaid?* she thought.

Sammi had never understood the rage. She didn't know the cause, but she looked at her stomach and pictured it getting bigger and bigger, an unwanted alien growing inside. She wanted to grab a knife, plunge it into her stomach, and dig the beast out. Instead, she rolled over onto her side and cried herself to sleep.

Less than two hours later, her alarm clock woke her. She scrambled to put herself together in time to meet Sarah who was going to take her to where Brent had told her to meet him. She knew she couldn't go through the front door. The two of them had discussed it and that was out of the question. Her mother would want to know where she was going, and Sammi knew better than to lie to her – she was in no condition to pull off such a move.

She climbed on top of a bookcase and opened the small basement window high on the wall that would allow her to wiggle through into the front yard. It took a good deal of scrambling and effort to get through the small opening, but she managed. Once out of the house, she snuck around the side and waited beside the corner of the garage.

Minutes later, Sarah slowed to a stop outside of the house with headlights off. Sammi ran and jumped into the car, and the two drove off on their way to the Usher farm. Sammi wore a smile on her face, desperately clinging to the faint hope Brent might somehow get them both out of this mess. It was all she had to hold onto, and hold on she did. Sarah turned down the radio and asked her, "Are you alright?"

"I guess. I'll feel better when this is over." The clock on the dashboard said it was 8:15. "Are we going to make it in time?" she asked.

"Plenty of time. Now remember, I'm going to drop you off. He's going to meet you there around nine o'clock." Sarah reached into her purse and removed a cell phone. "I have my phone," she said. "Take all the time you need, but call me when you're ready for me to pick you up, okay?"

Sammi dug through her purse and held her phone up as well. "I don't know how long we're going to be. It could be pretty late. Are you sure you don't just want Brent to take me home?"

"No. You're going to want to talk to someone after all of this. Just call me. It doesn't matter how late it is." Sammi agreed to do just that and the two drove on in silence. A million variations of the conversation that she and Brent were about to have flooded her head.

-4-

Meanwhile, Brent was busy getting ready as well. He was running behind - not because he had overslept, but rather because he had spent so much time staring into the mirror telling himself what a royal screw up he was. He finished tying his shoes and was just about to walk out of the door when the phone rang.

He considered not answering it, but feared it might be Sammi telling him that she was going to be late - or worse, not able to make it at all. The last thing he wanted to do was sit in a barn all night waiting on someone who wasn't going to show up, so he picked up the receiver.

It wasn't Sammi on the other end – it was his father. The last voice he wanted to hear, and the tone was stern as usual. "Brent? Listen, I need you to come and pick me up. Something's happened with the patrol car and I'm stuck at the Texaco station in Wicklow."

"Dad, I can't. I have a date in 45 minutes. Can't someone from the station pick you up?"

"No." His father's cut him off. "Your damn girlfriend can wait on you. Get your ass down here and pick me up or you can kiss that car of yours goodbye."

Brent slammed the receiver down and rushed into the kitchen for a pen and piece of paper, quickly scribbling out a note for Sammi before hurrying out to his car. He raced down to the barn where he had told Sammi to meet him and stuck the note to a nail on the front door. He hopped back into the car and floored it.

He needed to hurry. He had much bigger problems to deal with than his father and his broken down patrol car. As he sped down the highway, his thoughts returned to the situation he was in. He replayed the short conversation he'd had with Sarah earlier that afternoon. '*Sammi's pregnant*' echoed repeatedly in his head. The words hit him like a hammer – over and over.

Something about the conversation hadn't seemed right to him, though. It wasn't until he pulled into the gas station where his father had told him to pick him up that he realized what it was. There had been a click on the line towards the end of the conversation. He was sure of it. He couldn't be certain if his father had been home when the call had come in, but he knew one thing, his father was nowhere near that gas station.

Brent spun the car around and slammed the accelerator to the floor, leaving a couple of dark tire marks on the pavement in the process. He feared the worst. He knew what his father was capable of, and he was positive something was wrong – *very wrong*. He decided to take a series of back roads to get back to the farm, positive that if his father was indeed trying to keep him from meeting with Sammi, he would have someone lying in wait to stop him on his way back. He knew it might mean a few extra minutes, but it was worth it if it meant he could get there at all.

-5-

Back in Jones Chapel, Sarah pulled to the side of the road and pointed to a rickety structure in the distance. Small shafts of light shone through the gaps of the wall slats making the barn look like some kind of bizarre jack-o-lantern.

"That's it," she said. "He's going to meet you there. Looks like he's already inside. Are you okay? Sure you don't want me to go with you?"

Sammi shook her head. "No, I'm fine, really. I'll call you when this is over." With that, she got out of the car. Sarah sat beside the road with the car idling and watched as Sammi fiddled with the chain and hook keeping the gate latched. Once she'd made it through, Sammi was visible for a few minutes longer before she was swallowed in the darkness.

Sammi didn't like walking through fields at night. There were snakes in fields. There was cow shit in fields. She could step into a hole, twist or break her ankle, and it would be hours before anyone came to get her. Behind the curtain of night, she heard something move. It sounded big, and she picked up her pace.

The barn seemed so far in the distance, and she wondered if she could make it before the thing behind her caught up. Her imagination raced with images of monsters staring at her from behind the tree cover surrounding her – slimy things with big teeth and appetites to match. In her mind, the fireflies were eyes – a pair here, a pair there – three on that one.

Five minutes later, she reached the barn and peered through a crack in the door. There didn't appear to be anyone inside. Everything was quiet aside from the whine of cicadas in the trees. Dead quiet. She opened the door; it groaned on old hinges as it swung open. Hanging from a pole in the loft was a kerosene lantern. Its bright light blinded her from being able to see anything in the lower part of the barn. The sweet scent of alfalfa filled her nose, causing her to sneeze. Even without the use of her eyes, she knew the barn must be full of hay bales.

"Brent?" She whispered, looking up into the loft. "Brent, are you up there?" She felt along the wall for a ladder. She found one and grabbed hold of a rung just above her head. She placed her foot on a lower one, but froze when something moved among the hay bales behind her.

Before she had a chance to turn around, a hand held a moist rag over her mouth and nose and pressed down hard. She slung her elbow backwards in a futile attempt to fight back, but whoever it was that had grabbed her proved much too powerful. Her screams came out muffled from beneath the rag, which smelled of a combination of rubbing alcohol and gasoline. She was suffocating and fought desperately for what little air she could get. Her head felt light and fuzzy. Double vision set in, and things became blurry. Another deep breath and the world went black.

-6-

Brent reached the barn and through the wall slats he saw movement inside, but he couldn't make out what it was. He grabbed a flashlight from the back floorboard of his car and opened the barn door. Inside, the beam of light sliced through the darkness and the dust.

"Sammi!" He shouted. "Sammi, where are you?" He heard a noise from behind a row of hay bales and went to investigate. Sammi lay behind it; her legs were bound, and her hands were tied behind her back. "Jesus Christ!" he shouted, reaching out for her.

Just then, he was jumped from behind, but managed to free himself and deliver a swift kick to the assailant's mid-section, knocking the wind out of him. The mysterious attacker fell to the ground and Brent dropped to his knees, raising his flashlight above his head like a club, fully intent on bashing in the man's skull. Another hand seized his wrist and slapped on a pair of handcuffs before forcing Brent onto his stomach and cuffing his other arm as well.

"Goddammit, Perry," a voice said. "You aren't worth a shit, you know that?" Brent knew that voice, knew it well. Actually, he'd known who grabbed his wrist before the voice had ever spoken; he'd felt the calluses on his father's right hand and the thick gold ring he wore on it.

Perry struggled to get back on his feet. "Sorry, boss. The boy's stronger than I thought. Just surprised me, that's all."

A.J. was in no mood for excuses. "Just bring the bitch out here!" Perry disappeared behind the row of bales and appeared again, dragging Sammi like a rag doll.

Brent shouted, "Let her go! Be easy with her motherfucker!" Perry shoved Sammi onto her knees, and in the light from the kerosene lamp, Brent saw that her mouth had been gagged. Her eyes looked heavy and tired. "What the hell did you do to her?" he asked. "She looks drugged!"

"Take it easy boy," Perry said. "She's just a little groggy from the chloroform."

"Chloroform?! Sweet Jesus! What's wrong with you people?!"

A.J. stepped in front of him and said, "I know all about your little secret, son."

"What secret?" Brent looked at Sammi again. She seemed to be coming out of the chloroform haze. Her eyes widened in panic when she realized that her hands and legs were bound. She jerked this way and that trying to free herself, but to no avail. Her eyes cut up towards Brent again, and in them, there was a pleading.

"You couldn't keep you dick in your pants long enough to make something out of your life – *that's* the secret I'm talking about! Don't play stupid with me, son." A.J. walked over to Sammi and snatched a handful of her hair, pulling her head backwards. "You went and got this little bitch pregnant!"

It was all starting to clear up for Brent. His father *had* been listening in on the telephone call. None of that mattered now; he had to stall. "Where did you hear that?"

"Oh Christ, Brent! Are you really going to play this game with me? I told you a long time ago that there isn't a damn thing you can do in this town that I won't find out about." Pointing a finger at Sammi, he shouted, "Did you really think I wouldn't hear about *this*?"

"Okay... okay... you're right. She's pregnant," Brent finally admitted. "Listen, I know it looks bad, but..."

"LOOKS BAD? *LOOKS BAD?!* It doesn't *get* any worse than this!"

"C'mon, dad! Let's talk this out! Why are you doing this? I mean, look at her! You knocked her out and tied her up! Did you really have to go that far? I mean... I screwed up... I'm sorry. Punish *me*, not her!"

A.J. flung Sammi's head forward again and walked towards his son. Brent smelled the liquor on his breath and a quick glance in Perry's direction told him that there was going to be no help from him.

A.J. leaned into Brent's face and hissed, "I'm not going to let you fuck your life up over some little small town whore! I didn't raise you to be a goddamned ditch digger! You've got your whole life ahead of you. You've got your football scholarship..."

Brent's eyes narrowed, and he screamed, "That's *YOUR* dream!! *NOT MINE!*"

A.J. back-handed him across the side of the face and said, "Don't you raise your voice to me you little bastard!"

"I'm not going to school, dad."

"What did you say?"

"You heard me. I'm not going to school. Sammi's pregnant! You just expect me to leave her? Hell no, I'm staying here."

A.J. was absolutely livid by that point. He drew his gun from its holster and pressed it hard against Brent's cheek. "Like *hell* you are. Why do you think I brought you out here tonight? Huh? To have a little chat?" He pulled the gun away from Brent's cheek, cocked the hammer, and pointed the barrel at Sammi's head.

Perry stepped forward, frantically waving his hands. "Whoa, whoa, wait a sec, boss. You didn't say anything about killing the girl! I thought we were just gonna, you know, strong-arm the boy or something. Scare him a little."

A.J. turned the gun on Perry and said, "Get *back!* I don't need any advice from you! You're in this up to your ass, so I suggest you keep your mouth shut and get on board!"

"Dad, don't! Look, we can work this out! Nobody has to get hurt, okay? Just put the gun down. Please! Don't hurt her!"

His father walked over to where Sammi was kneeling and held the gun against the side of her head. Tears were streaming down her cheeks, and Brent could hear the strained sound of her screams from beneath the scarf Perry had used to gag her. She rocked back and forth on her knees, utterly terrified.

She couldn't believe any of this was happening. She thought it had to be a dream. The cold steel against her head, the smell of Jack Daniels, alfalfa, and sweat... all a dream! She tried to convince herself she had overslept – that she was still laying on her bed at home with her teddy bear against her body – not here, not tied up and kneeling on a dusty barn floor.

From what seemed to be a million miles away, she heard a voice: "Hold him." Perry ran to hold Brent back as he tried to bum-rush his father. Handcuffed or not, the boy fought before another gun was placed against his head, this one held by his father's henchman.

"Son," A.J. said. "You can watch or you can turn your head. Your choice."

"Dad, please – *Don't!*" Sammi looked up at him again. Tears streamed from her eyes and in them, he saw reservation – something inside Sammi had given up. He mouthed the words: *'I'm sorry. I love you.'*

Her ears had started to ring, and her mouth was bone dry. She glanced around the room and thought, *Oh God, let me wake up, let me wake up, please let me wake up!* She was feeling dizzy again and there was a tremendous lump in her throat. *Mom? Mom, where are you? HELP ME...*

Click

"DAD NO!!!!!!!"

POP!

A fiery cone of sparks erupted from the muzzle of A.J.'s pistol. Brent screamed as the side of Sammi's head exploded outward. Shards of bone, blood, and brain splattered against one of the bales of hay. Sammi's body crumpled onto the dirt floor. Brent broke down in tears as an ever-expanding puddle of blood pooled around her head, soaking into her blonde hair.

"YOU FUCKING BASTARD!!!" He screamed. "YOU CRUEL FUCKING BASTARD!!!"

A.J. didn't respond. He just removed a white handkerchief from his back pocket and wiped the blood from his revolver. He holstered it again and threw the wadded piece of cloth onto the ground. It landed beside Sammi's head and gradually turned red as it lay in the puddle. He shook his head and said, "One day you'll thank me for this, son."

With that said, he nodded to Perry who removed a rag from his pocket and held it over Brent's mouth and nose, just as he had done to Sammi not thirty minutes before. Brent fought against him, but the strength had left his body. He held his breath as long as he could, but before long, he drew in a deep breath and the lights went out.

-7-

Perry lay Brent onto the floor. He turned to A.J. and said, "Boss, how the hell are we going to get away with this? I mean, the boy saw the whole thing! People are gonna notice the girl's missing. It's gonna leak out!"

"No it won't. I can promise you that."

"Jesus, boss... *you shot her!*"

A.J. grabbed a blanket he'd brought with him. He spread it on the ground and rolled Sammi's body onto it. "Don't get judgmental on me, Perry. This is no different than what you did. Besides, we're square now. It's what you wanted."

"But not like this! How can you say this isn't any different? Mine was an accident!"

"Do you really think a judge would agree with you on that? Vehicular homicide, driving under the influence, obstruction of justice... do you know what they do to cops in prison, Perry?"

Indeed Perry did. It had been the determining factor that had caused him to go along with this plan to begin with. He shook his head. "She was so pretty."

"None of that matters. It had to be done. C'mon, Perry, you know her family. We did her a favor. I'm surprised she wasn't begging for the bullet." A.J. bent down and wrapped Sammi's body in the blanket before reaching into Brent's pocket and removing his keys.

"What are you doing?" Perry asked.

"Making sure that you don't have to lose any sleep over this. Let's call it insurance." A.J. put on a pair of rubber gloves and tossed a set to Perry. "Put those on."

"What's your plan?"

A.J. wiped the gun clean of prints and placed it in Brent's hand, curling the boy's fingers around the pistol's handle. He carefully placed Brent's index finger on the trigger and his thumb on the hammer. "Roll him onto his back," he commanded.

Perry did as he was told, and A.J. dipped his gloved right hand into the pool of Sammi's blood and flicked it over Brent's face. "I woke up this morning and my gun was missing," A.J. explained. "I wrote up a police report and you signed it."

"Jesus, boss! You're framing your own kid?"

"No, I'm just making sure he doesn't talk. Now, help me move her. You get her head, I've got her feet."

The men lifted Sammi's body and carried it out of the barn. A.J. popped the Mustang's hatch and the two of them hoisted her body inside. After patting the pockets of her jeans, A.J. reached into one of them and removed her cell phone. He held it up for Perry to see and then tossed it onto the floorboard.

"Now the boy," he said.

Brent proved to be considerably heavier than Sammi at a muscular 190 pounds, but Perry and A.J. managed to get him into the passenger's seat where Perry gave him another dose of chloroform.

A.J. asked, "Do you have any blood on you?""

"No, sir," Perry answered. "I'm clean." He peeled the latex gloves off his hands and handed them to A.J. He gestured towards the barn and asked, "What about the mess in there?"

"I'll come back later and clean it up. Trust me. This'll all blow over. Just try not to panic and act surprised when the phone calls start rolling in about her, okay?"

"Surprised. Got it."

"Good. Now, let's get the hell out of here. You take the squad car - the keys are on the dashboard. Follow me up to the house. I need you to stay with him until I get back." A.J. climbed behind the wheel of the Mustang, and Perry got into the squad car, which had been neatly hidden in a tangle of thick underbrush several yards away. Seconds later, the two cars headed off in the direction of the house.

What they didn't know was that Sarah had decided to wait by the side of the road instead of going home after she'd dropped Sammi off. The position of the barn in relation to the road behind it obscured her vision quite a bit. She hadn't seen Brent pull up, and she hadn't seen the bodies being carried out, but she did see two sets of tail lights pull away. It struck her as odd, and she was somewhat concerned. But she didn't want to interfere, so she chose to wait about an hour longer before walking down to investigate.

-8-

While Perry sat in the living room with an unconscious Brent, A.J. headed to the only spot he could think of to dispose of a body where it would most likely never be found. He shut off his headlights and slowly pulled into the driveway at the Bailey farm. He steered the car behind the tobacco barn, careful to place it where it wouldn't be seen by anyone driving to or from the house.

He still wore the latex gloves, and inside them, his hands were hot and sweaty, but he knew well enough to leave them on. The last thing he wanted was to leave a bloody fingerprint in Brent's car. One stupid move like that and the whole plan would fall apart. He opened the back hatch and pulled Sammi's body from it. He threw her over his shoulder and started to walk. He had his flashlight with him, but he wasn't going to turn it on until he was well out of range from the house.

The cave was about a mile from where he'd parked, and a cross-country hike with a dead body over his shoulder made the going that much tougher. After about five minutes, he looked back to see he had covered quite a good distance. His eyes searched for the tree line, but it was hidden in the dark.

"Sammi," he said, shifting her body from one shoulder to the other. "This is your fault, you know that, don't you? You couldn't keep your knees together and here I am hiking your dead ass across a field in the middle of the goddamn night!"

He turned his flashlight on. The tree line looked to be about fifty yards from where he was standing. His right shoulder had started to cramp, so he shifted her body back to his left. About ten yards ahead, his flashlight illuminated grave markers. He got closer and shined the light on one of them in particular.

"Jacob Bailey," he said to no one at all. "Doesn't *that* name bring back memories." He bounced Sammi on his shoulder and told her, "You're in good company, my dear." He stepped over the tombstone and continued on into the trees.

Arriving at the cave, forward progress proved difficult. The previous day's rain had made the rocks wet and slippery. Time was passing quickly, and Sammi's body was only getting heavier on his shoulders, which were tight and cramping with pain. He lost his footing on a moss-covered rock and went tumbling.. Sammi's body fell from his shoulder and rolled down the hill until it came to rest just outside the mouth of the cave.

A.J. cursed under his breath, retrieved his flashlight, and cautiously made his way down the slope until he reached the spot where the body lay. Her head rested on its right side, which made the gaping exit wound all-too-apparent along with the blood and brain matter. The blast had practically severed her ear. It hung on the side of her head by a small flap of skin.

He made sure that he was on stable ground before bending over and hoisting Sammi onto his shoulder again. His lower back seized, and he let out a low growl. *"Can't stop now,"* he told himself. *"Made it this far. Just a little longer."*

Thick carpets of moss grew on several boulders near the cave's entrance. The walls deeper inside dripped with rainwater seeping in from above. A.J. heard flap-like rustling over the heavy smacks of droplets striking the rocky floor. He directed the beam of his flashlight to the ceiling above and saw hundreds of bats – small, furry bodies swinging from side to side as they awoke for their evening hunt.

Ten minutes into the cave, he stopped, swearing he heard a voice, but dismissed the idea and pressed forward until he reached a spot where the floor opened into an enormous sinkhole. Shining the beam of his flashlight into the pit revealed the walls were sheer, and he knew he could never make it down. The pit was deep, so deep the flashlight beam never hit bottom.

A.J. set Sammi's body down on the cave floor and prepared to toss her in. From inside the pit, he heard what sounded like screams. The story was that this cave was the gateway to hell. He had no intentions of lingering to find out. His reputation as the meanest individual in the county did little for him here. He understood the history of this place and the need to get out.

He grabbed the waist of Sammi's jeans and placed his other hand under her neck. Her body made a raspy noise as air that had been trapped inside her lungs escaped. In his head, A.J. counted to three and then hurled her body over the edge of the sinkhole. There was a heavy thud as she hit one of the walls on the way down, but then... nothing. He waited for some indication she had hit bottom, but no such sound ever came.

Confident the task was now complete, he picked up the flashlight that lay at his feet. The bulb flickered a bit as though it was about to burn out. He smacked the flashlight on the palm of his hand a couple of times hoping there was enough juice left in the batteries to get him out of there.

A bright beam of light blazed forth from the business end of the flashlight, and A.J. began to make his way out of the cave. He had to stop a couple of times and take careful note of his surroundings; the network of underground passages was nothing short of a maze. He tried his best to look for landmarks, which would point him in the right direction.

After an hour of wandering, he conceded that he was lost. For the first time in many years, A.J. Usher was scared. He knew he might wander those passages for days or weeks and never make it out again. He certainly wouldn't have been the first one to suffer such a fate. Similar stories peppered the annals of town folklore. For a fleeting moment, he wondered if he would become another statistic – a simple morsel digested in the bowels of this place.

His shoulders were thankful to be rid of the load they had been forced to bear for so long, but the ache in them was deep. It would surely punish him for weeks to come. That was when he looked down and saw a sight that filled him with hope. It was a boot print – *his boot print.*

He followed the trail for several minutes more until he saw the opening of the cave again. Relief should have overcome him, but instead it was a sense of dread. He stopped mid-stride, knowing he wasn't alone. Further ahead, a creature was sitting on one of the moss-covered boulders as if it had been waiting on him. Its eyes were glowing, yellow marbles – the glow was not a cat-like retinal reflection, but rather a light source all its own that came from within them.

A.J. shined his flashlight's beam in the creature's direction and saw a coyote. The animal let out an angry snarl and began to move towards him. It was foaming at the mouth – lathery drool poured over its teeth and made smacking noises when it hit the rocky floor.

Instinctively, A.J. reached for his gun, but found his holster empty. He remembered leaving it on the floorboard of Brent's car. The only weapon he had – the only thing between he and the mad beast – was the flashlight he held in his hand, the one that was dimming more and more with every passing second as the batteries gave out. He cursed Sammi again for putting him in this position.

The coyote cocked its head and looked at A.J. Its eyes glowed brighter, and he felt a spear of pain rip through his head, just behind his eyes. It was piercing, almost unbearable, and it hurt down to the roots of his teeth. The flashlight dimmed again as a second bolt of pain hit, bringing him to his knees. It felt as though the coyote was trying to dig into his brain.

The flashlight dimmed... dimmed... and finally went out. A.J. was cast into darkness; all he had left was what little milky moonlight filtered into the cave. Before him stood the animal's silhouette and its eyes – *those yellow eyes that seemed to hold in them an eternity of knowledge and evil.* A.J. couldn't help but be drawn to them, almost mesmerized and completely unaware as the creature gradually closed the distance between them.

-9-

Still sitting beside the road, Sarah decided she was going to check up on Sammi after all. It had been three hours with no word, and she was worried. She'd seen two cars pull away from the barn an hour before and neither had returned. Calls and texts were getting no response. She had a bad feeling, but hoped she was wrong.

Her first thought was that Brent had done something. Certainly, he had motive, but Sarah didn't think he would try to hurt Sammi. Not when she could testify that the two had met... it didn't make sense. *Moreover, why had* two *cars pulled away from the barn?* She wondered. *Who would have been with him?*

Unable to wait any longer, she climbed from her car and went through the same gate Sammi had used. Her mind swirled with uncertainty and the horrors she might find. She didn't know it, but she came close to imagining Sammi's fate a couple of times, but had quickly dismissed the notions as too horrible to contemplate.

As Sarah worked her way across the field, A.J. Usher – *or what little was left of A.J. Usher* – was headed in her direction, weaving all over the road. His head was pounding and the backs of his eyeballs itched. He couldn't remember much. He remembered tossing Sammi's body over the lip of the sinkhole, but everything after that was a total blank. His stomach hurt, too, and he had a nasty sensation of something crawling beneath his skin.

A.J. had been careful not to wear his watch that evening. He wondered what time it was, if Brent had yet woken up, and whether or not he had given Perry any problems. One thing he did know was that too much time had passed, and he needed to get back to the barn and clean up what was left of Sammi Pridmore with a garden hose.

Back at the farm, Sarah slid through the barn door, which was propped partially open. She snatched her hand away from the door when she felt something sticky and wet. Not knowing it was blood, she wiped it onto her jeans and went further inside. There was no sound, no movement, nothing to indicate that anyone was or had been there at all.

An odd smell hung in the air, and it only got stronger the further she went into the barn. Sarah heard something squish beneath her shoes, and she took her penlight from her pocket and saw a dark smear of red across white shoe leather. She screamed, realizing that she was standing in a puddle of blood. Her hands started to tremble, and she knew then something horrible had happened to her friend.

She turned to run, but A.J. was standing six feet behind her, his tall body little more than a black shape of man with a cowboy hat on his head. She hadn't heard him come in. As he moved into the light, his white T-shirt was matted with the same inky, red fluid as the puddle she was standing in. A long object extended from his right hand, but she was unable to make out what it was. He wore a pair of sunglasses, which was odd enough as late as it was, but he removed them to reveal his eyes, and she couldn't look away from their glow – luminescent yellow orbs floating inside empty black sockets.

"You shouldn't have come here," he said in a voice with an echo all its own.

"I... I'm looking for my friend Sammi."

"She's not here."

"I don't understand," Sarah said. "Where is she?"

A.J. moved closer to her, fidgeting with the object in his hand. "She's where you'll be soon," he said. "I suspect the worms have found her by now. They work quickly." He moved even closer until Sarah was able to smell his sweat.

She was too terrified to move. His eyes held her in place, they seemed to speak to her, and they promised to relieve her of her pain. They convinced her she wanted that relief more than anything. She was too entranced to pay any attention to the machete A.J. held in his hand. It made a whipping noise as it cut through the air, slicing Sarah's throat with ease. The expression on her face never changed and she never made a sound.

Her head fell backward as a fountain of blood spurted into the air, peppering the hay bale behind her with bright, red droplets. She fell to her knees, and in another swift motion, A.J. came back down with the machete and finished the job, severing her head completely. It flipped into the air and came to rest next to his foot where her eyes blinked one last time. Sarah's headless body lay in a prone position on the floor. A trail of her blood flowed into the pool of Sammi's where the two merged.

A.J. accepted that cleaning up was probably a fool's errand – there was simply too much blood. To his left, he spotted a five-gallon can of gasoline. He grabbed it and started spreading the fuel over the hay bales. When that was done, he emptied half of the can on Sarah's body, which he had hurled atop one of the closest bales and wedged her severed head between them.

He climbed the ladder to the loft and grabbed the kerosene lantern from its hook. He climbed back down and walked out of the barn, stopping only to toss the lantern back inside. It hit the floor and smashed. Fingers of fire crept into the hay, quickly engulfing Sarah's body in flames. The barn filled with the sound and stench of sizzling flesh.

-10-

Back at the house, Perry was waiting on the porch. A.J. climbed the steps and followed the deputy's gaze into the distant valley, which shone with a sinister, orange light. Perry asked his boss what was going on, and A.J. said, "I had to clean up."

"Clean up? What'd ya do? Burn the sonofabitch down?" His comment was punctuated with a nervous laugh.

"Yeah," A.J. admitted. "I did. There were some unforeseen complications, but I handled them. How's the boy?"

Perry wanted to know the rest of the story, but the look on his boss' face told him that it wasn't the best time to be asking such questions. "He's fine. Still asleep."

"Still asleep?!" How much chloroform did you give him?!"

"Sorry, boss – I don't know. I just did what you told me to. I never used that stuff before."

A.J. gave Perry a surprisingly patient look and patted him on the shoulder on his way inside the house. "It's alright. You did well tonight. The problem's solved. I'll go in and take the cuffs off of him. You dust the gun for prints, take some blood samples, and write up a preliminary report. When the boy wakes up, I'll fill him in."

"Boss, he's gonna talk."

A.J. stopped in the doorway. "I don't think so. Think about it... he had motive. He got his girlfriend pregnant and organized a meeting in a secluded location. The girl turns up missing after my gun was reported stolen. It's later found in his car with his prints on it. Her hair is in the car... her blood is in the car... her blood is on his clothes… and you think he's going to say that daddy did it? No, he'll keep his mouth shut, I can promise you that."

"I hope you're right." Perry responded as the screen door slammed shut. He rose from the chair he had been sitting in and fished his keys from his pocket. He headed back to the station after collecting a few pieces of evidence.

A.J. uncuffed his son. The part that was still A.J. wanted Brent to live. The part that was the thing from the cave didn't care either way, but it thought the boy might be useful later. Until he proved otherwise, it was probably best to keep him around. There was still a small detail that needed to be taken care of, though...

A.J.'s eyes started to glow again as the cave thing under his skin worked its way into Brent's mind. It wormed inside and crawled around, careful not to disturb the boy's dreams. It was looking for something it could take, something that would make this whole problem disappear. Once it had found the memory, it took it and slowly retreated from the boy's head.

The memory was a minor annoyance that served only to derail the plan and the purpose for which this creature had come – a plan that involved a bloodline as ancient as its own – one that had kept him at bay for so many years. But now he was out, free to roam, and he had no intentions of going back. His mission now was to find the Keeper – whoever that may be – and put a stop to this once and for all.

CHAPTER NINE

-1-

A few days had passed since Erin had come back to Jones Chapel. For Brig, the days had grown long, the nights longer, and his investigation into the records surrounding Jacob's death had reached a dead end. There were leads. There were plenty of leads, but each one had proven fruitless leaving him with a web of roads that went nowhere at all. He wondered if the mystery would ever be solved. Whoever had buried the truth had buried it well.

To complicate matters, the spirits Kaitlyn alluded to had fallen silent. The house seemed empty without them, something for which Erin was quite grateful. Brig on the other hand had half-hoped to rely on them for some sort of guidance, but it looked as though he was on his own for the time being.

He rubbed his temples and set a stack of papers aside on the table. The sober silence was interrupted when the clock in the living room struck midnight. Brig stood up and stretched. Erin was sleeping soundly in the master bedroom holding Kaitlyn tightly in her arms. These sleeping arrangements had become the norm in recent days. At first, Erin hadn't been as willing as Brig to accept the idea that ghosts might be roaming the house. But following her initial introduction to Jacob, a few strange occurrences had changed her mind and she refused to entertain the idea of Kaitlyn being upstairs alone at night.

The first incident occurred the night after she'd arrived. Following a long, hot shower, the bathroom mirror had fogged over, but scrawled across it she found the words:

PROTECT THE CHILD

No sooner had she read the message than a gust of air blew past her, causing the steam in the room to circulate like a small cyclone. A chill ran over her body, and she'd hurried from the room only to return a few seconds later, dragging Brig in tow. By that time, the message had disappeared, but Erin insisted it had been there. Brig reminded her of all the things that had happened to him and assured her he believed her.

Now, two weeks later, the message still bothered him. 'Protect the child.' "*Protect the child from what?*" He asked the house as he prepared himself a rum and coke. No answer came. He picked up the cordless phone and stepped onto the back deck. Had he looked to his left, he might have seen a small circle of light bobbing across the distant field as A.J. Usher made his way to the cave to dispose of Sammi Pridmore. Instead, he sat down in a chair facing the opposite direction and looked once more at the slip of paper bearing Blackwind's telephone number.

Brig had given a lot of thought to the advice Harv had given him: '*Let the past die...*' Once or twice, the frustration of attempting to unravel a decades-old mystery had almost made him give in and heed the advice, but something more powerful was urging him to push forward.

Brig was apprehensive about making the call to Blackwind. He didn't feel as though he was any closer to the truth than he had been when he'd started, and he hoped the man would have the answers he was seeking. His fear was that the call would be just another in a long line of false hopes and he didn't know where to turn after that.

Halfway into his cocktail, Brig found the courage to make the call. He was disappointed to hear the outgoing voicemail message, but took some solace in the fact that the number had been the correct one. He left a message and downed what was left in his glass along with a couple of tablets.

His anxiety attacks had been blessedly infrequent over the past few weeks. His new project had been successful at keeping his mind occupied, but he was having trouble sleeping, and while ill-advised, the pills did the trick.

The door to the master bedroom was cracked slightly and Brig peeked in on Erin and Kaitlyn. They were sleeping soundly within the glow of the bedside lamp and the safety it offered. After everything that had happened, Erin was no longer able to sleep without it. She, like most people, had learned early in life that an apron of light is the best defense against monsters that roam the house at night and watch from dark corners. Brig didn't want to disturb their sleep by crawling into bed with them, so instead, he sat down in the recliner and let his pharmaceutical concoction work its magic.

-2-

The next morning, the three of them were sitting at the kitchen table eating microwaved pancakes when the doorbell rang. Erin looked at Brig and asked, "Are you expecting someone?" Brig shook his head and got up to see who it was. The front door was open, but through the storm door, he saw a tall man standing on the front porch with his back turned.

Brig estimated the stranger to be at least six and a half feet tall. His gray hair was neatly cut, and he wore a red polo shirt tucked into a pair of dark blue jeans. Hearing approaching footsteps, the man turned and the deep grooves on his face made him appear to be in his late 50's, early 60's.

Brig opened the door and asked, "May I help you?"

The stranger smiled. "I suppose I should be asking you the same thing," he replied in a deep voice. "Are you Brig Bailey?"

Brig offered a handshake without thinking, and the man took it. "Yes, I am," he replied. "Who are you?"

"John. John Blackwind. You called and left me a message last night. I wanted to come over first thing. Sorry I didn't call first." Brig stepped onto the porch and looked the man up and down. John asked, "Is something wrong?"

"No, no," Brig said. "I guess you look a little different than I expected, that's all."

John laughed, clearly amused by Brig's reaction. "Would it have made you feel better if I'd worn moccasins and feathers on my head?" he asked.

Brig liked him immediately and invited him inside. He was busy telling John how happy he was to finally meet him when Erin emerged from the kitchen, wiping her hands on a dishtowel. Brig motioned to her and said, "John, this is my wife, Erin." Fumbling with his words he corrected himself. "EX-wife. She's my ex-wife." He waved the whole thing off and said, "Long story. We'll get to that."

John shook her hand and said, "Pleased to meet you, ma'am."

Erin took his hand and said "Likewise." John made no comment about the bruise on her eye or the cut on her lip, but she remembered them both and covered her eye with embarrassment. "I'm sorry," she said. "Brig's right - it's a long story, but none of this is his handiwork."

John nodded his understanding and Brig was happy she had explained it the way she did. About that time, Kaitlyn came running up the hallway. The little, white sundress she wore swished playfully around her. She stopped and stared up at the tall man standing before her. She tilted her head back and her lips formed the word '*whoa.*' "You're *tall*," she said matter-of-factly.

John looked down at her and asked, "What might *your* name be?"

"Kaitlyn."

"Well, hello, Kaitlyn. My name's John." He knelt down so the two of them were at the same eye-level. Taking her hand into his, his eyes widened and his face took on a strange expression. "I've been looking forward to meeting *you*," he said.

"I know you!" Kaitlyn exclaimed. "You were in my dream. You chased away the bad man!" She threw her arms around his neck and gave him a tight squeeze. In that moment, they appeared to be old friends.

Brig said, "I don't understand. You two know one another?" Erin pulled Kaitlyn close to her in typical protective fashion. John waved his hands apologetically. "I'm sorry. I should explain. I'm probably getting ahead of myself here." He motioned to the couch and said, "Why don't we sit down and talk. Hopefully I can clear some things up for you."

Brig went to his recliner, Erin to hers. John took a seat on the couch and Kaitlyn hopped up next to him. "First," he continued, "let me say how sorry I was to hear about your father's death, Brig. I didn't know him very well, but he seemed like a good man. Rare nowadays."

Brig thanked him and said, "Yes, he was."

John settled back into the couch and propped his ankle onto his knee. "I'd talked with your father a couple of times – once shortly after your brother's death and again a couple of months ago. I'm sure he told you about the nature of our conversation."

Brig frowned. "No, I'm afraid we didn't really get a chance to talk about it before he died."

"Really? How did you know to get in touch with me?"

Brig went on to tell him about finding the slip of paper with the phone number in the hospital room. He also told him the story Harv had conveyed to him, but the narrative was slow and calculated. John suspected Brig was leaving key pieces of information out of the story, but he let it slide, confident that once a certain level of trust had been established between them, more details would come.

"I remember speaking with Harv a long time ago," he said. "I'm surprised he remembered so much of the story. But then again, I suppose something so fantastic would be hard to forget." He looked at Erin and said, "You haven't said anything about all of this, ma'am. I'd like to hear your thoughts."

Erin shook her head and said, "I don't know what to think. Some strange things have been happening around here, and I've been hard-pressed to find a rational explanation. I'll admit that much, but this all seems a little far-fetched to me if I'm being perfectly honest."

What she wanted to say was that she was scared to death. She wanted to tell him she was afraid to walk down dark hallways, because she didn't know what might be waiting around the next corner. Instead, she told him about the message on the mirror. She tried to tell him about Kaitlyn's dreams, but the little girl insisted on telling the story herself. John listened patiently, nodding his head at all the appropriate times.

Brig was the last to tell his tale, and John seemed most interested in the details. He probed for as much as he could get. Brig told him about the lady in white, the messages he was seeing, Jacob's tombstone, etc... When he'd finished, he looked at John and asked, "So what do you think?" not sure what reaction he would receive.

John's expression only grew more intent and serious. "The spirits are talking," he said. Erin buried her face in her hands and let out an exasperated sigh. "Is something wrong?" He asked.

"I just don't get it. Why would the spirits be talking to us? And what spirits are we talking about, anyway?" She looked over her shoulder as if one might materialize at the mere mention of it.

John drew in a breath and moved around the room, closing his eyes at times while breathing slowly. Placing his hand on the banister and peering up the staircase, he said, "There are many spirits in this house."

Kaitlyn piped up. "He's right, ya know! There's a whole bunch of 'em. They talk to me all the time!"

John smiled back at her. "I'm sure they do, little one."

Brig had managed to get used to the idea that his immediate family still roamed the house, but he wasn't sure if he liked the idea of too many more than that. "Good ones or bad ones?" He asked.

"I suspect both," John replied. "Of course, it's hard to be sure. Before I go any further, I'd like to take a look at your brother's tombstone, if you don't mind. Sometimes the voices of the spirits are strongest where they rest."

Brig agreed and all four of them climbed into the cab of Gabe's pickup. Erin sat in the middle of the two men with Kaitlyn on her lap. It was a tight fit, but the drive to the cemetery was a short one. Brig got back out and lowered the tailgate to allow Buster to jump into the bed.

Once there, they all hopped out of the truck and walked over to the two rectangular blocks of granite. It was a clear day, and the bright morning sun sparkled on the drops of dew still hanging from the blades of grass. John knelt down beside Jacob's and ran his fingers across the dates engraved on it.

He turned back to Brig and said, "His voice is strong. He's been speaking to you, hasn't he?"

Brig shrugged his shoulders. "Beats the hell out of me. I guess he has. To be honest, I don't know who's been doing the talking. At times, I think it's him. Other times, I think it might be mom or it might be dad."

John closed his eyes and held out his hands a few feet above the ground. "They all are," he said finally. "They're trying to warn you. Trying to guide you." He stood up and dusted off his hands. "The time is drawing near. Much to be said. Things will begin to clear up for you. You'll hear their voices soon. It's important that you not be afraid."

Erin spoke up. "Drawing near? What are you talking about."

"The Battle."

"Battle?" Brig heard laughter in the distance and looked up. Kaitlyn had lost interest in the conversation and had gone off to chase butterflies in the field. Somewhere in the distance, a bird whistled its song. The little girl twirled round and round, her arms held out like airplane wings. Buster made a move to run and join her, but Brig held onto his collar, and the dog sat back down. Brig looked back to John and said, "Dad never said anything about a battle. What does this have to do with us?"

"I tried to tell your father. The battle is yours to fight. It's pre-ordained, you could say. It's in your bloodline. It's no coincidence your house sits where it does. Your family has been here for generations doing just what you were ordained to do."

"If that's true, why don't I know anything about it?"

"Unfortunately times have changed. Science is the religion of the twenty-first century. Religion and the old ways have taken a backseat. We have operated under the misconception that we have been advancing our species, but by neglecting nature and the forces that exist in this world – *seen and unseen* – I worry we have done more harm than good. Religion has been reduced to superstition, and as time has rolled forward, the stories – the history – have been forgotten. You see, your family has certain gifts. They will help you defeat the evil one."

Brig laughed. "I think you give us too much credit, John. We're just normal people experiencing some very unusual things. We don't have any 'gifts.' And even if what you say is true, how am I supposed to fight this thing?"

John looked at the little girl running and jumping in the field. He lifted his hand and pointed in her direction. "Not you... *HER.*"

"WHAT?" Erin and Brig asked simultaneously. "You have to be kidding. She's a child!"

John wasn't at all fazed by their reactions. "Yes, such a heavy burden for a girl so young, but she's the one. I can sense the power all around her. I felt it the moment I took her hand. She may not know it yet, but she has talents you can only dream of. Typically, they develop to their peak around adolescence, but she's already a strong one. She'll do just fine."

Brig ran his hand into his hair. "This is bullshit!" he said turning away. "There's no way I'm putting her in any kind of danger. Forget it."

John hung his head. "Without her, nothing else matters."

"What's that supposed to mean?"

"If she doesn't fight, The Evil One will use her to open the Gate. If that happens, we all die."

Erin asked, "How is a little girl supposed to make a difference? What can she possibly do?"

"Her body is young, yes," he agreed, "but her soul is very old. When the time comes, she'll know what to do. The dreams she told me about – the things that have been happening to her - *she's a Keeper*. With practice, she'll be able to see things before they happen. She will commune with the dead. She will be a weapon like no other. There are a great many things she must learn, but the blood is in her veins, make no doubt about it. The power need only to be awoken."

"Why her?" Brig asked, leaning in. "Why don't I have any of this? She's my daughter!"

John took his eyes away from Kaitlyn and turned towards him. "Oh, I suspect you do have some. It's obvious considering the things you've been seeing, but your abilities are weak compared to hers. You have the hardened shell of an adult. Secular cynicism has blinded you. For whatever reason, it has lain dormant inside of you all these years. Be glad it hasn't manifested itself until now. If it had, it's doubtful you'd still be alive."

John continued, "The power was strong in your brother – *very strong*. I can sense it even now, so many years after his death. It pulses from his grave. That's the reason he's dead. The Evil One can see many things. He knew your brother would grow stronger with time. He had to stop him. The only way to do that was to kill him before he learned the old ways."

"It has been difficult to find the one that escaped through the portal in the cave. You see, while our two religious beliefs are somewhat different, the difference of one does not invalidate the other. God has many faces just as evil has many faces. It changes forms to evade us. To put things into perspective, you need to understand that this is but one battle in a much larger war between good and evil. In this war, like all others, there are rules. This is the physical world. The one of which we speak is a spirit. In order for it to impose its will upon the physical world, it must possess a body. Flesh and bone. It's hard for us to know where it is or who it is or what it is at any given time." John pointed to the tree line. "Since your brother's death, it's been brooding in that cave waiting for another opportunity to possess a body and escape. I fear that opportunity has come."

"What makes you say that?" Brig asked.

"Two girls were reported missing this morning. I fear the worst – that the bloodbath has begun and the body count will only get higher. The reason we must act – the reason we can no longer wait – is because the time of prophecy is upon us. The moon is in the sixth house, and the skies have fallen. Like a boulder rolling down a steep hill, this chain of events will be impossible to stop. They will lead us on toward the Final Battle. We have the opportunity to seal the monster and his minions behind the Gate for good or the Reality Gradient will forever be thrown out of balance. We must be ready. I suspect we'll be seeing a great deal of death in the days to come."

-3-

Erin's attention was drawn away from the conversation when she noticed a dark shape moving through the field in Kaitlyn's direction. She squinted and shielded her eyes from the sun trying to see what it was, but it was difficult at such a distance. The shape looked like an animal of some kind, but it was hard to tell because it was hidden in the tall grass. It wasn't simply strolling through the field, either; it was stalking her little girl, and getting closer quickly.

Erin screamed and took off running for her daughter a hundred yards away. Just as quickly, Buster broke from Brig's side with wild barks, running towards Kaitlyn at full speed. Brig's head snapped around, and he saw the shape, too. He grabbed the rifle from the truck and peered through the scope to see the coyote he had hunted and shot so many days before. It was clearly hurt and limping. There seemed to be emptiness in its eyes, and the same lathery foam dripping from his mouth.

Kaitlyn heard something approaching and turned around, squealing with delight as Buster quickly drew closer and completely unaware of the coyote moving towards her only yards away. She ran towards Buster with her arms open and the coyote picked up its pace, ready to make the attack. Erin was never going to be able to reach Kaitlyn in time.

John cried out, "That thing is rabid!! Shoot it!"

Buster and Kaitlyn were ten yards from one another when Brig chambered a bullet and took aim. He feared he was his daughter's only hope. He held the rifle steady and prayed for accuracy. His last attempt had been far from precise and there were far too many things that could go wrong if he sent a bullet downfield. Erin was zigzagging back and forth as she ran, crossing into his line of fire. His window of opportunity was closing. He had to take the shot, but he was waiting for a clean one. Time was a luxury he didn't have.

His finger curled around the trigger just as Kaitlyn froze and looked to her left as the coyote lunged for her. Buster leapt at the same time and the two animals collided inches before it would have had a hold of the little girl. The fight was fierce. Wild barking, pained yelps, blood splattering and fur flying. Buster was fighting as hard as he could to protect her, but Brig feared it might not be enough.

His eyes still trained through the scope, he watched as Kaitlyn ran for her mother. Comfortable she was safely out of danger from an errant rifle shot, he centered the crosshairs on the coyote and fired, praying all the while he wouldn't hit Buster by mistake.

Kaitlyn heard the shot and screamed, "NOOOOOO!" Brig felt the ground quake just before she thrust her hands forward. The bullet stopped in midair halfway to its target, suspended in midair before it fell to the ground like a stone.

Behind her the fight between Buster and the coyote had taken a nasty turn. Kaitlyn turned to see the two animals both rise onto their hind legs and snap at each over and over. Finally, the coyote won the advantage and clamped its teeth around

Buster's throat. The brown lab cried out in pain, falling to the ground with the coyote on top of him before it yanked its head back and ripped Buster's throat open in one powerful move. The dog lay silently bleeding in the grass.

Even from that distance, Brig witnessed an expression come over her face unlike anything he had ever seen – a sort of rage no child should ever have reason to know. The coyote turned and ran for her with Erin only ten yards away. In a swift motion as though she was throwing open the drapes, Kaitlyn's hands swept through the air. What followed was a pump-like booming sound and a powerful blast that radiated out in all directions knocking the coyote back and throwing Erin back as well.

Kaitlyn then held out one arm and clenched her right hand around an invisible throat. The coyote yelped and struggled as she raised her arm and lifted it off of the ground. She gritted her teeth and twisted her wrist. The animal's neck snapped and Kaitlyn flung it through the air where it landed dead in a heap fifty yards away.

Not even acknowledging what had just occurred, the little girl ran towards her friend Buster as fast as she could. Erin reached her before Kaitlyn had a chance to touch him and scooped her up. Together, they watched the animal slip away. Buster twitched several times, but eventually fell still.

By the time Brig and John caught up, Buster lay dead. Brig handed the rifle to John and kissed Kaitlyn, who sobbed uncontrollably. He set her down and she ran to kneel over the dog's body, where she cried out, "Busser! Busser, wake up!" She put her hands over the throat wound, and the air filled with an electric buzz.

Brig reached for her, but John pulled him back. "No," he said. "This is it. This is what I told you about. This is her awakening."

The feeling of electricity continued to build as the buzzing sound transformed into a sort of high-pitched whine, and a bubble of blue light formed around the little girl and the dog, encapsulating them within it as it expanded and contracted. Kaitlyn's rate of breathing increased, now more rapid and shallow.

Erin held her hands over her mouth as Brig shouted to John over the noise. "What the hell is this?? What's happening?" John motioned for them all to get on the ground and lie flat. They did as they were told, and the high-pitched whine lowered to the now-familiar bass, rumbling across the ground.

Erin felt the hairs on her arms stand on end just as the bubble of light turned from blue to brilliant white. Peels of thunder roared across the blue sky in every direction. The bubble grew in size and intensity, and inside of it, Kaitlyn wrapped her arms around Buster as though she were hugging him. Just then the bubble exploded outward with another deafening thunderclap and it was gone.

Kaitlyn collapsed onto the ground. Her skin was flushed and her hair was damp with sweat. Erin ran to her and cradled her in her arms, using one finger to brush the hair from her eyes. She looked up at Brig, demanding an explanation without saying a word.

John pointed to Buster's body and shouted, "Look!" The dog's shoulder twitched, his eyes blinked, and he let out a yawn. "The wound's healed! The dog's alive!"

"It's not possible," Erin protested. "He was dead." She looked to Brig again. "You saw it! *You saw it!*"

"I... I don't know," he said, "I thought I did." Buster rolled over onto his belly and sneezed. He looked up at the group of people standing around him as Brig knelt down and ruffed up the fur on the dog's head. "It's him!" He shouted. "I'll be damned if it isn't him! He's alright!" He wrapped his arms around the dog's neck, giving him a squeeze.

Buster looked at Kaitlyn, who was limp in her mother's arms. He rose up, walked over to her, and licked her cheek. He bumped his head against hers in an attempt to wake her, but Kaitlyn was out cold.

Brig turned to John and asked, "What just happened? Did *she* do that?" There was blatant incredulity in his question, but John didn't seem to mind. In fact, he responded as if he had expected that sort of reaction all along.

A simple nod and he said, "She did. I told you, she's the Keeper. There is great power in her."

Erin, still stunned, was trying her best to accept what had just happened. "But how did she know what to do?" she asked. "She's never done anything like this before... *nothing!*"

"It's like I said before, her body is young, but her soul is very old. These abilities aren't new to her. They have simply been forgotten. Oftentimes, they need to be relearned - *awakened*, and pain can be the greatest teacher." Pointing to Buster, he continued. "She loved this dog. She wanted it to live. That was enough."

Brig took another look at Buster who had curled up next to Kaitlyn, his head in her lap. "What does this mean?" He asked. "Is she going to be okay?"

"She's one step closer to becoming."

"Becoming what?"

"What she is destined to be. The Protector. The Keeper. This girl is precious. We have waited for her to come for generations."

"This monster you mentioned, the one that escaped. Does it have a name?" Brig asked.

"Yes, he does. His name is Malocere." The name rolled off of John's tongue as though its very pronunciation produced a foul taste. "He ranks at the top of the demonic hierarchy. In his world, he commands many legions. His duties are simple – death and misery. His thirst for blood is unquenchable, his methods ruthless and cruel. He will leave behind him a path of suffering and death which should be easy to follow."

Brig shook his head. "And what if we don't do anything," he asked. "What then?"

John's face turned cold as stone. "That option is one you can't allow yourself to choose," he said.

"And why not? Why can't I take my family and get the hell out of this town? Huh? What's stopping me?"

"Nothing is stopping you from leaving, but you must understand, this creature's only goal is to kill those who are a threat to it. You can turn away – that's your choice, but it won't stop until it finds you, and it will kill anyone who gets in the way. Many innocent lives will be lost because of your selfish decision. Before now, its only goal was to remain in the Earthly Realm, free from the dimension where it belongs, even if that meant eternity in a cave and being held prisoner by those of your bloodline. But as I have said, the time of prophecy is upon us, and its intentions are far more sinister. There is a great deal more at stake than a few human lives. The creature craves power. Both in this world and the others."

Erin's lower lip was quivering. She tried to get Brig's attention, but he held up his hand and cut her off. His head was already spinning, and he was doing his best to process all of this. Finally he shrugged and said, "So what do we do?"

"Unfortunately, planning is difficult. We must take things as they come, but above all else, we must protect the child."

Brig raised an eyebrow and Erin exclaimed, "That's what was written on the mirror!"

John said, "I told you, the spirits are trying to guide you if you'll only listen."

"And how am I supposed to protect her when I don't even know what I'm protecting her from?" Brig demanded.

"Today, your daughter has opened a floodgate. The spirits will rush through it to help her – to help all of you. Expect strange things in the days to come, but as I said, try not to be afraid. The spirits will aid us in clouding Malocere's vision. It will not be easy for him to find her. He will lash out with anger and many will die. Regrettably, such sacrifices must be made in war. You must understand the good spirits are not all that will be searching for your daughter. The evil ones will come as well – it is crucial you are able to recognize the difference."

"Kaitlyn needs time to develop her abilities. While she grows, we will wait for the enemy. When the time is right, we will lure him to us. His arrogant confidence will work to our advantage. And then - when Malocere is close, we will strike."

Erin broke down in tears. She pulled Kaitlyn close and rocked her back and forth repeating "My baby, my baby!"

Brig put his arms around both of them and said, "It'll be okay, Erin. I won't let anything happen to her." He knew it was an empty promise. Certainly, he would sacrifice his own life for that of his daughter's if it came to that. There was no doubt, but in his heart, he knew there was no way he could guarantee Kaitlyn's safety in all of this and it terrified him.

"But she's just a little girl!" Erin sobbed. "I don't want to lose her, Brig. I can't stand to see anything happen to her. Why can't all of this just go away? Why can't things just go back to normal?"

John tried to comfort her. "Things *will* go back to normal. Once the battle is won."

Erin glared at him and said, "Fuck you and fuck your battle! How dare you come here. How dare you put us in this position. This is my daughter we're talking about."

"I understand your anger and your fear. Believe me, I wish it didn't have to be this way, but I'm afraid we have no other choice."

It was nearing noon, and the sun had climbed high in the sky. Brig suggested that they go back to the house so Kaitlyn could rest. He gave two quick slaps to the tailgate of the truck and Buster hopped in. Brig looked once more at the dog, which was nothing less than a walking miracle in his opinion. It would have been easy for Brig to blow off everything John had told him if it hadn't been for Buster.

In his mind's eye, he watched again as Kaitlyn had levitated the coyote into midair, snapped its neck, and flung it away like so much trash. He leaned into the cab and told the others to wait there as he walked out into the field to where the coyote lay, chambering one more round and firing a round into its skull.

Climbing back into the cab, the four of them headed back toward the house. When they arrived, they went inside and Erin took Kaitlyn into the master bedroom where she dressed her in a pair of white pajamas and laid her down on the bed. The little girl was sleeping peacefully, but Erin wondered what she might be dreaming. With all Kaitlyn had been through, she didn't dare imagine what nightmares might be plaguing her. The possibility that an unseen world was in contact with her daughter – that one existed at all – bothered her greatly.

After she'd covered her daughter with a blanket, Erin went back into the living room and closed the bedroom door behind her. John and Brig were sitting in the living room, and she offered to get them something to drink. John asked for a glass of water, Brig the same. When she'd left the room, Brig posed the question weighing on his mind:

"What can you tell me about Jacob's murder? Harv suggested that the sheriff's brother did it, but if I understand you, you're telling me that this Malocere thing did."

John leaned forward, his voice a whisper. "Do you remember what I told you about the demon's ability to impose its will on the physical world? It has to be inside a body. *Whose* body it was in at that time, I don't know. Maybe Harv was right. I don't suspect that it really matters, though."

"It matters to me..."

"You were close to your brother, weren't you?" John asked.

Brig picked a figurine off of the table beside him and tested its weight in his palm for no reason at all. His eyes cut to the floor, no longer looking at John. "Yeah, we were very close."

"And it would ease your mind to know what happened?"

Brig looked up again and nodded his confirmation. "Yes, it would."

John closed his eyes and drew in a deep breath. "Your brother is here with us now," he said. "He knows what you're going through and he wants you to have the answers you seek. Kaitlyn has opened the door; your answers will come. Just be ready to accept them when they do. The rules are different now. Nothing is as it was. You can't take anything for granted."

Erin came back into the room with the two glasses of water. She put one on the coffee table, and handed the other to Brig. John quickly downed his and rose from the couch.

"Thank you for your hospitality," he said. "I'm really quite sorry to have thrown so much of this at you the first time we met. I know this is all very intense. I just hope you'll keep an open mind – for all of our sakes."

Brig looked to Erin and saw a blank expression. He turned back to John and said, "I won't lie to you. This is a hell of a story to swallow. Give us a little time to let it soak in, okay?"

John nodded and said, "If that's the way it has to be. Just understand that time is short..."

-4-

Shortly after John left, Erin went into the kitchen to finish washing the dishes she had been working on when he'd arrived. Housework was the last thing she wanted to do, but it was the only thing that seemed normal to her. She wanted normal. She needed normal, and maybe busywork would distract her.

She looked out of the window and the world looked different somehow. The feeling was like being inside a plastic bubble. She feared she was being unfair to John. After all, he had merely pushed the curtain aside to show them a larger world and she all but attacked him for it. All because the world he wanted them to believe in didn't fit neatly into her own.

The suds in the sink had dwindled to a thin film of twisted rainbows floating on top of cold, murky water. She drained the sink and filled it up again by the time Brig came into the kitchen and put his arms around her. She stared at his reflection on the windowpane and said, "This is all a dream, you know that, right?"

"What makes you say that?" He asked.

"It has to be. It doesn't feel real at all. I mean, you saw what she did out there! ...to that coyote?! Our daughter just brought a dog back to life for Christ's sake! I'm supposed to believe that actually happened? I'm supposed to believe that some monster is coming after her?"

Brig turned her around and said, "It's not a dream. You don't know how much I wish it were. Denying that any of this is real isn't doing us any good. Dad trusted John. I think I trust him, too. Everything that's been happening has happened for a reason. We have to accept what's going on if we're going to help her."

Erin buried her face into his chest and started to cry. The lump in her throat reminded her of the nights her father had put her to bed without turning on the nightlight. She remembered lying awake, watching shadows creep across the walls, and how she had listened intently to the sounds of the monsters she knew were rustling beneath her bed.

She felt alone, just as she had then, like a tiny rowboat tossed about by giant waves. The world had changed for her. Things were no longer simple, tangible, or rational. There were no wise old men to whom she could turn for comfort. They were alone – forced to fight an enemy none of them had ever seen. There were a million things she wanted to say, but all she could come up with was: "I'm scared."

Brig held her close and said, "I know. I am, too." And he was. Not so much afraid for himself, but afraid he wouldn't be able to protect them when the time came to do so. He put his arm around Erin's waist and led her out of the kitchen. They turned into the hallway and stopped. Kaitlyn stood at the other end, still dressed in her white pajamas, which were clinging to her sweaty little body. An undetectable breeze tossed her hair about.

Erin held her arms out and said, "Baby? Are you alright?"

Kaitlyn gave her a brief glance before looking to Brig. She pointed a finger at him and when she spoke, the voice was not her own. It was large, hollow, and deep. She said, "*Hide the woman and the child. Danger is near.*"

Erin covered her mouth and screamed, but Brig took action. He scooped Kaitlyn into his arms, grabbed Erin by the hand, and led them upstairs into his old bedroom. He sat Kaitlyn on the bed and moved a small bookcase away from the wall. Behind it was a recessed panel about two feet square.

Brig pulled on the molding that surrounded the panel and pulled it away from the wall. It was an entrance to the upstairs attic. Brig motioned for them to get inside. "It's okay," he said. "Jacob and I used to play in here all the time. It's the perfect spot to hide."

Erin didn't have time to think about the voice she had just heard. The urgency of the situation made sure to clear her head of that. She helped Kaitlyn through the opening first, and then as she was crawling through herself, she asked, "What do you think it is? You don't think it's *him*, do you? You don't think it's that Malocere thing?"

"I don't know," Brig admitted. "I'm just doing what I'm told." He didn't know what he'd do if it *was* Malocere, that was for sure. How do you fight a demon, anyway? Outside, Buster was barking from within his pen. Brig said, "Someone's coming. Get inside." He gave Erin a shove; she fell into the attic with a thud. He reached into his pocket and handed her the slip of paper with John's number on it along with the handset for the cordless phone. "If anything happens to me," he said, "you get out of town as fast as you can. Kick this panel out and run. You call John first. Understand?"

Erin now looked even more worried than before, and Brig saw deep concern on her face. "Please be careful," she said.

He assured her he would and replaced the panel. He moved the bookcase back into place and hurried downstairs where he removed a 12-guage shotgun from the coat closet. He grabbed the box of shells off the shelf and slid them into the gun one by one. Whoever was headed toward the house was in for one hell of a fight.

A blue Ford Taurus pulled up in front of the house. Brig peered through the sidelight window and saw Erin's husband, Tom, climb out of the car. He was instantly filled with rage remembering the way Erin had looked the day she had come back to Jones Chapel. He remembered the cuts, the bruises, and the tears she'd cried on his shoulder. The only thing on Brig's mind at that moment – the only thing he wanted to do – was to crack the bastard's skull open.

Somehow, Tom had been much larger in Brig's mind – his imagination had conjured the image of an ogre, but the reality was quite different. Tom was skinny as a rail, and he couldn't have been more than five foot nine. Brig didn't think he looked like much of a threat at all, but he was quickly walking towards the front door with intent and his right hand behind his back.

Brig heard Erin's voice from the day before. *"He's got a gun... he'll kill you!"*

Brig stepped out onto the porch with the shotgun in his hand. Tom stopped dead in his tracks. Through gritted teeth, Brig said, "You're trespassing."

"I'm here for my wife. I suggest you step aside." The comment was cocky, but Brig detected a hint of uneasiness in Tom's voice and he wondered what the little twerp had hoped to accomplish by showing up here. Surely he didn't think that Brig would just turn Erin over to him.

Brig stepped forward. "Like *hell* you are," he said. "The only thing you're leaving this house with is my foot up your ass, you wife-beating sack of shit."

"What did you call me?" Tom asked.

"You heard me just fine, motherfucker." Tom's face drew up, and he walked forward with his fists clenched. Brig squared his shoulders and said, "You think you can get past me? Take another step."

Tom said, "You screwed my wife! You expect me to just walk away?"

That was exactly what Brig expected him to do. As far as he was concerned, there was no middle ground here. "You can walk or you can crawl," he told him. "I don't really care which one you choose." Understanding the importance of the element of surprise, Brig stepped forward again and fired an unexpected blast into the air before swinging the gun towards Tom and cracking the stock across his face.

Tom fell onto his back, his hands cradling a shattered cheekbone. The revolver he had been carrying in the waist of his jeans tumbled out onto the sidewalk. Brig bent over to pick it up and tossed it away.

Tom's face flushed with anger. That's what Brig wanted. He wanted Tom to get mad; he wanted a fight. "What makes you think I'm going to let you get away with what *you* did?" Brig asked. Tom steadied himself and threw a sucker punch into Brig's stomach, igniting a blast of pain, which caused Brig to double over. He hadn't expected that one. He didn't think Tom had the balls to hit him, but he had.

The chain of events that followed was a blur. Brig straightened up and threw an uppercut, which landed squarely on Tom's chin. The large, middle knuckle on Brig's right hand struck hard bone, and Tom's jaw popped. It wasn't a well-placed blow, and it hurt Brig more than it did Tom.

A powerful right hook which planted Tom face-first onto the sidewalk immediately followed the uppercut. The impact was centered on Tom's cheek, already swelling from the blow it had sustained from the stock of the shotgun. It was punctuated by a meaty squish. A fine spray of saliva and blood flew from Tom's mouth just before he hit the ground.

Not one to waste a good opportunity, Brig delivered three swift kicks to Tom's mid-section, causing him to cough up thick, snotty mats of blood onto the sidewalk. Brig reached down and took him into a headlock. He led him back to the Taurus where he grabbed a handful of hair on the back of Tom's head and proceeded to slam his head onto the hood a couple of times.

He spun Tom around and pinned him against the hood with a hand clenched over his throat. Brig leaned in a couple of inches from his face and said, "Get off of my property, you son-of-a-bitch. If you *ever* come back, if you *ever* get near Erin or Kaitlyn again, *I'll fucking kill you.* So help me god I'll kill you and they'll never find your body! Do you understand?"

Tom nodded and Brig released the grip he had on his throat. He climbed into the car, and pointed at Brig. "I'll have your ass for this," he said.

"Get your ass out of here!" Brig shouted. "NOW!" And he fired another shotgun blast into the air and then another. He lowered the barrel, pointing it into the driver's side window and Tom pressed the accelerator to the floor, spraying gravel in every direction as he turned the car around. For a moment, Brig forgot that Erin and Kaitlyn were hiding in the sweltering attic, no doubt panicked over the sound of gunfire and Buster barking like mad.

He hurried back upstairs to move the bookcase and attic panel. The two of them crawled out and Erin asked, "Are you alright? What happened? I heard gunshots!!"

Brig helped her to her feet. "It was Tom."

The name struck Erin unprepared. "Tom?!" she said as if it weren't possible. Her safe haven had been violated. She never would have imagined that Tom would come for her here, much less drive up to the front door. She felt watched, like an ant under a magnifying glass. Everything she had come to believe in was turning upside-down. "What was *he* doing here?" She asked. A million possibilities raced through her mind, few of them good.

"He came to take you home."

"You're kidding," Erin said with a sarcastic laugh. "What did you say to get him to leave?"

"Say?" Brig scoffed. "I didn't *say* anything. I kicked his ass! He might be good at beating on a woman, but isn't worth a damn otherwise."

"Did he have his gun? Was that what I heard??"

Brig shook his head. "No, I fired a few rounds from the shotgun to scare him, that's all."

Erin's face turned cold and expressionless. She turned her back on him and led Kaitlyn downstairs. Brig followed, utterly confused. "Are you actually angry?" He asked.

She looked back at him and said, "Yes. Yes, you could say that."

"Why? Why would you stick up for him after what he did to you?"

"I'm not sticking up for him. I just don't think that you're going to solve anything by fighting. It'll only cause more problems in the end. You were lucky this time – what if next time he shoots you in the back before you ever see him? You think he's just going to give up??"

Brig looked to the couch and saw Kaitlyn sitting with her arms crossed – she was a pro at pouting. He walked over to her and said, "What's wrong, honey?" Somewhere in the back of his mind he was afraid that he would hear that other voice again, but the one that came out was all her own.

"I don't like when you guys fight," she said.

Brig squeezed her hand and said, "Honey, we weren't fighting. We just had a difference of opinion, that's all." Of course the two were one in the same, but he hoped he could slip the distinction past a child. It seemed to work.

She smiled and asked, "Can I go and see Busser?"

"Kaitlyn, do you remember what happened to Buster?" Brig asked. "Do you remember what you did out there?"

She turned her eyes up at him and in them he saw deep pools of timeless wisdom. Her eyes were not the eyes of a five-year-old behind which danced the dreams of candy canes and Barbie dolls, but windows into a much wider world.

"Busser was hurt," she said. "I helped him and I made that mean dog go away."

Before Brig had the chance to continue, Erin broke in. "Let her go outside." Kaitlyn didn't wait for her father's approval. She sprung from the couch and burst through the front door.

"Don't you want to know what happened out there?" Brig asked. "Aren't you the least bit curious?"

"Listen," Erin said, "I've seen enough today. All I want is to sit on the front porch and watch my daughter play with the dog. I want to forget all of this for a little bit, okay? Can you at least understand that?"

Brig nodded and they went outside and sat on the porch swing. Kaitlyn and Buster rolled and wrestled in the front yard, the best of friends. Erin was silent; small talk seemed pointless. Brig looked towards town and thought about the things John had told them. He wondered if Malocere really had escaped – how close he was – and when he would be coming for them.

Evening came quickly. Brig and Erin played a game of Candyland with Kaitlyn after they had finished dinner. Oddly enough, the little girl seemed unaffected by the day's events. Erin and Brig, however, were unable to rid themselves of the image of their daughter holding her hands on Buster's body, healing him in a way that had yet to be explained. In addition to that, there was the memory of the booming voice that had echoed from her tiny body. It was difficult for them to look at her in the same way.

About the time the clock struck nine, Kaitlyn declared victory, but her triumph was short-lived. Erin told her it was past her bedtime, and the little girl begged for ten more minutes. Brig promised her she could stay up late another night, but said that they all needed to go ahead and turn in.

Erin walked down the hall and turned into the kitchen when she saw something in her peripheral vision. She quickly turned to get a better look, but nothing was there. She thought she had seen the pale outline of a woman and a small boy standing in the dining room. John's voice spoke up in her head: '*There are many spirits in this house.*' Her mind wasn't so quick to dismiss the possibility of ghosts that time. They had been warned to expect strange things in the days to come and to try not to be afraid. She was trying her best now.

The three of them crawled into bed shortly thereafter. Brig found himself in the middle, lying on his side with Kaitlyn in front of him and Erin behind. A gentle thunder rolled in the distance, and small drops of rain pecked against the bedroom windowpane.

No one was awake when the bedroom door opened. Slow, soft footsteps made their way to the side of the bed, and an unseen hand brushed the hair from Kaitlyn's face. The little girl opened her eyes and she smiled.

CHAPTER TEN

-1-

Brig opened his eyes only to find himself in total darkness. The air smelled of plywood, spray paint, and latex. He stumbled about, unable to see where he was going. He extended his arms and felt the walls on either side of him. It was some sort of hallway. Moving forward, the floor beneath his feet felt uneven as though he was walking up an incline. He turned a corner and a small section of the floor gave way about an inch. A jackhammer sound followed, sudden and loud, and just as quickly, a blast of compressed air shot up his leg, causing him to scream with surprise.

Further down the hallway, overhead black lights cast an inky, purple glow, disorienting when combined with pulsing strobes. The flickering light made him appear to be moving in slow motion. Just then, a skeletal figure hurled itself against a panel of bars beside him, wielding a chainsaw, buzzing at full speed. White hair hung from the monster's skull, and the gaping, black cavities it had in place of eyes flashed with red light. Its mouth hung open in a silent scream baring crooked, yellow teeth.

Brig looked around and soon realized where he was. The room was large, and mirror-filled corridors ran in all directions. Each one appeared to twist and bend into infinity. The mirrors were eight to nine feet high. Cheating the maze wasn't an option since it was impossible to see over the top of each one. But Brig didn't panic; quite the opposite - he relaxed, because he knew this room well. He was in the Haunted House on Hillbilly Hill, and he'd been here many, many times as a child.

Once inside the maze, he remembered just how difficult it was to negotiate. Each mirror appeared to be the entrance to another corridor. For the first five minutes, he groped his way forward, bumping into one after another. Just as he began to get frustrated, he looked up and saw a little boy ahead and hurried in that direction calling to him as he did. The child offered no response, but rather turned a corner and disappeared from view.

Brig ran to the spot where the child had been, and saw him again, but this time only ten feet away, facing the other direction. Brig reached out and touched solid glass. It seemed as though the boy was *inside* the mirror. The boy turned to face him, and Brig was stunned to see his brother standing there.

Jacob spoke, and for the first time since his disappearance, Brig heard his brother's voice – only now it was in his head:

[Hello, Brig.]

[Jacob? What is this?! What's going on?] There were so many questions he wanted to ask, so much he wanted to say, but those simple questions were all he was able to find.

[No time to explain. It's back and it's coming.] Brig's memory was foggy, but he recalled the conversation with John earlier that day. He knew what was coming – at least he had an *idea*. But his desire to know what had happened to his brother so many years ago seemed to push the other back in his mind. It must have been clear to Jacob that his brother would never find peace until he knew the whole story of his death, and so he pointed to the mirror behind his brother and said, [Watch and see.]

Brig turned to face the mirror behind him. Images flashed upon it, and he heard what sounded like muffled voices. Soon, the images and sounds converged into something more akin to the news footage Brig had seen on TV days before where he was little more than a passive observer. Before him, the scenes unfolded, his concentration focused, and he quickly was immersed in what he saw, as though he had traveled back through time to 1978.

Max Usher, the sheriff's youngest brother was driving down the highway on his way toward the Bailey farm. Two other boys, roughly the same age, were in the car with him - one whose name was Johnny Kilgore was asleep in the back seat.

Brig knew from reading in the police reports that Max and his friends had skipped school the day Jacob died. Their plans had been to hike back into the woods just south of town and polish off a bottle of whiskey Max had managed to swipe from his father's liquor cabinet.

Muscular and tall, Max was the quintessential thug. With a family reputation like the one he had, the townsfolk gave him wide berth - a sort of freedom to do as he pleased that appealed to some. Lackeys were easy enough to come by. Few kids in Jones Chapel could afford a car in those days, and affiliation with Max meant access to his.

Any hunk of junk with wheels and an engine that ran was a status symbol to be admired in those days. Max drove a beat up Chevy. Max's father had pieced it together for him from various spare parts the summer before his 16th birthday. There had always been a problem with the carburetor, the passenger seat was broken, and the paint was sanded down and primer gray.

Brig watched as Chris, Johnny, and Max headed south on the highway toward an old logging road leading back to a secluded patch in the woods. The three of them never made it to their intended destination. A tire blew and the car swerved violently. Max slammed on the brakes, sending the car into a spin, killing a gray squirrel that had the misfortune of being in the wrong place at the wrong time.

After skidding to a stop, Max beat his fist on the dashboard and cursed out loud to no one in particular. He got of the car and leaned back in, barking an order: "Chris, help me get this son-of-a-bitch to the shoulder before we get our asses rammed."

Johnny asked, what had happened while rubbing a knot on the side of his head caused by his head slamming against the rear window during the skid.

Max said, "We blew a tire."

"No shit," Johnny replied. "I mean what are we gonna do now?"

"You're gonna slide your ass behind the wheel and steer while we push!"

Johnny did as he was told. Without a word, Chris opened the door and walked around to the back of the car. Max joined him, cursing under his breath. "Fuckin' piece of shit... PUSH!" The two of them shoved the car towards the shoulder with Johnny in the driver's seat making sure it didn't slip into the ditch.

Once they were safely clear of traffic, Max stopped pushing and looked around. He produced a cigarette from his pocket and fired it up. Leaning against the trunk, he surveyed the surrounding landscape and asked, "Isn't there a cave around here someplace?"

"Yeah, right back there." Chris motioned with his head back towards the thick patch of woods bordering the Bailey farm.

"Whatcha say we go back there and polish off this bottle? The tire can wait. It's hotter than hell out here." Not waiting for a response from the other two, Max leaned in through the open passenger window and grabbed a small flashlight from the glove box.

Before Chris had an opportunity to respond, Johnny walked back to join the two of them and asked, "So what now?"

"We're gonna head back to a cave over there." Max pointed in the direction Chris had indicated a few moments earlier. "We'll throw back a few and then we'll change the tire."

A silence settled upon them – an uncomfortable one atypical from the standard quick agreement Max was used to with his proposals. Johnny looked at Chris and shook his head, not realizing that Max had seen him do it.

A lungful of smoke rose into the air, and Max motioned for the tree line with the bottle he held in his hand. "What's the problem? Let's go…"

"No one goes back there," Johnny piped up. "You know that."

"Jesus Christ," came the response as Max flicked his cigarette out into the road. "You believe all those bedtime stories? Boogeymen? All that shit? Are you serious??" He gave Johnny a shove on the shoulder and told him to get his balls out of his mother's purse and fall in line.

"A lot of people died in there, Max."

"People die every day, Chris."

Johnny hung his head and started down the hill with Max at his side, glancing back at Chris who hung a few yards behind the rest.

"Which way is it?" Max asked no one in particular. The three of them stopped and scanned the trees, looking for some sort of a trail leading back to the cave. Max pointed up ahead about 150 yards. "There!" He shouted. "Do you see that big boulder? It's just to the right of it!"

The other two followed up the hill until the mouth of the cave appeared as a wide crack in the cliff face. From that elevation, they could see miles into town where small country roads snaked off into nowhere, and a white church steeple pierced the sky.

Max unscrewed the metal cap on the pint of Dickel he had brought along and took a gulp. His face puckered, and he coughed.. "Good shit!"

"Let me have a go." Johnny took the bottle and put the bottle to his lips. He took three short swigs before he passed it on. It made a full circle before returning to Max who spun the cap back on and placed it inside his jacket. He produced a joint from inside his cigarette pack – fat in the middle and tightly twisted at both ends.

He put the joint in his mouth and fumbled through his pocket. "Chris, where's my lighter? Did I hand it to you?"

"Here," Johnny said, removing a small box of wooden kitchen matches from his pocket. He held it to his ear and shook it, holding the box out to Max. "Only got about three, though. Make 'em count." Max struck the match against the side of the box and the head burst into flame. He held it to the end of the joint and puffed on the end until it was lit, passing it on to Chris.

Then, a strange sound – almost a roar – came from somewhere inside the cave. All three stood silent, looking into the pit for a few seconds before Johnny asked, "What the hell was *THAT?*"

Max shrugged his shoulders, and took another drag, more out of habit than calm. "Hell if I know." Puffs of smoke came from his mouth as he spoke. He exhaled what was left of the drag through his nose. "Let's check it out." He made a move toward the cave only to turn around and see the other two standing like statues. "C'mon," he prodded. "Let's go!"

Chris shook his head and Johnny followed suit, "No way. There might be somethin' down there, man."

"What? You really believe that bullshit, don't you?"

"I dunno. What do *you* think that was?"

"Well, if I knew, I wouldn't be going down there, now would I? But I don't believe in ghosts, so let's go!"

Inside the cave it was cold and damp, like an old basement with no windows after a heavy rain. The sound of dripping water echoed from deep inside. Max reached into one of his many pockets for the flashlight and switched it on. The small beam sliced through the darkness, allowing them to move deeper into the cave – Max in the lead with Chris and Johnny making sure to stay close together.

The passage they were in was more of a tunnel. There appeared to be no end, just a craggy path into never-ending black. The flashlight illuminated another passage on their left, and from it came the sound of a snarl. Max dropped the flashlight, casting the three of them into darkness. Immediately, he dropped to his knees and felt along the floor as something moved among them, producing a foul stench, but an undeniable sense of presence.

Max's fingertips found the flashlight, and he shined the beam in all directions, searching for some source of the stench and the noise. What came into view caused Chris' knees to buckle and Johnny's round of Dickel to dribble down the leg of his jeans. A figure sat on a bolder halfway down the tunnel, cloaked in brown rags. Its head was shrouded beneath a hood such that the only features that could be discerned were two yellowish-green balls of light where its eyes should have been.

It sat still, and made no immediate move toward the boys. Johnny and Chris fell over one another in an attempt to get out of there. They didn't look back; instead, they ran until they saw daylight – *blessed daylight* – and they didn't stop running until they had reached the car.

-2-

Brig watched across the span of time as Max stood still, unable to move and seemingly too terrified to breathe in the face of what must be Malocere – or one of his many forms. Jacob spoke to his brother and told him to place his hands on the mirror's surface. Brig hesitated, afraid of what might happen if he did as he had been told. However, he eventually did as instructed, trusting Jacob would never do anything to harm him.

Malocere spoke in the same telepathic manner Brig had just been introduced to. With his hands on the mirror, he was able to hear the voice in his own head as Max had all those years ago:

[*You're the one the other entities call Max, aren't you?*] The words came without a sound. Brig gritted his teeth just as Max did – when the creature spoke, it felt like razors ripping through his scalp.

[*I've been waiting for you, Max. There's a job I need to do, but I need your help.*] Malocere got down from the rock, and took his eyes – *or whatever they were* – off of Max for a second.

It moved quickly; the sound it made was like that of a crab walking across a marble countertop: *click-clack, click-clack.* Malocere's eyes met Max's once more; they had changed color to red.

[*I'll make this simple for you,*] he said. [*You help me, and I'll kill you quickly when I'm done with you – you won't feel a thing.* Don't *help me and I'll kill you slowly.*]

Further down the path came sounds of screams – thousands and thousands of screams. Malocere drilled into his head again, [*Those screams... they are melodies compared to what I can do to you. That pit leads to horrors you can't conceive of. You're already dead, Max. The only question is how do you want this to go? Do we have a deal?]*

Max lifted his head and lowered it again in submission. Malocere's eyes turned back to that eerie shade of yellowish-green. [*Goood,*] he hissed. A picture appeared in Max's mind. It was of a place he knew well. [*Do you know this place?*] the creature asked. Max's eyes shut, and once more, he bared his teeth against the pain in his head and nodded. [*You take me there and this will all be over. We don't have much time.*] With those words, the cave went dark, and Max was knocked into the cave wall behind him.

Outside, the other two had pried the trunk of Max's car open and had begun to change the tire. Neither of them made mention of what Max would do when he saw the damage. At that moment, neither cared. Johnny was tightening the lug nuts when Chris called out for him to stop. "Listen," he said.

"What? I don't hear anything."

"That's what I'm talking about! I don't hear *anything!* No birds, no wind – nothing!"

About that time, Max emerged from the cave. Johnny looked up from beneath the trunk where he was placing the blown out flat. Behind him, Chris had spotted Max as well. Through the mirror, Brig was able to sense their unease and their suspicions that there was something very wrong with their friend. There was something altogether inhuman about him. His eyes were vacant. There was a robotic determination in his gait, and an unseen shroud of darkness all around him.

Chris and Johnny stood on the far side of the car – Johnny with the tire iron in his hand and Chris with a look of dread on his face. Perhaps it was intuition or just plain fear, but both knew that they had to take Max down. It was Johnny who made the first move.

He ran at Max with the tire iron raised, and when he was within striking distance, he put all of his weight into a downward stroke aimed at Max's head. With lightning speed, Max caught his arm on the way down and flipped him over. The move looked rehearsed. Johnny landed flat on his back, the breath knocked out of him. Max snatched the tire iron from his fist, just as Johnny lifted his head off the ground for the last time.

The tire iron reflected the noontime sun as Max swung it at Johnny's head. It came down across the bridge of his nose with a meaty *pop* and a hollow *crunch*. Bone fragments flew into the boy's brain, killing him instantly.

Max hadn't noticed Chris rapidly approaching him from behind and was caught off-guard as the boy came down upon his back and forced him to the ground. Max rolled out from under him, still holding the tire iron and swinging it wildly. One blow shattered Chris's kneecap sending skyrockets of pain through his body. He fell to the ground, screaming.

Max was about to deliver the deathblow but stopped in mid-swing as a strange grin crept across his face. He took Chris's wrists and put his foot between the boy's shoulder blades, raising the boy's arms until they were perfectly perpendicular to the ground. Every tendon groaned with agony, but Max continued to pull the arms upwards until they finally tore, and the arms separated from their sockets. Chris' screams went unheard.

Max then reached down and grabbed the collar of his shirt and pulled him towards the highway. Once they reached the car, he placed Chris' head in front of the rear tire with his face towards the tread. He climbed into the driver's seat and started the car. Once the emergency brake was engaged, he pressed his foot on the accelerator.

Beneath the Chevy, the spinning tires tore a sheet of skin from Chris' face from just below his left ear to just beneath his nose. Max released the emergency brake, and the car took off with tremendous speed, crushing Chris' skull in the process. His brain would lie baking on the highway for two hours before his body was found.

The car sped down the highway on its way to route 72, a clear picture in the mind of the driver, a picture of a lake – a lake Max knew well. Malocere had not told him why they were going there; he knew the boy could still back out. After seeing what had happened to his friends, it was doubtful he would, but possible nonetheless. Malocere needed time to get inside Max's head – *to take control* – and the thirty-mile drive to Barren Lake would be time enough.

The next few scenes that flashed in the mirror told Brig his questions were about to be answered. He was no longer inside the car with Max, but on a sandy beach at the lake. He looked and saw his mother lying in the sand. Jacob had managed to paddle his inner tube a good distance from shore.

Rose shouted, "Jake! Jake, come in a little closer to the beach, sweetie! Mommy doesn't want you to get out too far!" Obediently, Jacob started to pull himself to shore using the ropes, marking the designated swim zone. With every pull, he made sputtering noises with his lips like the sound of an outboard motor.

Rose turned to lie on her stomach. Jacob splashed about in the water as he made the tube spin round and round. As the minutes passed, Brig watched his mother's weariness take over as sleep fell upon her. After about five minutes, Jacob had pretty well spun himself silly and exhausted. On any other day, his mother would have told him to come into shore and rest a while; Jacob would have protested, but eventually obeyed.

But this day was to be unlike any other...

Jacob sat in the tube with his legs draped over the side – they weren't quite long enough to allow his feet to touch the water. His arms hung over both sides, and his head rested upon the back. He was spent. The hollow *pinging* sounds of water hitting the tube were like a lullaby. Within minutes, he was asleep and floating slowly out of his mother's view.

Across the gulf of time, Brig shouted to his mother – *begged her*, "Wake up! Wake up!" but the distance was too great, and he watched Jacob continue to drift away.

Twenty minutes later, Jake and his tube had found their way into a tributary, and had passed beneath several highway overpasses along the way before finally getting beached on a sandbar just below route 72 – a truly bad stroke of luck if there had ever been one.

The thing that had once been Max Usher, was well under Malocere's control. It was nearing 1:30 in the afternoon when the car blew through the red light marking the intersection with Westover Street, barely missing a pick-up driven by one Kyle Bannard and his wife, Faye, by a matter of inches. Had Kyle not taken a second to change the radio station after his light had turned green, he would have been T-boned for sure.

Five miles further down the road, Malocere turned south onto route 72. He passed a sign which read: LIVE BAIT, TACKLE, N' BEER, and he stamped the accelerator to the floor. The Chevy lurched forward, and the speedometer started to climb – 60, 70, 80...

Unbeknownst to Malocere, the tire Chris and Johnny had replaced was short a couple of lug nuts and the rear end of the car was shaking. After only two miles, the coolant temperature started to climb as well. There was a loud explosion from beneath the hood, and steam poured out from beneath it with a hissing sound and the smell of pancake syrup.

Unfamiliar with modern mechanics, he accessed that part of Max's mind to diagnose the cause of all of this. He released the hood latch and opened the driver's side door, completely oblivious to the 18-wheeler, which had swerved into the oncoming lane to avoid running him down. The trucker gave a long, blast on his air horn, to which Malocere responded with a sideways glance. He lifted the hood and a thick cloud of steam belched from beneath it. Max's brain told him there was no fixing this with anything they had on hand.

From somewhere up ahead, came the sound of running water and he went to check it out. Where the grade of the land sloped downward, there was a stream. In that stream was what Malocere had come for – a small boy bobbing along in an inner tube – half on shore and half in the water. He appeared limp, lifeless, but the thing inside Max knew what needed to be done.

Brig yanked his hands back from the mirror, wanting to feel no part of what was about to happen. Jacob insisted he put them back, and Brig complied, less than eager to do so. When he did, he was able to see into Jacob's mind, too.

Jacob had been dreaming childhood dreams of ice cream cones and race cars when he was awakened by an overpowering sense of terror – a terror he had felt before moving about in his room like a vapor. He opened his eyes to a blurry world in the brightness of midday. On the opposite shore, Malocere stood watching him. Their eyes met, and Jacob started to cry.

Brig remembered how his mother had always said that Jacob was an "old soul." "Been around the block a time or two," she'd said. Brig couldn't help but remember that John had said the same thing about Kaitlyn, and on some level, the story began to make sense.

It was that "old" part of Jacob that recognized the abomination standing fifty feet away from him – an entity as old as time. The tears Jacob shed were not only for what he knew was about to happen to him, but for the world entire, knowing he wasn't strong enough to stop it.

Brig turned his head away again. Jacob told him: [*This is going to be hard for you to see, but this is what you wanted: this is what* really *happened.*]

Brig turned back to the mirror and watched Malocere take a step forward. The creature's foot came down upon the surface of the water, but didn't submerge. He moved slowly and with deliberation toward the small boy in the inner tube, walking on the surface of the water as he drew ever closer.

Jacob's face twisted with pain when Malocere spoke up in his head. [*It's been a long time since I've encountered a Keeper. I thought I had finished this the last time. I thought your kind was dead,* but here you are... *Looks like I was wrong.*]

Watching from the Mirror Maze, Brig gasped when Jacob stood upon the water's surface just as Malocere had done. The young boy did it automatically, without even giving the appearance of realizing what it was he was doing. The creature approached and Jacob turned to run. Malocere grabbed his arm, but released it, hissing with pain.

Jacob looked down, equally surprised to see his forearm glowing. He thrust one hand forward and pushed Malocere away using a much less powerful technique than the one Kaitlyn had used on the coyote. It came as unexpected and caught Malocere by surprise. The pulse that followed was easily deflected as a defiant sneer crossed the creature's face. [*Weak. You haven't discovered your gifts yet, Keeper. You're no match for the likes of* me.]

With blinding speed, Malocere grabbed Jacob and slammed him back into the inner tube, using tremendous force to push the boy's body downward, wedging him tightly in the tube so he couldn't move. Jacob lay trapped, hands raised as if in surrender, but screamed and sent a curtain of fire forward that wrapped around Malocere like a wet sheet. Max's skin sizzled and blistered, but the creature laughed through it all, seemingly oblivious to the pain,.

[*I was cast into fire,*] Malocere spoke again. [Your *kind saw to that. This just feels like home.*]

Jacob struggled to dislodge his body, but all his strength wasn't enough; the inner tube wouldn't yield. A strong hand shot forward, clutching Jacob's throat and forcing both him and the inner tube beneath the water's surface. Steam rose from Malocere's arm, extinguishing the fire as Jacob looked upon the creature from beneath the churning surface.

Malocere plunged his face into the water, again extinguishing the fire to reveal a hairless head with gruesome burns and looked into the boy's eyes one final time. He took pleasure feeling the little boy's body fight for its life. He leaned in, inches from Jacob's face and said [*It ends now,*] he said, [*You can't understand this yet, but soon you'll meet your maker and you tell Him* it ends now.]

Jacob's body lurched but to no avail. Malocere held him beneath the surface and watched the boy fight. In actuality, it took very little time. Jacob's body strained one final time and the water around him boiled before a burst of bubbles rose to the surface. Beneath the water, the boy gasped, and water rushed into his lungs. Thunder rumbled in the sky above.

Back in the Mirror Maze, Brig fell to his knees, coughing and gagging as he too experienced the burning sensation in his lungs. Only seconds after it had started, it ended, and Brig lost the psychic connection he'd had with his brother. Jacob Bailey was dead.

Malocere released the boy and the inner tube popped above the surface. Malocere flipped it over, submerging Jacob's head again as he put one foot on the side of the tube and gave it a shove downstream where a man in a small fishing boat would find the body, still lodged inside of it, six hours later.

Brig was torn between rage and crippling grief as the scene unfolded before him. He was unprepared for the emotional void that had accompanied his brother's passing as though a single candle in a dark room was blown out, leaving only darkness. He had hoped knowing the truth would bring him peace – a long-desired shelter from his maelstrom of emotions, but that respite hadn't come.

-3-

Deputy Lance Tillman knelt beside the disabled Chevy intent on the blood-like splatters covering the car's right, rear fender. He didn't see the figure approaching him from behind, but the sound of a knife being unsheathed made him all-too-aware of the presence. He didn't even have time to turn around before a hand reached around his throat and pressed a cold, steely blade against his skin.

A grating voice in his head said, [*Slowly turn around.*] Without a word, the deputy did as he was told and raised his hands to prove to his assailant that he had no aggressive intentions.

[*Any bullets in that gun?*] Malocere hissed. The creature stood before him, singed and hairless, but Max's facial features remained intact. Lance hesitated, confused. The boy standing before him was most certainly Max Usher, albeit a crispier version, and he tried to tell himself that this was some sort of prank. Stranger still, he had heard the voice, but it wasn't Max's voice and the boy's lips never moved.

"What?!" he asked. The question was rhetorical, more of a stall for time than anything else; all cops kept their weapons loaded. It was standard protocol, and what's more, Max knew that, so the question caught Lance off guard.

"Of course it's loaded," he said. "What's this about, son? Are you okay? Do you need an ambulance?" The knife pressed harder against his throat, and a small drop of blood escaped from beneath the deputy's skin; it ran down the side of his neck. *What the hell is this kid going to do*? The deputy's mind demanded. He was sure if he went for his sidearm, the kid would slice his throat.

This was the day he had feared ever since he'd joined the force. He'd heard a great many stories about the things that go through your head at times like this – how everything clears up and comes into perspective – how your life flashes before your eyes. He thought about his wife at home:

It was getting late, and he knew she was probably preparing dinner for them that evening. Was he going to allow his life to be cut short, or was he going to do something? He felt the blade start to slide across his throat, and in that instant, he made the decision that his wife was not going to get that phone call – the one that began with: "Ma'am, I hate to be the one to tell you this, but ..."

No. No way. Not today.

He was angry that Max had put him in this position to begin with. It was as though a seed of hate had been planted in his skull, and it was growing very quickly. He heard a whisper on the wind, [*Do it.*] *and he wanted to.* Something inside him wanted to watch the little prick's head bust open like a pumpkin dropped on concrete.

But fear remained... what would Max do if he reached for his gun? Much to his surprise, the thing he thought was Max Usher withdrew the knife and stepped back as if daring him to do something. Lance went for his gun and drew the hammer back, the pistol shaking in his hand. In a second provoking gesture, Malocere stretched its arms outward and exposed his palms. With one finger, he pointed to a spot between his eyes, telling Lance where he wanted the bullet.

[*Release me.*]

The deputy held his weapon as steadily as he could and said, "Drop the knife, Max!" He couldn't believe that he was holding a gun on the sheriff's brother. There was no way this could end well. "I don't want to have to shoot you!"

The whisper came again, only stronger this time: [*DO IT! RELEASE ME!*]

Feet not touching the ground, Malocere lunged at him with the knife raised in the air. The deputy acted on a combination of instinct and years of training. Cracks of gunfire ripped across the nearby fields. Max Usher's head blasted open; his body fell backwards and bounced once on the highway's gravel shoulder.

Within seconds, a thick, smoke-like mist rose from his mouth, which hung open, dripping blood. Lance distinctly heard the sound of beating wings. A dragon-like creature materialized before him, transparent and surreal. The creature lunged at him and threw him back onto the hood of the car. It melted into his chest like water soaking into a sponge.

Terrified and confused, but still fully aware that he had just killed the Sheriff's youngest brother, Lance stood up and felt a cyclone of panic come over him. He looked around, hoping no one had seen what had happened. Convinced that no one had, his next thought was disposal of the body. It had to be done. That much he knew, but before he could do so, there was one small thing that needed to be taken care of first... *and it wasn't going to be pleasant*. Lance holstered his sidearm and grabbed a hold of Max's feet.

He dragged the body fifty yards into a patch of tall grass where he was sure he would be able to conceal the body from view. Lance removed a pocketknife and studied the small entry wound in the boy's forehead. He took a deep breath and whispered, "Here we go..."

He locked the blade into place with a click and started to dig. The skull was much thicker than he had first thought, and the sound of the blade grinding against bone sent shivers up his spine. Minutes later, the mushroomed pellet of lead was between his thumb and forefinger. His hands were caked with blood, but he had somehow managed not to get any on his uniform. He had to dispose of the evidence – *and quick.* His first thought was the river.

He walked down to the bank and took one last look at the bullet before tossing it in – the *ploop* sound it made when it hit the water was a relieving one. He knelt down beside the water and dipped his hands into it, rubbing them together furiously in order to remove all traces of blood and gunpowder. With that done, he stood up, shook his hands, and wiped them on his pants. He drew his pistol out of the holster and opened the cylinder from which he removed the spent bullet casing and tossed it into the water as well. He made a mental note to clean his gun at the first opportunity.

Back at the cruiser, he reached in and opened the glove compartment where he always kept a spare box of rounds for his revolver. He took one from the box and slid it into the empty chamber. With the gun re-holstered, he took one last look in the direction where he had dragged Max's body, and felt confident he had hidden it well.

A call came over his radio on Channel 5. It was the voice of a state trooper – a frantic state trooper at that – the voice declared that he had just discovered two bodies on the western side of Jones Chapel. Lance knew what would happen next: the dispatcher would call on a landline and try to reach the sheriff, who would then radio to all of the deputies to report to the scene.

This would most likely be his only opportunity, so he took it. He climbed into his car, and turned the key in the ignition. The cruiser's engine roared to life, and the vehicle fishtailed as he spun it around and headed back towards Jones Chapel.

Just as he had expected, A.J.'s voice soon crackled over the radio, informing Lance of what he already knew. The deputy picked up his C.B. radio's mouthpiece and responded: "Ten-four.

I copy. Unit enroute. E.T.A. ten minutes. Over." He was breathing hard, and sweat was rolling down his face. He didn't want to think about what he had done, but his mind wasn't going to allow him to escape from it, either. His stomach had started to hurt; violent cramps caused him to buckle over and groan.

What happened back there? He thought. *My God, how am I going to explain this? I just shot a seventeen year-old kid between the eyes and left his body bleeding beside the highway!*

Malocere had accomplished his mission. The present danger had been averted. Jacob Bailey and his "gifts" would no longer be cause for concern. He rested and let Lance think his human thoughts without interference. In fact, Malocere was quite amused by the paradox of emotion flowing through the deputy's mind. He had acted in self-defense, and yet he felt guilty about it. *Curious creatures, indeed.*

Lance blew past LIVE BAIT, TACKLE, N' BEER; the parking lot was full of bass boats and pick-up trucks. Coincidentally, the same one belonging to the man who would find Jacob Bailey's body a few hours later was there as well.

Back in the Mirror Maze, Brig watched with great interest as the cruiser rocketed into Jones Chapel. Lance crested a hill beside the Bailey farm and pulled over to the side of the road. In the distance, red, white, and blue pulses of light appeared to hover above the highway, mingling with the bolts of lightning snaking through the black thunderclouds building in the west. The sight of those lights had always filled him with a sense of urgency, but also one of hope. It was a signal that salvation might still possible.

Another set of lights set a more somber tone: a single rotating, green strobe mounted on top of the car belonging to the county coroner. It was that green beacon that cinched the deal – someone was dead. Somewhere a family would have to be notified, and Lance was usually the man charged to do it. It was a wretched job.

The wind from the approaching storm had picked up. Lance drove on until he reached the cluster of police cruisers, ambulances, and fire trucks. He slowed the car to a stop and sat surveying the situation when a tap on the passenger window startled him.

A.J. Usher leaned down and peered into the car. He tipped his Stetson back and said, "Lance! What the hell are you doing? We've got ourselves goddamn situation here! We could use your help!" At that time, A.J. was only twenty-four years old. He had just taken over the sheriff's department less than a year prior – the youngest High Sheriff the town had ever elected.

His youth had not insulated him from the temptations of corruption, though. There was great speculation around town that the county's top law enforcement officer had his hands deep in the town's piggy bank. The rumors were never proven, largely because all witnesses had mysteriously died of various causes – some had disappeared altogether.

A.J. was the stereotypical cult of personality – no matter what he did, the majority of people seemed to like him. Add to that the fact that the townspeople continued to reelect him time and time again for the two and a half decades, and you have yourself a genuine "*what the hell*" Jones Chapel mystery.

A.J. had brought with him quite a reputation; his family was considered bottom of the barrel, and somehow genetically predisposed to mischief. His administration ruled with a heavy hand, just this side of dictatorial, and those who didn't like him were far too afraid to say so. The repercussions for such comments were most always severe.

Lance knew all of this. Somehow he had managed to stay on A.J.'s good side since he had won the election, and therefore, had only seen the sheriff's wrath from a distance. His gut seized knowing that was all about to change. If he was lucky, A.J. would kill him – if he was *LUCKY*. There were many worse fates that could befall him.

He rubbed his temples; his head hurt terribly. Doing his best to hide his panic, he opened the door and stood up. "What the hell happened here?" he asked. Two bodies lay on the ground covered in white sheets; blood was seeping through one of them.

A.J. said, "Real fuckin' mess if you ask me. Looks like a double murder. Damn nasty one, too. The coroner says the time of death was about four hours ago – 'course those boys don't know their asses from a hole in the ground – we both know that."

"We got the call from a state trooper who discovered the bodies, and we've been combing the scene for the last twenty minutes." Lance scanned the field, which was littered with evidence flags and men crisscrossing the field. Thunder rumbled in the distance. Its sound mixed with the low hum of voices all around them.

"Any suspects?" Lance asked.

A.J. noticed beads of sweat rolling down the deputy's forehead; his hands were shaking as well, and it looked like he was breathing a little too hard. "Nope," he replied. "Just heard about a couple up the road who was damn near run over by some punk who blew through a red light in a goddamn hurry."

"What model car was it?" Lance was stalling again; he knew what kind of car it was and what's more, he knew who had been driving it.

"Don't know," A.J. said. "They say the son-of-a-bitch blew through the light like a bat out of hell. You got any ideas?"

Lance thought to himself, *Yeah, I know who did it – the same bastard who held a knife to my throat. The same bastard I just shot at point-blank range...* your brother, *A.J. I shot your goddamned brother!*

Instead of saying that, Lance pointed to the shapes beneath the white sheets and asked, "Who are the victims?" He noticed that his boss was giving him a strange look and he asked, "What's the matter?"

A.J. responded with a laugh. "I was just about to ask you the same thing. You look like hell. Somethin' the matter?" Lance pointed to the bodies again and cleared his throat. A.J. nodded his understanding. "First time ya seen a body, huh?" Lance agreed that it was – of course he was lying. He had seen another one less than fifteen minutes before and had even crouched over it while he'd dug a bullet out of its skull.

A.J. took a stick of gum from his pocket and popped it in his mouth. He balled the wrapper up and tossed it to the ground. "No shame," he said. "You'll get used to it."

Desperate to steer the conversation in any direction other than the one in which it was currently headed, the deputy asked about the bodies again: "So, who are they?"

The sheriff didn't appear to suspect a thing; he went right along with Lance's manipulation of banter. "Don't know for sure," he said. "No positive ID's yet. Cliff seems to think he recognized one of 'em. Johnny somethin' or other. Says he hung around with the other one."

"What happened to him?"

"Poor bastard had his faced ripped off! Worst thing I've ever seen. It'll make your stomach turn."

Lance was actually startled: "Ripped off?" He asked.

"Oh, wait..." A.J. said, "it gets worse. His head was run over, too. Crushed like a freakin' melon. Brains and shit everywhere. Did you ever fry eggs on the sidewalk when you were a kid?"

"Yeah, sure. Why?"

"Well, that's about what it looked like. When I got here, there they were just bakin' in the road. Awful, just awful."

"How did the other one die?"

"Swift blow across the nose, I think. Bashed it in good."

Lance stood silent; something inside him desperately wanted to confess what he had done, but instead, he walked over to the nearest body and knelt down beside it. "This one bad?" he asked.

A.J. shook his head. "Nah, I've seen worse – a lot worse. Go on, take a look."

Lance pulled the sheet back and saw the blue, battered body of Johnny Kilgore. The blow to his nose had crushed his face. The ants had wasted little time in going to work on him – he was covered with them. Lance pulled the sheet back over the body.

Inside his head, Malocere was taking over, wanting control again. Before that happened, Lance turned to the sheriff and said, "The boy that you're looking for is dead."

A.J. laughed the statement off as ridiculous. "C'mon Tillman, how could you *possibly* know that? We don't even know who did it."

The deputy faced his boss and tried to confess. "I know who it was. The kid was bat shit crazy. I killed him… Shot him right between the eyes." He laughed a maniacal laugh, which actually made A.J. uneasy. Not an easy task. "It was him, I'm tellin' you. You should have seen him!"

A.J. reached out and put a hand on his shoulder. Lance brushed it off and turned his back.

"You killed him? Where? When? I don't understand. Who was it? Why did you do it?"

Lance desperately wanted to say the name. He wanted to get it over with, get it off his shoulders. "He was holding a knife to my throat, A.J.!"

"He attacked you?"

"Yeah... no... hell, I don't know. I guess not, but he wanted me to kill him." Lance reached up to his neck and felt the cut that had already scabbed. "Yeah... he wanted me to kill him. If I didn't he would have killed *me*. Fuckin' nuts, I'm telling you!"

A.J.'s voice took on a stern tone, which was almost parental. "We're friends, right?" He asked.

"Yeah, of course we are."

"I'd never steer you wrong, would I?"

"No, no you wouldn't."

"Then listen to me. You keep your mouth shut. If this kid did it, we'll find out. But you know what these state boys will do if you go running your mouth – they'll lock you up for sure. I need you, bud. You're one of the few I can count on. Can I count on you for this? Will you keep this quiet?"

Lance frowned and sadness fell upon him. Twelve years on the force and not once had he ever pulled his weapon in the line of duty. Over the years, he'd pulled over his share of speeders and drunks – had himself quite a record of bringing in revenue for the city on traffic fines, but he had never feared for his life.

At least, not until today.

He had taken another person's life, and the guilt was overwhelming. From deep inside his head, he felt something like an itch. It was then that Malocere's voice came through loud and clear:

[*You're a killer, Lance. Nothing more than a cold-blooded killer, and a* child killer *at that. Can you go home tonight and kiss that pretty wife of yours after what you've done? How can you go to work tomorrow? Do you honestly think this sheriff is going to stand by you? He'll turn on you when he finds out. One look at the body and he'll turn on you. You'll lose it all. It's lost* already. *What's the point? Let's end it. You have six shots in that gun. Let's just do it.*]

Lance shouted, "STOP IT!!!!" A.J. turned around and looked at him with an expression of dumb shock. "Leave me alone! Can't you just leave me alone?!!" His hands were balled into fists, and he held them against his temples; his revolver was in his right.

A.J. moved towards him. "Lance, give me your gun!"

Malocere fought against the deputy's will and rotated his wrist so that the gun's barrel was pointed directly at A.J.'s chest.

"Calm down, Lance. It doesn't have to be like this. Just give me the gun and I won't say a thing. You have my word. I understand, really I do. You're all mixed up right now. A boy is dead and you're feeling guilty. It's alright, really it is."

[*KILL HIM!!!*] The voice inside Lance's head commanded. [*KILL HIM!!!*] But the deputy still had *some* control over his own body – it was something he was losing rapidly, but it was still there. He screamed, "NO!!!" bending his arm back as though pulling against a great force. Lance pulled with all he had until the barrel rested against his own temple.

"Lance, listen to me," A.J. said in artificially calm tone. "I told you, it *doesn't* have to be this way. I'm giving you a choice."

Lance shook his head. "No choice." A tear formed in his eye and he said, "The boy was your brother, A.J. It was Max." He squeezed the trigger and the bullet tore through his head, splattering brain matter across the hood of the state trooper's gray cruiser.

His body fell to the ground like a sack of grain. Everyone stopped what they were doing and turned in the direction of the gunshot. A.J. dropped to his knees. The sheets covering the bodies of Johnny Kilgore and Chris Abrams started to flap like flags as a cyclone of wind swirled around the crime scene. Years later, those who were there still swore they had heard laughter in the wind.

The image in the mirror started to fade. Soon, Brig could see his own reflection again. Jacob was patiently waiting behind him when he turned around. [So that's how it happened?] He asked, now comfortable enough with the whole telepathy thing that it didn't seem strange to him at all. Jacob nodded, confirming that it had been the truth.

From somewhere a million miles away... "*Brig*..."

All of a sudden, it seemed like he was moving. He could no longer feel the floor beneath his feet, and when he looked up again, Jacob's image was fading in the mirror. Brig cried out to his brother. There were more questions, *so many more questions*. But his brother didn't answer. He continued to fade until he had disappeared completely.

Now half a million miles away... "*Brig*...!" The world bleached white and his eyeballs throbbed with sharp stabs of pain. He felt himself shaking.

Erin's voice..."Brig! WAKE UP!!!"

He sat up with a gasp and rubbed his face. "What!? What's the problem?"

Erin pointed into the living room where the front door was standing wide open. With a voice of tear-filled terror that only a mother in the grip of hysteria can muster, she screamed: "KAITLYN'S GONE!"

CHAPTER ELEVEN

-1-

Brig jumped out of bed and ran into the living room where he started to frantically flip on light switches. Erin hurried upstairs and did the same. Within minutes, every bulb in the house was glowing. They checked under beds, in closets, everywhere they could think of, but Kaitlyn was nowhere in to be found. Panic mounted and minds raced with possibilities and all those horrible scenarios parents are able to conjure in the face of a missing child.

Where should they search? Had someone come into the house and taken her out of their bed? Had she run away? Brig's first instinct was that Tom was to blame. *What had he said?*

I'll have your ass for this...

A hurricane of emotions churned within him; he felt violated and unsafe in his own home. Anger swelled from deep within, the kind of territorial, animalistic rage that, if left unchecked, could score a person twenty-five to life.

He reached into the closet, grabbed the shotgun and pumped a shell into the chamber. Startled, Erin asked him what he was doing. Her mind hadn't been to the depths his had been. Her initial fear was that Kaitlyn had simply wandered off. She was all-too-aware of the child's propensity for sleepwalking, so the prospect of foul play had not yet occurred to her.

Brig stepped into an old pair of sneakers when Erin pressed him again, questioning his intentions. His expression frightened her; it was one of determination, concealing the dark underbelly of parental wrath. She was unable to remember ever having seen him like that before.

"I'm going to get my daughter." There was nothing else to say. He grabbed a flashlight and turned to walk out the front door. Erin called out for him to wait; she wanted to go with him, but he told her to stay in the house. "Someone needs to be here in case Kaitlyn comes back." He told her there was a pistol on the top shelf of the closet. He told her to load it and to keep it close by. He was about to instruct her to call the sheriff's department, but had a flashback from the vision Jacob had shown him and a gut feeling urging him not to even consider that as an option, so he let it go.

That was when Erin started to cry again, just as she always had whenever she was frightened. Brig walked outside as though he hadn't even heard her. Tunnel vision had taken over; all he wanted was to find his little girl.

After she'd closed the front door, Erin locked the deadbolt and put the chain on just to be on the safe side. As soon as she did, she rushed to the closet. The pistol was right where Brig had said it would be, but it was high on a shelf and she had to stand on a chair in order to reach it – a small, nickel-plated, .38 revolver. She knew a thing or two about guns; Brig had insisted she learn about them before they had moved to New York. The sheer size of the city had been enough to intimidate the both of them, Erin especially. From behind every dumpster, she'd feared an attack, and the small Derringer she carried in her purse in those days had eased her mind somewhat.

There was a box of bullets on a lower shelf; she opened the pistol's cylinder and loaded six rounds. With a flick of her wrist, the cylinder snapped back into place. The sound was enough to calm her down somewhat; that simple *click* was the sound of security. She checked to make sure the safety was off, and sat down on the couch to wait. She felt useless, but she understood that waiting was all she could do.

-2-

Outside, the fog was thick, dense and white. Brig switched on his flashlight, but it proved of little use. Visibility was close to zero. Beside him, Buster pawed wildly against the sides of his pen, but Brig decided not to take him along. He feared the dog might be more of a hindrance than help. He still suspected Tom in the deep recesses of his mind, and stealth very much needed to be on Brig's side tonight.

He stood at the end of the sidewalk, his heart pumping rapidly in his chest. Unsure what to do next, he did the only thing that came to mind; he closed his eyes and thought of Kaitlyn. A clear image of her formed in his mind, and he saw her standing in the fog. A strange, luminescent haze surrounded her body.

She wasn't alone, either; that much he knew, but try as he might, he was unable to see who was with her. This feeling was new to him. More than imagination, it had the same feeling about it as the telepathy had between Jacob and him. Still, should he trust the picture in his head? It could just as easily be a false lead. But, it felt real enough, and it was all he had to go on.

Not only could he see her in his mind, he could feel her. He was sure the haze surrounding her was radiating what he felt... it was *her aura* and it moved around him, through him, and at one time he swore he smelled the scent of her hair pass by him. "Baby it's me," he whispered. Where are you??"

Brig turned this way and that as her presence moved around him. It carried with it a pulse, but a different one than he'd heard that day in the meadow. This one was gentler, more playful, and devoid of the rage he had seen in her face before. He followed it like a needle on a compass. Kaitlyn had become his magnetic north and he no longer doubted his intuition at all. Her aura vibrated in his mind so strongly that he stepped into the fog, turning off the flashlight with full trust what he felt was real. She was leading him – he was sure of it. He walked blindly into the fog with only that feeling to guide him.

From high atop a hill in the distance, a coyote howled. The sound was haunting, and it made Brig think again of the day's events though he knew that particular animal was no longer a threat. Kaitlyn and her newfound abilities had made sure of that. He gazed up into the cloudless sky through random thin spots in the fog to see a fuzzy crescent moon hanging there. Surrounding him however was a thick, white wall; the entire world had been reduced to the six feet of visibility he had in every direction. He closed his eyes and focused on Kaitlyn's energy again. Its pulse was like that of high electrical voltage, and he felt it deep in his bones. He was getting closer.

The gravel crunched beneath his feet as he walked down the drive. He sensed Kaitlyn pass by him again with a giggle and in his mind he saw her chasing a small rabbit through the field. Her presence was soothing, and it relieved his anxiety, wrapping him in a strange sort of calm.

He thought about the dream he'd had before this new quest had begun. It had yet to fade as most dreams do, and he thought that might be because it wasn't *just* a dream. It occurred to him there were a great many things he was taking on blind faith lately, and it seemed the more he accepted, the stranger the next thing was.

Brig remembered Jacob's voice in the dream. It had been so long since he'd heard it and yet the sound of it had seemed perfectly natural to him at the time… and *it was in his head, wasn't it? That was how they had talked… In their* heads!

A snapping sound, like a twig breaking in two, caused Brig to turn. He listened for something more, but there were only the grating sounds of the crickets in the grass and the gentle rustle of the wind in the trees. Beneath it all was a nagging feeling of being watched. He tried, but was unable to shake it. He did his best to convince himself he was just being paranoid.

Kaitlyn's pulsing aura had led him off the road at some point. He stopped, no longer sure where he was. His eyes had adjusted, but the fog still severely limited his vision. Each footstep resonated against the silence of the countryside. He reached out, his fingers moving through the fog, but unable to push the curtain aside. Then, somewhere on the other side of it, he thought he saw the reflection of a pair of eyes, but just as quickly as they had appeared, they were gone.

Brig's mind conjured images of the creatures that might be lurking about, watching him stumble through the darkness like a blind fool. They were biding their time. Of that he was sure. Soon the beasts of eventide would emerge from behind the cloak of night and then... He shook the thought away. He couldn't be worried about himself at a time like this.

He wanted to scream out Kaitlyn's name, but remembered his dream and thought about how it had felt to talk to Jacob... *in that special way*... and the mental tingle that had accompanied it. *But that was a dream. He couldn't actually* do *that, could he?*

He concentrated on his daughter as hard as he could, and he called out her name in his mind. [Kaitlyn...] The tingling sensations returned only they were much stronger this time; he felt them throughout his body and called out again: [Kaitlyn...]

[Daddy?] The reply was distant and faint, but it was her voice. His relieved sigh sent fog before him swirling. *She's alright,* he thought. *Wherever she is, she's alright. Thank God!*

[Sweetie where are you?]

[I'm with the spirits I told you about.] She paused. [This is how Nanna talks to me, Daddy. When did *you* learn how to do it?]

He didn't know how to answer. He just knew. It was as simple as that. So many things were different now. He didn't feel like the same man who had driven up from Birmingham just weeks ago. He had changed in some way, grown somehow.

[I don't know, sweetie, but your mommy and I are very worried about you. I need to come find you.]

[NO! Don't try to come here!] Her thought projection was intense – like a shout. [I'm with the good ones, but the bad ones are somewhere out there, too. I'll come to you.] Brig felt her mind pull away from his until there was no connection at all.

As he stood, waiting in the mist, he saw something in the distance – a human shape moving towards him. Before he was able to get a good look at it, it evaporated in a delicate zephyr swirl as if it had never been there at all. Whatever it was, it had become part of the fog again. Whispers were all around him, but each time he turned his head, they fell silent. The sensation that he was being watched had only grown stronger.

He felt a finger slide down the side of his neck. He spun around and lifted the shotgun, but no one was there. Fear had found him once again. He wasn't sure who the *'bad ones'* were, but he suspected they had found him, too.

The sensation passed quickly as Kaitlyn's aura returned. He felt it approaching from behind and he turned to see her shape in the mist, transparent and surreal. She lifted a finger to her lips in a silent 'shhhh' before looking to her left and to her right. Brig reached out for her, but his hand passed right through. She pointed into the distance with her free hand, and Brig knew to stand still. Something was moving in the mist, a shape darker than the rest, and Brig raised his gun again. Kaitlyn shook her head no, and it was clear to him in his mind that no weapon he could bring to bear would help them now.

In time, the shaped disappeared, and Kaitlyn's form solidified. Brig took her into his arms and hugged her as hard as he could. He was both relieved and outraged at the same time. Kaitlyn pulled away, and it was then he noticed something different about her. She seemed... *older*.

"Why did you run off?" He demanded to know, hands on her shoulders. "Your mother and I were worried sick!" He waited for his answer, but Kaitlyn seemed distracted. She kept looking over her shoulder as though listening to something just below Brig's level of perception. When she failed to offer an explanation, he insisted on one again. Kaitlyn turned her eyes up at him and held her finger over her mouth as before in a soundless '*shhh.*'

Brig mouthed the word, 'What?'

[Talk to me like *this* right now,] she said. [The bad ones are looking for us. We have to be quiet.]

It struck him as odd how natural this mode of communication was. [Why were you out here all alone in the middle of the night?]

In the silence of the meadow, her aura vibrated again in a sort of giggle. [I wasn't *alone*, Daddy. Nanna was with me. She said the *bad ones* were looking for me and we had to hide. She took me to see the others, too.]

[The others?]

[The other spirits.] She was speaking clearly, and now, her voice sounded much more mature.

[Where did you go?] He asked. [Where did they take you?]

Kaitlyn's face contorted a bit. She appeared to be groping for the right words. [We had to... We had to *jump*.] It came out just like that with no further explanation.

[I don't understand. What do you mean '*jump*?']

Kaitlyn shook her head, unable to expand upon the concept any further than she already had. Brig accepted her answer for the time being; there were other questions on his mind.

[Were they protecting you or something?] He asked. Kaitlyn nodded. [How? How did they hide you from the *bad ones*?]

Kaitlyn grinned and there was a hint of mischief in it. She made a circle in the air with her index finger and said, [Just like they're protecting us now. Don't you see, Daddy – I didn't step out of the fog. I pulled you *IN*.]

Brig looked up and saw the two of them were standing in the middle of a rapidly rotating funnel cloud, which appeared to be about twenty feet high. Small orbs of light moved about inside of it, each one following a different path.

Brig moved closer to the funnel, and a face formed before him. He reached out to touch it, but it dispersed as soon as he did, like grains of sand blown from the palm of his hand. He heard something then, and it sounded like laughter – genuine laughter, light-hearted and kind. He stepped back and saw a host of shapes surrounding them as ever more faces formed and vanished just as quickly.

Out of nowhere came the sensation of a familiar presence, and he heard a voice behind him calling his name. He turned and saw his mother there. She reached out and touched the side of his face, an eternity of kindness in her eyes. In that one touch, just before the fog absorbed her again, she communicated something to him. It wasn't a spoken word, but pure emotion. A sort of peace settled over him, and he moved one step closer to accepting the new reality revealing itself with every passing day – the true reality of the universe and where they all fit in.

Kaitlyn took his hand and said, [They're gone now – the bad ones, I mean. We can go home.]

[Will they be back?] He asked.

[I don't know, but tomorrow we need to call John. There's something he needs to do.]

Brig liked that idea. The thought of having John around made him feel a lot better, safer. The man seemed to have all the answers, which was exactly what they needed now. He wondered how he was ever going to explain all of this to Erin – if she would even believe him for that matter.

The funnel cloud was gone; all that remained of it was the same thick, soupy haze through which Brig had come. The visibility was every bit as poor as it had been earlier, and so it would remain until the morning sun peeked over the horizon and burned away the fog.

He took Kaitlyn's hand and they walked back to the farmhouse, paying no mind to where they were stepping. They simply moved forward, and their feet found solid ground. There was no light, no beacon to guide them home. Brig relied on instinct to guide him, nothing more. He had often gloated that he knew the layout of the farm well enough he could walk from one end to the other blindfolded. He was getting that chance now.

[Daddy?]

[Yes, sweetie?]

[I like talking like this.]

[Me too.]

[Do you think Mommy can do it?]

[I think it's just you and me for right now.]

Kaitlyn seemed to like that answer very much. The two of them had their own special thing to share – something that was theirs and no one else's. She held onto her father's hand and skipped beside him as they made their way down the gravel drive. Brig was delighted to see the little girl in her again.

-3-

From the couch where she had been sitting the entire time, Erin caught sight of two figures emerging from the fog. She sprung from the couch and ran outside. Tears of joy rolled down her cheeks at the sight of Brig with Kaitlyn beside him. Erin clapped her hands with excitement and ran towards them with arms open. She met them at the end of the sidewalk and fell to her knees in front of her daughter; covering the child's face with kisses.

Kaitlyn turned away and wrinkled her nose. "Mommy, that's gross!" She squealed.

Erin pulled her close and looked up to Brig. "Where *was* she? Where did you find her? Is she okay?" The questions came out in the kind of jubilated excitement that so often resonates in the aftershock of fear.

Brig's voice was sedate by comparison. "She's *fine,*" he said. "As for where she was... *well* that's going to be a little harder to explain."

Erin's expression changed to one that said, *Oh, no. Don't say it. Don't tell me it's more of* that *crap, again.* Please *don't tell me that.* But Brig's face bore her answer. "I'm going to have to sit down for this one, aren't I?" she asked.

Back inside, Brig told her the entire story. He left out no detail, regardless of how insignificant it might have seemed at the time. He told her about his dream, about Jacob, and what he had seen in the field. Erin listened and stared at him through skeptical eyes until he had finished.

While her parents discussed the recent events from the seclusion of the kitchen, Kaitlyn remained in the living room with a five hundred piece jigsaw puzzle scattered about, carefully separating the border pieces as her father had taught her to do.

Back in the kitchen, Erin shook her head. "Where does this end?" She asked. "I mean, the dog, the voice, it's all too bizarre. And now you're telling me that the two of you can communicate *telepathically?* For the love of God, Brig, are you listening to yourself?"

"I know," he said. "I know, but it's the truth. I swear it."

"Well, when did it start? How did *she* learn it? What's more, how did *you* learn it?"

"I don't know where she picked it up," Brig admitted. "It's like I told you before, she said my mom talks to her like that. Who knows how long this has been going on. She started having those dreams a while back, right? Maybe then? As for me, Jacob spoke to me that way in my dream – the one I was having when you woke me up. That was the first time I had ever done it." He paused, trying to decide if Erin was any closer to being convinced. It didn't look like she was, but he continued, anyway. "It's easy to do. I just wish I could prove it to you."

He tried to think of a way, but it would be impossible without Kaitlyn. Holding out a hand he said, "Take my hand. I think I have an idea." Reluctantly, Erin placed hers inside of his and together they walked into the living room where they both stopped abruptly in the doorway.

Kaitlyn sat on the floor with her back to them, seemingly unaware of their presence or at least disinterested in it. In midair before her hundreds of puzzle pieces floated in the air. She carefully moved her hands this way and that, fitting them together as gradually, a picture began to form.

Erin covered her mouth and let out a squeak of a scream. It was enough to break Kaitlyn's concentration, and when she turned towards the source of the sound, the pieces fell to the ground instantly. Kaitlyn's shoulders sagged and she began gathering the pieces with her hands, dumping them back into the box.

"Now I have to start all over, mommy." She pushed the box aside in favor of an open Tupperware container full of crayons and magic markers beside her. She took a coloring book from the coffee table and opened it halfway, not once acknowledging what her parents had witnessed with the puzzle.

Erin moved into the room with caution, side-stepping around her daughter and settling down into her recliner. She watched Kaitlyn color, happy to see puffy clouds and nothing more sinister.

The little girl put the marker down and looked up at her father. [I know you want to play a game, Daddy. I don't want to play.]

Brig walked over to the spot that Kaitlyn had claimed on the floor and sat down in front of her with his legs crossed. He reached down and tore a sheet of paper from the middle of a legal pad and pulled a fine-tipped marker from the Tupperware container. [C'mon, sweetie. Let's show Mommy how we can talk... you know... *that way.*]

Kaitlyn frowned. [Daddy, that's *our* secret. No one else can do it, but us. You said so.] She got up and shuffled around the corner in a huff.

Erin, having heard nothing of the conversation between the two of them, but still wide-eyed, looked at Brig and whispered, "Did you see that with the puzzle? It's... it's..."

"Incredible, I know," he said, finishing the sentence for her. "But do you believe me now?"

"I don't see how I couldn't," she admitted. Her hand went to her forehead and she sank back into the recliner. "It's just so much to take in. This kind of thing isn't supposed to happen."

"You're right, it's not. But it *IS* happening." Kaitlin had wandered back into the living room, and plopped down onto the carpet. Soon, the sound of rustling paper drew Brig's attention to the floor where Kaitlyn was scribbling furiously. When she had filled one page of her coloring book, she tore it off and began another. The small pile of paper grew larger and larger.

"What's she doing now?" Erin asked.

"I don't know." He bent down to see the blank expression Kaitlyn wore on her face. When his attempts to snap her out of it proved unsuccessful, he took one of the sheets from the pile and saw two words written over and over again:

HELP ME!

Brig picked up another page - on it was a single name - written repeatedly as before:

SAMMI

All of a sudden, Kaitlyn's eyes bulged. She fell to the floor with her hand clasped to her throat. She started to gag, and her parents jumped out of their chairs and rushed to her side. "WHAT'S WRONG WITH HER?!" Erin cried.

"I don't know!" Brig tried to pry Kaitlyn's hand from her throat, but her grip was too tight. "Kaitlyn!" He shouted. "Kaitlyn, what's wrong!?" Never in his life had he felt so helpless, so out-of-control. "Baby, talk to me!!"

Kaitlyn's little body convulsed, and her face turned red, then peculiar shade of blue. A vase fell from the coffee table when she started kicking her legs in a frenzied panic. Her hands went to the sides of her head and she shrieked.

Then, just as quickly as the episode had begun, it ended. Kaitlyn took her hand from her throat and rolled onto her back. She lay there drawing in deep, wheezing breaths. Erin ran her fingers through her daughter's hair and asked again, "What happened, sweetie? Are you okay?"

Kaitlyn nodded, to which she added, "Couldn't breathe." A croupy volley of coughs erupted, but quickly died off.

Brig asked her, "Did you choke on something?"

The little girl was about to answer when her head snapped violently to the left. She fell to the floor again, clawing at the right side of her head. Her shrieks were so loud that, outside, Buster heard her and barked. Brig snatched her up and held her to his chest – he didn't know what else to do.

The second episode ended just as the other one had in a matter of seconds – seconds that felt like hours. Erin pleaded with Brig for answers, but he had none to give her. He hoped Kaitlyn might. It didn't surprise him when she spoke up and answered his question without him even having to ask it.

"It was her," she said, pointing to the sheet of paper littered with Sammi's name. "She's a new one. I've never talked to her before."

They had not been watching the news or reading the papers, so Sammi's name meant nothing to them. John had spoken of a couple of missing girls back in town, but as far as Erin and Brig were concerned they were nothing more than nameless, faceless tragedies – something you come to take in stride after living in Jones Chapel for any length of time..

"Why did she try to hurt you?" Erin asked.

Kaitlyn shook her head. "She didn't mean to. She's scared because she's lost."

Brig remembered what Kaitlyn had said while they were out in the fog, and he asked her, "Is Sammi a bad one?"

Kaitlyn's denial was adamant: "No, no. She's a good one. I think she was trying to talk to me, but I don't guess she knows how, yet."

Outside, the carpet of fog was slowly turning a brighter shade of white as the sun rose. Soon it would be stained orange and then be gone. Brig glanced at the clock, surprised so much time had passed. Erin kissed her daughter on the forehead and asked if she was going to be okay. Kaitlyn assured her that she would be, and Erin got up and walked back into the kitchen.

After a couple of minutes, Brig went to investigate. From the doorway, he saw the half-empty bottle of Bacardi sitting on the counter next to the stove. Erin was standing at the sink, staring out the window. A floorboard creaked beneath his feet, and she turned around. In her hand, she held a glass filled halfway. It appeared she was drinking it straight without so much as an ice cube. He nodded towards the glass and said, "A little early for that, isn't it?"

Erin turned back to face the window. "Don't start preaching to me," she said. "It's a little early for *that,* too."

He walked up to her and took the glass from her hand. After downing a large gulp, his face drew up in a sneer. "I'm not preaching," he said. "You don't look like you're holding up so well."

"Gee, thanks."

"No, I'm serious. I know this is a lot to take in, but I'm worried about you." He kissed her on the neck and she gave him a hug.

"I think I'm on the verge of a nervous breakdown," she admitted. The glass was less than an inch from her lips when Brig took it away from her. He took another glass out of the cabinet and filled it with water from the tap. "Liquor isn't going to help you," he said. He was holding the bottle of Xanax in his hand when he turned around. He opened it, shook one into his hand, and held it out to her.

"What's that?" She asked.

"It's a sedative. It'll help."

"Is it going to knock me out?"

"Do you care?" She answered his question by taking the tablet from his hand and swallowing it. Brig pulled a chair out from the kitchen table and motioned for her to sit. "Wanna talk about it?" He asked.

"Not really."

"It might do you some good..."

She knew he was right, but she didn't know where to begin. Brig sat across the table from her and waited patiently for her to start talking. Finally, she said, "I guess I feel a little responsible for all of this."

"Are you serious? How could you possibly be responsible for any of this?"

"Maybe if I hadn't come back up here, none of this would be happening. What if it all got stirred up simply because Kaitlyn is here?" She saw a rebuttal coming, but she cut him off before he had the chance. She pointed an indignant finger at him and said, "Don't you tell me that I'm talking nonsense, either. There's no way you can prove me wrong."

"No, I don't guess I can. But if you think that you're coming back here caused all of this, it's still not your fault. If that's the case, *Tom's* the one to blame."

"But if you and I hadn't – you know."

"No!" He pounded his fist on the table. "We can play this 'what if' game all day. It's not going to get us anywhere. This isn't your fault; this isn't my fault, and it sure as hell isn't *Kaitlyn's* fault. It is what it is and we have to deal with it."

"It is what it is, huh?"

"That's right."

"Then, tell me... what is it?" The question was a good one. Truth be told, Brig didn't really know what it was. All he knew was that something very big was on the horizon. What John had told them wasn't enough; Brig was sure there was more to it, and that things were going to get much stranger – *very soon*.

"I don't know," he said. "I guess we'll figure it out soon enough. Until then, we're just going to have to take things as they come." Erin nodded her head in unspoken agreement as she fought to keep her eyes open. The pill was kicking in and she was feeling a bit woozy. She had always been a lightweight when it came to medication and if Brig's estimation was correct, soon it would be light's out.

Brig helped her up and led her out of the kitchen. When they made it into the hall, Erin stopped and said, "Do you *hear* that?" The sound she heard was a low grumble, almost a steady growl. "Is that her?" They continued into the living room and found Kaitlyn asleep on the couch, snoring. They both laughed a quiet laugh that such a big noise could come from such a small person.

Erin reached out and took a few strands of Brig's hair between her fingers. After a quick examination, she said, "Have you looked in the mirror lately? You're going gray!" Her comment took Brig by surprise, but he was quick to refute it, nonetheless.

"Am not!" In a nervous show of self-consciousness, he ran his fingers through his hair. "I mean, I have a little, sure, but it's not that bad."

Erin took his hand and led him into the guest bathroom where she flipped on the light and pointed into the mirror. "Take a look," she said.

He stared at his reflection, and his eyes opened wide with alarm. She was right; he *had* gotten grayer. "I look like an old man!" He said. "I'm thirty-three, not *sixty!*"

Erin mussed it up and said, "I don't know... I think it's kinda sexy. Gives ya that distinguished look." His reaction let her know that her approval had done little to diminish his own displeasure. He decided right then and there that he was going to be making a trip to the drug store to buy some youth in a bottle.

-4-

It was nearly ten-thirty by the time Brig got back to the house. It was shaping up to be another hot day, and the sun had successfully burned off the previous evening's fog. The bright sunlight and cloudless sky were a welcomed sight.

Erin and Kaitlyn were snoozing in the master bedroom, so he was careful to be quiet when he came back inside. Behind the closed bathroom door, he removed the item he had bought from a paper sack. The instructions on the box of men's hair dye sounded easy enough to follow, but after he had opened it, he started to think otherwise. Not to be undaunted, he donned the clear, plastic gloves and went to work.

Not long after he'd started, he heard a noise outside. The sound was too familiar – the squeak of brakes – and he walked to the front door, uneager to see who might be there. He was still wearing the gloves as well as a matching plastic cap, the elastic of which was snug against his scalp.

Harv was slowly lumbering up the walk when Brig stepped outside to meet him. The old man stopped dead in his tracks and gave a look of disconcertion when he saw what Brig was wearing. Nothing was said for a second or two, but finally Harv spoke up and asked, "What the *hell* are ya doin'?"

Brig tried to laugh the whole thing off, but eventually confessed that he was trying to "get the gray out." He left it at that. There was no doubt in his mind that he should keep as much information from Harv as possible. The old fella was still on the home team, but Brig respected his decision to sit this game out. If riding the pine was what Harv wanted, that was *exactly* what he was going to get.

Somewhere amid a series of deprecating glances, Harv said, "To each his own, I guess." Brig looked past him and saw a couple of wooden crates in the back of his pickup. They were both about the same size as a large suitcase.

He pointed and asked, "Whatcha got there?"

Harv looked back, even though he knew what Brig was referring to. "Oh, that. Dynamite."

"Dynamite?! What for?"

Harv removed a handkerchief from his back pocket, lifted his cap – the same one that said *'No time for sleepin', I'll rest when I'm dead'* on it – and wiped the sweat from his forehead. He pointed to a distant spot on the other side of the farm and said, "Tree stumps," as if it was no big deal.

"Jesus!" Brig said. "You're gonna blow them up?"

"You know a better way to get rid of 'em?"

Brig admitted that he didn't. It was obvious Harv was trying to get back into the swing of things. Getting back to work was probably a big step toward that goal. That good-old protestant work ethic is a hard thing to keep down.

Brig asked him, "You're not going to do that today, are you? I mean, it's not something that has to be done right away is it?"

Harv looked a bit puzzled by the question. "Well, no. I don't s'pose I have to do it today. Any particular reason ya don't want me to?"

Unprepared to have the ball knocked back to his side of the court so quickly, Brig scrambled to come up with an answer. The truth was that he wanted Harv to go home; he didn't want him there when John came back, because it would totally jeopardize the secrecy he was trying to maintain. As a last resort, he pointed to the window of the master bedroom.

"Erin and Kaitlyn are asleep. They sort of had a late night. I want to let 'em sleep. If you'll come back tomorrow, I'll help you out." As soon as the offer had left his lips, he regretted it. In the grand scheme of things, he had much bigger fish to fry and very little time for manual labor. But that moment was the most important thing to him right then, and if getting Harv out of there meant he spent the next day blowing up tree stumps, then so be it.

Harv accepted the offer. He asked where he should store the dynamite in the meantime, and Brig told him to put it in the tobacco barn. A moment's hesitation and a downward cast of eyes led Brig to suspect something was weighing heavily on the old man's mind. He realized that the whole time the two of them had been talking, Harv had only taken his hands out of his pockets once, and that had been to wipe his forehead. The lines on his face looked deeper, the circles under his eyes, darker. He looked tired. He looked depressed.

Brig found himself caught between what he knew he had to do and the longing to help an old friend. His father used to say that it was times like these that revealed the fiber of men's souls, and for the first time, Brig understood what that meant.

Harv turned to leave, but when he did, Brig stopped him. "Are you alright?" He asked.

In a rare display of vulnerability, Harv admitted that he wasn't. Such confessions were not in his nature. In his day, you were a man at eighteen, and you were expected to act like one. The week after his own eighteenth birthday, he had enlisted in the army. Within months, he found himself in the heart of the Korean peninsula south of the 38th parallel. One day, pinned down in a rice paddy, having just lost three of his best friends in an intense firefight that lasted hours, Harv fired his last round. He lay on his belly, silent and waiting for the enemy to draw in close. When they had, he hacked three of them to death with the small hatchet he wore on his belt. Harv's life was teeming with such stories. Harv was not a weak man.

Brig suggested the two of them should step into the house and talk; Harv agreed. The house was gloomy inside with all of the blinds closed, a stark contrast to the glaring light outside. Harv took a seat on the couch and Brig flipped on the floor lamp beside him before excusing himself to go and rinse his hair. Surprisingly, nothing was said when Brig emerged from the bathroom some five minutes later with a full head of dark, brown locks.

The men talked for an hour, and Brig concluded from what was said that Harv was going through a crisis, that's really all it was. Harv had always found his identity in his work. When Gabe died, despite Brig's assurance of continued employment, Harv's world had been thrown into a state of turmoil. Before, the workload had always been a joint-effort between he and Gabe; now it had become a solitary one and somewhere along the way, its meaning was lost.

While Brig had never thought of himself as having anything remotely in common with the old man, he was able to listen with a sympathetic ear. He too had been consumed with his job at one time, and for months after his decision to retire, he'd been little more than a shadow on the wall. His professional life had been so tightly entangled with his personal one that he had found it virtually impossible to separate the two. But he told Harv that he had made it through the rough patch, and that was proof enough it could be done.

Brig hoped that what he was saying didn't sound outwardly condescending; he felt odd offering life-advice to a man some forty years his senior. Still, Harv listened to what Brig had to say and even affirmed the validity of many of his statements.

The conversation ended without any uncomfortable questions being raised about Brig and Erin's relationship. Brig wondered if Harv was just being polite or if he didn't want to ask for fear of what the answers might be. Nonetheless, he left the house in much better spirits than those in which he had arrived.

Harv climbed back into his truck; after a quick wave, he headed up the drive. Brig watched him unload the crates of dynamite in the tobacco barn and drive off before going back inside to admire his hair in the mirror.

He was elated that he now looked ten years younger, rather than twenty or thirty years older. The temptation to wake Erin and show her was eclipsed by a renewed urgency to call John. Kaitlyn had stressed that point the night before. She'd said John needed to do something. Try as he did, Brig couldn't imagine what that something was, but he was determined to find out.

CHAPTER TWELVE

-1-

The noontime sun was baking down on Brent as he stood in the front yard holding a bottle of carpet shampoo his father had given him, insisting he clean up his own 'goddamned mess.' He stared into the rear hatch of his Mustang, his stomach in knots, looking at the mats of dried blood there. The pain and guilt were overwhelming, and he had already cried so much. The thought of having to do this deed – the idea that he had done the one that had made this even necessary – was psychologically crippling.

A million questions churned in his mind: *What had come over him? Had he just snapped? And why couldn't he remember doing it?* He had often heard the term 'temporary insanity.' It was a common defense thrown around in courtroom dramas for heinous deeds such as this, but he had never actually believed it to be a legitimate phenomenon, rather just something cooked up for TV shows. There didn't seem to be any other rational explanation, though – he *must* have been out of his mind – or worse – he was more like his father than he had ever realized.

He tried to mentally retrace every step he'd taken that day. Oddly, everything was crystal clear – his conversation with Sarah, the tumultuous hours that followed... everything – to a point. His last clear memory was of turning his car around at the Chevron station. After that, everything was a blank until earlier that morning when his father had woken him in what seemed to be a blind rage. Perry had been there, standing in the doorway not saying a word. When Brent asked what the fuss was all about, his father told him what they'd found in his car – the blood, the gun, the hair, the cell phone...

"Brent," he said. "Sammi Pridmore is missing! *WHAT DID YOU DO?"*

Brent pleaded his innocence, wearing a dumbfounded expression. His initial reaction had been concern for Sammi, not for himself, and that alone was enough to distinguish him from his father who was bound to find the rest out sooner or later. He went ahead and confessed to him about Sammi's pregnancy. A.J. acted surprised – shocked even. He'd even managed to feign a few tears to complete the effect. Once the dramatic display of emotion was over, A.J. sat down beside his son and told him he would do everything he could to throw the dogs off of his trail.

Brent was terrified – in part because of what he'd done, but also because there was a small part of him that was happy it had happened. *Was he* that *much of a monster – so much of one that he was actually* happy *he had killed his girlfriend – simply because the responsibility of his prior mistake was now erased?* This was the part of himself that resonated similarities with his father – a side he had fought hard to hold down, but was no longer able to deny existed.

His father had asked him if anyone else knew about the pregnancy. Brent told him the only other person who knew about it was Sammi's best friend, Sarah. Looking back, Brent could have sworn a smile crept across his father's face, but it was difficult to tell since his eyes were hidden behind a dark pair of sunglasses. A.J. patted him on the chest and said, "Then you should be okay. You killed her, too. We found her body in the barn." Again, his father assured him that he would do all he could. "Perry and I will get rid of the body. Where'd you dump the other one?"

Brent shook his head. "I... I don't know. I swear to you, dad, I don't remember any of this." That's when A.J. tossed the bottle of shampoo in his lap and suggested he remember and damned fast.

"Prison ain't no playground, boy."

Now, six hours later and fully convinced of his guilt, grief and fear held him in their grips and a weight unlike any he had ever felt pressed upon him as he shook the bottle of shampoo, sprayed on a layer, and started to scrub. As he did, the white foam slowly turned a shade of pink. The insulation shock offered him was the only thing keeping him going. None of this seemed real yet, and it was that very disconnect keeping him from curling into a fetal position. This was all a nightmare – it had to be – and all he wanted was to wake up.

-2-

Back at the sheriff's station, Perry sat behind a small wooden desk in a creaky chair with casters that tended to stick whenever he rolled from place to place. The office had been flooded with calls about the missing girls in the few hours that had passed since they'd become front-page news. Perry had been the one fielding most of those calls, and he'd managed to send the other deputies on a score of wild-goose-chases, just to keep them busy. He understood quite well that idle men have time to think and thinking men ask questions.

After the initial confrontation with Brent that morning, Perry had asked his boss why the boy couldn't remember any of the details. A.J. told him not to worry about it and that everything was taken care of. Try as he might, Perry couldn't make sense of it. The boy had seen everything, but if he was faking amnesia, it was a damn impressive performance.

What Perry didn't know was that A.J. Usher was no longer in control of his own body. Malocere had taken the reigns sometime in the early morning hours. The possession had taken much longer than Malocere had anticipated, despite his foreknowledge that the Ushers were a strong-minded lot, difficult to break due their resilience under pressure.

Still, Malocere won out in the end, and had even managed to keep his bloodlust at bay for the time being – no easy task as it went against the creature's very nature. He had accessed the sheriff's thoughts and memories with full intentions of playing the role and going undetected, at least for now...

Malocere was going to make sure things turned out exactly the way he wanted them to – nothing less. Things needed to be clean – when people turned up missing or dead, the waters tended to get muddy. Until he found the Keeper, things needed to remain uncomplicated and status quo.

Everything was going according to plan until one of the other deputies called in and reported to Perry that they had found Sarah's car. "Oh, and one other thing," he added. "It's on the side of the road next to the boss' farm." Perry panicked, sure they were busted, but Malocere took it all in stride.

He followed standard procedure – dusted the car for prints, that kind of thing. The car was towed away as evidence, but A.J.'s property was never searched. His subordinates knew better than to call his character into question. Had they investigated, or even walked fifty yards across the pasture, they would have seen the burnt shell of the barn. In it, they would have found the charred remains of one of the missing girls.

It was now widely known that Brent and Sammi had been dating. Had protocol been followed to the letter, Brent would have been among the first to be questioned. But Malocere told the deputies he had already spoken with the boy and that Brent knew nothing. Privately, some of them smelled foul play, but no one said a word.

-3-

John showed up at Brig's front door a little past one in the afternoon. There was a cool confidence about him that Brig picked up on right away. He invited John inside and started to tell him about everything that had happened since they'd last spoken.

It didn't appear as though much of what he said surprised John, who listened and nodded in his usual way with an occasional raised eyebrow. He seemed amused Brig had discovered the ability to speak with his daughter telepathically, but admitted such things were to be expected. In fact, John didn't show any outward emotion at all until Brig suggested that he might be able to handle Malocere on his own.

John told him it was out of the question. "Your abilities alone simply aren't enough," he said. "I understand where you're coming from, you don't want anything to happen to Kaitlyn. I assure you I will do everything in my power – the spirits will do everything in theirs – to protect her. Didn't they prove that to you last night?"

"Yes," Brig admitted, "but what if all of that isn't enough?"

"It's like I told you before; if we fail at this, we all die. It really doesn't matter."

It was an answer Brig didn't particularly like, but he accepted it just the same. The sheets of paper from the night before still lay on the floor. He picked them up and handed them to John. "Last night, Kaitlyn spaced out," he said. "That's the only way I know to describe it. It was like she wasn't there at all. She just started scribbling on this pad of paper… page after page. What does it mean?"

John turned on the lamp beside the couch and studied the pages. After looking at the first one, he flipped through the others quickly by comparison. He set them down on the coffee table and leaned back in the couch. "Spirit writing," he said. "Your daughter is in almost constant contact with the spirit worlds. It may seem strange to you, but to her, it's quite normal." He pointed at the sheets of paper. "This often happens when a spirit tries to communicate. They all have their own methods of getting through, but with this method the spirit takes over and guides the person's hand as if it were its own."

Brig examined them again. Indeed, the handwriting was different than Kaitlyn's and while scrawled, it had a sort of penmanship about it. He asked John his thoughts on the violent episode that had accompanied the writing.

"Simple. This spirit... I believe her name was Sammi?" He asked, picking up the pages to confirm and then setting them back down. "She took over in hopes of getting a message through. The problem is that when a spirit passes into another world, they are often confused at first - even scared - because they are desperately trying to hold onto some semblance of their mortal lives. They don't understand that they've passed over. Usually, the disorientation passes quickly, but they carry a great deal of emotions and physical pain with them at first. It's difficult for them to let go of it, and sometimes that pain is felt by the person they're speaking through."

"So you're saying Kaitlyn was possessed?"

"If you choose to use those words, but it's really much more than that. This Sammi is a new spirit. She is swimming in a sea of darkness right now - eternal darkness - the kind that swallows you and doesn't let go. In the midst of all of this - the pain, confusion, and fear - she saw a speck of light."

"Kaitlyn."

"Exactly. Sammi's reaction was not unlike anyone else's would be if they were drowning. She panicked and held on. When she did, what she was feeling spilled over into your daughter. I suspect what Kaitlyn felt had something to do with the circumstances surrounding this girl's death."

"So you think she died violently."

"I do. I believe she's the spirit of one of the girls they're looking for back in town. I've heard rumblings, but I haven't had a chance to read the papers, so I don't know their names."

"Then we should call someone!"

John smiled and leaned forward when he spoke, "Who? I suppose you'll just call the police and tell them your daughter is able to channel the spirits of the dead and that she has been in contact with one of the missing girls?" He shook his head and laughed. "You have to understand that while you may be getting used to all of this, the rest of the world is as it has always been – at least on the surface. The last thing you want to do is to draw attention to yourself by making people think you're crazy. You don't know who you can trust – you don't know who Malocere might be."

Brig stood up and paced the room with his hands against his head. "What about her parents?" he asked. "They have to be out of their minds right now."

"Believe me, I understand where you're coming from, but if you draw attention to yourself, you'll only be endangering your own daughter. It's not worth it. There's too much at stake here."

Brig slung the stack of paper across the room. The pages landed in scattered piles. He folded his arms and looked out the living room window. John addressed his aggravation by saying, "You told me you were finally given the answers regarding your brother's death. Aren't you at least satisfied with that?"

Brig turned around and said, "No. Don't you see? It's happening all over again. I had to wait for over twenty years to find out what happened. Do you have any idea what that's like? Not knowing?" He pointed to the papers lying on the floor. "Now you're asking me to put someone else in the same position when I have the answers right here?"

John stood up and walked over to him. "Look, you can tell them anything you want when this is over, okay? You just have to trust me now and keep quiet. He's out there – somewhere. You have to keep a low profile." John paused, eyeing Brig with an uncertain expression. Always self-conscious about such things, Brig asked what was wrong.

"I don't know," John said. "Maybe it's just the light, but you look different."

"It's the hair. I dyed it." It was the first time Brig had ever heard John laugh – at least a genuine, belly-shaking laugh.

"Are you serious?" he asked. "Why did you do that?"

Brig went on to tell him about the rapid graying process, and John doubled over, his face a bright shade of red. "Well, I'm glad you think it's so funny!"

John took a deep breath and said, "No, I'm sorry. I shouldn't laugh at you. It just caught me off guard, that's all. The problem isn't with your hair, Brig. It's all the spirit activity around you. The spirits require a great deal of energy to operate in the physical world. They get that energy from the life forces of the living... whoever happens to be close by. If you don't take care of yourself, they'll drain you before too long."

"But I feel better than I've felt in years!"

"And you *will*... at first. But before long you won't be any good to anyone. You have to take care of yourself. Erin and Kaitlyn have the right idea." He pointed to the bedroom door and said, "You should join them. Get some sleep."

Brig resigned to do just that, and he thanked John for coming by. Before he left, John explained to Brig what Kaitlyn had alluded to the night before when she'd told him there was something that needed to be done. John assured him he would return that night to perform a protection ritual that would further shield Kaitlyn from Malocere. The bad ones, as Kaitlyn called them, had gotten uncomfortably close, and it was more important than ever to put the protection in place.

-4-

Three hours and four bottles of carpet shampoo later, Brent had managed to rid his car of any visible evidence that could tie him to Sammi and Sarah's murders. He stumbled through the house overcome with a sense of loss. Nothing made sense anymore and it appeared he was not the person he thought he was, but had proven to be an Usher, after all.

In the end, it was more than he could handle. Malocere had stolen his memory, but not his morality. The idea from the night before and the release the razor blade had promised him was even more tempting than it had been then. He went back into the house and poured a glass of lemonade when the phone rang. A quick glance at the handset display caused a thick knot to form in his throat. The name spelled out on the screen was 'PRIDMORE.'

It was Sammi's mother; he was sure of it. There was no way he could talk to her – no way in hell! She'd hear the guilt in his voice. *Mothers have that kind of intuition, don't they?* She'd know immediately what he'd donc and that would be it – game over. Checkmate.

The phone continued to ring, but Brent backed away from it. Each ring was painful, and he wanted it to stop. He wanted her to give up and leave him alone. On the third ring, he felt his burden grow heavier and he even considered answering the phone and confessing. *I did it! I did it! Sammi's never coming home! Now leave me alone!* On the forth ring, the answering machine picked up. What followed was the sobbing, snot-sniffing voice of a mother in the grip of extreme emotional turmoil. "Brent? Brent, are you there? If you are, *PLEASE* pick up!"

In actuality, Sammi's mother hung up not long after that, but Brent's imagination was in high gear and it gave him something else to listen to. He heard the tone of her voice drop much deeper and he imagined that she was hissing through her teeth when she said, *"I* know *it was you. You killed my Sammi, didn't you? You're just like your father, you soulless* bastard*!"*

Brent grabbed the answering machine and tore it away from the wall. It broke into five or six pieces when he threw it to the floor, and he screamed "WHY CAN'T I REMEMBER ANYTHING????"

Ten minutes later, Brent sat in front of his computer upstairs. His word processor's white screen bore only one letter – an 'I' – and a blinking cursor beside it. He didn't know what to say; last words were proving difficult to choose. Finally, he stopped thinking and started typing. The words that appeared on the screen were honest, from the heart, and they came quickly. He wrote about his initial reaction to the news of Sammi's pregnancy, his determination to do the right thing, and his complete lack of memory of the events that had taken place during the span of time from seven thirty that evening until eight o'clock the next morning.

By the time he was finished, he had summed up his final thoughts into a few neatly crafted paragraphs. He was happy with the result, because it said what he had wanted to say. He closed the letter with an apology for the pain he'd caused, and he stared at the blinking cursor for another couple minutes longer before printing it. The machine's gears whined as it spit out his suicide note. The machine fell silent, and the only sounds that remained were the lonely creaks of bedsprings and the low hum of the computer fan.

It surprised Brent that he wasn't afraid of what he was about to do. His fear of living had surpassed his fear of dying. All that was left was to do the deed. He told himself there was no time like the present – best to get it done.

He crossed the hall on his way into the bathroom he and his father shared. Once there, he opened the medicine cabinet and rummaged through it, reading the labels of various prescription bottles until he found three he believed might do the trick. He took the cap off of each one and poured the tablets into a paper cup adorned with yellow daisies before disposing of the bottles in the trash.

Five minutes and a half a glass of lemonade later, he had taken three times the lethal dose of the various pain killers he had found in the cabinet. He sat on his bed with the crumbled paper cup on the floor. The tablets' bitter aftertaste lingered on the back of his throat.

It wasn't long before the pills took effect. Brent lay on his back, blinking slowly, his respiration slow and labored. *So this is what it feels like to die,* he thought. *Not so bad.* He wondered how long it would take before it was over. *Would he feel his heart stop? Had it stopped already?* Mostly, he wondered what Hell would be like – it's where he belonged and no doubt where he was headed. Such would be his punishment, and he felt that he deserved it.

He stood up when his stomach cramped, and found his legs were rubber beneath him. His thoughts were a foggy mix of euphoria mixed with nausea. He swayed from side to side as the light ran from the room and darkness came. Then there was a sensation of falling.

-5-

A voice in the darkness: "*Brent...*"

"Who's there?" He asked. "Where am I? *Am I dead?*" The voice didn't respond.

His feet felt like they were on solid ground, but he didn't dare move. A crimson moon hung in the sooty sky above him, and it stained the canvass of low-hanging clouds a sinister hue of red. Black silhouettes of large, winged, dragon-like creatures darted in and out of the cloud cover.

A much smaller creature swooped out of the sky with tremendous speed. Its paper-thin wings beat so fast they were little more than a blur accompanied by a faint droning sound. The creature was about the size of a softball – green and covered with scales. Its teeth were disproportionately large for its body and as sharp as knives. The gums surrounding those teeth were black and moonlight reflected off the streams of saliva dripping from them. The chattering sound it made in Brent's ear was almost hysterical laughter. He swatted at it as one would an annoying June bug; it flew away and disappeared somewhere on the other side of a tall, cone-shaped mountain belching plumes of yellow smoke into the sky. To this, Brent attributed the choking, sulfurous air in his lungs. The soil beneath his feet was red, like the pictures he'd seen of the surface of Mars. Just as he had imagined, the landscape was barren with no vegetation in sight, only that bloody soil strewn with rocks and ash.

The voice was closer now and insistent. "*Brent!*"

He was on top of some sort of mountain. In the valley below were the bodies of thousands of pale-white, hairless people floundering in a sea of antifreeze-green water. At first it looked like they were trying to claw their way up the mountain so that they could pull him into the water with them. But he realized that wasn't so when a gentle rain started to fall, and the first drop landed on his arm, singeing his skin. *Acid rain*, he thought.

A white-capped wave washed over the masses below, and when their screams reached his ears, he understood they were only trying to escape. Another drop of rain landed on his cheek and he winced with pain. His mind shouted, *they're swimming in this stuff!* Just then, one of them managed to grab hold of a rocky outcropping on one of the vertical walls. A look of intense relief came over the man's scabrous, sore-ridden face. But the relief was short-lived.

The handhold broke away from the wall, sending the man tumbling back into the lake of acid with a splash. Even the rocks seemed bent on torturing them. The man surfaced again, and his earsplitting scream convinced Brent that the pain was even worse than before.

Ribbons of lightning divided the sky, illuminating the red clouds above. In them, Brent saw the shadows of hundreds of winged creatures, where before, he had seen only five or six. In the bright flare of a second bolt, he saw one of them plunge from above and snatch one of the thrashing bodies from the water with claw-like talons.

The creature flew back into the air with its catch securely in its grasp. A second one swooped in and tried to snatch the prize away. It dug a hooked talon into the man's chest and a morbid tug-of-war ensued. The two creatures hovered in place, snapping at one another's throats.

The dragons were about three hundred feet in the air when the man's body twisted and tore into two asymmetrical pieces. The severed upper torso slid from the dragon's grip, and fell through the air. The second creature abandoned the fight and dove for the scrap of meat. It caught it in its teeth and lighted on a hilltop some fifty yards away. Brent watched as it tossed the torso into the air and gobbled it down. The monster's triumphant roar shook the ground. Small rocks bounced like pebbles on the surface of a beating drum.

Now fed, the dragon flew back into the clouds. Brent had not moved an inch. The fear in him was too great to allow him to do so. Anxiety was the air he breathed. It was everywhere... a part of everything.

The voice spoke again, only this time it was right behind him: "*Brent!*"

He didn't want to turn around, terrified of what might await him. His nightmares had taken physical form – there could be nothing good in this place. Eventually, he resigned himself to the fact that it was probably better to face whatever it was – *best to look your demons in the eyes than allow them to attack you blind*. But before he had a chance to do so, he felt a cold hand touch his shoulder. He spun around and stumbled backwards.

Sammi walked towards him, but for every forward step she took, Brent took one in the opposite direction. He was too horrified to think. The very sight of her repulsed him. Her blue jeans were caked with large splotches of blood, her T-shirt the same. The sockets of her eyes were sunken and dark. The skin on her arms and her face was a pale, sickly white; her lips the deep purple of a bruise.

Her left arm hung limp at her side and she drug her right leg behind her when she walked, relying on it for little more than balance. She turned her head and Brent saw a gaping hole above her half-severed ear twice the size of a man's fist. The skull that surrounded it was jagged and fractured. Light shone through it, and loose flaps of skin hung over the hole like a grisly curtain. Every now and then her head bobbed to the side; when it did, her brain – *or what was left of it* – protruded outward, sending pink fluid from inside her skull cavity dripping down the side of her face. Brent was convinced that she had come to pour out all of her vengeance upon him.

Sammi called out again; her voice bubbled through a throat filled with fluid: *"Brent!"*

He had retreated as far as he could. On one side, a cliff dropped off into the acid lake; behind him and to his other side, the rock wall shot straight up for another sixty feet. He was cornered – trapped. All he could do was scream, and that's exactly what he did.

She reached out for him with a white, bloated hand. Her fingernails were broken and bloody, and he wondered if she had clawed her way out of the lake and up the mountain just to get to him. The last thing he wanted to do was to touch that hand – he'd sooner jump.

He found his voice again and begged her for mercy... for *forgiveness*. The look she gave him was one of confusion. "I don't want to hurt you," she said. "I'm here to help." Brent wasn't sure if he should trust her. Why would she want to help *him?*

"Why?" he asked. "I killed you, Sammi! Why would you want to help me?"

"You didn't kill me," she said. "That's what they wanted you to think." She held out her hand, but his aversion to her touch must have been evident, because she withdrew it and said, "You shouldn't be here."

"Where is *here?*" He demanded. "Am I in Hell?" Whatever her answer was going to be, he hoped she wouldn't shake her head. He didn't want to see that yellow glob of brain pop out of the side her head again. "This isn't Hell," she said. "But you're a lot closer than you were before." She extended her arm, pointing to the mountain belching yellow smoke. "Hell is through those gates, I think. These are The Borderlands. Now take my hand, and I'll show you the truth."

That time, he took it. Sammi's skin was cold and she gripped Brent's hand with crushing force. He stared into her glassy eyes, unable to look away. The events of Sammi's murder began to play in his head. She was kneeling on the barn floor, and it was his father holding a pistol to her head, not him. The shot rang out, and Brent jerked his hand away, unable to watch any longer.

He was furious. His father had lied to him. The bastard killed his girlfriend and then *framed him for it!* "But I was there, wasn't I?" he asked. "Why can't I remember?"

"The memory was taken from you. Darker forces are at work here. Your father went somewhere he shouldn't have. He got too close..."

"To what?"

"He got too close to a door... there isn't time to explain. Your father is possessed. The thing controlling him is preparing to wage war against everything good. It needs your father to carry out its plans. You were a threat, but without your memory, it was able to convince you that it was your fault."

"Why didn't it just kill me, too?"

"Your father still had some control - He couldn't kill his own son. The demon had to do the next best thing. You're the only one who knows its identity. *That's* why you have to go back."

"I'm dead, aren't I?" He asked. "How can I go back?

Sammi opened her hand and in her palm was a glowing, yellow ball the size of a marble. "Yes, you're dead. But you *can* go back. There is very little time left - you *have* to hurry." She held her hand out and said, "Swallow this. It's the memory he stole from you and it will take you home."

"What am I supposed to do when I get there?"

"You'll know. Spoil its plans somehow." The ground beneath their feet shook and rocks from high above fell around them. "The Gate is closing," she shouted with an urgency only the dead can have. "There's no more time! You'll be trapped here! This is your only ticket back! SWALLOW IT!"

Another shower of small rocks rained down from the cliffs above. Brent snatched the glowing object from her hand and popped it into his mouth. It tasted surprisingly sweet and slid down his throat easily. Then, as if carried on wings, he rose into the air, climbing higher and higher into the sky, all the while worried that one of the dragons might snatch him out of the air. His body felt heavy – much too heavy to stay aloft for long. He was sure he would plummet into the acid sea, but somehow he kept rising.

Sammi stood on the ledge of the cliff and watched him; he watched her as well. She appeared to get smaller and smaller the higher he climbed. When she was little more than a point on the horizon, Brent heard her repeating a word over and over in his mind as her voice gradually faded.

[Remember... Remember... Remember...]

Brent turned and faced the other direction. In the starless sky above, he saw a tiny, shimmering crystal ball. He wanted to go to it, and just like that, he started moving with no physical effort on his part – his mind was doing all the work.

The ball was just within his reach – he wanted it badly, but didn't know why. The faceted surface reflected the light so perfectly that he was sure a touch – just a simple touch – would yield enough ecstasy to last him a hundred lifetimes. His desire intensified, and he reached out and touched it with the pad of his index finger.

It moved away from him with tremendous speed. It wasn't long before he realized that *he* was moving away from *it* – and fast. He turned to see a huge, rotating mass of darkness in the sky ahead of him. The rotating portion was much darker than the rest of the sky, and it reminded him of the black holes he'd seen in science books his mother had shown him.

The anomaly was pulling him in. Its intense tug was centered on his chest. Another one of the softball creatures flew alongside him and bared its teeth. Brent was thankful for the loud roar of wind rushing past his ears, because it meant he didn't have to hear its god-awful chattering. The creature accelerated until it was little more than a green streak and disappeared into the swirling blackness.

Brent noticed small, white things pouring out of the black hole, which seemed odd because its suction was so great. His first impression was that they looked like tiny maggots. Groups of them spilled out of the void, occasionally five or more at a time. They tumbled to the ground where they writhed and squirmed in ever-growing heaps. A small number of dragons stood around the various piles, feeding. Some of the maggots scurried away in several different directions, all trying to elude fate.

Another tug... moving faster now...

Brent was now close enough to see the little white things weren't maggots at all. They were humans! Thousands and thousands of humans! One of the dragons watched him move across the sky; it opened its mouth and trumpeted a roar like an oncoming train. The other creatures joined in with roars of their own. The volume was deafening, and Brent was relieved when it died down. That is, until he saw three of them spread their wings and take flight to intercept him.

Brent and the dragons were moving towards one another quickly. The creatures assumed a sort of attack formation, and they positioned themselves between him and the black hole. His thoughts turned to evasion when he remembered how he had moved toward the crystal ball using nothing more than his own will. He wondered if it would work again.

Now twenty feet in front of him, the lead dragon opened its mouth wide, ready to devour Brent whole. In that mouth was a large, triangular tongue and rows and rows of long, curved teeth; it was no place Brent wanted to be. The dragons were just about on top of him. He could see their nostrils flaring and their bat-like wings cutting the thick air, leaving behind curled, white contrails. He closed his eyes, and pictured himself nose-diving toward the ground.

It worked.

The creatures zoomed over his head. Before they even realized what had happened, Brent had accelerated and become a streak of color just as the softball creature had. He headed in the direction of the black hole and within seconds, he was inside of it.

The black hole became a tunnel that wound around itself like a roller coaster tearing from its track. Much to Brent's surprise, there was a light inside of it, and he tried his best to avoid the bodies as they tumbled past him on their way down. They fell like paper dolls strewn from a skyscraper – legs and arms waving about.

So many of them!

Their faces said that they didn't know where they were or where they were going. Brent thought about the monsters feasting on the bodies, and he decided that not knowing what was in store at the end was probably better for them. Their ignorance of this place would be the last good thing they would ever know. It was a place he hoped he could eventually forget.

-6-

Brent felt like he had been gone for days, but as he hovered in a corner near the ceiling of his room he saw the clock on his nightstand, and it appeared as though only ten or fifteen minutes had actually passed. The body on his bed was his own – there was no doubt about that. It lay on its back, legs bent over the sides, with its mouth agape. A wet spot had formed on the bedspread, and it was growing larger with every passing second. Brent looked closer and saw saliva flowing from his mouth in a steady stream.

He knew he needed to get back into his body, but something told him it was going to be an *extremely* painful thing to do. That aside, he didn't want to get back in there because he was just beginning to enjoy the freedom of being out. Getting back inside would be the equivalent of taking a hot shower and then slipping into a pair of muddy jeans. Further complicating matters, he didn't have the slightest clue how to do it.

His suicide note still lay in the printer tray, and as he looked at it, he felt discouraged. When he had sat down to type that letter, he'd had doubts about the existence of an afterlife. Those doubts were gone now, but he wondered if there was more than what he'd found. There had to be. Over the course of his short journey, he had seen many horrible things, but nothing to suggest the afterlife consisted of anything other than varying degrees of misery. His eyes had been opened, and he realized just how stupid an idea suicide had actually been.

He heard Sammi's voice in his head: [Remember...]

There were things to be done, weren't there? After all, that's why she had sent him back. Part of him wondered what would have happened if he had chosen to shoot himself, instead. *Could I have come back* then? He looked down at his body again and saw his eyes blink.

I'm still alive! His mind shouted. *Holy shit! I'm still alive!*

It all made sense to him then. Not only had he returned from the afterlife, Sammi had sent him back in time as well. He also understood that he couldn't get back into his body until he died.

Jesus Christ! He thought. *I have to watch myself* die?

He tried to think back and remember his death, but couldn't. He told himself it was just a drug overdose, after all. *How gruesome a death could that possibly be?* It wasn't like a gunshot where you repainted your room in your own blood – *with pills you just went to sleep, right?*

What happened next changed his mind about that, too.

A geyser of vomit erupted from his mouth; some of it ran up into his nose, some down the sides of his cheeks, but most if it went straight up into the air and came straight back down. *Oh, great,* he thought. *I'm gonna drown in my own vomit.* Another fountain spewed, and Brent resigned to his fate. At the same time, he knew that once he got back into his body, he would only have time to do one thing – the only thing that was going to save him.

His mouth hung open, filled to his front teeth with chunky, brown fluid. A bubble escaped from his throat and then another, and he gagged. Brent expected something dramatic to happen – sparks, or trumpets, or something that would give him a clue as to when it was time to get back inside.

But that wasn't the way it happened. One second later, he instantly snapped back into his body and it was every bit as painful as he had imagined it would be. His head felt like it weighed five hundred pounds. *And the throbbing!* The pain was far beyond any hangover he'd ever had. Hangovers were nothing compared to what he was feeling now.

Somewhere in the haze and the aching pain, he remembered where he was and what was going to happen if he didn't do something soon. His body didn't want to obey at first. It was as though it knew that it was dying and that he wasn't supposed to be in there at all. But his will not to return to that awful place was stronger than his body's willingness to send him there. One final try was all he had left in him, and he threw everything he had into it. His body rolled over onto its side, and the vomit poured out onto the bedspread. He coughed and spat out the rest just before passing out again.

CHAPTER THIRTEEN

-1-

About eleven o'clock that night, Brig awoke to the sound of someone knocking on the front door. He got out of bed, wearing a T-shirt and boxer shorts. Through one of the front door's sidelight windows, he saw John standing on the front porch amid the shadows of a dozen insects fluttering around the front porch light, spectral wings dancing in a sort of chaotic ballet.

The door was opened, and John stepped inside. A few of the bugs entered with him. Brig rubbed his eyes and asked, "What's going on?"

"I told you I'd be back," John said.

Brig nodded his head. "Right, right, the ritual." He motioned toward the bedroom door and said, "Let me go get them. They're still asleep."

John held up his hand: "No need to wake anyone, just yet. I have to get some things together before we can do this. Best let them sleep. I just wanted to let you know that I was here and that I hadn't forgotten."

"Do you want me to come with you?" Brig asked.

"No, that won't be necessary. I do need some tools though – an axe, a hatchet... something like that. Do you have one I could use?"

Brig didn't think to ask why John needed an axe. He was too tired to care. Moreover, John seemed to be in a bit of a rush. "Yeah, of course," he said. "Dad kept tools like that in the barn you passed on your way up here. You should be able to find what you need."

"Great, I'm sure I will. Go back to sleep and I'll come get you when I have everything ready."

Brig's intended to do that very thing as he shut the door. The entire conversation lasted less than five minutes, well short of the time necessary for Brig to break free of sleep's grasp. He stumbled back into the bedroom and flopped onto the mattress. In less than ten seconds, he was out again.

John pulled up to the barn and killed his truck's engine. He walked in front of the bright headlamps, and they painted a large silhouette on the barn's double doors. His shadow's legs were long and spindly, his arms the same. As he walked through the field, his footsteps caused small creatures in the grass to scurry away, but John paid them no mind. From a nearby tree, an owl hooted before taking flight.

He went into the barn and scanned the space which had been illuminated by his headlight beams. Inside was a tractor and an unhitched wagon, but nothing he needed, so he switched his flashlight on and searched the rest of the barn which was still shrouded in darkness. In a far corner, he saw the retinal reflections of a dozen prying rat eyes just before they disappeared beneath the barn walls with typical rat-like urgency. In the rafters above, he heard the sound of flight – a bird, or maybe a bat.

John found the tools he was looking for, and turned to leave. The beam of his flashlight revealed a couple of wooden crates beside the entrance. He went over to them to get a second look, and a smile crept onto his face.

"What's *this?*"

He ran his hand across the top of the crate where 'DYNAMITE' was written in large letters enclosed inside a rectangular border. Below that it read: 'DANGER! HIGHLY EXPLOSIVE!' A penchant of affection glistened in his eyes as his fingers traced the letters. "Well, hello, beautiful," he said. "It's been a long time."

John grabbed one of the crates and put it in the truck bed, hiding it beneath a tarp on top of which he placed a spare tire. He put the tools in the back as well. Before climbing back into the cab, he patted the crate and laughed a mischievous laugh.

Perfect, he thought, *Perfect*.

The truck's engine roared to life, the sound of which was amplified as it bounced off the side of the barn. The transmission engaged with a metallic *click*, and John drove forward. His red taillights pitched and rocked across the field, eventually vanishing into a low valley like a ship overtaken by the waves of a black sea.

-2-

Four hours later, at three in the morning, John knocked on the front door again. The same heavy-eyed Brig who had opened the door the first time greeted him again.

"You just left," he said.

John laughed, "That was four hours ago! I found what I needed. I'm ready when you are." He checked his watch. "I hate to rush you, but we don't have much time. We really do need to get going."

Brig groaned as he turned towards the bedroom. "Just warning you – the girls aren't gonna be chipper."

John replied, "I'd be surprised if they were."

Brig disappeared through the bedroom door and emerged a few minutes later wearing a pair of sweat pants and sandals. Kaitlyn was still dressed in her white pajamas; her long, blonde hair hung haphazardly about her face and was flattened on one side. Erin didn't look much better, but out of the three of them, she was the only one who was fully dressed.

Brig, now fully awake, apologized to John and invited him inside. The small group exchanged idle chitchat while Erin struggled to slip a pair of purple tennis shoes onto Kaitlyn's feet.

The little girl craned her neck and cried out, "Hi, John!"

John stopped what he was doing and went to muss up her hair. "How ya doin', little one?"

"We slept a long time," she told him. "Mommy says we were just being lazy."

"Well, I guess you all were pretty tired then, huh?"

Kaitlyn nodded to which she added, "Bushed!"

Erin patted Kaitlyn on the leg and said, "Okay, sweetie, you're ready to go." The little girl hopped down and hurried to give John a hug, one he willingly returned.

He straightened back up, and saw Brig eyeing the duffle bag he held in his hand. John set the bag down and unzipped it. From deep inside, he removed three small pouches - each of which were attached to long, thin strips of leather and identical to the one he wore around his own neck.

John handed one to each of them and said, "These are medicine bags. You wear them around your neck. Go ahead, put them on." They all did as they were told and a round of laughter erupted when they saw that Kaitlyn's hung down to her knees. John's chuckled and said, "I guess I should have thought about that when I made these." He took a small knife from his hip pocket and cut the leather strip, reaffixing it such that it hung properly.

"What are these for?" Brig asked, twisting the pouch back and forth between his fingers.

John said, "These are your first line of defense."

Erin fumbled with her own and asked, "What's in them?"

"Cedar wood. Tradition holds that the wood of the cedar tree contains powerful protective spirits. The wood is also placed above the entrances to the house, and the needles are burned to protect against the entry of evil spirits. We'll need to nail some wood above each of your doors when we get back."

Brig tried to lighten the mood and said, "Hell, you can hang a whole tree over the door if you think it'd help!"

"This is serious," John said. "Please don't take it lightly."

Brig apologized, but John waved off it off as unnecessary and bent over to grab the duffle bag. "Well, are you guys ready?" They all confirmed they were, each in their own way, and the four of them stepped outside. A question was heavy on Brig's mind and it had been haunting him since the night before in the fog. "Why was it so important to do this tonight?" He asked.

"Aside from the obvious?" John asked, not expecting a response. "Everything is taking place according to an ancient timetable. Certain rituals are performed at certain times. This is true for practically all religions, so I'm sure you're comfortable with the concept."

Brig agreed that he was.

John pointed to the sky and once again, Brig looked upon the moon's crescent shape. It hung like a fingernail in the sky, and it appeared thinner than it had the night before. John continued, "The protection ritual must be performed in the light of the waning moon." He shook the duffle bag and said, "I have everything that we'll need right here."

To Erin, all of this sounded more akin to witchcraft and voodoo – certainly not the kind of thing she had learned growing up sitting in creaking wooden pews each Sunday morning, but ultimately she concluded all religions boiled down to pretty much the same thing: ritual and superstition. It was simply a matter of picking the poison that tasted the sweetest.

John asked Brig to drive them out to the cemetery. Remembering Brig's recounting of the events the night before,

Erin shifted uncomfortably. Kaitlyn picked up on it immediately and did her best to reassure her.

"It's okay, Mommy," she said. "They're the good ones, remember?"

They arrived at the cemetery where a large pile of cedar branches lie beside the headstones. John checked his watch again and said, "Time's short. We need to get started." He knelt down next to a bare patch of dirt and opened his duffle bag. He removed a handful of dried grass on top of which he built a pyramid with a few small twigs and several strips of tree bark.

Brig held out his hand and said, "Wait - you're building a fire?"

John looked up for a moment, but went back to work. "That's right."

Brig objected. "Wait a second. You're building a fire on top of my family's *graves!* That's desecration!"

John was quick to counter. "No, no! Not at all. In fact, this is the farthest you can get from desecration. This is... well... *consecration*. We're calling on the spirits for help. The fire also shares the essence of the Creator, the All-Mystery." Busily checking the bearings on his compass, John drew a line in the dirt with the toe of his boot, and pointed. "East is said to be the direction of triumph. My people believe the red light immediately preceding sunrise is impregnated with miraculous creative power. East is the heading for hope, determination, and life. It is the direction from which comes the life-giving force, which stirs all beings into motion with the coming of the new dawn. The direction is important in a number of religions. I'd explain further, but we really need to hurry."

He picked Kaitlyn up and sat her in the bare patch, facing the direction of the line he'd drawn in the dirt. He knelt down beside the pyramid and repeatedly struck two pieces of flint together until the ball of tinder started to glow. John fed the infant flames, blowing on them until they grew hungrier and hungrier.

Kaitlyn clapped her hands with excitement. John smiled back at her before adding some larger branches to feed the growing flames. With the fire well on its way, he reached into another pouch, this one larger than the medicine bags each of them now wore around their necks and began spreading white powder in a circle around Kaitlyn. He went on to adorn the circle with directional arrows and various shapes.

Finally, he stopped and motioned for Erin and Brig to join Kaitlyn inside the circle, one on either side of her. They did as instructed, sitting with their legs crossed. Again, John reached into his bag of tricks. This time he removed three small canisters of paint – red, blue, and yellow.

He dipped his index finger into the red one first and drew a line down the bridge of each of their noses, his own included, and a horizontal line under each of their eyes. He switched fingers when he switched colors, and this time he drew blue lines under the red ones. Then came the yellow, and it was applied in the same manner as the blue.

Kaitlyn watched with great interest as John added more wood to the fire, which was growing hungrier by the minute. The hot flames drew small beads of sweat from their foreheads. She reached out and took each of her parents' hands as John began speaking in a language that neither Brig nor Erin could understand. The speech graduated into a sort of chant, a chant John decorated with dance and the sound of some kind of rattle.

It's hypnotic, Brig thought. The more he tried to shut it out of his head, the harder it became to do so. Before long, the three of them – Kaitlyn included – fell into a sort of trance. John's voice was the only sound they heard aside from a constant crackle of burning wood.

John raised his hands high into the air. The flames seemed to follow his movements - dozens of forked tongues twisting upon themselves, lapping at the night sky. Brig watched the flames morph into faces just as the fog had done the night before. The faces were everywhere - in the flames, in the shadows, even in the glowing embers. Erin saw them too. She thought she should be afraid, but she wasn't.

John put the rattle down and reached into the larger pouch again. He held his hand out, and in his palm was a mound of the white powder he'd used to make the circle. It scattered when he blew into his hand, and the small, white grains stuck to each of their faces, which were now dripping with sweat.

After a few more minutes of chanting, John knelt and clapped his hands in front of the three sitting on the ground - one clap for each - and just like that, they all snapped back from wherever they had been, now relaxed... much too relaxed to move, or even speak. Erin's sat silent, staring into the eastern sky where she saw the first indications of dawn - red fingers of light creeping over the hills. She remembered what John had told them, and it *was* spiritual - there was something profound and pure about the first light. It struck her at such a basic level that she started to cry.

John reached for a bucket and poured water over the coals. White steam swirled skyward, and the ever-present roar of flame was replaced with a sizzling hiss. Turning back to them, he said, "The ritual is complete," he said. "The rest is up to us."

-3-

Back at the house, John nailed a strip of cedar wood atop the doorframe of each window and exterior entrance to the house. Brig approached him when he had finished and asked, "What now?"

"Now," John replied, "we wait."

"For what?"

"For the right time. The ritual we performed this morning will cloud Malocere's vision, just as I told you it would. He won't be able to find Kaitlyn until we *want* him to find her."

"Wait one goddamned minute!" Brig shouted. "You plan on using my daughter as bait?!"

John rubbed his face and said, "I really hate when you characterize things that way. We're not using her as bait. You have to understand that Malocere is out of that cave for one purpose and one purpose alone – to get your daughter! She is the only one who can send him back where he belongs, and believe you me, he *does not* want to go back."

John continued, "So long as he doesn't know where she is, she's safe. I told you that all of this is taking place according to a timetable. We have to wait for the right time. Our strike must be swift. It must be precise, and it must be devastating."

"Is she going to be alright?" Brig asked. It was one of those questions that slips past the lips without you even realizing it. In his heart he knew John couldn't give him guarantees, but he was in real need of reassurance.

"I would give my own life before I let anything happen to that little girl," John assured him. "But I can't make you any promises. What we have done tonight will greatly anger Malocere and his forces."

"Malocere's forces? I thought you said that he was the only one."

"Ah, yes, but there are spirits everywhere. Malocere is one of those who was banished to The Lower Afterworld long ago. He was supposed to remain there for all time for the very reason we seek to send him back – his only purpose for being in the physical world is to tear it apart. As for his forces - you call them spirits, so that's the term I have been using. My people call them *Invisible Agents* – they come in two forms – The Dark and The Light. They roam the Earth, unnoticed for the most part, but when called into duty, they are savage warriors. Tonight, we called to the Agents of the Light. They will protect Kaitlyn as I have said, but with our forces mobilized, Malocere will be forced to do the same." John pounded his fist into his palm and said, "Then the Battle will begin."

Kaitlyn burst through the front door and ran out to meet Brig and John on the porch. John scooped her up and sat her on his lap. She presented him with a picture she'd drawn of the two of them. He studied it, and as he did, he felt the child trying to get inside his head to read his thoughts. A look of surprise crossed her face when he spoke up in her head: [I know what you're trying to do, little one. *Don't try*.]

Her little face drew up with frustration, causing her nose to crinkle at the bridge. She said, [I didn't know *you* knew how to talk like this, too!]

[There are a great many things you don't know,] he said.

[You're hiding something. I can tell. *Let me see it!*] Her thought projection was akin to the ranting demands of a spoiled child.

John was patient with her, though. [I'm afraid I can't tell you everything, little one. You have to trust me.]

Kaitlyn didn't like that answer at all, but after another unsuccessful attempt at cracking the barrier John had erected inside his mind, she resigned to accept it. She wiggled off of his lap and went back inside without saying another word. John turned to Brig and asked, "Do you have any more questions before I go?" Brig thought about the term John had used before – 'The Lower Afterworld' – and decided to ask him to explain.

"It's kind of complicated," John said. "But I'll do my best. The Lower Afterworld is simply another Realm – The Lowest Realm. I'm afraid that too much emphasis has been placed on the belief that when we die, we go somewhere else. The Afterworlds are every bit as real as this one. They exist around us every minute of every day, only in different dimensions. There are three Realities: the one you and I are in right now, The Upper-Afterworld and The Lower-Afterworld. Our Reality lies in the middle. When a person dies, their energy is predisposed to either The Upper or The Lower."

Brig spoke up. "Heaven and Hell."

John shook his head. "I don't mean to sound insulting, but those are really rather elementary labels to assign to the Realities. The greater picture is much too large to fit into such crisp categories. The individual Realms are best described as areas of energy concentration, positive or negative. When people die, they can choose to go to their respective area of concentration, but most do not."

"Why?"

"Well, they're confused. Just as the spirit that contacted your daughter was confused. You see, spirits are not infallible. They can make bad decisions, too. Most are unwilling to abandon the lives they have led on Earth, so they choose to stay. Then there are others who fall victim to the pull of lies and wander through the Gate leading to The Borderlands. It's not a Reality of its own, but a trap that sucks the unfortunate into a realm of horror.

Brig interrupted to say, "The ones that stay here... are they the 'Agents' you spoke about earlier? Are they the ones I saw in the fog? In the fire?"

John's face lit up. "That's right!" He said. "Now you're catching on."

"And what about the Gate? What is it, a door or something?"

"Ah, yes," John sighed. "The Gate. Not really a door, more of an elevator. It's like I was saying before – The Afterworlds exist all around us, one on top of the other. It's not like they're millions of miles away. They're here. Right now. The Gate allows the agents to move between the realities – higher or lower. Believe it or not, it really is that simple."

Brig remembered his conversation with Kaitlyn that night in the field. She said they had needed to *'jump.' Was that possible? Could a human being actually move between realms? And was that what she had done?* He remembered feeling her presence move about him and through him. He asked John if that's what had happened – that she had simply moved into another dimension and the two of them were occupying the same space.

John confirmed that it was possible, "but only for very brief periods of time," he added. "The presence of a physical entity in a spiritual realm causes a sort of reaction, which threatens to tear apart the realm the person is in. It's similar to the way the human body rejects an organ transplant if the organ isn't the right type. If a positive entity is in a realm of concentrated negative energy, the realm will repel it."

"But if we close the Gate," Brig asked, "won't we be sealing off those other realms? All of the spirits will be trapped here, won't they?"

John shook his head. "No, no. But I like the way you're thinking. We're getting somewhere now. The Gate we seek to close is one that has existed from the beginning – it's a part of the very framework of the universe. You know the rest - it's how

Malocere escaped from the Lower Afterworld, and it's how his minions move about. This town has a dark history, Brig and it can all be traced to the forces moving in and out of that cave."

"So how many Gates are there?"

"Many more, and just like the one in the cave, they are all part of the natural framework of the universe – part of what you might call The Divine Plan. The Agents are typically the only ones who can freely move between The Realms, but somehow Malocere managed to get through."

John continued, "The important thing to remember is that once Malocere is sucked into The Lower Afterworld, he cannot escape. He and his ilk are bound there unless they are set free, and only a Keeper can do that. So right now, even if we send him back – *if Kaitlyn sends him back* - but we fail to destroy that Gate, he can easily find his way back"

"But Malocere isn't stupid. No strategy we come up with, regardless of how ingenious and crafty it might be, will get him to step back through on his own. Because once he does, he knows the Gate can be destroyed."

"So what do we do?" Brig asked.

"I can't tell you." It was the first time John had purposefully withheld information, and it caught Brig off guard. John tried to explain. "If I were to tell you everything you want to know, the risk that the Agents of the Dark might read your thoughts and thwart the plan is too great. I can't take that chance."

"What's keeping them from reading *your* mind?" Brig asked with a resentful tone that was as transparent as it was impolite.

John leaned forward and Brig did the same. "I know how to keep things from them," he said. "That's all I'm going to tell you."

Brig leaned back in his chair and said, "So we're operating on a need-to-know basis, I guess."

"You could say that," John agreed. "But you have my word that I won't let you down. All I ask is that you trust me and do what I tell you to."

Brig wondered what would have happened if he had not contacted John at all. *What if he had never picked that slip of paper off of his father's hospital room floor? What if he had never made the phone call? What then?* He put these questions to John and waited for the answers.

John crossed his arms over his chest and said, "You didn't have a choice."

Brig had been willing to go along with John's dogma concerning The Afterworlds, but he wasn't so willing to accept the concept of predestination. The idea that his actions were somehow planned out for him, and that he lacked free will didn't sit well with him. *And if that's the case*, he wondered, *why all the pomp and circumstance? Won't things just work themselves out? If everything is predestined, we're powerless to change it!*

Unbeknownst to Brig, John heard his thoughts. Not waiting for Brig to speak, he said, "I'm not saying that you were *forced* to pick up that slip of paper. I'm saying that if you *hadn't*, the Agents of the Light would have found another way to get through to you. That's all."

Brig was more willing to accept that explanation. "Are my parents, my brother, included in with these 'Agents'?" He asked.

"Yes, they are."

Erin stepped out onto the porch and said, "Brig, Harv just called. He isn't feeling 'up to snuff' today, so he won't be coming by to work on those tree stumps with you." Brig had forgotten about the chore, but he was relieved nonetheless. He thanked her and she offered to make them both some breakfast, but John declined.

"I have some things I need to take care of," he said. "I really should get going. I appreciate the offer, though." He assured Brig he would be back in touch and reminded them both to keep the medicine bags around their necks at all times. He got into his truck and drove off with the crate of dynamite still hidden deep in the truck bed. He made a brief stop at his own house and unloaded it into his garage. After that, he headed towards Wicklow, stopping at The Electronics Barn to pick up a couple of cellular telephones and a spool of electrical wire.

Things are starting to come together, he thought. *Yes, things are starting to come together nicely.*

-4-

Brent had begun to emerge from his drug-induced sleep. He drew a deep breath though his nose and smelled something foul – something that smelled like a combination of hot dogs and bile. He lifted his head off the bed slowly and he saw the large puddle of vomit in which he had been lying. In it were several of the tablets he had taken, still intact.

The roof of his mouth was dry and seemed to be coated with paste. It was sticky, and his tongue peeled off of it with the sound of duct tape being pulled off a plastic bag. He ran the tip of his tongue over his front teeth; they were slimy, furry even, and he wondered how long he had been out. The bright shafts of light coming through the mini blinds suggested it had been quite a long while.

He ran to the bathroom where another violent eruption of vomit spilled into the toilet bowl. Countless dry-heaves later, he stood up and made his way to the sink to splash cold water over his face. It was something his mother had always done for him whenever he had gotten sick as a small child. It seemed to help, so he soaked a blue washcloth and held it over his mouth and nose, breathing through it in an attempt to settle his stomach..

All that time, he thought. *And no one checked in on me?*

[Remember...]

Of course not, why would anyone have checked in on me? I'm just a pawn in this game, right? My dad isn't even my dad, anymore. Something else took over – but... In a brief moment of doubt, he questioned whether any of this was actually *possible. Had it all been some sort of drug-induced hallucination? That was the most logical explanation, wasn't it?*

[Remember...]

He remembered hovering in the corner of his room, looking down at his own body. As well as the mangled version of Sammi who had helped him escape from The Borderlands. An image of a dragon flashed in his mind, and he remembered seeing it toss a man's severed torso into the air and gobble it down. Once again, he suffered all the fear of that place – the hopelessness, the anguish, the desolation. It had followed him here.

He held onto the sink in front of him, because it was tangible and tangible was exactly what he needed. He wanted to hold onto something and believe it was real – he no longer knew what was. He hoped The Borderlands were a figment of his imagination, but something inside him – *deep inside him* – assured him it was real and reminded him why he was back and why he was on borrowed time.

Everything came rushing back to him, and he knew what he had to do – just as Sammi had told him he would. No longer burdened with tunnel vision, he saw things clearly for the first time. In the greater scheme of things, his life wasn't really that important at all. Strangely, the realization didn't trouble him.

He reached into the shower stall and turned the water on. He undressed while he waited for it to warm up, and he tried to formulate some sort of plan. His father was most likely at the sheriff's office. Scratch that - what *used* to be his father was most likely at the sheriff's office. He couldn't allow himself to think of this thing as his father. If he did that, there would be no way he could go through with what he needed to do.

He stepped into the shower stall and relished the sensation of hot water on his face. He remembered how the acid rain had felt on his skin - the stinging, the burning, and the inability to escape from it. In The Borderlands, there was no cover, no shade, no isle of refuge. But Sammi had pointed to another place and told him it was Hell. He didn't dare imagine the horrors on the other side of that mountain.

He recalled the screams of the people thrashing about in the acid sea. The looks on their faces were clear in his mind. He tried to shake the images away, but they had become a part of him. He found himself unable to drown out the heartrending cries of the forsaken, so he started to sing. He lathered up his body and sang, savoring the sensations of fragile mortality. He wished things could go back to the way there were before when things were simple. But in his heart, he knew those times were gone forever.

CHAPTER FOURTEEN

-1-

Meanwhile, at the sheriff's station, Perry was half-heartedly sifting through a stack of reports the other deputies had filled out regarding the two missing girls. It was boring him, because he knew where they were – at least he knew where one of them was; nonetheless, he knew both were dead and that all efforts to find them were futile. This was busy work.

It was around lunchtime when one of the younger deputies on the force, a man by the name of Carl Pritchard, walked into the office and sat down on the corner of Perry's desk. Carl was a fairly tall man – he stood at about six feet and weighed somewhere around two hundred and twenty. He was cocky, like most of the young bucks beginning their careers in law enforcement, but he seemed capable enough and seldom called for backup, so the other deputies respected him.

He sat there on the corner of Perry's desk, smacking his chewing gum not saying a word while he watched Perry work. Perry continued to scribble, hoping his silence would serve as some sort of hint that he had no interest in conversation. After a few minutes, he looked up and asked, "Can I help you with something, Carl?"

The young deputy glanced around the office and asked, "Where's the boss?"

"Hell if I know," Perry said. "I haven't seen him all day. Why?"

Carl leaned forward and said, "Why don't you tell me what's goin' on?"

"What do you mean?"

Carl laughed and wiped his nose. "I think you know what I mean. We've been searching for these girls for two days now and have barely found a trace. We found one of their cars next to the boss' property, but that's the last any of us have heard about it."

Perry's neck muscles tensed up. He set his pen down and asked, "What are you insinuating?"

Carl held up his hands. "I'm not insinuating anything. No sir. Not me. Just seems a little fishy, that's all I'm sayin'."

"Fishy?"

"Yeah, you know..."

"No, I don't think I do. Explain it to me."

Carl looked around again, making sure no one was there to hear what he was saying. When he was confident of that, he continued. "The Pridmore girl."

"What about her?"

"Well, we know the boss' boy was dating her, right?"

"Yeah," Perry agreed, "but we've already covered that angle."

Carl scratched his nose. "I know you have. I know you have, but don't you think we might be taking the boss' word as gospel just a little too readily?"

Perry stood up, causing the wooden chair to roll back against the air conditioning unit behind him. It hit with a loud *clank*. "You had better watch your mouth," Perry warned. "You go bringing the sheriff into this and there'll be hell to pay – you know that."

Carl stood up and leaned forward on the desk, supporting his weight on extended fingers. "Okay, okay, Perry. Don't get all ruffled up about this. I just wanted to see what you thought, that's all." He adjusted his gun belt and scratched his nose again. He picked up a silver letter opener from Perry's desk and tapped it on the stack of reports in front of him twice before throwing it down. "You go on back to what you were doing, and let's just forget I said anything, okay?"

Perry nodded and went back to pretending he was doing something important. Carl walked out of one of the double doors just as Malocere entered through the other one. Carl tipped his hat, and the thing in the sheriff's uniform nodded in return. Once on the other side of the door, Carl turned back to face Perry and made the "zip your lip" motion with his thumb and index finger. Perry pretended not to notice. He put on an artificial smile and said, "Mornin,' boss."

Malocere waved, but said nothing. Perry got up and followed him into the office. Malocere looked at him through the dark pair of sunglasses he wore and asked, "Something I can do for you, Perry?"

The deputy pointed to a chair in front of the desk, asking for permission to sit. Malocere motioned for him to do so. The deputy cleared his throat and said, "Sir, I think we may have a problem."

"Really? What might that be?"

"The other guys, sir. I think they're beginning to suspect we're up to something."

"Up to something?"

"Yeah, you know, with the girls." Perry went on to recount the conversation he and Carl had shared minutes before. Malocere leaned back in his leather chair and scratched his chin, which was covered in coarse, black stubble. "I'll handle it," he said. "When Carl gets back into the office, bring him in to see me. We'll get this straightened out today. The longer we wait, the more people he's going to talk to and the rumor's just going to spread. Best to stamp it out now."

Perry laughed to himself when he thought about the tongue-lashing Carl was in for. The humor quickly faded when Malocere asked, "Do you keep a clean uniform here at the office?"

"Do I what?"

"You'll want to make sure you have a clean uniform on hand."

"Yes, sir." Perry closed the office door unintentionally hard. Its aluminum mini-blinds rattled against the glass. *Why would I need a clean uniform*, he wondered. *What the hell is he going to do?*

-2-

Brent stepped out of the shower stall and dried himself. His head still felt foggy, which made thinking difficult. It seemed as though the tinnitus in his ears had quieted down, but when the air conditioner kicked off, the sound was back again, every bit as loud as before.

Inside his room, he tossed the wet towel onto the floor. He reached into his closet and removed an old football jersey that he'd worn to most of the varsity pep rallies his junior year. He put it on over a white T-shirt. He wondered how everything was going to play out. It wasn't going to be pretty – that much he was sure of.

He snatched his suicide note from the printer tray and tore it into several pieces. The smell of hot dogs and bile still hung in the air like a bad memory. He stuffed the shredded remains of his last words into the hip pocket of his jeans and headed downstairs and away from the detestable stench.

-3-

John crouched in a dark corner of his basement, surrounded by cardboard boxes full of various things. He'd bellied-up to a small, folding table cluttered with screwdrivers and a hundred other odds and ends he'd managed to collect over the years. Perched over his right shoulder was a flexible lamp – the kind with an adjustable neck about three feet long. It provided all the light he needed for his current project, which consisted of two disassembled cellular telephones and the spool of electrical wire he had bought earlier that morning.

Affixed to the gray, cinder block wall in front of him was a map of Jones Chapel – two maps as a matter-of-fact. One was the most recent edition by the good folks at Rand McNally, the other was an older map – *much older* by the looks of it – the only things on it were a few winding dirt roads, a small settlement area, and vast expanses of pastureland and forest. Barely decipherable was a date written in the lower left corner, which read: 1865.

John was taking special care with his new project, moving this wire here and that wire there. All the while, humming to himself. After soldering a yellow wire to one of the cellular circuit boards, he began to softly sing out loud, keeping the rhythm by beating the eraser of his pencil against the side of his head.

On the floor beside him was the crate of dynamite he'd taken from Brig's tobacco barn the night before. He tapped his foot on the side of the box and made a long, drawn-out *'boom'* noise. He got out of his chair and walked over to a shelf from which he removed a roll of electrical tape. Still bobbing his head to the beat of the song, he moved back to the table and picked up a red marker. He drew a large circle around a corresponding spot on the two maps in front of him and then drew an 'X' through each of them. He sat back down and got back to work, singing as he did. It would be later that evening before the project was finished. Taped to the wall above the maps was an old news article which had yellowed with age. In the center of the clipping was a small, grainy picture of a young man dressed in camouflaged Army fatigues. The headline read:

LOCAL MAN AWARDED THE SILVER STAR FOR BRAVERY IN THE JUNGLES OF VIETNAM

The caption beneath the picture read: John Blackwind – Demolitions Expert, United States Army.

-4-

Brent climbed inside his Mustang, which smelled of pine cleaner, carpet shampoo, and ammonia. He was on his way to meet a friend of his who lived on the other side of the county line, some ten miles away. He rolled the windows down and opened the sunroof, hoping to rid the car of the stench filling the interior.

He flipped on the radio; *November Rain* was playing. The song brought back memories, and he felt a sinking in his chest when he thought of the trip he and Sammi had taken to the lake only weeks ago. The song had been playing then. He looked into the passenger's seat and saw Sammi there. Her skin was the pale white of death, and the stench was nauseating. He tried to tell himself she was a product of his imagination, but after all that had happened to him, he couldn't be sure.

He tried not to look at her gaping head wound, but was unable to resist the urge to do so. Her skull cavity was dark inside, and he thought he might scream when she started to bob her head to Slash's guitar solo, and the yellow glob of brain popped out of the side.

It's all in my mind, he told himself. *That's all it is – just my imagination. When I look back over there, she'll be gone.*

He looked back, but she was still there. As she leaned in towards him, he pressed himself against the driver's door. Her blonde hair hung in sparse strands, exposing flakes of white scalp. Her purple lips parted, and she tried to speak to him, but all that came out was a gurgling sound.

She reached for him, and he saw open sores all over her arm that looked like bite marks. He wondered what had been feeding on her back in The Borderlands. He hadn't been there long enough to learn what nightmares the place held.

The sight was ghastly enough, but more horrific was what she cradled in her other arm – a baby – *HIS* baby. Still attached to its stomach was its umbilical cord, which wound its way down, disappearing beneath the waistline of Sammi's jeans. The infant's body was the same purple color as its mother's lips; its arms were about two centimeters long, and its head was the size of a grape.

It's not possible, he told himself. *It's just not possible!*

Sammi's voice spoke up in his head. [*Anything* is possible...]

She put her lips next to his ear, and her voice was as seductive as it was dead. "Brent..."

He shouted, "*NO!!!!*" and swerved his car into the oncoming lane, missing a SUV by a matter of inches. To his relief, when he looked over to the passenger's seat again, Sammi was gone. *She's trying to rush me,* he thought. *I'm hurrying, Sammi. I'm going as fast as I can. Just give me time – PLEASE!*

-5-

It was around four in the afternoon when Carl came back into the office to fill out his end of shift reports. Perry gave him a look that said: '*Oh, brother – you've done it now,*' but if Carl recognized it for what it was, he didn't say anything. The three of them, Malocere included, were the only ones in the office right then. The second shift wouldn't arrive for about another hour.

Carl walked over to his desk, unbuckled his gun belt, and set it beside his computer keyboard. After a few minutes, Perry walked over there. Carl asked, "What's going on, my man?"

"Oh, you know," Perry said, stalling for time. "This and that. How was your shift? Did you find anything?"

Carl sat down in his chair and faced his computer monitor. He spoke to his fellow deputy without looking at him directly. "Hell no. It's like I told you – the trail's gone cold. We're not gonna find anything."

"They have to be somewhere."

"Oh, yeah," Carl agreed. "They're out there somewhere, but no one in this office is gonna find 'em. I can promise you that. I can tell ya what's gonna happen. About a year from now, some hunter or some group of kids will be out dicking around in the woods and stumble over their bodies. The funny thing will be that they'll be lying ten feet to the side of some road we will have checked a hundred and fifty times by then. *I guaran-fuckin'-tee it.*"

"Glad to see you're holding out hope," Perry said with a scoff.

"I'm just being realistic." A few clicks of his mouse, and Carl was on his way to wrapping up his shift. Perry jerked his head in the direction of the sheriff's office door and said, "Boss wanted me to send you into his office when you made it back."

Carl's eyes grew wide, and he asked, "You didn't tell him what I said, *did you?*"

"Of course not!" Perry replied. "You think I'm crazy?"

Carl relaxed and exhaled a deep breath he'd been holding. "Good," he said. "I knew I could count on you." He patted Perry on the knee and stood up. "Is he in there now?"

"As far as I know. I haven't seen him leave since he came in this morning."

Carl bent over his desk and finished typing the sentence he'd been working on. He palmed the mouse and selected 'print.' After straightening up, he brushed his hair back with his left hand. "Well," he said, "let's go see what this is all about."

Perry walked over to the sheriff's door and knocked twice. A somewhat disinterested voice rose from the other side and said, "Yes?"

The deputy opened the door and leaned in. "Boss, Carl is here. You said you wanted to see him?"

Malocere was still wearing his sunglasses, and from what Perry could see, it didn't look as though the piles of paper on the sheriff's desk had moved at all. A cigarette was burning in a large, red ashtray on the corner of the desk, which was practically overflowing with spent butts. Malocere motioned for the two of them to come inside. He held out a pack of cigarettes and offered one to each of the deputies. Both declined.

"So, what can I do for you, boss?" Carl asked.

Malocere leaned back and asked, "How's the investigation going?"

"It's not. It's like I told Perry," Carl explained, "the trail's gone cold. We're not going to find anything."

Malocere leaned forward as he pushed the sunglasses further up the bridge of his nose. He picked the cigarette out of the ashtray and took a short drag. "No suspects?" He asked. "No leads? Surely you guys have *something* to go on by now. It's been two days. We have some worried parents out there!" Malocere wormed into Carl's head, his unseen eyes hidden and glowing beneath the dark shades, and asked a question telepathically: [You think I did it, don't you?]

Carl jerked his head to the side, searching for the source of the voice he'd heard. His face flushed, and Malocere could see the deputy getting nervous. *The weak-minded are so easy to control.*

[*Admit it!* You think I killed those girls, don't you?]

Carl sat straight up in his chair and shouted, "NO!" Perry scooted away with surprise. Malocere leaned back in the chair and took another drag off the cigarette before flicking an inch of ash into the tray.

"No?" He asked. "No, what?"

Carl looked around, positive someone else was in the room – there wasn't anyone. He looked back at what he thought was the sheriff and saw his own reflection in the sunglasses. *Why the hell is he wearing those things?* His mind demanded. *We're* indoors *for Christ's sake!*

Malocere looked over to Perry and said, [You see that hunting knife on my desk? Pick it up.]

Now, Perry was searching for the voice.

[Pick it up, Perry!] Malocere shouted. [*Pick it up!*] Confused, but unable to disobey, Perry did as he was told. Malocere turned his attention back to the younger of the two deputies. "You want me to tell you a little secret?" He hissed just before crushing out what remained of the cigarette. "Do you *really* want to know?"

Carl was scared, and he didn't like the sheriff's tone. What's more, he'd heard enough rumors about the man to know he didn't want to be let in on any of his "little secrets."

Malocere removed his sunglasses, and both Perry and Carl looked upon the same black cavities Sarah had seen moments before her death. The balls of light floating inside them were red this time, but for all their brilliance, the black void around them remained.

"The first girl begged for her life," Malocere said. "You should have heard her cry. The second one... well, she didn't have time to scream." Malocere turned to Perry again. [*Kill him,*] he commanded. [Drive the knife into his goddamned throat and give it a twist.]

Carl stood up before he realized he had done so. It was as though every part of him wanted out of that office as fast as possible, but his legs felt heavy and didn't move. He couldn't have made it out anyway; Perry had positioned himself in front of the door, blocking the only escape route. The older deputy approached Carl, who slowly backed away.

"Perry?" He said. "Perry, c'mon. What are you doing?"

The fact was that Perry had no idea what he was doing. All he knew was that he wanted to bury the knife into Carl's throat more than he had ever wanted to do anything in his life. He raised the blade high above his head and started to laugh.

Malocere watched with amusement from the other side of the desk, continually feeding his accomplice's mind with thought projections of encouragement: [Do it, Perry! Kill him! Obedience will be rewarded in this life and the next.]

Perry lunged, knocking Carl to the floor. The two struggled, but the older deputy won the advantage and sank the six-inch blade into Carl's throat, slicing his carotid artery in two. Just as his boss had told him to, Perry gave the knife a twist and pulled it out again – the blade made a strained slurping sound on its way out.

Through no will of his own, Perry continued to raise the knife and drive it back into Carl's chest until he had inflicted thirty-four stab wounds. When he was finished, Perry stood up and grimaced at the sound of his shoes moving across the floor, which was tacky with the stickiness of clotting blood.

Malocere put the sunglasses back on and lit another cigarette. He walked around to the other side of the desk, careful to avoid the expanding puddle of blood, and patted Perry on the shoulder. "Good job," he said as he checked the watch on his wrist. "The next shift will be coming in soon. Make sure this gets cleaned up." He turned back to Perry and said, "I hope you brought that clean uniform I told you about." The comment was accompanied by a malicious smile Perry didn't care for at all.

"What do I do with the body?" He asked.

"I don't care. Stuff it in a trash bag and hide it in my closet. We'll take care of it later. The body won't start to stink for a while. Just make sure this blood gets cleaned up. It'll be a bitch once it dries."

-6-

Brig and Erin were busy getting ready for dinner that night. After everything that had happened, they'd decided that a night out might be a nice change of pace. Kaitlyn had fallen asleep on the living room couch while she waited for her parents. Brig had promised her a hamburger and crinkle-cut French-fries if she was good, knowing full well that his daughter wouldn't do anything that might cause her to miss out on those.

As Brig stood in front of the bathroom mirror shaving, he caught sight of the reflection of Erin's body in the shower behind him. He put the razor down and watched her lather up her hair and rinse the suds away. The silhouetted shape of her body was enough to excite him. It was the first time he'd been turned on since all of this craziness had started, and with Kaitlyn sleeping in bed with them each night, there had been very little opportunity for horse play. The moment just felt right. He finished shaving and washed the remaining foam off of his face before quietly locking the bathroom door.

He opened the shower door and stepped into the stall. Erin's voice echoed off the tile walls: "Hey! What's the big idea?" She asked, laughing. "I don't believe I said you could come in here!"

He made a *shushing* sound with his lips and planted them on hers. The smell of the shampoo in Erin's hair mingled with the steam making the balmy air aromatic. Brig's hands worked their way down along the curves of her body, finally coming to rest on her hips. He drew his lips away from hers and kissed her neck.

She asked, "What about Kaitlyn?"

"Don't worry," Brig said. "The door's locked. Besides, I promised her crinkle-cut French-fries – she won't budge from the couch."

Erin popped him on the shoulder. "You should be ashamed," she said. *"Bribing our daughter!"*

Brig grabbed the backs of her thighs and lifted her off of the floor with her back pressed against the wall. She liked the way his arm muscles tensed whenever he held her like this. She wrapped her legs and arms around him and pulled him closer. It was spontaneous, passionate, and a welcomed diversion from all that had consumed their minds in recent days.

When it was over, the two of them finished getting ready, exchanging playful looks in the mirror as they did. Erin turned to him and asked, "You dyed your hair didn't you?"

He blushed, but admitted that he had. "John laughed at me," he said. "I was waiting to see if you'd notice."

She ran her fingers through his hair and said, "I like it. Makes me feel like I'm having an affair with a younger man!"

Brig laughed and pushed her back. "Stop it."

"No, really! I can pretend you're my little boy toy! I'll teach you to clean the pool and we can make love next to the cabana bar!" The comment made both of them laugh – something that felt good to do again.

More playful glances in the mirror and Brig thought this was the way things were supposed to be. Something between them had just gotten screwed up along the way. They exchanged another kiss and went into the living room where Kaitlyn was still sound asleep on the sofa. Erin gently shook her to wake her up.

Kaitlyn rubbed her eyes and asked, "Time to go?" Brig nodded, and the little girl sprung to life almost immediately. "Have I been good?" she asked. "Do I get my hamburger?"

"And crinkle-cut fries," Brig added. Kaitlyn shook her little fist in the air and let out a triumphant cheer as the three of them walked out of the house.

On the way to the restaurant, Brig's Explorer crossed through the main intersection of town as the squad car driven by Malocere passed them in the oncoming lane. The medicine bag tucked beneath his shirt surged with heat, causing him to wince. He assumed Erin had felt it too, because she was frantically fumbling with her blouse.

"Did you feel that?" he asked.

"Yeah, what was it?"

"Beats the hell out of me. John said the only thing in there was cedar bark, right?"

Further up the road, the steakhouse came into view. Brig pulled into the parking lot, and the three of them got out and walked towards the entrance. Kaitlyn held her mother's hand and skipped playfully alongside her.

Once inside, the hostess seated them in a corner booth within eyeshot of the bar. The restaurant was dimly lit – each table was illuminated by a small oil lantern. Brig paid little attention to the ambiance. His eyes kept drifting to the bar, which was bathed in red, neon light from a Budweiser sign hanging above it. A beer sounded so much better than the Coca-Cola the waitress had sat in front of him, but this was a family night, so he brushed away the urge.

Very little time passed before Erin was forced to move the lantern out of Kaitlyn's reach, having told her several times not to try to light the straw wrapper on fire. The hostess reappeared with an activity placemat and a box of crayons, which succeeded in keeping the little girl occupied.

While their daughter colored, Brig and Erin perused the menu. Erin focused on the main courses, but Brig was more interested in the appetizers. When the waitress finally came back by, Brig told her that the three of them wanted to start off with a plate of mozzarella sticks. Kaitlyn wrinkled her nose, but Brig knew that when she saw it was a dish served fried, she'd take to it immediately.

The next hour proceeded pleasantly, with a great deal of casual conversation between the three of them - the kind of conversation Brig had always envisioned a "normal" family as having on such outings. Nothing was mentioned of spirits, of dreams, or of any of the other things that had so consumed their lives over the past few weeks.

It was a welcomed change.

The food came, and Kaitlyn dove into her hamburger, which came, just as Brig had promised, with a side of crinkle-cut fries. Her parents had ordered steaks, and the aroma was a welcomed departure from the smell of pizza. The three of them were so intent on the meals in front of them, that no one noticed the pair of eyes watching them from beneath the alien glow of red light at the bar. The eyes were hidden beneath a Cincinnati Red's baseball cap, the owner of which continued to hammer down shots of Kentucky bourbon.

Brig and Erin finished their meals, declining the waitress's offer for dessert, but not before requesting a doggie bag as Kaitlyn insisted in taking what was left of her burger home to Buster. Unbeknownst to them, the man in the red baseball cap had paid his bar tab at the same time and was only a few steps behind.

Erin buckled Kaitlyn into the backseat and climbed up front. No sooner had Brig started the engine than the driver's side window shattered inward with explosive force. The cab filled with the sound of screams, and a shower of glass rained inward onto Brig's lap – the result of a blow delivered by an aluminum baseball bat.

A hand reached into the driver's compartment and seized Brig's shirt collar. The person attached to that hand, the man in the red baseball cap, tried to pull Brig out through the window. Brig's shoulder was sliced on the shards of glass that remained, and he reached for the latch to open the door.

He spilled out of the SUV and looked up. Tom stood over him holding the baseball bat he'd used to smash the window high above his head. Brig managed to dodge Tom's downward stroke at his head. The bat hit the asphalt with a hollow *ping,* and Brig scrambled to his feet in time to throw a punch, which landed squarely on his assailant's jaw.

An older couple on their way out of the restaurant witnessed the punch Brig had thrown, and hurried back inside to report the incident. The hostess immediately called 911, and within minutes, the sheriff department's dispatched a couple of cruisers.

These were the times the deputies lived for. Speeding tickets were about the most exciting thing a cop in Jones Chapel could hope for – aside from the occasional and inevitable murder, but those were a relatively infrequent occurrence until recently. What they had here was a full-fledged disturbance of the peace, and the deputies were pumped up, because in such cases, they were allowed to turn on their lights and run full sirens.

Tom and Brig continued to slug it out in the parking lot. Brig managed to get the bat out of Tom's hand and sling it to the side of the highway. After that was done, it was just the two of them – mano y mano – and Brig was as sober as a preacher on Sunday, giving him a decided advantage.

Before long, he had Tom on the ground and was delivering an unmerciful volley of blows to the man's face. Splatters of blood sprayed this way and that as the punches landed one after the other. One well-placed lick succeeded in popping Tom's nose out of joint, eliciting a howl of pain from him as well.

"*Have* MY *ass, will you?*" Brig taunted. "I told you I'd kill you if I ever saw you again you sack of shit!" He grabbed Tom's head and pounded it onto the pavement. "Do you wanna *DIE?* Is that it? I'll fucking KILL YOU!" His rage was intense, and it had drowned out everything except the sounds of his knuckles striking the side of Tom's face. He didn't hear Erin's pleas for him to stop any more than he heard the approaching police sirens.

That was when Tom pulled his gun. From inside the Explorer, Kaitlyn must have seen the glint of light from the barrel, because her face instantly changed from a little girl who had just had crinkle cut fries to something far more terrifying. She screamed out for her father and when she did every window in the SUV exploded outward. The explosion masked the sound of the shot as Tom squeezed the trigger mere feet from Brig's head.

Kaitlyn reacted with amazing speed, stopping the bullet as she had before only this time she melted it in midair. She lifted her arm and the pistol flew from Tom's hand into hers before she sent a tremendous push his way that knocked him into the pickup one parking space away. It looked like Tom stood up, but Erin remembered the coyote, so when she saw him groping for his neck, she knew it was Kaitlyn who had him by the throat and she also knew what would come next.

"Kaitlyn!" She cried out. The little girl's teeth were gritted and her fierce stare directed at Tom with complete concentration.

"Kaitlyn, let him GO!" The little girl blinked and Tom fell to the pavement gasping for air.

The cruisers whipped into the parking lot and screeched to a halt. The deputies jumped out and ran over to the scene of the altercation, separating the two men after Brig had pounced again. Erin tried her best to convince the officers Tom had started the whole thing, but one of the deputies took one look at Tom's face and said:

"Well, it looks like your boyfriend finished it!"

The second deputy threw Brig against the side of the Explorer and pulled his hands behind his back. He fumbled with a pair of handcuffs he hadn't used in quite a while and finally managed to secure them around Brig's wrists. He led his suspect towards the cruiser's rotating red and blue lights.

Erin called out, "Brig!"

He shook his head to tell her to keep quiet. "Go home and wait for me to call!" he shouted. The deputy opened one of the cruiser's back doors and put a hand on the back of his head, shoving him down into the seat.

Meanwhile, the other deputy had managed to cuff Tom, and as he was leading him towards the other cruiser, he taunted him by saying, "Looks like you should have picked on somebody a little closer to your own size, little buddy!" Tom told him to 'fuck off.' The resulting headache would later cause Tom to reevaluate the comment after his head was abruptly pounded into the cruiser's doorframe. The deputy offered a half-hearted apology and shoved him into the backseat.

Meanwhile, Erin was busy trying to calm Kaitlyn down as best she could. The deputy who had put Brig into the back of the cruiser was hounding her for a statement. On his third request, he got what he was looking for, but Erin's statement contained a few more expletives than he was used to.

She recounted the details exactly as she remembered them. The deputy took it all down in a small, vinyl notepad that he had removed from his back pocket. He thanked her and walked back to his cruiser without asking any questions about all of the broken glass lying around the vehicle.

By that time, the other deputy had taken down the statements of several other witnesses and climbed into his own cruiser as well. The two of them tore out of the parking lot as if they had just apprehended Al Capone himself, and everyone standing within earshot of the restaurant heard their tires peel and sirens wail.

Erin hadn't mentioned the pistol. Explaining how it had gotten into her possession would require quite a bit more explanation than was necessary. For now, she tucked the weapon under the passenger seat and headed for home to wait for Brig's call.

CHAPTER FIFTEEN

-1-

The cruisers pulled up to the sheriff's station and screeched to a halt just as they had in the restaurant's parking lot not twenty minutes before. Over the course of the short trip, Brig had replayed the scuffle in his mind, and he smiled to himself despite the trouble he was in. The seriousness ascribed to the situation and the determination with which the deputies went about their work amused him as well.

These guys must be having a pretty slow day.

Both Brig and Tom were escorted into the station where they went through the standard booking procedures, which included fingerprinting, the cataloging of personal items, etc. Brig cooperated, so his processing went fairly quickly. Tom, on the other hand, had passed out in the car, and the deputy who had subdued him fought to obtain a decent set of prints and to hold the drunken bastard up at the same time.

Brig and Tom were placed into individual holding cells about the same time Perry emerged from behind the sheriff's closed office door holding a mop and a bucket.

"What's going on?" one of the deputies asked. "Boss got you on the janitorial staff, now?" The comment won a hearty laugh from the other deputy, but little more than a wary smile from Perry, who was thankful he had remembered to put on that clean uniform.

"Uh, no," he said. "Just had to do a little cleaning up for the boss." He pretended to hold an imaginary glass in his hand and tipped it towards his mouth three or four times. He made a gesture to imply vomiting and said, "Shit all over the place." The other two chuckled, and Perry took the opportunity to change the subject. He pointed toward the holding cells and asked, "What's the story with these guys?"

One of the deputies motioned toward the cells with his thumb and said, "Oh, nothin' big. They just decided they were gonna scrap it out in the steak house parking lot."

"Well," the other said, "we need to get back out there. You think you can handle these guys?"

Perry looked over to the cells and saw Tom passed out on his cot and Brig, who was quietly flipping through an issue of Hot Rod Magazine, which had been left by the cell's previous tenant. "Yeah. They don't look like much trouble."

"Alright then, they're all yours!" The two deputies disappeared through the double doors, and Perry watched their taillights fade in the distance. He went into a storage room in the back where he dumped the foul water into a large sink basin. He chased that down with a gallon of bleach, making sure to erase all traces of blood.

He removed the mop head, which he would later take out back, douse with gasoline, and burn. He scrubbed the mop handle with ammonia – it was a little trick the sheriff had taught him a while back. The ammonia destroyed the DNA evidence, making positive identification practically impossible.

Back in the holding area, Brig was standing at the door of his cell, trying to get Perry's attention. "Hey!" he shouted. Perry stuck his head out of the back room, but didn't say anything. "Don't I get a phone call?" Brig asked. "What about bail?"

The deputy walked over to the cell and squinted his eyes. *"I know you,"* he said. "You're the one who came in here a few weeks ago looking for all that paperwork on the Baxley boy."

"Bailey," Brig corrected.

"Yeah, that's it." Perry pulled up a chair and sat down, facing the cell. "The sheriff will be back in a couple of hours. He'll set your bail and you can make your phone call then." The deputy started to laugh, and Brig asked to be let in on the joke. Perry just shook his head and said; "You pissed him off pretty good when you were in here the last time. He won't be goin' easy on you."

Brig sat back down and spoke in a cocky voice. "Don't try and scare me with that shit! I know my rights."

The comment only made Perry's laugh stronger. "That's great!" he said. "The boss *loves* people who know their rights. Be sure and remind him that you pay his salary while you're at it!" He buckled over and laughed until his face was a bright shade of red, almost as though he had lost his mind. Little did Brig know, but on some level, he already had.

-2-

Erin had made it back to the farmhouse not long after she'd pulled out of the steak house parking lot. Due to the shattered windows, she'd pulled the Explorer into the garage to keep the interior from getting wet if it started to rain. Kaitlyn was having a difficult time understanding why the police had taken her father away.

Erin did her best to explain that it had just been a misunderstanding. She didn't know how much of the fight Kaitlyn had seen, and she wondered if the little girl remembered what it was she had done and how she'd done it. It didn't seem that Kaitlyn did, but as she talked with the child, she discovered that she had seen enough to know who her daddy had been fighting.

"Why won't Tom leave us alone?" Kaitlyn asked. "Why won't he just go away?"

Erin didn't know how to answer - in fact, she was wondering the same thing. The whole situation was turning into a sort of a tabloid talk show. She pictured Brig, Tom, and herself on stage bitch-slapping one another and throwing chairs around the room.

Kaitlyn turned to face her, and a in a voice as calm as it was disturbing, she told her mother "*Next time I won't stop.*" Erin knew what she was alluding to, and it frightened her to think what she had witnessed was merely Kaitlyn winding up. Eventually, the child fell asleep.

Erin took her into the bedroom only to return to the living room to wait for Brig's call. After about thirty minutes, she got up and went into the kitchen where she popped one of Brig's Xanax tablets into her mouth. She stood at the sink, holding a small glass of water as she watched the large, orange sun sink below the western horizon. She realized she and Kaitlyn would be alone in the house when nighttime fell. Of course, the term '*alone*' had lost its meaning over the past few weeks. There always seemed to be someone there with them – just out of sight and around the next corner.

Without warning, the icemaker dropped a load of cubes into the tray. Erin jumped, spilling her glass of water down the front of her dress. She was quick to soak up what she could using a dishtowel which lie nearby. She went back into the bedroom to change, careful to be quiet and not wake the child beneath the blankets. When she emerged again, she saw daylight had started to fade. She wandered around the house, room-by-room, flipping on every light switch before sitting down in Brig's recliner to wait.

-3-

An hour later, Tom lifted his head off the pillow for the first time since he'd been thrown into the cell. His headache was bad enough, but his face was also swollen due to the thirty or so punches Brig had planted there. The first thing he saw was the rust-stained toilet bowl three feet away. He rushed over to it, and Brig roared with laughter when Tom's heaved into it.

Once the heaves stopped, Tom lifted his head and wiped his mouth on his shirtsleeve. He looked around and slowly began to realize where he was. Brig watched with a wide smile, because he knew just what Tom was feeling.

All that separated the two cells was a partition of bars, which Tom used to help himself stand up. Brig was seated on his cot, covering his mouth and nose to keep from smelling the thick stench of vomit rising from Tom's toilet bowl. When their eyes met, Brig smiled and said, "Hey there, sunshine! How ya feelin'? How's about a courtesy flush?"

Tom groaned and swayed from side to side, still holding onto the bars for balance. He looked like a caged ape in a zoo, and the sight of him only made Brig laugh harder. The vertigo soon became too much for Tom to handle. He let go of the bars and staggered backwards, eventually collapsing onto his cot in a seated position.

Brig was itching to say something. He had managed to come up with several snide comments to throw Tom's way – *real zingers* as his father would have called them. It was pointless to waste such sharp wit while Tom was drunk, so he decided to wait a while longer. *He has to sober up sooner or later,* Brig thought, unaware of the unconscionable amount of alcohol Tom had consumed. Truth told, sobriety was still several hours away.

-4-

John pulled into his driveway a little past eight o'clock that night. He had taken an insanely irresponsible risk in order to ensure the success of his "Plan B." Luckily, he had succeeded in his mission without incident. Now, safely back home, he hurried inside to change out of his muddy clothes.

Things were coming together just as he'd hoped. The only thing he could foresee endangering their success had to do with the most important element of all – *Kaitlyn*. Truth told, he did have some concerns regarding her age, but he hadn't voiced them. Instead, he prayed she would have the strength – both physical and emotional – to do what needed to be done when that terrible hour was upon her.

He tried his best to rid himself of doubts – such thoughts served no purpose.

He was hungry. It had been over twenty-four hours since he'd eaten. After a hot shower, he got dressed and made his way towards the kitchen. It was then that a familiar feeling overcame him – he knew he wasn't alone. One-by-one, dozens of apparitions appeared, lining the hallway ahead of him. He tried his best not to look at them; they'd always filled him with unease, be they of the Light or of the Darkness, it made no difference. However, on this night, they were thankfully silent. John was pleased they chose not to speak to him. They seldom had anything good to say.

Towards the end of the hall, a woman dressed in a bell-shaped, antebellum gown reached out for him. John twisted his body to avoid her touch, and when he did, he saw red rope burns along the sides of her neck. He had always been able to handle the sight of their physical scars. What bothered him the most were their eyes.

The apparitions watched him through thick, bluish-white membranes. John never knew if they were looking at him or into him. Either way, he didn't like it in the least. Nor did he like the repulsive sensation of their touch. Ever since he was a child, they had sought him out whenever they needed a momentary charge of energy. It made him feel defiled, dirty, and drained.

He pushed past the phantom woman and into the kitchen where he poured himself a tall glass of milk. His ever-present indigestion was in high gear. The chewable antacids had long-since stopped doing the trick. Nowadays, milk was the only thing that helped.

He went into the den with his glass in one hand and a leftover roast beef sandwich in the other. He sat down in a leather wingback chair, propping his feet up on a matching ottoman. His tight back muscles thanked him, and he let out a relieved sigh.

He paid no attention to the elevated level of psychic commotion around him – over the years he had learned to tune it out when he needed to. Instead, he finished his snack and focused on the pseudo-intellectual ramblings of Alex Trebek as the game show host attempted to stump his guests with useless tidbits of knowledge in a sort of pissing contest for the brain.

It wasn't long before the hours spent on his project caught up to him and his eyes grew heavy. Eventually John surrendered his will and allowed sleep to take over. His only hope was that the dreams wouldn't come again. Oh, how he hated the dreams...

About the time Mr. Trebek was announcing a second round of Double Jeopardy – *when the scores can* really *change* – Brent was speeding back towards Jones Chapel. The meeting with his friend across the county line had been brief, but successful. A black, semi-automatic pistol now lay in the passenger's seat with six rounds in the clip and one in the chamber. Another clip rattled in the car's cup holder as the Mustang passed over the patched, rural pavement.

A series of images remained at the forefront of his mind. It was the one Sammi had shown him – the one in which his father had held the pistol to her head and pulled the trigger, splattering her brains over a six-foot radius. That scene kept replaying in his head – over and over.

He gripped the steering wheel, angry at so many things. He felt cheated and betrayed. He wanted revenge. His father could not be allowed to go unpunished, but Brent knew there wasn't a judge in the county that would convict him. His own hands would have to be the ones dealing the justice.

-5-

Malocere had grown angry in the absence of any trace of the Keeper – there seemed to be none whatsoever. He had sent out several Agents in search, but they had all come back empty-handed. He sensed other hands were at work here. Time was drawing short. The longer he waited, the stronger the Keeper would become, and the harder she would be to defeat.

Despite the fact that night had fallen, Malocere still wore his sunglasses. When he entered through the station's double doors, Perry was sitting at his desk, mulling over mounds of meaningless paperwork. The deputy looked up and saw his boss standing in the doorway, thankful he was still wearing the sunglasses. He didn't want to see those eyes again – or whatever they were. He had tried his best to forget them.

Perry put on an artificial smile and said, "How's it goin'?"

Malocere removed his Stetson and hung it on a hook beside the door. "Fine," he said. "How's everything here?" He sniffed the air, trying to detect the faintest scent of blood. An expression of disappointment crossed his face when no such scent was detected. "Did you get everything cleaned up?" He asked.

"Yes, sir. Everything's taken care of. The... uh... *package* is in your closet. Right where you told me to put it."

Malocere nodded his head approvingly. "Good job." He pointed to the occupied holding cells and asked, "What do we have here?"

"Just a couple of drunks who decided to duke it out in the steak house parking lot."

Brig stood up to protest, asserting that he was not, nor *had he been,* drunk. Malocere shut him down with a wave of his hand, and Perry went on with his explanation. "That one," he said, pointing to Brig, "wants to make a phone call. Says he knows his rights."

Malocere chuckled. "Does he now?"

He moved closer to the cell, and as he did, the medicine bag, which was hidden beneath Brig's shirt, started to heat up again. Brig fumbled with it, trying to keep it away from his skin, convinced it would burn him. He stared into the black reflection of the sunglasses, and knew what it was that stood before him.

Malocere.

Malocere cocked his head to the side, intrigued by what he had heard. [Say it again.] He said telepathically. [It's been eons since I've heard my own name spoken.] Brig's hands went to his head as pain flared within it. He drew further back into his cell, as though confident the metal bars would protect him. Malocere drew closer and asked, [You know what I am?]

Tom watched from the other cell with a blank expression on his face. For all he knew, this was just a bad dream – nothing that couldn't be taken care of the next morning with a hollow apology and half a bottle of Advil.

At that moment, Brent was five miles from the station. He looked into his rearview mirror and spotted a pair of flashing red and blue lights. "God-DAMMIT!" He shouted. The last thing he needed was to get pulled over with an illegal firearm in the car, especially when he wasn't sure what the other deputies had been told about his relationship with Sammi and his probable involvement in her disappearance. He knew he had one ace in the hole – the engine beneath the hood of the car – and he intended to use it.

His right foot pressed against the floorboard and the car accelerated with amazing speed. The eight cylinders roared, pushing him back into the bucket seat. He had driven these roads many, many times and knew every pothole, every turn, and every bump. If there was anyone capable of outrunning a couple of rookie deputies, it was him.

He watched in the rearview mirror as the rotating lights grew smaller and smaller in the distance. He decided to crank the game's level of difficulty up a tad, so he turned off his headlights and made sure not to use the brakes. Without those lights, the black Mustang was swallowed by the Kentucky night.

[How do you know what I am?] Malocere demanded. [I want to know!]

Brig had backed himself into a corner, and he slid down the wall, pulling his knees to his chest. Inside his head, Malocere continued to insist on an answer. Brig was waiting for the tingle to come, and when it did, he sent out a thought projection with all of the force he could find within himself:

[BECAUSE YOU KILLED MY BROTHER, YOU SON-OF-A-BITCH!]

A noticeable slit of a smile spread across Malocere's face. [The Keeper.] He said, as a mental picture of Jacob Bailey sprang forth in his mind. *If this guy knew Jacob*, Malocere thought, *he must know where the* new *Keeper is, too. Same blood in his veins.* [Where's the other one?!] He demanded.

Brig was defiantly silent, so Malocere sent spears of pain into his head in retribution. The medicine bag beneath Brig's shirt started to get even hotter, as if it contained a rivet fresh from the fire rather than a small chip of wood. Brig promised himself that no matter what Malocere threw at him - no matter how much it hurt - he wouldn't divulge the information or even think her name.

Has it come to this? He wondered. *Is* this *the battle John spoke of?*

Nevertheless, Brig tried to think of a way he might defeat this thing. *Was there something he could do? Something he could say?* He remembered the plots of a hundred different horror movies and he lamented the fact that he didn't have a crucifix and had never studied Latin. Still, there had to be *something* in his memory banks - a long forgotten prayer, a Bible verse - *something* that would make this monster back off.

Something that would piss it off...

Of course, he thought. *When you're angry, you make mistakes. When you're angry, you can't think straight. But what to say?*

All of a sudden, the answer was there.

Malocere picked up a chair and threw it across the room in a fit of rage. Perry remained seated at his desk, confused by his boss' display of anger. He hadn't heard a single word spoken between the two men, but the sheriff's face was flushed, and a vein had popped out on his forehead.

Malocere screamed, "TELL ME WHERE THE KEEPER IS!!!!"

The commotion had been enough to seize Tom's attention. He rose from his cot to see what was going on. The chair Malocere had thrown slammed against the bars of his cell, and

Tom stumbled back deeper inside, wanting no part of whatever was happening.

Brig started humming a tune – a childish tune: *Camptown Races* – and waited for Malocere to settle down. When he had, Brig looked up and sang the words the way Jacob had sang them when he was little. "I-know-some-thing-you-don't-know. Doo-dah. Doo-dah."

Malocere clenched his fists into tight balls and roared with throaty frustration. The sound was so loud that no one in the sheriff's office heard the bark of Brent's tires when he pulled into the parking lot and slammed on the brakes.

Perry jumped out of his chair when Brent burst through the front door with a black semi-automatic in his right hand. Without a word, Brent raised the weapon and fired. The pistol's roar came as a surprise, and at first, Brig thought that someone had set off a firecracker as some sort of prank.

Malocere spun violently to the left as a result of the bullet that had buried itself into his right shoulder. He fell to the floor and tried to crawl underneath the nearest desk for cover. He had to stay in a body – if he got sucked back to the cave, there was no telling how long it would be before he could get out again.

Brent stood in the doorway with the gun still raised. Perry foolishly went for his own sidearm. When he did, Brent fired a second shot, which struck the deputy in the chest, sending him to the floor where he lay, apparently unconscious. Brent lowered his gun and approached the thing that had once been his father. Malocere tried to reach for the gun in his belt, but his right arm was useless – the bullet had done too much damage.

Now, five feet away, Brent raised the gun again. He wasn't scared – not in the least. *This was justice. True justice. Not the kind they doled out at the County Courthouse. No plea bargains today.*

Deep within his mind, he heard Sammi's voice. [Do it, Baby! Shoot him!]

Brent saw her standing in the far corner of the room, next to the fingerprinting table. Her face had drawn up into a mass of wrinkles as if her skin had dried out. It peeled off in large, white flakes, which drifted to the floor like feathers. Her eyeballs rolled around inside their sockets like Ping-Pong balls, large white balls with hazy-blue irises.

In her arms, Sammi cradled the tiny, purple, under-developed fetus. Its umbilical cord had dried up, now a brittle, noodle-like twig attached it to its mother. Brent watched the child twitch in her arms. It turned its head towards its father and started to cry. The sound was like a kitten in pain, and it filled Brent with rage. He pointed the pistol at his father's back and fired three more shots.

Out of nowhere, another crack of gunfire sent a red-hot spear of pain ripping through Brent's abdomen. He fell to the floor, clutching the entry wound. Perry had lifted himself off of the floor long enough to fire the shot, and when Brent hit the floor, the two locked eyes.

Blood ran from the corner of the deputy's mouth; mixed with saliva, it trickled from his lips with the consistency of syrup. He smiled, and his teeth were stained pink. Brent raised his pistol again and pulled the trigger. Perry's head snapped backwards, and the white wall behind him was peppered with droplets of blood.

Sammi called out to Brent again: [You only have one shot left! *Make it count!*] She busied herself with trying to quiet the crying fetus. Brent watched her, remembering the way she'd begged for her life on the floor of the barn. He also remembered what his father had said to him that night: "*You can watch or you can turn away.*"

Brent pressed the pistol's muzzle against the back of his father's head. He pulled the trigger, and the shot rang out. The empty casing ejected from the chamber and spun in midair, smoke still rising from inside of it. It hit the floor with a *clink* and bounced a couple of times before rolling underneath the cell bars and coming to a rest beside Brig's foot.

Brent was losing blood quickly. He laid his head down, resting his cheek on the cold tile. Just before losing consciousness, he heard Sammi speaking to the fetus. [Not long, now, precious. Daddy's coming soon. Not long, now.]

Brig stepped back from the cell door when fingers of vapor started to rise from the sheriff's nostrils. It was strangely luminescent and thicker than smoke, but not quite as thick as fog. He continued to watch, unable to look away, as it took shape in front of him.

The first feature to form was a pair of wings, which spread to a span of about ten feet. A dragon-like head was the next thing to form, followed immediately by a snake-like body. The sight reminded Brig of the feathered serpent statues he'd seen in Mexico – but instead of feathers, this thing had scales.

The ghost-like apparition of Malocere hovered in midair. Its eyes were yellow, glowing, and reptilian. The monster extended its neck so that its head was only inches from Brig's cell door. [I'll ask you one more time,] he threatened. [Where is the Keeper?]

Brig's mouth was dry, but he puckered his lips and started to whistle the tune *Camptown Races,* again. It was all he knew to do.

Malocere sneered, baring his teeth. His forked tongue wiggled back and forth between needle-like fangs, and he hissed, [You had your chance.] His wings churned the air, and he lunged through the partition of bars as though they weren't even there.

He struck Brig's chest with tremendous force, but an impenetrable umbrella of blue light spread from the medicine pouch like a shield. Malocere reeled back and howled with pain. He then lunged at Tom, melting into his chest the way Brig had seen it do in his dream. The scene looked just as it had then, when he'd watched Malocere melt into Deputy Lance Tillman's chest.

Tom toppled to the floor and clutched his stomach. It looked like he was in a great deal of pain. In any other set of circumstances Brig might have been happy; however, he was struck with horror over what he had just witnessed. Tom threw his head into the toilet bowl again as another round of vomiting began. When it was over, he stood up and fell back onto his cot. He looked different, still pasty-white and sickly, but exponentially more menacing. But there was something else. He hardly blinked at all. He just sat in his cell, staring at Brig with a smirk on his face.

Unbeknownst to Brig, Malocere had quickly taken absolute control of Tom's body. Unlike the sheriff, Tom had been much more weak-minded, making possession simple. Unfortunately for Malocere, when he got the body, he got everything that went along with it. His ability to function inside a physical body was limited by that body's capabilities – and Tom was as drunk as a skunk. Malocere wasn't going anywhere for quite some time.

So, having nothing better to do, he sifted through Tom's mind, listening to random thoughts and looking at memories as one would when flipping through the pages of a photo album. The mental slideshow passed the time well enough, but not until he reached the video clip of tonight's events as well as a series of images spanning the past couple of years did his interest peak. What stood out the most was a little girl – a little girl with blonde hair.

Malocere watched the video clip and then stopped when the windows of the SUV exploded. He paused and rewound several times before moving forward to see Tom's bullet melted in thin air and the pistol yanked from his hand. Malocere smiled.

From the other cell, Brig watched thinking, *That's how he moves. He switches bodies!* He remembered John saying, *"It changes forms to evade us."*

Malocere was overwhelmed with elation and more than a little impressed by this stroke of luck. The person he was inside *knew* the Keeper, and he was sure that if he kept digging through the man's mind, he would find out where she was, too. In the process of digging, Malocere came across an image of Brig and immediately recognized him as the man in the next cell. Malocere already knew that Brig was the last Keeper's brother, but now it looked like he was also the *newest Keeper's* father.

It's too perfect! He thought. He wanted to jump up and run towards Brig's cell, howling like a victorious lunatic, but the amount of alcohol flowing through his veins prevented him from doing so. Instead, he just smiled.

"What the hell are you grinning about?" Brig asked.

Malocere tried to provoke him: [I know your secret.]

"You don't know shit."

Malocere responded by saying, [I know more than you think.] Then, in a kind of psychic fax, Malocere sent him the picture of Kaitlyn he had found in Tom's memory banks and asked, [Does this look familiar... *Daddy?*]

Brig jumped off his cot and threw himself against the cell bars, reaching through with one arm in a desperate attempt to get at the thing on the other side. Before long, he realized that all of his struggles were getting him nowhere. He threw the issue of Hot Rod Magazine through the bars where it landed in a wet spot next to Tom's toilet bowl.

[Tell me where she is.]

"Fuck you."

[TELL ME!] Fresh stabs of pain pierced Brig's head, and he gritted his teeth against them, trying his best to be strong.

"I'll let you kill me first!" He shouted.

When Malocere spoke again, his voice had calmed considerably. [Oh, no,] he said. [I'm not going to kill you first. No, sir. I'm going to kill that little girl, and I'm going to make you watch.]

"You can't kill her if you can't find her, motherfucker."

[Oh, *I'll find her*. But if you tell me where she is, I'll make it as painless as possible.] He crossed his arms and said, [The choice is yours. I got to your brother. I'll get to your daughter, too.]

All Brig wanted was to get out of the cell – to warn them somehow. He looked to the other side of the bars, but saw only blood and bodies. There was no one there to help him. *Surely someone will come back soon*, he thought. *This* is *a police station for Christ's sake!*

He looked at the clock on the wall and estimated the next shift would be arriving in about five hours – a long time, but of course Malocere was locked up, too – he wouldn't be going anywhere – not unless he figured a way out.

Brig looked back into Malocere's cell and saw quite clearly that there were no harrowing escape plots in the works. Malocere attempted to stand up, and he swayed from side to side in the center of his cell. He tried to send a few more thought projections, but they came across as garbled nonsense.

The alcohol must be getting to him, Brig thought.

Finally, Malocere's eyes rolled over to white, and his body fell to the floor. His head hit the concrete with a loud smack. A few minutes later, he started to snore.

Great, Brig thought, *now I have to listen to* this *shit all night.*

During the next three hours, Brig tried in vain to jimmy the lock on his cell door. He looked at Malocere lying sprawled out across the floor and wondered if there might be a way to kill him before he - or "it" as the case may be - woke up. After a great deal of thought, he came to the conclusion that there wasn't.

While Malocere slept, he saw a stream of images rolling through Tom's mind. He was unacquainted with dreams, so he didn't know what to make of them. Even still, he paid close attention when he recognized the little girl again. Tom's brain was dreaming about the day he had driven out to Brig's place with the intention of getting his wife back. Malocere took special note of the direction in which Tom was driving - he was sure the information would be of great value. The farmhouse appeared in the distance, and Malocere recognized it immediately. It had been his Watchtower - the bane of his existence for almost 200 years. Those who had lived there had managed to keep him locked in that cold, damp cave for all those years. Now, the newest one in their bloodline - the last in their bloodline - lived there, too.

A moment of consciousness came, and he tried to sit up, ready to get out of the cell. He had the answers he needed; the only problem was that his new body wasn't cooperating just yet. He called to his Agents for help - the ones John had called "the Agents of the Dark."

Brig was startled when loud, piercing wails suddenly filled his head. The sounds reminded him of a smoke detector wailing. There seemed to be a pattern in the wails. They sounded a lot like Morse code.

Holy Shit! Brig thought. *He's communicating! I have to get out of here - NOW! Kaitlyn and Erin! I have to get them out of there!*

He tried his best to get the tingle to come back into his head so that he could talk with his daughter, but something was wrong... he couldn't feel it. He was sure it had something to do with the goddamned noise coming out of Malocere's mouth. Just then, Brig remembered something else John had said: "*With our forces mobilized, Malocere will be forced to do the same. Then the battle will begin.*"

Brig buried his face in his hands when the panic came. *Not now,* he thought. *Not now, please.*

CHAPTER SIXTEEN

-1-

It was two o'clock in the morning when three hasty knocks on the front door woke Erin. She rubbed her eyes, unaware she had fallen asleep. The cordless phone still lay in her lap, and a quick check of the call history told her Brig hadn't called.

Outside, the wind had picked up. A couple of large maple trees in the front yard groaned against the force of the wind. Their leaves rustled furiously with every gust, adding to the melody. In his pen, Buster bayed long, mournful howls that went on without end.

Three more hasty knocks...

Erin stood up and stretched with a yawn and thought, *That's probably Brig, now.* An abrupt gust of wind... somewhere a tree limb snapped, and Buster's howl rose in pitch like a woman's scream.

Three more knocks... louder, almost impatient.

Erin's shouted, "I'm coming, I'm coming!" She reached for the knob and yanked the door open. The wind whistled through the gaps in the storm door with the sound of air blown over the top of a coke bottle. The porch was dark even though she had made sure to turn the light on earlier. *Probably a burnt out bulb.* Brig wasn't standing there as she had hoped, but through the glare in the glass, she saw someone was out there, but couldn't tell who it was. She flipped the light switch back and forth a couple of times with no luck and asked, "Who's there?"

The small voice that answered was practically inaudible against the whistling wind, but the voice sounded harmless enough, so Erin unlocked the storm door and leaned outside. On the sidewalk beneath the porch's overhang stood two small children, a boy and a girl, dressed in black, cracker-jack outfits. At first, Erin thought they looked like the cute, little Pilgrims that always graced the front of Thanksgiving Day greeting cards.

The girl was clearly the younger of the two; she stood much shorter than the boy did. Her straight, raven-black hair hung at shoulder length was tossed about carelessly by the wind. It blew this way and that, occasionally obscuring her delicate features. White stockings began below her knees and disappeared into a pair of black shoes.

She held hands with an older boy, who Erin estimated to be about seven years old – maybe eight. He was dressed similarly, in black shorts and shoes with white socks and a shirt to match. His features were much more chiseled and angular than the girl's; his hair was curly and thick.

Erin couldn't imagine why two children so young would be out at two in the morning. She asked them their names, and the boy said that his was Azel. The little girl must not have heard the question; she seemed preoccupied with Buster's howling and looked in his direction instead of answering. The boy told Erin her name was Lamia.

"Are you lost?" Erin asked. "Do you need me to call your parents?" The little boy replied that they were indeed lost. Lamia looked past Erin, pointing to something inside the house. Erin followed the little girl's gaze and saw Kaitlyn's container full of crayons. Some coloring books and a Barbie doll sat beside it on the living room floor.

"You have a little daughter?" Lamia asked over the wind. Erin nodded, and the little girl asked, "Can she come out and play?"

"Of course not!" Erin said, shocked by the request. "It's two in the morning! Why don't you two come inside and we'll see if we can't get a hold of your parents?"

Lamia stepped forward, but Azel pulled her back again. Erin noticed that he kept looking up towards the porch roof. The little girl did the same, and her eyes grew wide. She shook her head and said, "I don't think we should."

Erin didn't see the door to the master bedroom open behind her, nor did she see Kaitlyn walk out of it. But the children on the porch did, and she saw their eyes widen. She turned to see Kaitlyn standing behind her with a look of concern on her face.

"What's wrong, honey?" Erin asked as she bent down to give her daughter a kiss.

Kaitlyn pulled her mother's ear down to her lips and whispered, "Mommy... those are *the bad ones.*" Erin's back was turned, so she didn't see the children smile at Kaitlyn. Both bared mouths full of pointed teeth, and Kaitlyn covered her eyes.

Erin spun back around, and when she did Azel was pointing at Buster's pen. "If your daughter doesn't want to play," he said. "We can just play with the puppy."

"Yeah, the puppy," came Lamia's response before she broke into laughter. The two moved toward his pen just as Erin snatched the shotgun Brig had left propped in a corner near the front door. She pumped it and stepped out onto the porch, lifting the muzzle in their direction.

"Keep away from the dog."

The two turned and smiled, baring those pointed teeth. Erin held the gun firmly and prepared to fire. She remembered Azel's eyes and how they had cut up towards the roof of the porch. *Of course they didn't want to come inside,* she thought. *They couldn't walk beneath the cedar wood.* Kaitlyn called out again, and Erin took her left hand off of the gun and pointed toward the house. "You stay inside!" She shouted. "You're safe in there!" Turning back to the children, she said, "On your knees, you little bastards!" but the children were nowhere to be seen. It was as though they had vanished.

Another strong gust of wind masked the sound of what was rapidly approaching Erin from behind. Buster tried to warn her with loud, panicked barks. She turned around and saw two creatures flying towards her – the same big-teethed, softball creatures Brent had seen in The Borderlands.

Erin raised the gun and fired. The combined chattering of the two creatures hurt her ears. They separated and disappeared into the trees. Erin continued to move the barrel around this way and that hoping for some sign of them. *What the hell* were *those?* She thought.

Kaitlyn screamed, "Mommy look out!!!" just as Erin felt hands seize the legs of her jeans, pulling her back. She fell forward, accidentally squeezing the trigger when she hit the ground. The blast missed Buster and sent him into another barking frenzy as the two things that had hold of her dragged her away towards the back of the house, causing her to lose the grip she had on the gun. It slipped from her hands and lay in the grass.

"We gots one! We gots one!" were the cries from the strange creatures pulling her around the house towards the barn further down behind it. Erin twisted her body to see they were no longer children at all, but strange goat-like creatures that walked on two legs. Their hooves clicked and clocked as they ran. Their upper bodies were hairless and green with horns that protruded from bald heads sporting oddly human features.

They drug her into barn just beyond the backyard of the farmhouse. She lie in the doorway on her stomach, a powerful hand – she assumed to be Azel's – held her to the floor as the other creature hurried to tear slats of wood from the barn walls and began beating them together using a rock and rusty nails.

"We gonna cross you!" One shouted.

"We gonna hang you up!" said the other.

"Cross her! Cross her! Hang her up!" became the chorus sang over and over as the construction continued.

The ruckus didn't die down until a shadow fell into the interior of the barn, long and thin. Kaitlyn stood inches from her mother in the open doorway, her small body's shadow cast from the moonlight behind her. The creatures looked up and hissed.

"Keeeeeeeeeeeeeeeper!"

Erin screamed, "I told you to stay inside!"

Kaitlyn stood firm and said, "ENOUGH!" With that she threw her hands apart sending the two creatures through the air, colliding with the barn walls and bouncing to the back of the barn. Kaitlyn extended her hand and rotated her wrist, lifting it and levitating Erin to her feet.

"Mother?" she said, completely absent of emotion.

"Yes?"

"Run."

Erin did as she was told and bolted for the house, assuming Kaitlyn was on her heels. Not until she had run about fifty yards did she look back over her shoulder to see that Kaitlyn had walked deeper into the barn. Once her small figure was swallowed in shadow, every barn door and hayloft window slammed shut at the same time.

Inside the barn, the two creatures had managed to get back on their feet. They moved restlessly in the shadows, hissing and chattering. "Weeez found the Keeeeeeeeeeeeper! We gonna have fun with you!"

Kaitlyn didn't respond.

"Last time me seen a Keeper been long time!" said one.

"Jeeeeeeeeeeeeeeeeeeeeezus." Confirmed the other.

"Yes! Yes! Jeeeeeeezus! We killed him – yes we did! Crossed him! Hung him up!"

"Jeeeeezus no fight us. Too kind to fight, yessssssssssss."

The creatures moved toward her from the shadows and through the shafts of milky moonlight that made its way into the barn through cracks in the slats, their reptilian eyes sparkled. Kaitlyn stood still and lifted her right hand, pressing together the pads of her thumb and middle finger. A strange, red light radiated from them when they had touched.

She shrugged a shoulder as one corner of her mouth turned up. "I'm not Jesus," she told them and snapped her fingers.

The barn illuminated from inside with a brilliant orange light and a sucking sound as though all the oxygen surrounding it had been pulled inside. The farm fell silent. Then, Erin heard the two creatures scream just as the barn blasted apart in a violent explosion that sent boards, nails and tin roofing flying across the field and high into the air as the rest of the structure was engulfed inside a gigantic fireball.

Erin screamed and covered her ears just as Kaitlyn's shape emerged from the flames, unharmed. Behind her, the two creatures tried to escape by shifting back into their flying softball form, but fell back to the earth when their wings vaporized in the flames, rolling around like fireballs in the field until they retook their goat-like forms and ran about screaming in pain.

Kaitlyn stopped and turned towards them. She held her hands up, palms out, and began to make circles in the air in front of her. As she did, the area she manipulated swirled and churned inky black. The air filled with the sound of a jet engine as the rim of the Gate Kaitlyn had opened glowed red. The two creatures lifted from the field and howled as they were sucked into it, trailing long tails of fire. They and the Gate vanished as Kaitlyn's hand clenched into a fist with a resulting boom that roared across the fields.

"Oh my god!!!" Erin screamed. "That was amazing!! She scooped Kaitlyn into her arms and smothered her with kisses before cradling her daughter's little face in her hands. "Are you okay? Are they gone?? Kaitlyn nodded that they were, and Erin grabbed her wrist. Together they bolted for the front door of the farmhouse. Once inside, Erin grabbed the phone and dialed 911. She waited for an operator for what seemed like an eternity. Finally, a woman with a nasally voice asked her to describe the nature of her emergency.

Erin screamed, "I WANT THE FUCKING SHERIFF'S OFFICE!"

While she waited, she looked through the window into front yard, wondering how many more of those things might be out there. For all she knew, armies of the little bastards had already surrounded the house, just waiting for the right time to attack. She shivered, picturing the creatures' teeth and hunched over way they walked when on two legs. Not since she was a little girl had she wished for anything as hard as she wished for the morning sun at that moment. But a glance at the clock told her daylight was hours away. *Where* are *you, Brig?* She thought. *We need you* here!

-2-

A few seconds later, Erin's call connected, and the phone on Perry's desk rang. Brig peered through the bars, wishing he could reach it. Perry's body lay on the floor with its head partially propped against the air conditioner. Several splotches of blood had run down the white wall.

Over six hours had passed since Brig and Tom had been put into their respective cells. It would be another four before the deputies who had arrested them returned to close out their shifts. Meanwhile, Malocere was gradually beginning to sober up, and Brig was starting to worry. He looked at the sheriff's body lying face down on the tile floor.

There was something in the body's hand, and Brig squinted, trying to see what it was. His eyes strained to see a set of keys. *If there's any justice in the world,* he thought, *there's a cell key on that ring.* Even if there was, the sheriff's body was a good fifteen feet out of reach.

Just then, one of the station's double doors opened, and a little girl stepped inside similar to the one who had appeared at the front door of the farmhouse earlier. She stopped and surveyed the room, glancing only momentarily at Brig who was pleading for help. She wore a blank expression on her face, and when she turned towards the cells, her arms hung straight at her sides. The heels on her shoes proclaimed every step she took with a *click*. She appeared to ignore Brig, stopping only momentarily to glance at the bodies on the floor. Her hair fell over her eyes when she looked down, but with a brush of her hand, she tucked the fine, black strands behind her ear again.

Brig continued to ask for help, but he sensed something wasn't right when the girl stopped in front of his cell door. She looked at him without saying a word. There was something wrong with her eyes – her irises were the same color as her hair... black. *Black eyes?* Brig backed away, no longer wanting any help she might offer.

In the other cell, Malocere stood up and steadied himself. He had made several trips to the toilet over the past six hours. The bad part was that Malocere never flushed. The stench of liquor, vomit, and urine drifting into Brig's cell was almost unbearable.

The black-eyed girl walked over to Malocere's cell where he was leaning against the bars for support. She looked at him for several seconds in the same, inexpressive manner. Then, her mouth opened wide as though her jaw had unhinged itself. From it came that same Morse code-like wailing Brig had heard coming from Malocere before. Any doubt Brig might have had about it being a mode of communication left him when Malocere responded in kind.

The scene was surreal. Even though Brig didn't know what was being said, he felt quite sure that they were talking about Kaitlyn; he felt it in his gut. He feared they had found her, and that Malocere knew his secret after all.

The room fell silent, the conversation apparently complete. Malocere leaned backwards and cackled with laughter. He wrenched his neck to the left and looked directly at Brig. [Your house is two miles past the interstate, isn't that right?] he asked, taunting Brig for some reaction.

They know where she is! His mind shouted.

It was three in the morning – still another three hours before anyone would show up at the station. He looked at the sheriff's hand again and thought about the keys. *I've* got *to get them.* His mind insisted. *I've* got *to get out of here.* The room was bleaching white, and Brig realized he was hyperventilating. *Gotta calm down.* He told himself. *Gotta calm down.* He tried to slow his breathing. He knew if he didn't, he would surely pass out.

Malocere's laughter stopped. He turned back to face the girl and wailed out another unintelligible message. The wail was different that time – Brig detected a pronounced sense of urgency in it. The girl held her hand an inch away from the lock on the door. A red glow of light radiated from her palm and the room filled the hum of swarms of angry hornets. The door's lock broke with a loud *pop,* and Malocere kicked it open.

Brig gritted his teeth and spoke in a voice that shook with a mix of fury and fear. "Don't you go *near* her you son-of-a-bitch!" Without saying a word, Malocere bent over and took the keys from the sheriff's hand. He jingled them in the air and staggered toward the front doors.

The girl followed closely behind, but stopped to look at Brig again. She smiled, showing her sharp, jagged teeth. There was a bright flash of red light, a loud crack, and she was gone. One of softball creatures hovered in the air where she had stood.

Malocere opened one of the station's doors and the creature flew out of it at incredible speed, creating a small sonic boom. Brig screamed at Malocere as he stepped through the door so loudly his voice cracked. "Don't you do it! Don't you fucking touch her!"

Malocere winked with arrogant defiance. He reached over to a switch on the wall and shut off the lights. In the darkness, his eyes glowed brightly. He said, [I'll tell her that Daddy sends his love.]

-3-

Halfway across town, John jerked awake with Brig's voice screaming in his head. Along with the sound came several random thoughts and John understood what they meant.

KAITLYN!

He saw a picture of Malocere (actually it was an image of Tom, but John saw the eyes and knew who it was). Another image of Brig locked in a jail cell followed shortly thereafter. John tried to focus all of his thoughts and energy on Kaitlyn. He didn't know if he could reach her in time, but he had to warn her at the very least. [Kaitlyn... Kaitlyn can you hear me?] He had never tried to communicate like this at such a distance, but he had no other option.

[John?]

Thank God!

[Kaitlyn, he's coming! There's very little time. Where are you?]

[We're at Daddy's house.]

[You have to get out of the house, little one. Take your mother. Run! Run as fast as you can. He knows where you are and he's coming for you!]

She asked him where he thought they should go. John tried to think of a good place – somewhere they could pull a sort of quarterback sneak. His first thought was the tobacco barn, and that's where he told her to go. [You'll be safe there,] he said. [I'll come and get you.]

[The bad ones came to the house tonight. I took care of them. I'm ready if there are more.] Kaitlyn told him. [I'm not afraid anymore, John. I'm ready to fight him.]

[No, Kaitlyn!! Don't you even think it! You're not ready yet. Save your mother – get to the barn!! The good ones will protect you. There's no time, Kaitlyn. Get out of there! *RUN!*]

Kaitlyn clapped her hands, attempting to get her mother's attention. Erin was still trying to reach someone at the sheriff's station for the third time in twenty minutes. "Mommy," Kaitlyn said. "We have to get out of here. He's coming. We have to go – NOW!"

The little girl grabbed her mother's hand, and Erin asked, "Where, honey? Where are we going? We can't go outside; you know what's out there! Besides, what are you worried about? The bad man can't come in here, remember? He can't get past the cedar wood!"

Kaitlyn pulled her towards the door. "Oh yes he can!" She said. "That's why we have to go!"

Erin removed the pistol from the waistband of her jeans and mentally prepared for what she was convinced was going to be an all-out war. She reached into the box of ammunition as they passed the closet and snagged another handful, which she stuffed into her pocket, spilling random bullets onto the floor as she did.

Outside, Erin held the gun out and panned around the front yard. Remembering what Kaitlyn had done to the barn – to those creatures – she felt as though she was ready for anything. Kaitlyn pointed towards the dog's pen and said, "We can't leave Busser! He's coming, too!" Erin ran over and opened the pen. Buster wasted no time getting out of there. The three of them ran down the driveway toward the tobacco barn with the dog close to the little girl's side.

-4-

While John was speaking with Kaitlyn, Malocere climbed into A.J.'s squad car. The engine roared to life – together, the eight cylinders and the four-barrel carburetor were a beast begging to be unleashed. Malocere dropped the transmission in drive, stepped on the accelerator, and let the engine do its thing.

The tires peeled, and the car fishtailed a couple of times – something Malocere had difficulty correcting due to the lingering intoxication, but it thrilled him just the same. Ahead, the streetlights, road reflectors, and dotted white lines were a wicked blur. The car weaved from the right lane into the left and back again several times.

It was three o'clock in the morning, and the downtown streets were deserted. The overhead streetlights cast strange, orange ovals of arc-sodium light onto the pavement below. The traffic light at the intersection of Main Street and First Avenue was red, but Malocere blew through it at nearly fifty miles per hour. On the other side of the intersection was the crossing for the railroad tracks. When the car hit it, the front bumper bottomed out with a shower of sparks.

The car went airborne, and slammed back onto the road ten feet beyond the tracks with another shower of sparks and the sound of grinding metal. Malocere's head struck the windshield and he fought to keep the vehicle under control, nearly hitting a utility pole head on. Any thrill he'd previously felt was now gone.

Further up the road, a red pickup truck swerved to avoid the squad car as it veered into the oncoming lane. The driver laid on the horn and shouted something Malocere was unable to make out when he passed. The softball creature from the station zipped out of the sky and flew alongside the squad car. Malocere waved it on, and it took off in the direction of the Bailey farm just as Malocere skidded through the intersection of Main Street and the main highway, making a hard right turn and flooring the accelerator again.

Erin, Kaitlyn, and Buster were about halfway up the drive. Every noise Erin heard elicited an over-exaggerated startle response from her. She held the pistol, waving it from side to side as she ran, determined to shoot anything that moved.

From the sky above them came a deafening bang, like a cannon's roar. Erin looked up and saw the softball creature swooping down at them. Kaitlyn pointed at it and shouted, "Mommy, look out!" Buster stepped in front of the child and growled defensively.

Erin raised her pistol and fired, but the creature dipped and dodged the bullet. Her second shot missed as well, but the third found its target. The creature shrieked and it fell from the sky. Before it even hit the ground, Erin emptied the pistol's cylinder and started loading again.

Kaitlyn called out, "Mommy, we have to go! He's close! I can feel it!" Erin grabbed her daughter's hand and they darted through the field towards the barn. Buster wasn't far behind.

Once inside, they looked for a good place to hide. Erin was frantic, but Kaitlyn assured her that everything was going to be alright. "The good ones are here now," she said. "They're going to protect us."

Erin gasped when she noticed that the barn was full of apparitions. They were everywhere – in the loft, in front of the doors – everywhere. Some floated among the rafters and one brushed by Erin close enough to graze her ear and whisper into it. Buster hid behind Kaitlyn with a whine. The little girl put her hand over her mouth and giggled.

"You should see the look on your face!" Kaitlyn laughed, pointing at her mother. "Are you afraid?"

Erin realized she wasn't afraid. Oddly enough, these spirits didn't scare her. They seemed peaceful, warm-hearted… *good.* After all, that's what Kaitlyn had called them – the good ones.

A roar filled the barn as the spirits moved about them faster and faster, creating a cocoon around Erin, Kaitlyn, and Buster. Erin started to feel the same electric buzzing she had felt the day Kaitlyn had her 'awakening' in the meadow, and just as they had then, the hairs on her arms stood on end.

Kaitlyn squeezed her hand and said, "He's here, Mommy. The bad man's here. We have to be quiet."

Through the gaps between the wallboards, Erin saw a pair of headlights turning into the driveway. She pulled Kaitlyn close, and the buzzing in the room grew louder. Suddenly, they were surrounded with what looked like clouds of blue light. Erin felt her stomach drop the way it does on a roller coaster. That's when she realized they weren't in the barn anymore.

"Where are we?" She asked.

"It's okay," Kaitlyn said. "We just jumped."

"Jumped? Jumped where?"

"We jumped up..."

Erin scanned the scene. The ghosts were still standing around them, but they no longer *looked* like ghosts. They looked like real people - solid, flesh and blood people. Far off in the distance were lush, green, rolling hills. Hanging above those was a white sun much different than the yellow one she had always known. The sky wasn't baby blue; instead, it boasted every color of the spectrum, almost like a rainbow, but the spectrum even reached what looked infrared. Erin reached down to scoop up some of the sugar white sand into her hand. A cool breeze blew through her hair, and there was music in the wind.

"Where are we?" She asked again.

The spirits answered her question by sending a message into her mind the same way that Kaitlyn and Brig had been communicating. Suddenly, she understood. They were still inside the barn - sort of - only in a higher dimension. The ghosts had taken them to a place where Malocere could never find them - somewhere he couldn't go - The Upper Afterworld.

-5-

The squad car Malocere was driving looked like a rocket sled as it sped down the gravel drive; giant plumes of dust kicked up in its wake. He was overdriving his headlights; the driveway was much too narrow with far too many twists and turns for him to successfully navigate it at such speed. Sure enough, when the car reached a bend about a hundred yards from the house, it kept going straight - *straight off a six-foot embankment.* The car pitched forward, and the front bumper dug a deep trench in the ground when it hit, throwing Malocere's head into the windshield. A blast of stars exploded in his field of vision, and the windshield shattered in an intricate spider web pattern. The car flipped onto its side and rolled three or four times, eventually coming to a stop some thirty feet later, resting on its roof.

When the car rolled, Malocere was thrown over into the passenger's side. He had to crawl through the open window to get out. Once he'd managed to free himself from the twisted wreck, he collapsed onto the ground where he lay, waiting for his head to stop spinning.

Meanwhile, John had reached the driveway, turning off his headlights before he turned into it. As he neared the barn where he had told Kaitlyn to meet him, he was very nervous. *Is she in there? Did she make it in time?* He pulled behind the barn, careful to position his truck so that it wouldn't be seen by anyone, and he left the engine running. He had seen lingering gravel dust hanging in the air when he'd pulled in, and knowing what that meant, he was trying to be careful. Still, a sense of urgency prevailed.

[Kaitlyn? Kaitlyn, can you hear me?]

In the Upper Afterworld, the little girl jumped for joy. She shouted, "John's here!" Erin saw her nod her head to one of the ghosts that responded with a knowing nod of its own.

"What do we do now?" Her mother asked.

Kaitlyn's response was simple: "We have to jump back."

The blue clouds surrounded them again and Erin felt the roller coaster sensation as though plunging down. Her stomach rose into her throat, and everything around her became a blur – everything except Kaitlyn and Buster. The spirits stretched and grew cloudy, forming more and more of a translucent haze. She remembered Brig telling her about the funnel cloud he'd been in the night Kaitlyn had wandered off. Erin was excited to think she was seeing the same thing now. *This is how they did it,* she thought. *This is how you hide.*

The blur cleared, and all of them found themselves back into the inside of the barn. The spirits were no longer solid – they had all returned to their previous spectral forms. Kaitlyn looked around, thinking John might be there waiting for them.

Kaitlyn thanked the spirits for their help one-by-one. As she did, each became a glowing orb that soared into the sky, bright at first, but dimmer and dimmer the further away they flew until winking out like a shooting star.

[We're here, John! We're ready.]

[We need to get going,] he told her. [I don't know how much time we have.] Erin's head peeked around the corner following the sound of creaking door hinges. She looked in all directions to make sure the coast was clear when she caught sight of John standing in front of his truck. She motioned for Kaitlyn and Buster to get moving. After they were safely on their way, Erin followed behind them.

Kaitlyn jumped into John's waiting arms. He hugged her tightly, but made sure to stress that they needed to be on their way. He handed her back to her mother, who helped her into the cab of the truck while John lowered the tailgate for Buster to hop in the back. Once he had, John climbed behind the steering wheel, put the truck into gear, and they were on their way.

Erin rested her head against the passenger window, clearly exhausted. She tried to tell John about what had happened at the restaurant and how the deputies had taken Brig away, but he stopped her, letting her know that he was well aware of the situation. Kaitlyn sat between the two of them, listening intently to the conversation. She turned her head towards John and asked, "Are we going to get Daddy?"

John frowned and said, "No, sweetie. I wish we could, but we can't take that chance. Don't worry, though. He'll be fine. I promise."

Kaitlyn asked, "Then where are we going?"

"I'm taking you someplace safe," John told her. "I have to hide you for now. The time isn't right."

-6-

Malocere hoisted himself to his feet a few minutes later with a groan. He looked at the car and then at the house. There were no lights on inside, and that bothered him. *If anyone were in there,* he thought, *they would have heard the crash!* He wondered if he had come all this way for nothing. Behind the house and still smoking, lay the burning remnants of what had been a barn. Wood still glowed hot with embers and the debris field told him something very big had occurred.

The house's windows were dark; the shades were partially drawn, making them look like sleepy eyes. A long, thin section of white siding shone brightly against the dark veil of the night sky. The house seemed unaware of, or unconcerned with, the menace that was approaching.

Malocere glanced back at the wrecked squad car. Jets of steam rose from the radiator. All four tires were spinning; the one on the front, passenger's side wobbled with the rhythmic, grinding sound of metal on metal. He was going to have to find another form of transportation.

His right ankle felt like it were on fire. He reached down to lift his pant leg, and saw a deep gash surrounded by a growing, purple bruise. The swelling made it difficult to walk, but he pressed forward. The only thing he cared about was getting inside that house.

The front door was wide open. It appeared whoever had been here had left in a hurry. Bullets lay strewn across the front porch, and he kicked them aside. Once over the threshold, he sniffed the air, but was unable to sense the Keeper. He flipped the switch next to the door, and the living room filled with light. Various items lay haphazardly on the floor, but the crayons and the Barbie doll were what interested him the most.

She is *here*, he thought.

Bending over to pick up the doll, he heard whispers in the rear part of the house. His lips stretched, forming an ugly grin, and he set the doll back onto the floor. He inched forward, floorboards creaking as he went. A *shushing* sound came from that direction, which made his grin grow even wider. He licked his lips and thought, *She's back there. I* know *she is.* He tried to imagine all of things he was going to do to her when he found her – after all, *this Keeper would be the last, and their blood is so sweet.*

The hallway was dark, but the light from the living room lamp was enough for him to find his way down it. He stopped and listened to soft whispers drifting from beneath Gabe's office door.

They're cornered!

He moved closer and reached out for the knob, whispering: "*Come out, come out wherever you are!*" He threw his body against the door with a loud *thump*. The door opened easily, sending him toppling to the floor. He cursed the pain in his ankle, which throbbed with pitiless agony. Hurried footsteps shuffled down the hallway, and he quickly got up and followed.

Arriving in the living room a few seconds later, he saw what appeared to be the legs of a child running up the staircase to the second floor.

Now I've got you!

Malocere rushed in that direction, turning to run up the staircase at a full sprint. Once he had ascended halfway, he stopped and saw Jacob standing at the top of the stairs. The ghost-child looked down at him with arms crossed and a defiant smirk on his face. Malocere recognized the child immediately and roared with rage. He bolted up the stairs again, but slipped on a puddle of water, falling face-forward, smacking his head on one of the wooden stairs. He heard Jacob giggling just as everything went black.

CHAPTER SEVENTEEN

-1-

Malocere regained consciousness about 5:30 that morning. He beat his fists against the stairs and roared with anger. He'd been tricked, and he didn't like it at all. This particular Keeper was proving to be quite elusive, which meant catching her was going to be an even greater challenge than he had originally thought. It appeared as though she had help from both the living *and* the dead – a formidable alliance to say the least. But he knew the latter could only hide her for so long... *even the dead make mistakes.*

He stood up, but sat back down almost immediately when his ankle screamed with knifelike pain. He could no longer pull his pants leg up to examine his injury – his ankle had swollen that much. He felt his left ankle and then his right, trying to make some sort of comparison. The injured one was much larger; however, he was sure it wasn't broken. If it were, he'd never have been able to walk on it – that much human anatomy he knew and he detested how fragile human bodies were.

Convinced it was just a sprain, he forced himself to stand up and get going. It was time to find this little bitch. The pain was intense, but bearable enough to allow him to walk. Transportation was the first order of business – he wasn't going to make any progress on foot. He needed a car, and stepping out onto the porch to see the smoking, twisted wreck lying in the ditch only caused his head to throb with recall.

Malocere panned around, looking for the solution. This was a farm, after all and that mean equipment – tractors, trucks, that sort of thing. It was then his eyes spotted a pickup truck further down the drive parked next to the tobacco barn. Its paint shone brightly in the early morning light as an older man was busily loading something into the back of it.

Malocere limped in the direction of the barn, fully intending to use his injury - not to mention the innate human response of sympathy - to his advantage. He didn't have to fake an expression of pain; the one he wore was one hundred percent genuine. He had learned a very unfortunate side-effect of possession and plugging into the host's brain wiring. Pain was part of the package deal.

Harv caught sight of someone approaching and it was clear to him right away the man was injured. He removed his cap and wiped the sweat from his forehead with a handkerchief he tucked back into the chest pocket of his overalls. "Hey there, young fella!" He called out. "You alright? You look a little banged up."

The approaching figure was close enough for Harv to make out his facial features. Harv remembered seeing pictures of Erin's new husband that Brig had shown him, and was fairly certain this was the same guy. He also remembered Brig telling him what Erin's husband had done to her. The memory caused a well of distaste to brew in his stomach.

Malocere grinned, and it made Harv feel uneasy. "Had me a little accident up the drive there," Malocere told him. "No one was home. I really need to get to a phone."

Harv's brow furrowed. "No one was home?"

Malocere shook his head. "No one. Do you know the folks who are living up there?"

Harv went with his first instinct and said, "No, I don't. I worked for Gabe Bailey before he died last week. I'm just wrapping some things up, that's all." He didn't know why he felt the need to lie, but he was compelled to do so just the same.

"Really?" Malocere asked. "You don't know them?"

"No, I'm 'fraid I don't. Gabe's son moved away years ago, long before I started working here. Never had the chance to get to know him."

Just then, two of the softball creatures zipped in alongside Malocere, their wings beating with the sound of angry hornets. They immediately transformed into the goat creatures and set about rummaging through Harv's toolbox in the bed of his truck.

"Hey!" Harv shouted. "What do you think you're doing? What the hell are those??"

One of the creatures removed a hammer and a handful nails. The other grabbed a small sledge hammer that it waved in the air, testing its weight with cackles of glee.

"Oh yessss!" it called out. "This one do a good job! BANG! BANG! BANG!"

Malocere looked back at the old man, never acknowledging the question that had been put to him and said, "So, you don't know them... I guess that means you don't have any idea where they might be?"

Harv shook his head and backed away. His hands started to tremble, sweat rolled down his creased forehead, and he strained to say, "No, I told you, I *don't* know them!"

Malocere shook his head and motioned with his finger for the creatures to follow. "Tsk, tsk, tsk," he said. "That's a shame. You know what? I think you know more than you're telling me. Unfortunately I don't have time for games." With a swift motion, he reached out and clutched Harv's throat, pressing the old man against the side of the truck. He looked deep into Harv's eyes and said, "Pity. I'd hoped it wouldn't come to this. Let's just see how much you *do* know."

Malocere released Harv and waved his hand dismissively, telling the goat creatures, "Do your thing." They closed in on

Harv, licking their lips and snorting like pigs. Before they were upon him, a lone rooster crowed in the distance.

-2-

Brig's attention shifted back and forth between the front doors and the clock on the wall. It was five till six, and his anxiety was raging. He'd been alone in the building for three hours, growing increasingly worried about Erin and Kaitlyn. Had he known John was on the case, he might have felt better, but as far as he knew, they'd had no warning at all.

Just about the time his patience had run out, he heard the sound of car engines in the parking lot outside. He stood up when the front doors opened and two deputies entered – the same two who had arrested him and Tom the night before. Both froze in the foyer. The taller one, whose name was Everitt, looked down at the bodies and screamed, "Oh, JESUS! It's the boss!!" Both deputies drew their pistols, and the shorter one ran back to lock the front doors.

Everitt looked at Brig with a mask of fear and a complete lack of composure. "What the hell happened here?!" he demanded. Before the words had even left his lips, he noticed the other cell door standing wide open. The deputy pointed to it and asked, "And where the hell is *that one?*"

Everitt and his partner Bill started searching the station, thinking the perp might still be inside, but hoping like hell he wasn't. Brig tried to explain what had happened, but neither of the deputies paid him any attention.

The two of them continued to search the premises, having seen the sheriff's body and that of his son lying on the floor in a lake of blood. Bill looked to his right and buckled over, covering his mouth. It looked like the guy was going to vomit and Everitt believed the hand-over-the-mouth trick might just succeed in keeping down the waffle he'd eaten thirty minutes earlier. Bill slapped Everitt on the arm and used his free hand to point to the corner where Perry's body lay with its head partially propped against the air conditioning unit; blood and brain matter were splattered all over the wall behind.

Everitt screamed, "HOLY SHIT! It's a goddamn massacre!" He looked back at Brig and demanded to know who was responsible.

"What do you think I've been trying to tell you?!" Brig shouted. He pointed to the empty cell next to him. "The other guy... Tom... he's gone after my little girl! Please, you have to let me out! It might not be too late!"

"No one's going anywhere!" Bill said. He turned to Everitt and asked, "What the hell are we going to do? Who do we call?"

"Hell if I know, man!."

"C'mon, guys!" Brig shouted. "You don't understand! It's a goddamned emergency!"

"You shut up!" Bill said, waving a finger in his direction. "The only thing I want to hear from you is who did this. Who killed the boss?"

Brig pointed at Brent and said, "It was him! The kid. He killed them both!"

"Who the hell killed *the kid*, then?!"

"That one!" He told them, pointing at Perry that time. "He got a shot off before the kid popped him in the head." Brig was about to start begging to be let out again when the taller one shouted out from A.J.'s office.

"God-fucking-damn! Bill! Get your ass in here we've got another one! *It's Carl!*"

No sooner had Bill gone into A.J.'s office than he ran back out and into the rear storage room. Brig heard him heaving violently; the sound was followed by several chunky splatters.

When those sounds quieted down, they were replaced by miserable, yet somewhat grateful, moans and the sound of running water. Soon after that, Bill emerged again and leaned against the doorframe.

The front door rattled a couple of times before the person on the other side decided to try knocking instead. A muffled voice called out, "Hey guys! Let me in! It's Sam!"

Bill, still leaning against the storeroom's doorframe, called out to his partner, "Get the door!"

Everitt stuck his head out of the sheriff's office and asked, "What?"

"Get the door."

"Are you okay?"

Bill looked at him and made an exaggerated gesture across the room of bodies. "Hell, no I'm not okay! Everyone's fuckin' dead! *Now get the door!*"

Everitt did as he was told, and Brig watched another deputy – this one of more average height, but slightly on the portly side, step through the door.

"Sorry I'm late," Sam said. "Carl was supposed to pick me up, but he never showed. Have you heard from him?"

Everitt motioned for Sam to follow him and both went back into A.J.'s office. The portly deputy ran back out almost immediately. He paced back and forth between the desks as if he didn't know where he wanted to go. Finally, he turned toward the cells and saw the other three bodies.

"What the hell *happened here?*" He asked in an amazingly high-pitched tone. "Christ, will you look at this mess!!"

Brig decided that if he was ever going to get out of his cell, this was his chance. Everyone seemed to be shaken up. The only one of the deputies who seemed to have it together at all was Everitt. Brig started demanding to be let out, his voice gaining volume with every request until it sounded like a full-fledged conniption fit.

"Will someone *shut him up*?!" Bill screamed. Sam asked what Brig was in for, and Bill responded, "Drunk and disorderly."

"Shit, Bill! Get him out of here. We've got bigger problems now!" There was a definite authoritative tone in Sam's voice, which surprised Brig, who had him figured for a timid fellow.

"He's a *witness*!" Bill countered.

It was then that Brig decided to plead his case. "Please... if one of you will take me home to make sure my little girl is alright, I'll answer all of your questions. *PLEASE*! It might not be too late!"

"What the hell is he talking about?" Sam asked.

Everitt pointed to the empty cell and said, "The guy who was in that cell there fished the boss' keys off of him and let himself out. *That guy* (pointing to Brig) says he went after his daughter."

"Take him home," Sam said. "Find out if his little girl is alright and then bring him back here. We need to get his story. In the meantime... no one touch *anything*! Bill, you call the state police. Tell them we have three officers and one civilian dead. Tell them to get their asses over here STAT. I don't want any excuses, either. Tell 'em the goddamned speeding tickets can wait!"

Everitt fumbled with his keys and unlocked Brig's cell door. "Okay," he said. "Let's go. Don't try anything funny." Brig stepped out of the cell and thanked Sam, who waved him off. Brig followed Everitt outside, and both of them climbed into the squad car. The deputy floored the accelerator and flipped on the lights and sirens. At six in the morning, the roads were still relatively clear of traffic, but what cars were on the roads quickly pulled to the side.

Everitt asked Brig to tell him exactly what had happened, and Brig did his best to modify the story in such a way as to appear at least partially sane. He described how Brent had come into the station and shot the sheriff as well as the other deputy before taking a bullet himself. Of course, he lied about Tom fishing the keys out of the sheriff's hand and letting himself out of the cell, but he stuck to that part of the story, too.

"Why do you think this guy wants to hurt your daughter?" Everitt asked.

"It's a long story," Brig admitted. "He's her stepfather and I'm kinda having an affair with his wife who just so happens to be my ex-wife." Brig thought his explanation sounded rational enough. Something told him Everitt was a 'play it by the book' kind of guy. He doubted the deputy would be willing to accept the notion that Tom had been possessed by the same something that had been in the sheriff's body before Brent had blown his brains across the station's tiled floor.

"You really think he'd hurt her?"

"Without a doubt."

"That's just messed up," Everitt said. "What is this guy? Some kind of psycho?"

Brig shook his head as the Haunted House on Hillbilly Hill zipped by in his peripheral vision. "You don't know the half of it," he said.

Everitt noticed Brig wringing his hands and that his face had gone pale. "Calm down, buddy," he said in his best consoling voice. "Everything's going to be alright. We'll find the son-of-a-bitch before he gets to your little girl. Don't worry."

I wish I could believe that, Brig thought. *If you only knew.*

Just then, Harv's pickup blew past them, headed in the opposite direction. Harv never drove that fast, and Brig's gut told him something was wrong. The encounter was too quick for the medicine bag around Brig's neck to have time to react. He let the thought go; his mind was preoccupied with thoughts of getting back to the house and making sure Erin and Kaitlyn were safe.

When the drive came into view, Brig pointed to it and said, "Pull in there." Everitt turned in and continued toward the house. After passing the tobacco barn, he made a quick, habitual glance in his rearview mirror and slammed on the brakes. "Sweet tap-dancin' Jesus!" He shouted.

Brig looked over his shoulder through the car's back window and drew in a shocked gasp. "Oh, shit!" He shouted. "Holy mother of God! *Back up*! *Back up*!"

Everitt put the car into reverse and stepped on the accelerator. Beneath the car, the tires spun, spraying gravel before they finally bit, sending the car backward with a jolt that propelled its two occupants forward. A hundred yards later, Everitt slammed on the brakes again. He and Brig flung the car doors open and jumped out.

The sight before them was horrific – the sort of stuff nightmares are made of. Harv was hanging on the barn door, three feet above the ground. His arms were outstretched, and nails had been driven through his wrists. Long trails of blood ran down the gray wood in random streams.

Everitt removed his hat and put his hand on his forehead. "Dear God!" He shouted. "He's been *crucified!* What's going on in this town?"

Harv's head hung with his chin against his chest. The bill of his cap concealed his face. The two men stood staring at the hired hand when they saw one of his legs move.

"He's alive!" Brig screamed. "He's alive!"

The two of them rushed forward. Brig looked at Harv's face and saw that he had been badly beaten. "Harv!" He cried. "Harv, can you hear me?" The old man's mouth opened and a glob of blood fell from his lips and splattered into the dust below. He let out a painful groan, and Brig told Everitt to grab his legs.

"Hoist him up!" he commanded. "Take the weight off of his arms!" Everitt did as he was told, and as soon as he did, Harv drew in a deep breath – the gurgling sound that accompanied it told Brig his lungs were filling with fluid. "We have to get him down!"

Brig hurried to pick up a hammer lying on the ground a few feet away. "Hold on, Harv! We're going to get you down." The old man's arms were a good nine feet off of the ground, so Brig searched for something on which he could climb. He grabbed the crate of dynamite and turned it onto its side, propping it against the barn door.

"Is that going to hold you?" Everitt asked.

Brig steadied himself and said, "I think so." Once he'd climbed on top of the crate, he found that the nails were still above his head, but within reach. "Harv," he said. "I'm afraid this is going to hurt, but we have to get you down." With that, Brig snagged the head of the nail in the hammer's claw and pulled with everything he had in him.

The nail came out of the door with a creak. Harv responded with a tormented moan, and his arm flopped to his side, causing the old man's center of gravity to shift. Everitt desperately fought to hold up Harv's two hundred and thirty pounds of near-dead weight. Before he managed to get it under control, Harv swung from side to side like some sort of morbid pendulum pinned to the barn by the remaining nail driven through his left wrist. He raggedly coughed up an oily ball of phlegm and howled with pain before mumbling something about the cave.

Brig was quick to move the crate to the other side of the door. "I'm know it hurts, Harv. I'm hurrying. Just stay with me!"

He climbed on top of the crate again and removed the other nail just as he had before. Now free, Harv's body fell forward, landing squarely on Everitt's shoulder. Both of them tumbled to the ground.

The deputy rolled the old man onto his back and took the cap off his head. Harv's face was bruised and bloody; his jaw was cocked to one side, and when Brig looked at it, he hissed through his teeth, imagining the pain. It had to be broken.

Brig took off his button-down shirt and wiped his hands on the white undershirt he wore beneath it, leaving behind smeared red handprints. He tore the shirt into long, wide strips, which he used to bandage the puncture wounds in Harv's wrists.

Everitt was busy checking for vital signs. His emergency training was rusty, but when he looked into the old man's eyes, he knew what he saw. One of Harv's pupils was larger than the other. The deputy lifted his eyes to Brig and said, "He has a concussion. His pulse is there, but it's weak. We have to get him to a hospital now."

Brig got down on his knees and put his lips next to Harv's ear. "Who did this to you?" He asked. The answer was a raspy noise Harv made as he exhaled. Brig took the old man's callused hand into his own and said, "Was it Tom? Squeeze my hand if it was. Tell me, Harv – was it Tom?" Harv's eyes rolled in their sockets, even more evidence of the pain he was in, but he managed to lightly squeeze Brig's hand.

Everitt watched the scene unfolding before him and asked,

"*Well?* Was it? Was it Tom?"

Brig nodded and growled, "Don't worry," he said confidently. "I'll take care of him. Help me lift Harv up. We'll put him in the back of your car. Get him to a hospital as fast as you can. I'll take care of the rest."

The two of them loaded Harv into the backseat of the squad car and Brig shook Everitt's hand, thanking him for his help. "Call all of your men," Brig told him. "Tell them who they're looking for. He's driving a white Chevy pickup with a red stripe down the side. Tell them he's *extremely* dangerous."

Everitt nodded and added, "Shoot first, and ask questions later." When he said that, Brig thought about what he'd seen back at the station – when Malocere had jumped into Tom's body after Brent had killed the sheriff.

"No," he said. "Don't shoot to kill. Wound him if you have to, but whatever you do, *don't* kill him. I don't have time to explain. You just have to trust me." Everitt agreed and promised to communicate the message to the other guys. He shook Brig's hand again and climbed into the car. After a quick turn, the squad car was wailing down the highway.

-3-

Brig had been so wrapped up with taking care of Harv, that he had momentarily forgotten why they'd come here in the first place. He took off running toward the house as fast as he could. When he reached the spot where Malocere had careened off of the embankment and rolled the car, Brig was filled with a desperate hope.

He reached the front door, tore it open, and rushed into the house calling Erin and Kaitlyn's names. The house was silent, and Brig prayed the two of them had made it out in time. After searching the back part of the house and coming up empty, he walked back down the hall towards the living room.

He stopped dead in his tracks when he saw a woman dressed in a flowing, white robe sitting in one of the living room's rocking chairs. There was a glow all around her, which covered her head and body like a long veil. She reminded him of the lady in white he'd seen on his first day back in Jones Chapel. Part of him wondered if this was her. There was something vaguely familiar about her, but before he could put his finger on it, she asked:

"Why do you look for the living among the dead? Your daughter is not here."

"Where *is* she?" Brig asked. The urgency was evident in his voice. "Is she alright?"

"She's *fine*," the woman said, rising from the chair. I wish I could tell you where she is, but as you know, there are other forces seeking the same information. Their ears are always listening, their eyes forever watchful."

"How can I reach her, then?" Brig asked.

The woman smiled. "I think you know." As soon as she said that, she started to dematerialize, growing fainter and fainter until she was gone. Brig went over to the spot where she had been and felt the temperature drop considerably.

He paused to consider what she had told him. *Of course*! he thought. *We can talk in our heads! But it hadn't worked back in the cell. Why hadn't it worked then*? He wondered if Malocere had something to do with it - *maybe he was blocking us somehow?*

There was only one way to find out. He closed his eyes and waited for the mental dial tone. It came quickly this time.

[Kaitlyn! Kaitlyn, this is Daddy. Can you hear me?]

[Daddy!] Came the reply. [Daddy, you're okay!]

A wave of relief washed over him at the sound of her voice. [I'm fine. I was so worried about you! Is Mommy okay, too?]

[Mommy's fine,] she said. [Busser's here, too.]

[Where are you, sweetie? How can I get to you?] When he asked the question, he sensed hesitation on her end.

[I can't tell you, Daddy. The bad man might find us. Where are you?]

[I'm at the house. How can I help you if I can't come to you?] he asked.

[You stay there,] she said. [We'll find you.]

Brig felt her mind draw away from his, and he fell back into his recliner, exhausted and somewhat relieved. He thought about Harv and wondered if Everitt had gotten him to the hospital in time.

Kaitlyn turned to her mother and said, "Daddy's safe! He's at home. We have to go get him."

Erin ran her hands down the back of the little girl's head and she said, "I wish we could, sweetie, but you know we can't go outside. We don't want the bad ones to find us."

Kaitlyn smiled and said, "We don't have to go outside." She put on her mischievous little grin again and covered her mouth to stifle the giggle that always seemed to go along with it. She turned to John and said, "Nanna taught me a trick. Wanna see it?"

John sat in a chair a few feet away, listening to the conversation. He wondered what the little girl was talking about and what 'trick' she had learned. He knew one thing - she had already surpassed his wildest expectations, so he didn't doubt her. Instead, he nodded and waited to see what happened.

Kaitlyn stepped into the center of the basement and closed her eyes, drawing in deep, meditating breaths. She lifted her arms into the air and made wide, sweeping circles with them. The air pressure in the room dropped, causing everyone's ears to pop. Buster barked and shifted this way and that, but didn't appear afraid.

Erin leaned in and whispered, "Wait til you see this," into John's ear. He watched Kaitlyn's hands moved through the air as though it was a canvass, and she was making the world's largest finger-painting. Something strange started to happen. A spot in midair began to ripple like a pool of water, shimmering with specks of light, which grew in diameter.

"Oh my God!" John exclaimed. "I've heard stories about this kind of thing, but I've never seen anything like it. I... I think it's a *portal*."

"A portal to where?" Erin asked

Kaitlyn turned around and said, "Nanna showed me how to make a door to the *Good Place*. You remember, Mommy. It's where we went when we were in the barn." The little girl motioned for the two them to get up and follow her. "C'mon," she said. "Let's go find Daddy."

"But Daddy isn't in the Good Place, sweetie. You said he was at home, remember?"

Kaitlyn rolled her eyes and answered her mother's question in a scoffing tone. "I *know* that. We have to jump like we did when we hid!" She motioned again for them to get up and said, "Follow me."

Erin looked to John for guidance. What she saw surprised her. On his face, he wore a wide smile dripping with eagerness. Knowing she had been there before didn't prompt him to ask her if it was safe to go. Instead, he grabbed her arm and led her towards Kaitlyn's "door."

Up close, the portal looked even stranger than it had at a distance. It was about six feet in diameter, round, and encircled with a brilliant, white ring. It hovered in the middle of the room, and Erin walked around to the other side to look through it. She was able to see John and Kaitlyn, but they appeared bowed and distorted. Looking at the portal edge-on, it was thin – razor thin. Its glowing border was the only evidence it was there at all.

John reached out and stuck his arm into the portal all the way up to his elbow. His joyful laugh sounded remarkably like that of child playing with a new toy. Erin looked to the other side again, fully expecting to see his arm poking out. It wasn't. At the point of his arm's insertion there was a circle of light swirling with color.

Kaitlyn grew visibly agitated, and she shifted her weight from one foot to the other before finally stamping one onto the floor and said, "C'mon guys, let's go! We're burnin' daylight!"

Erin laughed when she said that, because it was one of Brig's favorite phrases – *a few too many John Wayne movies*. "Okay, okay," she said. "What do we do?"

Kaitlyn said, "Watch me," and without another word, she jumped into the portal. Its surface rippled violently when she passed through, but a few seconds later, her little voice was heard coming from wherever it was that she'd gone. "Okay guys, who's next?"

John offered his hand to Erin and asked, "You want to go together?" Erin nodded and took his hand. "On the count of three," he said. "One, two, THREE!" Erin took a deep breath and held it the way one does when jumping into the deep end of a swimming pool.

The two of them jumped into the portal at the same time. They fell to ground on the other side, both rolling off in different directions as they hit. The six-foot drop from the portal to the ground came as an unpleasant surprise, but the ground was soft and absorbed most of the shock.

Kaitlyn stood a few feet away, looking around. John was busy dusting off his clothes and admiring the beauty all around him. Erin asked him if he knew where they were even though she had been there before and was sure that she knew.

"I think so," he said. "I think this is the Upper Afterworld."

"It's the *Good Place*," Kaitlyn corrected.

Diplomatic as always, John agreed with her. "Okay, that's what we'll call it, then. The Good Place." He drew air in through his nose and smiled. "Roses," he said. "The air smells like roses." Erin sniffed a couple of times and agreed that it did.

"I still don't understand how we're supposed to find Brig up here," she said. "What are we supposed to do?"

John knelt down and started drawing parallel lines in the sugar-like sand. When he had drawn three of them, he looked up and said, "If the legends are correct, I understand how this works. I explained it to Brig a couple of days ago." His laugh was uncertain, but he continued, "I guess we get to see if the theory holds water, huh?"

He went on to tell Erin about the Three Realities and how they occupied the same space, but existed in different dimensions. "Okay," he said, pointing to the top line he'd drawn. "We're here." He pointed to the line directly below it and said, "Brig is here. You follow me?" Erin assured him that she did, so he kept going. "If we walk five miles to the east in *this* world, we will have covered the exact same distance on Earth. So if we want to get from one place on Earth to another, we can come here and travel to the spot directly above it, dimensionally speaking. Then we just..."

"Jump back," Erin said, finishing his sentence for him. Despite the outrageousness of the theory, the things Kaitlyn had been telling them for the past few weeks started to make a bit more sense. "Okay," Erin said. "I'm with you. But how do we find the house? Everything looks so different here. What if we jump back and find ourselves in the middle of the Interstate?"

Kaitlyn had been quiet up until that moment, but she piped up and said, "Oh, don't worry about that. We'll find him."

While Erin could appreciate her daughter's optimism, she doubted Kaitlyn understood the difficulty of what they were trying to accomplish. "What makes you so sure we'll be able to find him?" she asked. "Do you know the way?"

Kaitlyn shook her head, "Nope, but *he* does." She held her arm out, pointing behind her mother. Erin turned around and gasped when she saw who was standing there. It was Brig's father, Gabe. She couldn't believe it, but threw her arms around him and burst into tears.

"Gabe!" she sobbed. "Gabe, is it you? Is it really you?"

"It's me, alright," he said. "I'm guessing this is all a little bit of a shock to you, isn't it?"

Erin pulled away and wiped the tears from her eyes. "Yeah, you could say that. So much has happened..."

"I know," he said. "The three of you are doin' great. It's almost over, I promise." He held out his hand and offered a handshake to John, who took it enthusiastically. "How are ya, John?" he asked.

"Fine, sir. How are you?"

"Not bad for a dead guy. Have you been taking care of my little granddaughter?" Kaitlyn ran up to her grandfather and wrapped her arms around his leg. He put his hand on her shoulder.

"Yes," John said. "I've been doing my best. She's really something."

Kaitlyn tilted her head back to look up at him and asked, "Paw-paw, where's Nanna?"

Her grandfather knelt down beside her and put his hand on her shoulder. "Nanna's at the house watching out for your daddy," he said. "Would you like to go see her?"

Kaitlyn's eyes widened and her face beamed with a smile. She started to hop up and down with excitement. "Uh-huh! Uh-huh!" she shouted. "Let's go! Let's go!"

Gabe faced the other two and asked, "How about you two? You ready to get this show on the road?" Both Erin and John agreed that they were. Gabe took Kaitlyn's little hand into his own and led all of them in the direction of the white sun hanging in the eastern sky.

A little while later, Erin stopped to take in some more of the scenery. She couldn't believe the beauty of this place. Beside her was a species of tree she had never seen before. It was tall and full; when the wind blew through the leaves, they made a sound that reminded her of the wind chimes that had hung on her grandmother's front porch. She closed her eyes and listened to the melody, breathing deep the rose-scented air.

She wanted to lie on the grass and daydream. She wanted to watch the clouds roll by in the sky above her as she'd done for hours on end when she was a little girl – back when things were simple and the world was good – back when things were pure.

A peal of thunder roared across the sky, snatching her from her fantasy and back into the here and now – except she wasn't exactly sure where *here* was. Two more peals immediately followed the first one. The sounds moved across her body like shock waves, one after the other, and her body throbbed with their energy.

Voices called to her from far away; she looked up and saw three small figures standing on the horizon atop a large, crystalline sand dune. She hadn't realized that she had fallen so far behind, and she hurried to catch up with them. When she did, she asked, "What was that thunder? Don't tell me there are *storms* here!"

Gabe shook his head. "No, no storms. The Thunder is The Voice."

"Voice?" she asked. "What did it say? What did the Thunder say?"

"I'm sorry, I can't tell you that," Gabe replied. "The living can't know what the Thunder says." He looked into the sky, studying the sun's position. Stars began to appear, almost miraculously. "Time is short," he said. "We have to go now." He pointed to a pool of water in a low valley that lie between the dune on which they stood and another just beyond it. "That's where we're headed."

The four of them walked down the far side of the dune until they stood beside the water's edge. Erin and John leaned over and saw that the pool was as clear as glass. It must have been 60 feet deep, but they could see all the way to the bottom. The pool was teeming with fish of every shape, every size, and every color. Erin bent down and scooped a handful of the water into her hands. She was about to drink it when Gabe slapped her hands, causing it to spill onto the ground. "Don't drink that!" He insisted.

His tone caught her off guard. Flowers bloomed instantly on the spot where the liquid fell. "Why?" she asked. "What's wrong?"

"You have to be *very* careful here," Gabe explained. "This place isn't for the living – The rules are different."

"What does that have to do with getting a drink of water?"

"If you drink that, you'll never die."

"And that's a bad thing?" she asked.

John chimed in, seemingly excited he could add something to the conversation. "Of course it would be!" He said. "Think about it... stuck in that body *forever*, no reprieve from the misery and wretchedness of life. Having to watch your children die, your friends, your grandchildren. On and on, suffering with the knowledge that you will be forever forced to drink from the chalice of pain, never knowing what the next tragedy will be – your only certainty being the fact that it will never, ever end.

Erin's stared into nothing, quietly contemplating what had been put to her. *Forever*, she thought. The concept sent chills through her body, and she wiped her hands onto her pants and thanked Gabe for the warning.

"I'm always looking out for ya," he said with a sly smile. "Are all of you ready to go back?"

Kaitlyn looked up at her grandfather, who towered over her. "Are you coming with us?" she asked.

"No, I have to stay here for now," he said. "But if you need me, just call." He held his thumb and pinky finger to the side of his face like a telephone receiver.

Kaitlyn giggled and wrapped her arms around him. "I love you, Paw-paw."

Gabe knelt down beside her, and her shoulders were swallowed in his hands. He looked into her eyes and said, "I love you, too. Everything is going to be alright. You're going to do just fine. You and your daddy are going to do just fine." He kissed her forehead and stood up again.

Erin asked him what it was, exactly, that Kaitlyn was supposed to do. The answer Gabe gave her was the same one John had given– she'll just know. "And what about Brig?" she asked. "Will he 'just know,' too?"

"Brig is stronger than you think –stronger than even he knows. He'll remember what to do. Tell him I said dreams are nothing more than windows into Realities. I've already told him what needs to be done. He knows. Just tell him that if he needs me, I'll be waiting at the window."

Gabe stretched out his arm and set it upon the water's surface. A pink glow started to spread from beneath his palm and fingers across the surface of the pool, concentrating into a pink ring around the pool's circumference. In the middle of that ring, the water rippled and danced the same way Kaitlyn's portal had done back in John's basement.

"This is the way back," Gabe said. "All you have to do is jump." John shook Gabe's hand and thanked him. Erin hugged him tightly; when she pulled away from him, he saw her wipe a tear from her eye. "It's okay, Erin," he consoled. "We'll see each other again soon enough." He pointed to the pool and said, "Go. Brig needs you. Take care of my boy for me, okay?"

She agreed to do so and took Kaitlyn's hand into her own. She grabbed John's hand with her other one. After scanning the world around her one last time she thought, *I wish I could stay here forever.* She called out, "Okay, this is it!" Just as John had done before, she started to count. "One... Two... THREE!"

They jumped into the air at the same time and vanished through the portal. As soon as they were through, it rapidly closed in on itself until it disappeared with a hollow *pop* like a cork pulled from a bottle of wine and a bright spark that died as quickly as it had been born.

CHAPTER EIGHTEEN

-1-

It came as quite a shock to Brig when Kaitlyn, Erin, and John materialized in the middle of the living room. He fell back in the recliner he had been sitting in with an unintended backwards somersault before rising to his knees with a look of bewilderment. Kaitlyn laughed and pointed at her father. "What the hell?" he said. "Where did the three of you come from??"

Kaitlyn went on to tell him they had just 'jumped back' in her *this is no big deal* tone she was growing ever-increasingly comfortable with using. Brig was quick to ask where exactly it was they had 'jumped back' from, and Erin was quick to launch into telling the story of their visit.

"Oh, Brig," she said. "I wish you could have seen it. It was *gorgeous*! The sand, the water, the sky..."

Her rambling continued a while longer before John broke in and said, "We were in the Upper Afterworld. You remember me telling you about it, right?" Brig agreed that he did, and John did his best to explain the need for the journey as a means to end in their effort to avoid running into Malocere, despite Erin's repeated interruptions about the scenery.

Finally the volume of her voice won out. Excitement sparkled in her eyes when she told Brig, "Your father was there."

All expression fell from Brig's face until he found his voice and stammered, "You saw him? Did you speak with him? How was he? Did he look the same?"

"Yes, we spoke with him," Erin confirmed. "And he's fine! He is so proud of you and all you have been doing." Brig seemed elated. Aside from a few dreams, hunches and a hallucination or two, it seemed through all of this, there had been very little contact between him and his parents at all. Kaitlyn certainly seemed to be in touch with his mother, but despite his vision in the fog that night, he had not been.

He went on to tell them about the woman who he'd seen sitting in the living room and the things she had told him. As he spoke, a smile crept across Erin's face and she bubbled with anticipation to tell him what it was Gabe had communicated to her while they were in the Upper Afterworld.

Brig continued his story, "There was just something about her... I don't know what it was, but I swear I knew her. Does that make sense? It's like the feeling you get when you pass someone on the street and you just can't place them. I mean, you think I would have been at least a little freaked out at the fact I had a ghost sitting in my living room, but I wasn't! I really wasn't."

"I know what you mean," Erin said going on to tell him about the experience in the barn and all of the spirits she'd seen there. "I felt the same way. I knew I should have been afraid, but I wasn't. Maybe it was because these spirits were the good ones, I don't know, but Brig... the woman you saw – the one who spoke to you – she was your mother."

Brig shook his head and held his hand out. "No," he said. "That was *not* my mother. I would have known it was her."

Erin walked up and put her arms around him. She kissed him and said, "But it *was* your mother. Your father said so. For all I know, she's probably still here in the house somewhere. Your father said she has been watching over you ever since you came home."

Flashes of memories burst to life and winked out as he replayed the last few weeks in his mind, and it began to make more sense. Not until he recalled one particular memory did his eyes widen. He turned to Erin and asked, "Uh... you don't think she might have seen us having – you know."

Erin drew in a mortified gasp, and she covered her mouth with her hands. Her voice came out muffled, but the message was clear. "NO!"

Brig threw his head back and laughed. "I tell ya, you never get away from it. It's like high school all over again!" The laughter rose in the room, and at first, no one noticed that Kaitlyn had wandered upstairs. It wasn't long before her absence was felt and her parents began calling her name. Her reply floated down the stairwell, asking her father to join her on the second floor. As Brig turned to head that way, Erin took hold of his arm and stopped him.

"There's something I forgot to tell you," she said, going on to relay Gabe's message.

A dream? Brig thought, furiously rustling through his mind for the missing file. *I don't remember any dream.* He paused, hoping the memory would come back to him, but again it failed him.

His father's voice spoke up in his head. [I'm waiting at the window...]

Brig told Erin that what she'd said meant nothing to him. She continued to try and jog his memory. "He said you'd remember! He said he told you what you have to do!"

"I'm sorry," Brig said. "I just can't remember."

John spoke up from the sofa on which he was sitting. "According to your father, you and your daughter must work as a team."

"So what am I supposed to do?" Brig asked.

John shook his head. "I don't know. Your father didn't tell me."

Brig moved to the stairwell and looked up to see Kaitlyn gesturing to him in urgent fashion to come up and join her before holding her finger over her lips in an attempt to communicate what she had to show him was a secret. Brig smiled at her, rather than nodding, to let her know he understood. He turned back to John and Erin and said, "You two wait here. I'll be right back."

Brig hurried up the stairs to see the door to his old bedroom had been closed. He turned the knob to find Kaitlyn sitting on the bed, combing her Barbie doll's long strands of blonde hair and singing a childish song.

"Whatcha doin,' sweetie?" he asked.

She jumped at the sound of his voice, not having heard him open the door. Once she realized who it was, she went back to grooming her doll and said, "Nothin,' just playing. You?"

Brig moved further into the room and sat down beside her. He gave her a quick squeeze and pointed to a similar doll with darker hair resting against one of the pillows at the top of the bed. Kaitlyn handed it to him, and he asked, "What this one's name?"

"That's Skipper," she said. "Barbie's little sister. You wanna help me brush her hair?" Brig agreed he did, so his daughter reached into a green pouch and handed him a small, yellow comb. She showed him how the grooming was supposed to be done, and Brig did his best to follow instruction.

"Sweetie," he said, "you called me up here. Is there something you want to tell me?"

"Soon."

Brig stood up and gripped the hair on both sides of his head. Kaitlyn picked her doll up again and went back to brushing. "All of this talk about spirits, The Bad Man, paw-paw, and..." He paused, thinking about what Erin had said. He thought how wonderful it would be to see his mother again – to look upon her and know who she was.

"And who, daddy?" Kaitlyn asked, interrupting his thoughts without looking up at him.

"And Nanna."

"What about them?" She asked.

"I just don't know what's going on. Mommy said paw-paw told her I'm supposed to do something – something to help you, but I can't remember what it is!"

The little girl stopped what she was doing and turned to face her father. "You don't get it?" She asked.

Brig shook his head. "Any of it! Dreams, Windows, none of it makes any sense. How can I help you if I don't know what to do?"

"You know," she said. "You just forgot." Kaitlyn set her doll and comb down carefully on the bed and looked up at her father. "We need to go to the window." Kaitlyn patted the pillow against which Skipper had been resting a few minutes before and said, "Lay down, daddy."

It was something Brig was more than willing to do; he was exhausted. Once his head hit the pillow, he asked, "Are you going to help me remember?"

Kaitlyn leaned over him and smiled compassionately, looking like the world's smallest psychiatrist. She put her hand on his forehead as though she were feeling to see if he had a fever. Brig felt her hand begin to heat up, and he tried to lift himself off of the bed, but Kaitlyn pushed him back down with surprising strength. "Sit *still*, daddy!" She commanded.

Brig felt a pulse of energy surge from her hand. It crept across his body, covering him from head to toe like a cocoon. Struggle as he did, he was unable to move. It was as though Kaitlyn had strapped him to the mattress. Her voice was soothing, but dampened as it passed through the energy field to fall upon his ears. "Settle down," she said. "You wanted help."

Brig asked his previous question again: "Are you going to help me remember?"

Kaitlyn shook her head. "No, daddy. She is." Brig's eyes went to the spot where Kaitlyn was pointing, and he saw the bedroom door slowly close to reveal the same woman he'd seen earlier that day standing behind it. She stood still, with her hands folded. The aura of white light surrounding her was brilliant, but not blinding. Her robe and her dark hair furled about her body in waves, tossed about by a breeze not of this world.

The woman moved closer, floating more than walking, and Brig recognized her for the first time. "Mom?!" he shouted. Tears welled in his eyes and spilled down cheeks.

No wonder I didn't recognize her before! He thought. *She's so* young*!*

He heard his father's voice again. [*I'm waiting at the window*...]

Brig's mother knelt down beside him. He wanted to speak, but the tremendous lump in his throat prevented it. She was beautiful – the way she'd looked when he was a child. Her smile beamed down at him, and her fingers of light plunged through the energy field and ran through his hair.

[I've missed you, son.]

Brig felt the dial tone in his mind, but found it difficult to speak telepathically. He was quickly growing tired, and he recalled what John had told him about the spirits and how they fed off the life forces of the living in order to operate in the Earthly Realm.

He wanted to ask her a million things, but the question at the front of his mind was whether or not she had been the lady in white he had seen his first night back in Jones Chapel. *Was she* really *here that day?* He wondered. *Has she been here every day since? Was it her voice on the tape singing that song?*

He felt sure it had been.

Brig struggled, now feeling very uncomfortable and considerably more claustrophobic than before. With what he had left in him, he shouted to his mother, [I don't like this! I want to get up! Let me up!]

His mother's expression didn't change. Kaitlyn's hand remained on his forehead, holding him in place as the energy was sucked from his body.

His father's voice again – [*Come to the window…*]

Brig sunk into the mattress, resigning to the fact he was losing his struggle. His mother had taken his head into her hands, and the energy drained from him faster and faster. He found the dial tone again and cried out, [Why are you doing this, Mom? *Why?*]

[Hush now . . . We're sending you to the window, son.]

Kaitlyn started humming a tune, the same haunting tune he and Erin had heard on the videotape. Her sweet, childish voice was even eerier than his mother's had been. His daughter started to sing to him, and his eyes grew heavier.

His mother took her hands off of him and arced them through the air, enveloping the three of them in a sparkling white bubble. Kaitlyn looked into his eyes and said, [She needs our energy to get us there, Daddy. Be patient.] Brig succumbed to exhaustion and his head collapsed into his daughter's lap.

-2-

Brig opened his eyes and found himself in a long hallway where glaring whiteness stretched forever in every direction. He walked forward, and the *clicking* sounds of his footsteps echoed loudly against the silence. It sounded as though he was in a huge, tiled room – *or a tomb.*

He called out, "Hello? Is anyone here?"

“Turn around son,” came the reply.

Brig turned to see his mother and his daughter side-by-side and he rushed to them, taking both into his arms. “Mom,” he said, “I’ve missed you so much! I’m so sorry I wasn’t there when you died. I never got to say goodbye.”

Rose waved him off. “No son. None of that matters - you had your own demons to conquer then as you do now. Let’s not live in the past.” She took his hand and began walking down the hallway. Ahead of them were countless rectangles with light streaming in through them that seem to float in midair.

Brig asked, ‘Where are we?”

His mother pointed to the rectangles. “In this world, there are windows, Brig. Glimpses into alternate realities, each as real as the next.” They continued forward, stopping in front of one of them. Rose motioned to it and smiled.

Brig turned his head and was amazed by what he saw. It was his family’s farm. The season was spring. The grass was a deep emerald green, and it covered the rolling hills. The green color bordered rectangles of turned earth like a frame - the fields were being prepared for planting.

The only thing out-of-the-ordinary was a large, white disk of light hanging in the cloudless sky - an alien sun. Wildflowers were in bloom; clusters of them were scattered about the landscape, adding to it splashes of pink, yellow, and white where butterflies danced among the blooms.

Brig approached the window and debated whether he should step through the opening when he heard his father’s voice again.

[*I left the window open…*]

Brig turned back towards his mother, who motioned him forward. Taking Kaitlyn’s hand, he lifted his leg and stepped over the sill where his foot found solid ground on the other side. Once through, he found himself in knee-high grass that swayed in the warm breeze. He stopped for a second to take a look back. From where he now stood, the window was a huge rectangle – almost as though someone had erased a section of the sky.

Further ahead of him, sunlight sparkled on the surface of a pond. Beside it, a man sat in the shade of a large oak tree holding a cane pole. A thin strand of fishing line was attached to a red bobber that pitched and rocked on the water, occasionally exposing its white underbelly. The man's face could not be seen as it was obscured beneath the rim of a large, straw hat.

Despite Brig's heavy footsteps, the man in the hat offered no indication he heard anyone approaching and made no attempt to move. When Brig was about fifty feet from him, he called out, "Getting any bites?"

The man nonchalantly tipped his hat back with his thumb and said, "Nope. I don't think there's a single fish in this pond." He set the pole on the ground and stood up, turning to face Brig as he did.

It was Gabe.

Brig's feet suddenly felt as though they had become concrete blocks – heavy and useless. His father walked towards him with arms open and said, "Ya just gonna stand there? That's no way to greet your old man!"

Still unable to move, but having regained his power of speech, Brig asked, "Am I *dead?*"

Gabe wrapped his arms around his boy's shoulders and gave him a hug – a quick "Dad-hug" as Brig had always called them – which ended with two hearty slaps on the shoulder. "Nope. You aren't dead. Your mama brought you here – left your body back home, though. No need bringin' unnecessary baggage."

"Brig looked at his hands, just as solid as his father standing in front of him. Is any of this real?"

"Real?" His father laughed. "After all that's happened to you, to Erin, *to your daughter*, you still think you know what Reality is? This is as real as it gets, son." Gabe turned back to the pond and gave a whistle. From behind the tree a dog barked and came running.

Brig recognized the Collie-mixed mutt immediately. "Cricket???" Now free of the concrete his feet moved and he ran to meet the dog halfway as it jumped into his arms, licking his face. Brig squeezed her and the dog continued to bounce around him, desperately wanting to play.

"I haven't seen her since high school!" Brig remarked. "Look at her! She's perfect!"

Cricket quickly bounced over to Kaitlyn and her mother as Gabe wrapped his arm around Brig's shoulder and led him towards the pond. "When your spirit roams free and you aren't bound by your mortal shell, traveling between the dimensions and looking into them through The Windows is possible."

Brig held out his hands again, examining the tops of them and then doing the same thing with his palms. "So, I'm not *me?*" He asked. "This is just my spirit?"

Gabe laughed and said, "*Of course* you're you! Don't you understand? Your spirit *IS* you!"

Still looking at his hands, Brig asked, "Well, shouldn't I be able to see through myself or something? For that matter, shouldn't I be able to see through *you*? I mean that makes us ghosts, right?"

Gabe nodded his head and said, "Ah, *now* you're getting to the meat of it. John explained The Three Realities to you, right?" Brig nodded, "Well, together, all three make up the Total Reality. The whole she-bang, if you will. Lock-stock-and Barrel. Up until this mess started, you believed Earth was all there was. *Now* you know it makes up only a third of Reality."

Brig sat down and leaned against the tree, picking up his father fishing pole and tugging on the line to make the bobber dance. Gabe sat beside him and went on with his explanation. "Earth is the physical world," he said. "The other two are all spiritual. If a spirit materializes in the physical world, it will look like you said – transparent, ghost-like. But in the spiritual worlds, we look every bit as real as we did when we were in our bodies."

"So spirits can't make physical contact with the living?" Brig asked, remembering the feeling of his mother's hands on his face.

"Oh, no!" Gabe exclaimed. "I didn't say *that!* Can they have contact? You bet they can. The spirits just operate on a different set of rules, that's all. They're *liberated* from physical laws, not bound by them. What may be a wall to you might be seen as a doorway to them." He paused a moment to reposition his hat. "But I need to tell you about the most important thing – Time. It passes differently in all three Realities. Right now, you're in the highest one. Time passes very slowly here compared to the way it does on Earth. The further down a Reality is in the hierarchy, the faster time passes in relation to those above it. A day on Earth is like a thousand years in The Upper Afterworld. The flip side of that is that a day in the Lower Afterworld is a varying multiple of time on Earth. The time flow in the lower worlds is very unstable."

Gabe continued, "Understanding the time difference is *very* important. They can work *for* you or *against* you. Think about it this way, anytime you jump into another dimension, you're bound by that Reality's time flow – slower or faster, it doesn't matter. The thing you need to remember is the time flow on Earth keeps going as it always did. If you jump into a lower Realm, you could spend only a few minutes there, but return to Earth and find that *years* have passed."

Gabe stood up and held out his hand. "C'mon," he said. "Walk with me, there's still a lot to talk about."

Brig took his father's hand and rose to his feet. "But what about Erin and Kaitlyn?" He asked. "I can't leave them alone!"

"They'll be waiting for you when you get back. As far as they're concerned, you and Kaitlyn are curled up taking a nap together. Remember, time passes slower on Earth. Nothing will to happen to them."

Brig and his father started walking out of the valley. They neared the top of the slope, and as they did, the farmhouse appeared. Brig turned to his father and asked, "This is the Upper Afterworld? It's not anything like Erin described it."

"What Erin saw was a template," Gabe explained. "What she saw was what all spirits see when they arrive here. Each then creates a world all their own."

Brig looked up and noticed they were standing on the front porch of the house, which had been at least a thousand yards away only seconds before. He glanced back over his shoulder and then to the house again. His eyebrows drew together, and he stared off into space, trying his best to make sense of how they had covered so much distance in so little time without him even realizing it.

Gabe spoke up and it was obvious that he was reading his son's thoughts. "It's a lesson you need to learn," he said. "Knowing how to warp space will be a critical tool if you are going to fight Malocere."

"You've got to be kidding!" Brig scoffed. "There's no way I can do that! I've seen some of what that thing can do. And John said it himself – my abilities are dormant. The best I've been able to come up with so far is telepathy." Pointing to Kaitlyn who was playing with his mother in the front yard, he said, "I'm nothing compared to her!"

Gabe's reply was firm. "Dormant yes, but we're about to wake some of them up – for you and for Kaitlyn. Make no mistake about it Brig, you *can* fight him, and you *will*, though perhaps not in the way you're thinking. Your daughter's life depends on it!" When he said that, he turned and looked away from the house towards the end of the sidewalk. Brig did the same. "Give it a try," Gabe said. "It's all in your head. Just pick a spot past Kaitlyn out there, and imagine that space between this point and that bends so that the two points touch – just like you're holding a piece of notebook paper on both ends and you bring your hands together without letting go. When you can see that in your head, all you have to do is step across."

Brig still had his doubts. "You make it sound so simple," he said.

"It *is*. After all, you did it just a minute ago and you didn't even realize it – stepping across warped space, I mean. It's how we got here so quickly."

"And that's all there is to it, huh?"

"Simple as pie."

Brig decided to give it a shot, although he still had his doubts. He found a spot midway up the hill, which sloped upward from the house to the highway. At the spot he chose, there grew a large Frazier Fir, which had been the family's Christmas tree when he was nine years old. Just as his father had told him to, Brig pictured Reality bending between the front porch and the Fir tree. It felt strange, almost as if his brain was stretching inside his head. All of a sudden, space warped in front of his eyes, bending just as his father had said it would. The world around him looked wavy like something he'd seen in the reflection of one of the Haunted House's trick mirrors.

When the two points touched in his mind, Brig stepped across the rift as one might step over a puddle. Once he did, space snapped back into place with the violent elasticity of a large, rubber band. A loud *cracking* sound followed.

Brig reached out and touched the tree's waxy, green needles. He looked back in his father's direction with evident amazement that he had been able to pull it off after all. He decided to try for someplace a little further away, and he chose the shady spot beside the pond where his father had been fishing.

Again, he pictured space bending between where he was and where he wanted to go.

S – t – r – e – t –c – h . . .

A quick step forward and another loud *crack* later, Brig bent over and picked up his father's cane pole, which lay on the ground where Brig had left it. He shook his head and thought, *Amazing.* For the hell of it, he tugged on the fishing line again, but there was still nothing on the other end.

Brig looked back and saw the backside of the house. He wondered if this whole 'space warp' thing would still work even if you had to pass through solid objects to get where you wanted to go. No sooner had the thought entered his mind than Gabe shouted:

[NO!!]

Heeding the warning, Brig imagined himself standing beside the front porch merely feet from where he had been two warps ago.

S – t – r – e – t –c – h . . .

Space bent just as it had the previous two times. The house itself sank, a casualty of the Reality vacuum now well within Brig's control. The house went down quickly, like a battleship whose hull had been blown open by an enemy torpedo. In a blink, nothing remained – almost as if the house had never existed at all.

Brig stepped forward – *Snap! Crack!* – and he was back at this father's side.

"I told you it was easy," Gabe said.

Just then a lightning bolt crashed into the roof that overhung the porch. The force was tremendous and both Brig and Gabe covered their heads. Out in the driveway, Rose held her hand over her mouth as Kaitlyn stood beside her with a palm out, electricity still buzzing all around it.

"Sorry about that!" Rose called out. "Little Bit here needs to learn control."

Gabe shook his head and turned back to Brig. "Are you ready for lesson two?" Brig nodded that he was. "It's going to come as a bit of shock!" His father warned.

Full of confidence from his recent success, Brig said, "Give me what you've got. I'm ready for anything!"

No sooner had he spoken those words, than the face of a dragon materialized out of thin air and lunged at him with a sharp snap of dagger-like teeth. Brig screamed with surprised and fell backwards, tripping over his feet and landing on his butt.

Gabe shook his head with disappointment and a sprinkle of chastisement. "I told you it was going to come as a shock! You have to be ready for that kind of thing."

"*Jesus!* Brig shouted. What was that?!"

"That is the kind of thing you should expect from Malocere. He's going to try and do everything in his power to throw you off guard. You have to be ready for whatever comes."

Brig was more frustrated than ever. "Well, what the hell am I supposed to do??"

"Try this." Gabe said, holding his hand out like a traffic cop trying to stop oncoming cars. Again, the dragon appeared and a surging pulse of bluish-white light erupted from Gabe's palm, like an umbrella turned inside out by a vicious wind. It reminded Brig of the light that had emanated from the medicine bag back in the jail cell when Malocere had tried to leap into his body. The monster reeled back and shrieked before it evaporated and blew away like particles of dust on the fickle wind. Gabe turned to face his son and said, "It's not a dagger through the heart, but it'll buy you a few seconds. Sometimes, that's all you need."

Gabe's face grew solemn. "I can teach you to protect yourself. I can teach you to protect Kaitlyn when it's necessary, but you need to know you don't have enough ability to go on the offensive against Malocere. If you try, I promise you, you'll fail." Then, just as he had lectured Brig so many times in his teenage years, Gabe beat his fist into his palm and said, "A man must know his limitations. Kaitlyn must wage the battle. Not you."

Brig nodded and in a humble tone, he asked, "Can you teach me to do what you just did?"

"It's really not that difficult," Gabe assured him. "You just have to imagine what you want to happen, believe that it will happen, and watch what does happen. Reality exists in your mind. *Remember that.* The only reason things are as they are is because you perceive them to be so. To shape Reality into what you want it to be, all you have to do is to imagine it as you want it. What I just did is a simple defensive technique – you can use it to protect others as well, but be cautious with all of these abilities, they will drain you."

Gabe pointed to Kaitlyn back down the sidewalk who was busy sending lightning bolts zigzagging through the air. "Do you remember the twist in your gut you felt the day that coyote was about to maul her in the meadow?"

Brig nodded. "I felt helpless. I was too far away. I couldn't take the shot. There was nothing I could do."

"Exactly." Gabe replied, poking Brig in the abdomen. "Right there. Right where you felt that twist. That's where I want you to go. Distance is meaningless – I've already proven it to you, but you had the power to help her all along – you just didn't know it." He tapped his finger against his temple and then wagged it at Brig. "I think I know what you need. Now get ready and remember what I told you."

The dragon's head appeared again, only this time it swooped from above, its mouth agape, headed straight for Kaitlyn. Brig didn't have to think that time. He dropped to one knee and swiped his hand through the air. His mind reached out and he saw himself between the dragon and his little girl. A silver shield glimmered in the air and the dragon collided with it, causing it to reverberate and wobble. Again and again the dragon lunged, but Brig stayed focused and the shield remained.

Kaitlyn turned towards the thing snapping at her and sent forth a power pulse that knocked it back far enough for her to wind up and cast ribbons of lightning directly at it. The apparition reeled back and howled. Two more power pulses and she seized it with her hand, yanking it to the ground where she thrust a fist forward in a downward punch, that resulted in a meteorite-like crater in the driveway and a shower of gravel dust.

"YES!!!" Gabe and Rose clapped at the same time. "YES!!! You're working as a team!"

Kaitlyn looked back at Brig and winked before giving him a quick 'thumbs up' sign. "Nice shield, Daddy."

Gabe hugged his boy and said, "You seem to be getting the hang of this. That's enough for now; I need to show you something." He took Brig by the arm and led him into the house.

The first thing Brig noticed was that all of the interior walls were missing, making the house one large room. The ceiling above the first floor was gone as well and the bookcases soared twenty-five feet to the ceiling of what would have been the second story.

"What's this?" Brig asked. "Some kind of library?"

"Sort of," Gabe answered. "Remember what I told you, we create our own worlds here. For our purposes, I just tweaked the house a little bit, because there are some things you need to learn. A library seemed like the obvious place for that kind of thing."

Gabe removed a large, leather-bound tome from one of the bookcases and blew a thick layer of dust from the cover. The book's spine cracked and the leather creaked like old, tired bones. Brig wondered how long the book had been sitting on the shelf as Gabe dropped the book onto the table, sending dust billowing all around them. He held his finger on a section of the page bearing large, bold type written in a language Brig could neither read nor understand.

"What is that?" He asked. "Hieroglyphics?"

Gabe looked at the page. "Oops," he said. "Sorry about that. This is the original text." He waved his hand over the yellowing pages, and the type font changed to a sort of Old English styling Brig was a bit more familiar with. "The information in this text should help you."

Brig pulled up a chair from beneath the table and sat down to read. Written at the top of the page was "Malocere." The words below that weren't so much written on the page, rather they floated above it, making his head swim with motion sickness. He rubbed his eyes and tried to focus, but only grew more frustrated until he finally shoved the book aside.

Gabe laughed and said, "Not an easy read, is it? I guess I should have told you that reading is a little different here, too." He reached out and scooted the book back in front of his son. "All you have to do is touch the page."

Brig put his hand upon it, and he felt the words squirming beneath his palm. They jumped from the pages and crawled up his arm like thousands of busy insects. His skin was quickly covered with inky nouns and verbs, which marched up his arm and wiggled into his ear.

His mind soon filled with images – images of the Great War between the Dark forces and the Light – the same ancient war that had managed to rip the very fabric of Reality, fragmenting it into the three Realities, which Brig had only recently come to understand. The great battle had taken place millennia before man's first one-celled ancestor appeared in a shallow pool of primordial soup somewhere on an inhospitably hot and primitive earth.

Brig watched the horror and the destruction caused when Reality folded in on itself the way a child makes an accordion fan out of a piece of paper. Some of the Dark Forces were trapped between the folds – some on the dimensional plane, which would later become Earth, some in The Borderlands, and a far greater number became locked in the Lower Afterworld.

The Dark Forces which remained in the Upper Afterworld were few in number and were quickly overpowered by the Forces of the Light. They were driven to the edge of the Upper Realm and cast from its walls. They fell into the lower worlds by the thousands, trailing long, bright tails of fire like meteors plunging to their death – unspeakable pain shrouded in a façade of brilliant beauty. Malocere was in this latter legion.

Brig watched the creature fall just as the others had. He came to rest in The Lower Afterworld where he remained for millions of years, his anger simmering and his intentions growing darker and darker. Those intentions finally came to fruition when he found the portal in the cave, allowing him to escape and rage forth upon an unsuspecting Earth, unleashing eons of festering bloodlust, before he was chased into his cave and held there against his will.

Slaughter came to Jones Chapel the day the miners came upon him deep in one of the many cave passages. Malocere communed with the men the only way he knew how – their blood was his wine; their bodies, his bread; their screams, music to his ears. The next century and then some passed before Brig's eyes in a blur. The next thing he knew, he was watching his brother's murder again, only this time, he recognized the creature inside Max Usher's body for what it was, and he finally understood the creature's dark motivations.

After another time jump, Brig saw Kaitlyn running across a field as fast as her little legs would allow. Her dress twisted around her body with every move she made – the sounds of the fabric's cries were *zip*-like swishes of chiffon and the rustle of lace. Brig saw fear in his daughter's eyes each time she looked over her shoulder at the unseen beast pursuing her.

A dark shadow hovering menacingly over the little girl was the only evidence of the creature's existence, but Brig knew who it was just the same. Consumed in the moment and no longer able to distinguish illusion from reality, he cried out to his daughter:

"RUN KAITLYN! RUN! DON'T LOOK BACK! *JUST RUN!*"

The little girl continued on, oblivious to her father's commands. She tripped on something in her path and toppled to the ground. The shadow drew closer and closer until her quivering little shape was engulfed by it. Kaitlyn rolled over onto her back in time to lock eyes with the beast.

Her terrified scream snatched the vision away from Brig, and he staggered about in a fog of confusion as though he had woken from a nightmare and was still caught between reality and fantasy, unsure what was real. The mental fog lifted, and Brig found himself sitting in the makeshift library again. His father sat across the table holding the closed book in his hands; a calm, but serious expression on his face.

Brig's hands trembled as he spoke, "What *was* that?

Gabe's response was hollow and lacking the comfort Brig had hoped to draw from him. "It's what will happen if you don't help Kaitlyn in her fight with Malocere. You can't go into this battle with false hopes, Brig. You *must* be willing to give your life to protect hers, if necessary."

"Of course I'd give my life for hers! She's my child for Christ's sake!"

Gabe rose from his chair and patted his son on the shoulder. "I'm glad to hear that," he said. "We need to get you two ready then. You both still have a lot to learn." He placed the book back onto its shelf and moved toward the front door. He motioned to Brig and said, "C'mon, let's go. There's a neat little trick I want to teach you both that might just come in useful."

CHAPTER NINETEEN

-1-

Brig stepped back through the window at Kaitlyn's urging. He woke to find himself back in his body, feeling heavy and drained. On the other side of the bedroom door, the wooden stairs creaked, heralding Erin's arrival. She pushed open the door and asked, "What do you think you're doing? I thought you were coming up here to check on Kaitlyn – not to take a nap! John and I have been waiting on you."

Brig rubbed his face and looked around the room before turning back to Erin. "How long was I gone?" he asked.

"I don't know – ten, fifteen minutes maybe?"

That can't be right, he thought, remembering all he had done and all he had learned while in the Upper Afterworld. It seemed more like days. He remembered what his father had said about the Realities' different time differentials and how a day on Earth was considerably longer in The Upper Afterworld.

Kaitlyn sat on the floor, combing her Barbie doll's hair just as she had been doing before the two of them had left on their little adventure. She looked up at him at shot a quick smile that told him the secret was theirs and theirs alone if they wanted it to be. His father had impressed upon him the necessity of keeping some of the details 'hush-hush', and Brig decided that maybe it was best for now. Meanwhile, Erin continued to drum her fingers on the bedroom's heavy wooden door with impatience.

"Sorry," he said finally. "I didn't mean to nod off on you. Give me a second, and I'll be down." Erin turned and left without saying a word. Brig gathered his strength and swung his legs over the side of the bed, scooping his daughter up and squeezing her tightly.

He was home, but the gravity of what they were facing had never felt so real. Looking at the little girl in his arms, the apple of his eye, he remembered with stark clarity the oath he had sworn to his father to protect her at all costs, even if it meant his own life, and he intended to live up to that promise.

Self-sacrifice wasn't the only thing that weighed heavy on Brig's mind. While in the Upper Afterworld, he had spent untold hours poring through ancient texts, researching something remarkable -- something about his bloodline - something incredible about what flowed through his veins. Still, he needed more details. He needed to talk to John.

He made his way down the staircase, eventually settling into his recliner where he sat silent, arms crossed. John's eyes met his, and Brig asked, "Why didn't you tell me?"

For the first time since they'd met, a confused and slightly concerned expression crossed John's face. Brig asked the question again.

"Tell you about what?" John asked.

By this time, Kaitlyn had descended the staircase and stood at Brig's side. Erin's voice rose in volume the more she insisted to be let in on whatever secret the two men shared. Incredibly calm and without taking his eyes off of John, Brig said, "I'm just curious why John neglected to tell me that we're related, that's all."

Whatever confusion John might have had melted away. He sat back down on the couch and buried his face in his hands. His voice muffled as it passed through his fingers. "I'd hoped to talk to you about that after all of this was over. I wasn't sure how you'd react."

Erin laughed a cautious laugh. "You're joking right?"

"This is going to take a little while to explain," John said as he leaned back with a sigh. "Long ago, when The Great War was at its peak, Reality fragmented." Of course, Brig knew this part of the story already.

John continued, "When the Dark Forces were driven from The Upper Afterworld, the concentration of energies across the three Realities was thrown out of balance. Ideally, the Light Forces should be in the Upper Afterworld, the Dark Forces should be in the Lower, and as we are well-aware, on Earth, there is a volatile mix of humans - both good and bad. That's the ideal. That's true balance, but what resulted from the fragmentation was quite different. A great number of the Dark Forces ended up in the Earthly Realm as they found ways to escape into it. The end result was that the Reality Gradient became lopsided and top heavy."

Brig asked, "What's so bad about that?"

"It all goes back to the fundamental laws of physics. Ever since The Great War, the universe has been struggling to bring the energy concentrations back into balance. Therein lies the nature of the ongoing battle. To over-simplify, the forces of Light and Dark are fighting for celestial real estate. Ultimately they want nothing less than to conquer the Upper Afterworld."

"In order to bring things back into balance, all the Dark Forces must be confined to The Lower Afterworld once they are all driven from the Earthly Realm. Only then can Reality come back into balance and The New Age begin."

"So where do we fit in?" Erin asked. "I mean, let's say all of the Dark Forces end up in The Lower Afterworld, what's to say they'll stay there?"

John held up a finger, acknowledging she had brought up a crucial point, but he purposefully withheld an important detail of his plan. "Once the Dark Forces are driven into The Lower Realm, they must stay there. There will no longer be a way out. That's where we come in. You see, the First Keeper descended to Earth with the goal of sealing the main Gate the Dark Forces were using to move about at will. He succeeded, but only after great personal sacrifice. Unfortunately, a much smaller Gate remained open to the Earthly Realm – the one Malocere used – the one that's in your cave."

Erin stood up and pulled Kaitlyn close. "The First Keeper…" she said, her voice unsteady. "You don't mean *Him*."

John nodded. "Yes. I'm referring to The One. The First Son of the Thunder." He leaned forward, resting his elbows on his knees. "What I have to tell you next may come as a shock, maybe it won't – the idea has been around for ages. Still, I don't know if you'll be able to accept it, but I swear to you, it's the truth."

"Just spit it out!" Brig said.

John drew in a deep breath and said, "History has propagated many untruths regarding The First Son. You must understand that the books detailing His life were written by men with their own agendas. Certain key facts were left out. The greatest oversight is probably the hardest for most people to accept."

"He had a child."

"Pfffffft! That's a bunch of Hollywood nonsense, John," Erin waved him off. "Biblically, historically… there was no child!"

John dropped his head, and said, "I think Napoleon put it best – *'What is history, but a fable agreed upon?'*"

"But if He had a child…" Erin broke off.

"There must still be a bloodline," Brig finished for her.

John smiled. "Yes, and it still exists to this day." He pointed to Brig. "The blood is in your veins. The blood is in your daughter's just as it was in your brother's – just as it's in mine."

"You must be kidding! I'm related to *Him?*" Brig asked, stopping to consider what John had said. His eyes widened, and he asked, "What about mom?"

"Your mother is of the bloodline. She was as we are – a descendant. An Heir to the Thunder."

"Why are we here?"

"That's the big question, isn't it? For most, the answer is hard to come by, but for us, it's quite clear. As Descendants of The Thunder we are charged with the task of keeping things in check, so to speak. Each Keeper has the capability to send the Dark Forces into The Lower Afterworld. For thousands of years, they have hunted them down, picking them off one at a time. It was this hunt that drove Malocere back into the cave. Our ancestors teamed up and imprisoned him, and we have all been on watch ever since. Still, until Kaitlyn, none has possessed the power to send Malocere back – he is far too crafty, far too powerful.

The struggle will continue until The Reality Gradient returns to a state of equilibrium. As I told you when all of this started, the time for the final battle has come. The signs are all around us. Malocere's days are numbered. Soon we will look upon the dawn of The New Age."

Erin held out her hand, pausing John's explanation. Remembering what Kaitlyn had done to the creatures in the barn and how she had opened a Gate that sucked them in, presumably into the Lower Afterworld, she put her initial question to John a second time. "What's keeping them down there if you all pull this off? That thing got up here once – what's stopping it from doing it again?"

"The First Son descended into The Lower Afterworld where He battled for the keys to the Gate. He succeeded. Ever since, our bloodline has been responsible for protecting those keys. If we were to fail, the Gate would swing open and all would be lost."

"This seems like a pretty big deal," Brig laughed. "It's hard enough to keep secrets when there are only two people in the room. Why have I never heard of this before?"

"The established Church has done all it can to pervert the teachings of The First Son and to twist them into a framework capable of being used as a means of social control. Somewhere amid the multiple translations and outright subversion of texts, the truth was lost to all but a few."

"In the centuries following His ascension, an underground brotherhood was formed to protect the keys and the oral history of events. They too were descendants. They called themselves The Blood Knights. We are all that's left of the line."

"What happened to the rest of them?" Erin asked. "After two thousand years, I would think there should be quite a few of you guys running around."

John nodded his agreement. "You would think so, wouldn't you? Indeed, there were a great many of us at the beginning of the second millennium, but the Church had grown in political power. In the mid-fourteenth century, our people were discredited, branded as heretics, witches and summarily burned at the stake. The Church thought they had exterminated all of us and buried the truth, but a small group escaped from England and sailed along established Viking routes until they landed in the new world."

"The Blood Knights quickly assimilated with the North American natives and began to intermarry in an attempt to perpetuate the line. The native's strong tradition of passing down history orally has served us well.

As the years rolled by and the New World developed, some of the knights' descendants migrated into the American colonies.

Once again, intermarrying took place, and before long, white skin reappeared in our line. Your family descended from this colonial branch of the bloodline, Brig."

"But you're telling me that the entire line can be traced back to one man?" Brig asked.

John nodded. "Yes, except He was no man. He was the first Keeper. Kaitlyn is the last."

"And His blood is in our veins?"

"Indeed it is. Amazing, isn't it? That you could be an Heir of The Thunder?"

"But that means you and Brig are Keepers too, right?" Erin asked.

John's denial was emphatic. "No, no. There can be only one Keeper at a time – often there have been long gaps between their appearances, some are stronger and blessed with more talent than others, but all pale compared to the first and the last. That's what makes Kaitlyn so special – it's also the reason we must protect her at all costs.

Brig and I are Kaitlyn's protectors, as the knights have always been. The reason that little girl is so special – the reason she must be protected at all costs is because she holds the keys. No matter how much Brig and I do, it won't make a bit of difference without Kaitlyn, she's the only one who can open Gates. She is also the only one worthy of wielding the blade to strike Malocere down."

An image flashed in Brig's mind of a page in a book back in the library and he spoke up before he realized he had done so. "The Blood Sword."

"Yes," John acknowledged. "Little is known about the The Blood Sword. All I can tell you is that it was created for one purpose and one purpose alone – to be wielded by the Last

Keeper in the Final Battle before The New Age. Kaitlyn *is* that Keeper, and the battle is just over the horizon.

Everyone turned and looked at the little girl sitting on the floor. “Inside her?” Brig asked. “What are you talking about?”

John knelt down to squeeze her hands. He touched her forehead with his index finger and said, “The keys – they’re right here. Remember what you did in my basement? When you opened the portal? Your Nanna taught you that, didn’t she?”

Kaitlyn nodded.

“That wasn’t just a trick. She taught you how to use the keys. They’re inside you. They’re part of you. You *ARE* the key! You are the only one who can open the Main Gates between the Realms.” Kaitlyn wrinkled her nose, unable to comprehend the significance of what she’d been told, but John paid it no mind, turning instead to face her parents. “Malocere cannot be allowed to get a hold of her – he could very well force her to open a Gate to the Upper Afterworld, and I shudder to think what that would mean for Reality.

“So you and I,” Brig said, “we’re just pawns?”

John answered with a quick nod. “Yes, compared to Kaitlyn, that’s all we are. But that doesn’t diminish the significance of the role we play. We’re very important to all of this.” He interlaced his fingers and tapped them on his chin a couple of times as he chose his words. “So, the time has come. I want you to consider carefully what I’m about to tell you, Brig. We need your help, but only if you’re willing.”

He went on, “Please understand this is no game. The stakes are high and very, very real. The good guys don’t always win in the physical world and the spiritual worlds are no different. I can’t guarantee your safety. If the choice comes down to protecting you or protecting Kaitlyn, I’ll choose her. Make no mistake about it.”

Brig's face was sedate. "I wouldn't want it any other way," he said. "And the same goes for me – don't count on any of that 'one for all' bullshit. I'll sacrifice my life for hers, and I'd gladly do the same with yours. Count me in."

John clapped his hands and said, "Good. We agree then."

Erin broke in. "Don't I get a say in any of this?"

"I'm afraid not," John told her. "You aren't part of this, I'm sorry."

"The hell I'm not," she shouted. "Your Keeper just so happens to be *MY* daughter!" She pointed a finger at Brig. "And you... I don't want anything to happen to you, either." Her voice broke when the tears came.

Brig knew she was frightened – with good reason – and feeling more than a little out of control, something Erin despised. He took her hand into his and wiped a tear from the corner of her eye. "I understand how you feel," he told her. "Really, I do. You care a lot about Kaitlyn and me, and we're both going to be in danger. I know how terrified I would be if it were the two of you, instead. That's why you can't come with us."

Erin snatched her hand away and stood up. "What?! *Oh, I'm going, Brig*! There's no way in Hell I'm going to sit here and think happy thoughts while you all are out there fighting that, that THING!"

"Okay, okay," Brig said in his best soothing voice. "Let's all just settle down. We're getting ahead of ourselves here." He pushed down on her shoulder for her to sit. When she had, he suggested that a drink might calm them all down.

Brig walked towards the kitchen, listening to the sounds of the voices in the living room behind him. Once he was there, he leaned forward, placing both hands on the countertop as he drew in deep breaths. He looked down at his shoelaces and spoke in little more than a whisper. "Dad," he said. "Take this responsibility away from me. I'm not strong enough. You've picked the wrong man."

He stood up a short while later and opened one of the nearby cabinets. He removed three glasses and set them on the counter when he spotted the bottle of Xanax. He took the bottle in his hand and exhaled a defeated sigh as he shook four tablets into his palm. He set them on the counter and placed ice in the glasses, adding rum to two of them.

He emerged from the kitchen doorway a few minutes later, struggling to balance all three glasses. Erin hurried to help, taking one in each hand. Brig pointed to the glass with colorful cartoon characters painted on the side and said, "That one's yours. It's the strongest, and you need it." The two of them went back into the living room, and Brig gave John the Sprite he'd requested. "Sure you don't want something with a little more kick?" he asked.

John shook his head. "Dulls the senses," he said. "I need to stay sharp. The same goes for you, but I suppose if it calms you down, a little won't hurt."

"Indeed it does." Brig's eyes searched the room for Kaitlyn, but came up empty.

John watched his gaze and said, "If you're looking for your daughter, she went upstairs to play, I don't think she likes seeing the two of you argue."

Brig hung his head. "No, she doesn't like that very much at all." Erin was already three-quarters of the way through her own glass. He sat back in his recliner and jiggled the ice cubes in his glass. Thick, brown clouds of rum floated weightlessly in the yellow soda.

"How long were you up there?" John asked.

"What makes you think I was actually there at all?"

"You knew about the bloodline, the blade... besides, you look different – wiser even."

Brig laughed. "That's lack of sleep. But you're right, I was up there for a long time. I'm estimating several days."

"*Upper Afterworld time,*" John interjected.

"Whatever, it was a long damn time. I learned a lot while I was there – some things I wish I hadn't. Life was so much easier before I knew." His eyes found their way back to the glass in his hand. "I don't know if I'll ever be the same again." John nodded his head knowingly, and the two of them made eye contact for a brief second. For the first time, Brig sensed the bond between them. The bond of brothers – the bond of blood.

Erin's snoring drew them out of the fragile trance of mutual reverence. Brig stood up and used his T-shirt to wipe away a thin line of spit trickling down her chin. After another explosive snore, John exclaimed, "Wow! She's out cold. Fifteen minutes ago, she was all gun-ho and ready to spit bullets. What happened? Can she not handle her liquor?"

Brig reached into his pocket and pulled out the Xanax bottle. He gave it a quick shake and said, "Sedatives."

"You drugged her up??"

"I had no choice! We can't take her with us, and we both know she'd never let us go without her. I'll admit it wasn't the best of solutions, but it was all I could think of." Brig considered the situation for a moment and said, "I know we can't take her with us, but I don't want to leave her here, either. She won't be safe. You know as well as I do that Malocere was able to get into the house – cedar wood or no cedar wood. What's stopping him from coming back?"

"He was in a human body," John explained. "It insulated him from the spirits in the cedar. There is a stronger defense we can use, though."

"I'm listening."

John grabbed him by the arm and led him to the front door where he opened a lock-bladed hunting knife. "We can seal the house. Without a word, John drug the stainless steel blade across the palm of his hand. Bright-red beads of blood rushed forth from the severed vessels, forming a small puddle in his palm. John closed his hand into a loose fist and tipped it over as if he were pouring water from a pitcher. Large drops splattered on the door's threshold.

John looked up and said, "The power is in the blood. Malocere can never enter this door again. The blood is to him as water is to fire." Then, in a blur of motion, John took Brig's wrist and sliced his palm with the blade. The cut was clean, precise, and after a couple of seconds, blood came to the surface. When it did, it flowed out readily.

Using his other hand, John pointed to the back of the house and said, "Every threshold, every windowsill! A couple drops in each spot should do the trick. Hurry, we don't have much time!" John headed upstairs where he met Kaitlyn on the second story landing. She was holding her blonde-haired Barbie doll by one of its legs, letting it dangle carelessly at her side.

"What's goin' on?" She asked.

"The time has come," he said. "It's time to fight."

Kaitlyn didn't appear at all upset by the news. She seemed more interested in the way John was cradling his left hand. He saw the concern in her eyes and assured her everything was alright. "We have to seal the house," he explained. "Your mother won't be coming with us, so we need to make sure she's safe when we leave her."

Without another word, he hurried through the two rooms on the upper floor, dripping blood on every windowsill. Kaitlyn waited patiently for him to finish the task. When he had, he took her hand and led her downstairs. Brig nearly tackled the two of them as he burst through the master bedroom door.

Kaitlyn saw that her father's hand was cut, too. She reached out and took it into her own as well as John's. She looked back up at them through tear-filled eyes, and Brig thought, *she can feel our pain.* They both felt something like a tickle begin in their palms. A bluish haze enveloped their hands, and Brig tried to pull away, but Kaitlyn held on. The tickle quickly turned to heat – more and more intense until she let go a few seconds later. The two men checked over their palms and found them completely healed.

Kaitlyn gave no indication she had done anything warranting thanks, but Brig and John offered theirs just the same. A smile crossed her face, but it disappeared when she saw her mother passed out in the recliner. She walked over and placed her hand on Erin's forehead, examining her with deep concern. She looked back at Brig and asked, "Is she asleep?"

"Yes," he said, "she is. I had to give her something to put her to sleep. She wanted to come with us, but..."

Kaitlyn interrupted him, "She can't go where we're going, can she?"

"No sweetie, I'm sorry."

She leaned forward, and gave her mother a gentle kiss on the cheek. "Sleep tight, mommy," she said. "When you wake up, everything's gonna be okay."

Brig watched with tears in his eyes and a lump in his throat. The gravity of the situation had become all-too-real. He was angry – angry that Reality was as it was. *She's too young for this,* he told himself. *It's not fair.*

Kaitlyn faced John and said, "We need get going. He's headed this way."

John checked his pockets, making sure he had what he needed. "Brig," he said, "you have a gun, don't you?" Brig nodded and went to get it, making sure it was fully loaded. After that, he went over to the recliner and gave Erin a kiss before returning to the foyer where John handed him a folding knife similar to the one that he had used to slice their hands.

"What's this for?" Brig asked.

"This is for all the things I can't imagine. Remember your blood has power."

Brig took it and slid it into his hip pocket. "So what now?"

"At present, Malocere is blinded. He doesn't know where Kaitlyn is, because of the cloud put in place by the Agents of the Light. We have to lift the veil and lure him to us." The three of them stepped onto the porch, and Brig locked the deadbolt behind himself. They climbed into the cab of John's pickup, and he said, "I hope we haven't waited too long to leave. I'm afraid we're cutting it close."

"Are you ready, little one?" John asked before starting the engine. She looked so innocent, so young. Her blonde hair rested on her shoulders, and her blue eyes were large and moist with tears, which made them appear swollen and glassy. The little pink sundress she wore fell across her lap in generous pleats where she scratched at one knee, clearly irritated by the lace rubbing against it.

"I'm ready," she said. "Let's get this over with."

Brig sat in the passenger's seat, overcome with a crippling sense of dread. The pink dress Kaitlyn was wearing - swishy chiffon, itchy lace, and all - was the same dress he'd seen when he'd touched the book in The Upper Afterworld. He remembered watching her running into uncertain, never-ending darkness, attempting to elude whatever it was that was pursuing her.

He heard his father's voice in his head, telling him that what he'd seen was what would come to pass if he didn't intervene. A chill ran over his body when he remembered her tripping and falling to the ground just as the thing caught up. Her screams echoed down the primitive corridors of his mind.

Just then and without warning, his ears popped, and the sound of a mighty wind washed over him. He looked to his left where John was holding hands with Kaitlyn. "What the hell was that?" he asked.

"We've lifted the veil," John told him as he started the engine and dropped the transmission into gear. The truck lurched forward, and they picked up speed. A few minutes later the truck reached the highway. John stared through the windshield at the road ahead and said, "We're no longer protected. Malocere knows where we are."

-2-

Malocere had been searching Jones Chapel for days – searching for any sign of the Keeper. Despite the torture exacted upon him, Harv never gave up any secrets. After all was done, Malocere had stolen his truck, which was running low on gas, and he knew he would have to find her soon or he would be back on foot once again.

It was about this time the veil was lifted, and Malocere's perceptions cleared. In his mind, he saw Kaitlyn sitting between two men, and he knew they were speeding towards him from the opposite direction.

Only moments before, Malocere had decided to head back to the farmhouse for one last search – after which he intended to eliminate the Keeper's hiding place altogether by burning it to the ground and dancing among the ashes. He thought back to the times – *so many over two hundred years* – that he'd peered out from the despised confinement of his cave, looking at the house with disdain. He remembered the way its white siding glowed beneath the light of the full moon, making it look like the tip of an iceberg floating amid a sea of rolling hills.

Oh, how he had wanted it to burn.

Just about the time John had turned off of the gravel drive onto the highway, Malocere stamped the accelerator to the floor and listened to the truck's engine roar as the speedometer climbed. Less than a minute later, he crested a hill, and John's truck was on the other side of it. The two vehicles zipped past one another too quickly for the drivers to get a good look at one another. Just the same, each knew who the other was.

Malocere slammed on the brakes and jacked the steering wheel to the left, sending the truck into a violent, skid. The back-end of the truck fishtailed, sending the tires chewing into the shoulder, spraying grit and gravel as they did. He steered into the skid, and one much milder fishtail later, brought the vehicle back under control. His face stretched to each side as a grin spread across it. He floored the accelerator again and sped off in pursuit.

When the two trucks had passed by one another, John's head snapped to the left and he beat his fist on the steering column. He accelerated, hoping against hope that his old truck still had enough muscle to outrun their soon-to-be pursuer. "He's found us," he spoke to the occupants of the cab through a tensed jaw and gritted teeth. He looked in the rearview mirror and saw Harv's truck gaining on them. A dark figure sat behind the wheel. One of the truck's headlights shined brightly, but the other winked on and off like some kind of warning light.

Brig peered out the back window. "He's gaining on us!" he shouted, "Faster, John! Faster!"

Annoyed but highly focused, John growled, "I'm going as fast as I can. I hadn't planned on a car chase!"

"Where the hell are you taking us, anyway?"

John kept his eyes on the road. "It doesn't matter now," he said. "We'll never make it."

Hillbilly Hill appeared from behind a grove of roadside trees, and Kaitlyn pointed at the park with a great deal of enthusiasm. "There!" She shouted. "Pull in there! *Go! Go! Go!*"

John jerked the wheel to the left and skidded into the main entrance. The road leading up to the park was a considerable uphill grade; the truck's engine bogged down, and John shifted into a lower gear which caused the vehicle to buck and groan.

Kaitlyn pointed at the Haunted House. She was growing more and more frantic the closer they got to it. Abruptly, John slammed on the brakes, parking the truck at an angle that spanned three parking spaces. The mood in the cab had reached fever pitch as if all their plans and preparation were unraveling before their eyes. Brig and John threw open their doors and jumped out.

An angry squeal of tires drew John's attention back towards the entrance. Harv's truck, with Malocere inside, was in the process of negotiating the hard left with considerably less success than John's truck had done - the back end whipped around violently and knocked over a wooden fence post before straightening out again.

John pointed to the Victorian structure perched atop the hill and cried out to Brig, who was pulling Kaitlyn from the cab. "RUN!" he shouted. "Run as fast as you can! Get her into the house! Don't look back - JUST RUN!" It was the first time Brig had ever heard such strained urgency in John's voice.

Brig obeyed and sprinted for the house as fast as his legs would carry him. He was amazed by the strength he found within himself, despite the added weight of his daughter in his arms. Nonetheless, he ascended the concrete steps with ease, and used his shoulder to bust through the front door of the house. The wooden door casing shattered in response to the blow, and both Brig and Kaitlyn toppled to the floor.

Less than a second after he had told Brig to get going, John hopped back into the truck's cab, depressed the clutch, and dropped the gearshift into neutral. Malocere was roaring up the hill as John hopped out and ran around to the front of the truck, giving it a strong shove. He didn't wait to see if his plan would work. Once the truck was moving, he took off running for the house as well. He had made it halfway up the concrete steps by the time Brig and Kaitlyn had burst through the front door.

Kaitlyn lifted her head and frantically waved her hand, shouting, "C'mon, John! Hurry!"

John did just that, not even looking back towards the sound of squealing tires and the deafening crash that followed. His truck had rolled backwards into Malocere's path, which had been moving at too great a speed to avoid the collision. The two vehicles slammed into one another, stopping Malocere in his tracks and sending him, once again, headfirst into the windshield. The hood buckled, and the radiator whined as multiple jets of steam poured out of it.

Not willing to be thwarted again, Malocere opened his door and fell out. He looked upon a distorted world through blurry eyes and saw John running up the steps to the Haunted House. He picked himself up and stumbled off in the same direction.

John rushed through the doorway and pulled Kaitlyn to her feet, leaving Brig to fend for himself just as he'd said he would do.

None of that *'one for all'* bullshit..

Malocere was halfway to the top of the steps when he looked up to see Kaitlyn standing in the doorway. His lips pulled back in a sneer. John grabbed her arm and tried to lead Kaitlyn deeper into the house, but she stood firmly in place. "Let's go, little one!" he screamed.

Her answer was a defiant, "No."

"We have to hide!"

"There's no time for that," she replied, speaking in a deep voice, which was throaty and brimming with determination. She balled her little fists up at her sides and locked eyes with the abomination running in their direction.

John pleaded again: "We have to RUN!"

"Yes, you do." Came her reply.

An anger had started to gather within her small body, filling her with hot, righteous hate and all the persecuted anguish of untold generations - *so much misery* - all of it caused by the thing hiding in her stepfather's body.

The slight afternoon breeze lifted blonde hair from her forehead, her bangs tossed about her face as she stepped forward towards Malocere, who was only a few hundred feet away and closing fast.

"I'm tired of running," she said.

John detected a faint scent of ozone building in the air around them. The scent was accompanied by a tingling sensation crawling across his skin, similar to what he'd felt before in the midst of severe electrical storms. Part of him expected to see a bolt of Lightning drop from the clouds, but the sky was blue, and what sparse cloud cover there was looked puffy and white.

Malocere looked once more at the small child standing in the doorway, and his mouth watered in anticipation of freedom. He tripped on the last step and fell onto all fours in a sort of sprinter's position. He lifted his eyes to Kaitlyn and reached out with his mind, groping for the faintest indication of fear in her. He found none, and fury boiled within him.

Brig watched as Malocere drew closer. The fear welling inside caused him to briefly forget everything his father had taught him, and he fell prey to a panicked reflex. He pulled the pistol from beneath the waistband of his jeans, and cocked the hammer back, squinting as he stared down the barrel with the raised site squarely in the middle of Malocere's chest. He hesitated.

"What are you waiting for?!" John shouted. *"Shoot him!"*

Brig's finger curled around the trigger and was just about to squeeze when Kaitlyn's voice made him stop.

"Wait."

Malocere sprung from his sprinter's position, covering the distance between himself and the house in mere seconds. Kaitlyn lifted her arms as a misty, orange haze surrounded her. Malocere charged towards her, raising his arms, ready to hit her like a linebacker sacking a quarterback. When he was within ten feet of her, Kaitlyn dropped her arms.

A tremendous blast came from somewhere deep within the House. It moved quickly, snaking down the plywood corridors and vibrating the floorboard planks as it passed over them. It struck John and Brig from behind and swept them off of their feet. Kaitlyn didn't move. She stood firmly in place, anchored by a much stronger will.

Now five feet away, Malocere's eyes widened when he saw Kaitlyn open her fists and expose her palms to him. Instantly, a rolling fireball formed between. It was about five feet in diameter, rippling with different shades of reddish-orange flames and smoky, black ash. She willed it forward, and Malocere was blown backwards. He soared through the air and landed fifteen feet away on his back.

The explosion was so powerful, the porch railing and support posts splintered, causing the small roof that overhung it to come crashing down as the ground beneath quaked and shifted. A crack appeared just in front of the house that zig-zagged out into the parking lot where it spread to a width of about ten feet. Harv's truck teetered on the edge before falling in with a loud crash as it hit bottom.

"Dear GOD!" Brig shouted. "Did you see that?!"

John struggled to get back onto his feet, but he had indeed seen what had happened and said, "I told you, there's great power in her. But we still have to come up with some sort of plan. You know what has to be done – we can't defeat that thing here. We have to send it back where it came from!"

Brig became distracted and ran his hands across the rough, plywood walls, which were painted black – just as they had been when he and Jacob were kids. The layout of the house appeared to be just as it had been back then. In the parlor, an animatronic ghost sat at the dusty pipe organ, frozen in a position that made it looked poised to start playing again at any moment.

The doorways appeared smaller, the hallways more narrow, but everything else was pretty much the same. He could almost see himself chasing his brother down the twisting hallways, weaving through the crowds of people, ignoring the warnings that they needed to slow down.

The park was now empty – not so much as a janitor in sight. It seemed fitting that they were here, battling evil in the purest place Brig had ever known. He missed the smell of peanuts and cotton candy, but most of all, he missed believing the world was a good place. He doubted whether he could ever rediscover his childhood eyes.

Outside, Malocere lay beside the steps in a small flowerbed. His eyebrows were singed and he was knocked out cold. John didn't know how long they had, but he wasn't willing to waste another second. He prodded Kaitlyn, insisting that they needed to retreat deeper into the house. After a couple more insistent requests, she turned and started down the main corridor.

John didn't immediately follow. Instead, he walked into the parlor and searched the walls until he found what he was looking for – a small circuit breaker the size of a shoebox with a long, bright-red, rubber-tipped handle. He reached for it and pulled. The switch made a loud, *popping* sound, and the parlor, once dark and dreary, sprung to life with light, sound, and motion. The organ-playing ghost sprang to life, hammering out dissonant chords with its thin, bony fingers. Occasionally, the robotic apparition let out a wicked cackle, and its eyes flashed beneath the hooded cloak it wore.

John pulled on Brig's arm and screamed, "We have to go!" He strained his voice so as to be heard over the carnival-like commotion. "There's no time left!" Brig turned away, taking his eyes off the figure sprawled across the front lawn with its face planted in a bed of marigolds. Now looking at the ghost hammering away at the keyboard, it was as though the creature was searching his soul with its haunting, yellow eyes, further confirming his fears that he was not up to the task at hand. The phantom cackled again, and Brig felt sure it was laughing at him.

John led him down the twisting corridor, chasing after Kaitlyn who had disappeared around a corner a few minutes earlier. Rubber pipes, which felt like arms reaching through the walls, slapped against their legs. They hurried on until they entered a room with chains hanging from the ceiling. John thought he'd finally found her. Twenty feet ahead was the shape of a little girl silhouetted in neon-red light emanating from a large, keyhole-shaped doorway.

As they passed a display depicting a Lizzy Borden, hatchet-style murder, they called Kaitlyn's name, but received no response. John was six feet from the little girl when he reached out to touch her shoulder. Just as soon as he did, a galaxy of pulsing flashes erupted. The little girl spun around, and the brilliant strobes revealed her gnarled, misshapen face. No sooner had she turned, than an old, wooden coffin burst through the floorboards behind her. Its lid sprung open, exposing a green and moldy corpse.

Brig screamed, "JESUS CHRIST!" and tripped over his own feet, sending him to the floor in a heap, dragging John along with him. In that moment both of them had forgotten why they were there, and they rolled with excited laughter.

They lay on the dusty floor, struggling to catch their breath, when Kaitlyn passed in front of a distant doorway. Her slow, mechanical movements made her appear to be just another horror-house prop, biding its time while it waited to jump out at them. Brig knew better, and he scrambled to his feet, racing towards her with John close behind.

When Brig reached the doorway, he peered around the corner to see Kaitlyn standing in front of the second story bay window. He rushed over to her and looked out of it as well. "Whatcha doin', sweetie?" he asked. "What do you see down there?" Her answer sent adrenaline coursing into his bloodstream. Its implications were terrifying:

"Nothing."

He looked through the window again, which was situated directly over the main entrance to the house. Malocere was no longer lying on the ground below. The only evidence that he had been there at all was the small patch of flowers, which had been pressed down in the shape of a human body.

John appeared behind them, slightly out of breath. He saw the blank expression on Brig's face and recognized it for what it was. "What's wrong," he asked. Brig didn't say anything; he merely pointed towards the ground. John's eyes followed Brig's gesture, and he reacted instantly.

He grabbed Kaitlyn's hand and started down the hallway. What light had managed to find its way through the old, wavy glass was snuffed out when they turned to venture down yet another long, black corridor. Brig was overcome with another warped sense of déjà vu. It wasn't until he stepped on a spring-loaded section of the floor that he remembered.

The floor gave way about an inch, and a jet of compressed air shot up his leg, just as it had in his dream a few days before. A skeletal figure lunged at him from behind a panel of bars wielding a chainsaw. Brig jumped back and screamed. John and Kaitlyn hurried on toward the flickering strobes at the end of the corridor. Those lights were their only beacons, and John hoped that salvation might be crouching somewhere in them.

Brig rushed ahead, seeking further proof that his dream had been more prophetic than just a hodgepodge of random memories. He turned the corner and saw the same lights the other two had seen. They filled him with hope, just as they had John, but for a much different reason: A little further past those strobes was the mirror maze. Brig was convinced that if they were to have a chance at tricking Malocere into jumping through the Gate, the mirror maze would be the place to do it.

Brig ran past the other two and waved them forward. "C'mon! Let's go! I've got a plan!"

They caught up to him, and John asked, "Really, you've got a plan? That's great! Let's hear it."

Brig pointed up ahead and said, "Follow me. I'll show you." The three walked on, and about ten paces later, Brig warned them to brace themselves. Before John had a chance to do so, the strobe lights shut off, and the hallway went dark.

It was quiet – *too quiet.*

From somewhere in the darkness came the sound of creaking hinges – low and lonely – unsettling and foreboding. A bright light appeared in a nearby doorway, and all three squinted their eyes just as a clown popped out laughing a sinister laugh. Its eyes were not happy eyes, but instead were narrow and slanted inward, punctuated with a deeply furrowed brow. Its lips were pulled back in a nefarious grin to reveal crooked, rotten teeth. Soon enough, it retreated back behind the door, and the light died out. Seconds later, the disorienting, yet somewhat comforting strobes started flashing again, making it safe for them to press on.

Brig was the first to notice they had started walking up another incline. This one was much steeper than any of the previous ones had been. Just as the floor sloped upward, the ceiling sloped downward and the corridor's width got more and more narrow. It was a portion of the house aptly named "Fat Man's Squeeze."

Brig and John turned sideways and wiggled through until they were able to continue on. Once they were through, they found themselves in the mirror maze. For Brig, it was a welcomed site; however, his relief was short-lived. John reminded him Malocere was inside the house, and for all they knew, just seconds behind them.

Further still, Brig stopped at a point where the maze forked in two different directions. John's agitation was apparent, and he was more than ready to get the plan into motion.

"Don't tell me we're lost!" he shouted. "That thing is going to be here any minute!"

"We're not lost," Brig assured him as he tried to decide which of the two paths to take. Panic crept into his throat at the sound of approaching footsteps. Eeeny Meenie Miney Moe... it had really come down to this? Why can't I remember the way?!

[*Help me, dad! It's been so long. I don't think I remember!*]

The footsteps were closer, and John wasn't willing to wait any longer. "Go!" he shouted. "Take her wherever you were going to take her. I'm going back!"

"Back?" Brig asked. "Back where?"

"To buy you both some more time. Now, get going!"

"But John..." Kaitlyn pleaded, holding onto his hand to try to keep him from leaving.

"No, little one. Don't worry about me. I'll be fine. Your daddy is going to take good care of you. I'll try to find you if I can, but if I can't, I want you to promise me that you'll listen to the voices in your head." He poked her stomach with his finger. "And listen to your gut. Do those two things, and you'll be just fine, okay?" Kaitlyn promised she would, and with that, he hurried off back down the path by which they'd come.

Brig looked down at his daughter who was standing by his side, and he feared once again that he was going to fail them all. Even with Kaitlyn there, he felt alone. It was as though his father had turned his back on him.

A glimmer of light caught Brig's eye, and when he turned his head, he was filled with renewed hope. What he saw was a bright ball of light at the end of the right-hand path. The ball burst into a million tinier ones, like the sparks of an exploding skyrocket. The little balls of light faded out as they cascaded to the floor; some of them bounced, having tasted flight and desperately wanting to spread their wings once more.

A misty figure appeared. Brig recognized his brother immediately. Jacob's face was long and sullen as though he were in a great deal of emotional pain. It was an expression Brig had seen on his own face many, many times before. During those lonely days when it had taken everything he had to drag himself out of bed. He remembered looking into the mirror and seeing an empty shell of his former self – swollen eyes underlined by dark, purple rings and a permanent frown whose corners were held down by the oppressive weight of regret and self-loathing.

Indeed, Brig understood what was tormenting his brother's soul. Even still, it did little to squelch the anxiety already churning in his stomach. Jacob felt responsible for the burden which was being placed upon his brother and the niece he never came to know. He was racked with guilt, because he felt this should have been *his* battle to fight, and he cursed himself for not having been strong enough to defeat the evil when it had come for him.

Jacob motioned for the two of them to follow. He turned and disappeared around the corner as he did. Brig and Kaitlyn hurried, following him around corner after corner as he motioned to them just as he had done before. Several minutes later, they emerged into the hub of the mirror maze.

It was a round area, ten or twelve feet in diameter through which an indefinite number of paths intersected at bizarre angles. The perimeter of the hub was made of mirrors the same as the corridor walls – reflections of reflections of reflections stretched infinitely into every direction, making it appear as though there were millions of versions of Brig and Kaitlyn, each one facing a different direction.

Jacob cast no reflection, however. In the center of the room hovered a halo of golden light. Before Brig had a chance to speak, Jacob's voice filled his head: [I know what you've been thinking,] he said. [But your father hasn't forsaken you.]

Brig hung his head, ashamed for having conjured the thought at all. [Why won't he answer me?] He asked.

Jacob continued, [He can't. The Gate to The Upper Afterworld has been closed. The Agents of the Light have all been called back. When I leave, The Upper Gate will close again. There will be no one left to help. The three of you will be on your own.]

Despite Jacob's assurance to the contrary, Brig's feeling of abandonment only intensified. At least he'd had a scrap of hope before. Now, even that was gone. [But why?] He asked. [Why did they close The Upper Gate? Why did they call the Agents back?]

Jacob shook his head, leaving behind faint contrails of light. [There was no other choice.] He said. [What Kaitlyn is about to do is extremely dangerous. Opening the Gate to The Lower Afterworld threatens to destroy Reality. Every Agent, Light or Dark, not dwelling inside a human body, will be sucked into the abyss once Malocere passes through. Think about magnets. Positive and negative energy. This struggle is due in part to that fact that positive and negative energy –]

[Attract.]

Jacob nodded, [That's right. The earthly Realm serves as a buffer between the two extremes. So long as the Gate to one extreme is closed, the other can be opened without the threat of Reality being destroyed.] He continued, [If both Gates were left open, the positive energy would be attracted to the negative. This Realm would be crushed as the two energy concentrations clashed together. If that were to happen, they would annihilate one another. Earth would be torn to shreds. After that, Reality would implode.]

Jacob's expression changed. [I'm sorry,] he said. [I'm out of time. I must go.] Without thinking about what he was asking his brother to do, Brig begged him to stay and help them fight. Jacob's apparition faded into a fine mist. When he spoke, his thoughts sounded as if he were sending them from a great distance.

[I can't,] he said. [Don't worry, you'll do fine. Remember what dad taught you.] He condensed into a glowing orb and took off through the air with tremendous speed, headed straight towards one of the mirrors. Brig was sure he would smash into it, but when the orb hit the surface, the mirror soaked it up like a pebble in a pond. The room shook with a violent roar.

Kaitlyn tugged at her father's pants leg; Brig looked down at her, and she said, "The Gate's closed. We're on our own."

Brig pulled her close and squeezed her. "We'll be fine, sweetie. Daddy's going to come up with something . . ."

-3-

John had been carefully inching down the corridor through which they'd come. He pressed his back to the wall and stepped sideways through Fat Man's Squeeze. He felt Malocere nearby; the malevolent stench was incredibly thick – so much so that it made his stomach turn. From further up the corridor, the sound of footsteps approached.

That was when the Gate to The Upper Afterworld slammed shut. John hit the floor and covered his head. The loud noise had caught him by surprise, and he'd misinterpreted the source.

Soon enough, he uncovered his head to see a pair of dirty, black boots two inches in front of his face. The figure wearing the boots also wore a pair of mud-caked blue jeans and a bloody T-shirt. His face was red and blistered, sporting singed eyebrows and charcoal-black smudges.

"Hello, medicine man," Malocere said. He opened his mouth and patted it with his hand, making the stereotypical *woo-woo-woo* sound.

John didn't respond. Instead, he lay still for a second before attempting to scamper away as quickly as he could. Malocere seized him by the collar and lifted him off the floor with a degree of strength that came as a surprise. John was slammed against the wall, feet off of the ground, with Malocere's hand around his throat. John gagged and choked as his heart thundered in his chest, viciously working double-time in order to provide his starving brain with the blood and oxygen it needed to remain conscious. John had to do something, and he knew he had precious little time to do it.

Malocere's eyes had started to glow, and John felt the creature burrowing into his brain. He quickly slammed all of his mental doors shut. He fully intended to live up to his promise to never divulge Kaitlyn's secrets – even if this was his end.

[Where is she?] Malocere hissed. [I know she's in this house. It's only a matter of time before I find her. Why not make it easy on yourself and tell me now, so I don't have to rip it out of you?]

[Kill me if you want to, but I'll never give her up.] John's words were bold, especially considering the fact he knew full-well what Malocere was capable of. As he spoke, he slipped his arm into his jacket, his hand fumbling to find the object hidden there.

[Have it your way, medicine man...]

John's fingers found what he was looking for, and he curled them around a piece of wood he'd stuffed into the back pocket of his blue jeans. He pulled it out and drove the sharp, cedar stake into Malocere's side, just below his ribcage with a great deal of force. The stake sank in deep – John hoped it was deep *enough*.

John fell to the floor as Malocere spun around and around, shrieking as he tried to extract the piece of wood. John raised himself onto all fours and gasped for air. When he'd caught his breath, he stood up and shoved Malocere against the wall.

He took hold of the stake, ripped it out, and punched Malocere in the gut. The creature buckled over, and blood spurted from the wound in his side. John raised a knee, striking Malocere across the bridge of the nose and sending him to the floor flat on his back.

The pain in the creature's nose brought tears to his eyes – he could neither breathe nor see. John hovered over him, with the bloody stake raised high in the air, ready to bury it into Malocere's chest. John's plan was simple. He intended to kill the body Malocere was inhabiting, thereby forcing the menace into the open. He would then tell Kaitlyn to open the Gate, and Malocere would be sucked into The Lower Afterworld along with his minions.

The stake plunged downward; its sharpened tip sliced the air with a *swishing* sound. Malocere caught John's wrist in mid-swing, and the two struggled against one another. The possession of advantage changed hands with almost every blow. Malocere eventually overpowered John, and drove the stake into his left shoulder. The screams made Malocere smile. He twisted the stake slowly, relishing in his victim's pain. [Does that hurt?] He asked. [I hope it does. But of course you know, this is only the beginning.]

Just then, a child's high-pitched scream filled the air, and Malocere turned towards it, smiling.

Kaitlyn had fallen to her knees. Her hands were covering her ears, and she was crying. Brig was at a loss as to why – she'd been fine up until that moment, and he hadn't heard anything that would have warranted such a reaction from her. For the sake of remaining hidden, he had to keep her quiet, so he put his hand over her mouth and whispered in her ear: "What's wrong?"

Unable to speak, she sent her thoughts: [It's John! The bad man got John! He's hurt!! I can't feel him anymore.] Tears continued to roll down her face. [Daddy, I think he's dead!]

Dead? Brig thought. *John*? He didn't want to believe it, but when he reached out with his mind. He felt no sign of his blood brother. If John was alive, his life force was terribly weak.

[We have to find him, daddy!] Kaitlyn cried. [We have to try to help him!]

Brig remembered what John had said about protecting Kaitlyn at all costs, as well as his own response: *None of that 'One for all' bullshit.'* [No sweetie, I'm sorry. We can't.]

[You're just going to leave him? Let him *die*?]

[I made a promise,] Brig explained. [It's what John wanted.]

Brig took his hand away from her mouth, and she wiped the tears from her eyes. He took her hand and led her over to one of the walls where he sat her down and pressed his forehead against hers. [It's time to get started,] he said. [Malocere is coming.]

Kaitlyn said, [I know; I can feel him, too. He's close.]

By that time, Malocere had made it through Fat Man's Squeeze and entered the mirror maze only moments before. The twists and turns unnerved him, and he wandered around for five minutes, thinking he was lost. He caught sight of an odd smudge on one of the mirrors further up the corridor. It was a small handprint. Malocere placed his hand over it. The size difference was significant, and he knew it had to be a child's. It radiated with a trace of residual energy, which told him the print didn't belong to just any child.

He crept on, careful to make his footsteps soft so as not to alert the Keeper of his presence. Every so often, he found another oily print upon which the light twisted into swirly, hand-shaped rainbows. Malocere knew full well what was said about rainbows, and he licked his lips thinking of the little blonde-haired pot of gold waiting at the end of his.

Several minutes later, he arrived at the hub. Directly in front of him, he saw what he'd come for – a little girl in a pink dress sitting on the floor with her back pressed against a curiously bowed mirror. It didn't appear as though she had sensed his presence, yet. She was sitting still with her knees pulled to her chest and sobbing uncontrollably.

The floor creaked and Kaitlyn jumped up. "Don't come any closer!" she said, lifting her arms as if she were threatening to unleash another fireball.

Malocere looked around the hub and understood why he'd had so much trouble finding her in the first place. All of these reflections that he'd seen in his mind had confused him. Now he knew why she'd picked this spot to hide.

"Mirrors. Very nice," he said, his voice filled with joyful menace. "Surely you didn't think I'd just give up and go away, did you?"

He took another step toward Kaitlyn, and she took a step back. "You leave me alone!" she cried. "My daddy is gonna be back here any second!" She waved her hands like a magician about to pull a rabbit out of a hat. The tips of her fingers sparkled, and Malocere ticked his index finger from side to side in a '*no-no-no*' motion.

"You caught me by surprise before. I'm not going to be so easy to knock down this time."

Responding to his dare, Kaitlyn released jagged bolts of lightning from her hands. Malocere crossed his arms in front of his face, creating a bright, red shield. The bolts bounced off of it and into the nearby mirrors at random. They bounced around the hub, finally flying into the ceiling and blowing a large hole in the roof.

Malocere threw his head back and laughed. "You're going to have to do better than that!"

Age-old uneasiness consumed him at the sight of all of her reflections. They looked like an army – *an army of Keepers surrounding him*. Memories of The Great War flooded his mind.

He remembered the fall and how much it had hurt. He blamed Kaitlyn's kind for causing him so much pain, and he intended to pour out no less upon her.

The moment of recall brought forth a surge of rage, and he was about to charge her when he saw something out of the corner of his eye. Kaitlyn's reflections, which had all been facing in so many different directions before, all turned their backs on him at the same time. He looked back at the Keeper and saw the first hint of a grin stretching across her face.

"Smile all you want," he said. "The battle's just getting started."

Kaitlyn stretched her arms out, assuming the crucifixion pose, and she levitated into the air. The sight of the little girl in the pink dress hanging, pinned to an invisible cross reminded him of the First Keeper so very long ago, and how difficult *that* battle had been.

"No," she said. "It's done."

Her head fell limp and seemingly lifeless against her chest as though her neck was no longer able to support the weight. The floor shook and rattled as peals of thunder filled the room. All of Kaitlyn's reflections turned back to face the crucified child. Malocere watched them fall to their knees and fold their hands in a strange sort of prayer. Small drops of blood began seeping from non-existent cuts on Kaitlyn's forehead, just below her hairline. The drops trickled down her face in thin streams.

Malocere covered his eyes and shouted, "NO! This isn't real! It's a trick!"

When he looked again, Kaitlyn was standing in front of him, laughing as hard as she could. Her mocking made him angry – *very angry*. He opened his mouth wide and roared – the sound was strong enough to shatter a few of the nearby mirrors, but despite his rage, Kaitlyn continued laughing. She put her little hand over her mouth and giggled while pointing at him with her index finger. She had pushed him to a point where rational thought dared not tread.

He charged and wrapped his arms around her body with full intentions of crushing her against the wall. The two of them plunged through the mirror's surface. Where Malocere had expected to hear breaking glass, he found the Gate instead.

CHAPTER TWENTY

-1-

John fell to his knees, horrified as he watched Malocere and Kaitlyn disappear through the Gate. "Oh, god," he whispered. "I'm too late. I've failed." The arm holding the stake fell to his side and dangled there like a limp rope. He had developed strong feelings for Kaitlyn – almost parental feelings – that was true enough, but in light of what her disappearance meant to the world, the fact that she was gone was merely incidental.

She was so young – far too young, and he feared she wouldn't be strong enough to survive The Lower Afterworld or even the fall for that matter. If she died before her task was complete, the Gate to The Lower Afterworld could never be closed. For it was written, 'Once a Keeper opens a Gate, only *that* Keeper can close it. A triumphant Malocere would return to the Earthly Realm, accompanied by every last Agent of the Dark capable of making the journey.

John's mind continued to analyze the problem, and he discovered its true, apocalyptic inverse: If the Gate to The Lower Afterworld could never be *closed*, that meant the Gate to The Upper Afterworld could never be *re-opened*. Meanwhile, Malocere and his legions would possess full, uncontested reign over two-thirds of Reality.

The Agents of the Light would have no recourse whatsoever – their only option too horrific to consider: They could open the Upper Gate, but doing so would destroy everything, just as Jacob had told Brig it would. In short, if Kaitlyn were to die before closing the Gate, the war would be over and Malocere would have won.

-2-

Malocere held Kaitlyn tightly in his arms as the two of them began their descent, tumbling wildly through a roaring tube of rotating flames. The heat was tremendous, having built up like a blasting furnace over the course of two thousand years.

Malocere realized immediately what was happening, and he panicked. He let go of the little girl and tried to spread his wings, but he had forgotten he was trapped inside a human body and was thus, unable to fly. Powerless to do anything else, he fell for the second time.

Their two bodies emerged from the fiery vortex into The Lower Afterworld. Kaitlyn's dress snapped and popped about her body as she plummeted through the algae-green sky. Malocere flipped head over heels again and again before finally smashing into the side of a mountain covered with dusty ash, thorns, and razor-sharp brimstone rock. A thick, red fluid poured out of faults in the rock face like blood from a gaping wound.

He looked into the sky above and saw the little girl floating down towards him, seemingly held aloft by giant, invisible wings. Behind her were what looked like falling stars. Millions of them poured out of the vortex, trailing behind multi-colored tails of fire.

Malocere knew full well what they were – Agents of the Dark, sucked from the Earthly Realm to join him here in the basement of Reality. They shrieked as they fell, and the cocoons of fire surrounding them fed off the poisonous atmosphere's noxious vapors. They hit the ground dozens at a time, and the collective sound of their impacts was deafening.

Several small pebbles danced on the ground beside Malocere as the mountain shook and rumbled. A large boulder perched on a ledge further up the hill broke loose and rolled downhill, missing him by less than a foot. It collided with a larger rock at the bottom where it shattered into several large chunks.

The green sky surrounding the vortex swirled and churned. Malocere looked up and watched the Gate close with the *sucking* sound of an airlock sealing shut. A shroud of silence fell across the wasteland, all except for the anguished screams of the Dark Agents, the whistle of the arid wind whipping through the canyons, and... laughter.

Only one other had ever dared laugh here. And that had been long, long ago.

Malocere turned his eyes to the little girl who had lighted on a large boulder twenty feet from where he lay twisted and sprawled out across the living, bleeding rock. Kaitlyn crouched down and pulled her knees to her chest. He shook his head and added laughter of his own. Certainly, things looked bad, but he wasn't ready to abandon all hope just yet – after all, there was still another way out.

Kaitlyn's laugh gradually got deeper and deeper until it sounded like a man's. She morphed before his eyes – her small body quickly grew taller and taller. Her facial features morphed as well. In a matter of seconds, the little girl who had been sitting on the rock had transformed into a full-grown man.

Malocere could only watch in stunned silence. He didn't know what to think anymore – *was this person the Keeper or was it her father?*

Brig's laughter continued, but he stopped long enough to point to Malocere and shout, "Gotcha!"

The eternal creature stammered as he looked from side to side. "Where... where's the Keeper?? She was here! I saw her!"

Brig smiled and said, "Back in the Haunted House I would imagine. Safe and sound and as far away from you as she can get!" He was overjoyed. The realization of where they were hadn't quite set in, so he was able to relish in this small victory. Shape shifting was but one of the many tricks they had learned while in the Upper Afterworld. The creature before him used misdirection and deception to his advantage, and it seemed poetic justice that the tables had been turned.

-3-

Back in the mirror maze, the Gate started to wobble as it closed. Kaitlyn pulled the portal back into herself as she had done before, gripping her fist into a tight ball that resounded with a boom that shook the entire structure. Already on her knees, she fell to the floor.

John's face beamed, and he clapped his hands, unable to contain the deluge of emotion. However, his smile melted quickly when he saw Kaitlyn crying after she had curled herself into a ball. He rushed to her side and asked, "What's wrong? Why are you crying?"

"Daddy made me do it," she sobbed. "I didn't want to, but he said it was the only way!"

John's eyes opened wide and he asked, "What? What did you do?" He hadn't had time to wonder about the little girl who had disappeared through the Gate. But it began to make sense and he put two and two together. Brig was missing. He covered his mouth with his hands.

Oh, God.

Brig had failed to see one colossal flaw in his plan. Kaitlyn was the only one worthy of wielding the Blood Sword. He had been foolhardy and risked his own life to protect his daughter's. Noble, yes, but selfish just the same. The three of them were meant to work as a team. Alone, Brig didn't stand a chance. Worse still, his energy was positive and it had no place in the Lower Realm. His presence there threatened to unravel the very fabric of Reality.

Kaitlyn begged for forgiveness: "I'm sorry, John!"

He could find no reason to fault her – there was no way she could have known, and he partly blamed himself for not being more forthcoming with the information. But what's done is done, and Brig went into this knowing full-well sacrifices might need to be made. Malocere and his forces were now in the Lower Realm. It wasn't the victory he had envisioned, but it was enough. The time to make that sacrifice was now.

"It's alright," he said, reaching into his pocket and removing a cell phone as he spoke. "Everything will be fine. There's just one small thing that needs to be done before we can right the wrong." He began dialing a number on the phone's keypad. Kaitlyn sat up beside him, her eyes still puffy, but she wiped them dry. He was just about to hit SEND when his eyes met hers. He hoped she wouldn't be able to see into his mind and attempt to stop him from what he needed to do.

Kaitlyn asked, "Who ya calling?"

Unable to look her in the eyes any longer, John averted his and said, "An old friend." He pressed SEND with his thumb and pulled her close to him. In that brief moment, the doors in his mind flew open and allowed Kaitlyn to see inside for the first time.

She pushed him away and shouted, "NO!!!!!!"

The "Little Surprise for the Locals" that John had assembled in his basement and later placed deep inside Malocere's cave, exploded. Kaitlyn beat her fists against his chest again and again.

"You trapped him!" she screamed. "You blew up the other portal and trapped daddy down there! You didn't even give him a chance to use it!"

He grabbed her wrists and said, "It had to be done! We couldn't destroy it until you sent him back! Now he's trapped down there, don't you see? Nothing is coming back through that portal!"

"And that includes DADDY!" She shouted. The house shook when she spoke with such unrestrained force. She pointed at John and demanded to know how to get her father back.

John shook his head as he placed his hands on her shoulders. *How do I tell the child her father sacrificed himself for her benefit? How do I tell her that her father offered himself as bait? How do I tell her that her father might spend eternity in The Lower Afterworld?* "Your daddy understood the risks, little one. What he did, he did for you. His sacrifice was a brave one. But I'm afraid he's not coming back."

Kaitlyn slapped his hands from her shoulders and looked him in the eye with a mix of determination and rage. The issue was not up for debate, and the words that came next were quick to underscore her resolve. "Get your things, John. We're going after him."

John knew better than to argue. She had the ability to go it alone if she chose to, and her chances were better if he went along. Still, he knew there was little chance of getting Brig back, but the stern expression on Kaitlyn's face told him he needed to try. He knelt down and said, "Don't worry. I think I know what we can do." He took her hand into his and said, "Come with me, I'm taking you home."

-4-

John's bomb had rocked not only the Earthly Realm, but The Lower Afterworld as well. Brig was knocked off of his rock and tumbled down the steep, rocky slope, landing on a wide outcropping some sixty feet below with a meaty thud. He groaned and dusted himself off when he realized he was bleeding from several lacerations. A large drop of blood clung to his forearm as if it wanted no part of the world into which it had emerged. Brig shook it off and watched it fall. It sizzled when it struck the ground.

Malocere's head snapped around towards the explosion, and his eyes focused on the mouth of a cave far down in a distant valley – fire and debris flew out of it, making it look more like a cannon. He roared, not with anger, but thick, dark, hopelessness. The explosion had cut off his only escape route, locking him in desolation forever. Without the Keeper, Malocere knew there was no way back.

He squinted his eyes and glared at Brig, who had curled up on the ledge below. Visually tracing the path Brig had taken as he'd tumbled down the mountainside, Malocere saw something reflecting light from the bloated, red sun, which was quickly sinking on the horizon.

Interested, but cautious, Malocere moved towards the object, a hundred or so yards away. Brig saw him moving along the slope, and he reached behind his back and felt for his gun. It wasn't there. It didn't take him long to figure out what Malocere was after.

"Shit."

Malocere leaned over and picked the pistol up. He held it in his hand, testing its weight. He thought back to when he had been in the sheriff's body – more specifically the time that Brent had come into the station and shot him. That such a small object could wield such destructive power had left quite an impression in his mind.

The red sun had partially sunk below the horizon. It looked like a fiery dome sitting in the middle of miles and miles of swirling desert sand. A slight breeze whistled down the side of the mountain, blowing Brig's hair back and filling his nostrils with nauseating scents of sulphur and decaying flesh. His stomach seized as he inhaled the polluted air, and he buckled over, spewing vomit onto his shoes.

By the time he stopped retching and looked up, Malocere was pointing the gun in his direction. A shot rang out, and Brig hit the deck. A puff of dust rose three inches from his leg. He was shielded from Malocere's view under the protection of a rocky overhang. He crawled to where the ledge dropped into the canyon and peered over the edge. Below, he heard a voice, and as he listened closer, more voices rose to his ears. He soon realized that they weren't just voices, but screams – *millions of terrified screams*.

Six or seven of the softball creatures flew along the rim of the canyon. They reminded him of the dragonflies he'd chased around the ponds on the farm when he was a child. However, these creatures weren't just flying about at random; they were flying in a sort of squadron formation. It looked as though they were searching for something as they covered grid after grid of barren landscape. Brig's gut told him that they were looking for *him*.

A shower of rocks spilled down from the overhang above. Brig rolled onto his back and peered up. Malocere was standing above him, cocking the hammer back with his thumb. He closed one eye and pointed the gun at Brig's head.

"Get up," he commanded.

Brig rose to his feet and held his hands above his head, hoping the non-threatening gesture might buy him some time. "It's over," he said.

"I don't suppose it will do any good to kill you," Malocere said. "You're stuck here either way, but it'll sure make *me* feel a lot better."

Brig grinned and closed his eyes. There was a soft *swoosh* sound, like a basketball passing through a hoop – *nothing but net*

– and just like that, he disappeared. Malocere lowered the weapon and opened his other eye. He looked from side to side, trying to figure out where Brig might have gone.

Malocere told himself that this was just another one of Brig's tricks. He raised the gun again and fired at random. Four shots later, he stopped when Brig's voice called out from an indiscernible location:

"One bullet left!"

"Where are you?"

"If I tell you that, you'll shoot me!"

Malocere kicked the ground sending another shower of rocks over the ledge. He didn't like these games. More important was where Brig had learned them – the Keeper was proving to be a force to be reckoned with, but not nearly the pain in the ass that *this* guy was turning out to be.

He continued to point the gun at nothing, partly because putting it away would be admitting defeat. Malocere spun around, looking for Brig who continued on with his taunting, but the direction from which the voice was coming kept changing. This game went on for a few minutes longer before Malocere grew dizzy and staggered. Again, he was reminded of the limitations of the human body, and he decided he'd had enough of it. Still, he was trapped in this shell, and the only way out was...

As Brig's harassment continued, Malocere looked down at the gun in his hand. *One bullet left*, he thought. *Of course! Why didn't I think of that before*? Without another thought, he put the pistol to his head and fired the remaining round. The shot's report echoed off the sheer canyon walls. The pistol fell into the dirt, and the body Malocere had been inhabiting landed in a crumpled heap, striking its head against a large rock on the way down.

Brig, still invisible and quite happy to be so, watched as what looked like two wide ribbons of smoke rose from Tom's nostrils. The two ribbons were braided together like a ten-year-old girl's pigtails. Then, the two ribbons violently unwound, creating small, whirling dirt devils on the ground below.

One of the ribbons took shape, and Brig recognized what was happening right away. The transformation looked just as it had back at the sheriff's station when he'd seen Malocere – the *ghost-like* form of Malocere, that is – come out of A.J.'s body. Now, the REAL Malocere had materialized, and it hovered in the air before him.

The creature was a long-toothed, scaly, red dragon with glowing coals for eyes. His bat-like wings spanned twenty feet from tip to tip. Nostrils the size of a man's fist flared each time he exhaled double-barreled blasts of steam. Running down the ridgeline of his back from the top of his head was a bright yellow, fan-like fin made of the same membrane as his wings. It was supported by spiny protrusions about six inches high and spaced just as far apart.

Even though Brig was invisible to human eyes, Malocere was able to detect the man's infrared heat signature using his Afterworld eyes. Brig appeared as little more than a humanoid shape painted in blobs of neon pink, red, and yellow.

Malocere beat his wings as hard as he could. The resulting sound was the *chop-chop-chop* of helicopter rotors. Some grit flew into Brig's eyes, making them water and sting. He covered them with his hands, but peeked out through the small gaps between his fingers. The last thing he wanted was the surprise of finding his head clamped between the creature's teeth.

Malocere extended his neck so that his head was right next to Brig's, who could feel the hot, soupy air coming from the creature's nostrils. He licked Brig's cheek with his forked tongue covered with bumps and ridges, and Brig's face twisted up in utter revulsion.

Malocere spoke in his mind. [Have no fear. I won't kill you – not yet. The Keeper will come to save you. She won't leave you here. And when she comes...]

Malocere let the thought hang in Brig's mind as he envisioned the parade of horribles that ensued. He hoped John had survived and that he would be able to restrain Kaitlyn from any unnecessary rescue mission. Malocere was right about that – she would never leave him down here, and he began to consider that he might have unwittingly set the stage for the final battle in his desperate attempt to avoid it.

Malocere turned and plunged headfirst into the canyon at terrific speed. Brig knew he wasn't gone for good, so he quickly cleaned the grit from his eyes, wiping them on his shirtsleeve. He looked up to see Tom standing in front of him, taking in the scenery of this new world. He must have materialized from the second ribbon of smoke that had been intertwined with Malocere's. Brig hadn't witnessed the actual transformation, but it was the only explanation that made sense.

Tom's face took on the strangest expression of confusion Brig had ever seen. The shock of waking up in a place like this would be bad enough, but Brig sensed a much deeper fear. Tom looked him up and down before finally asking, "Brig?"

"Yeah, what of it?"

"Where are we?"

Brig laughed out loud. Tom's unfortunate stroke of bad luck had done little to ease Brig's hatred for him. Deep inside, he was glad Tom was here. As far as he was concerned, Tom deserved to be here.

"Welcome to Hell," Brig replied.

Tom's brow furrowed, and his eyes cut up to the sky, as he did his best to reconstruct the missing time. "No," he said, shaking his head with disbelief. "That's not possible. The cell... the police station... that kid came in and shot the sheriff. I was drunker than shit, I know that, but I'm not dead! No way! This has to be some sort of nightmare."

Brig pointed to the crumpled body lying in the dirt and said, "Does it feel like any dream you've ever had before?"

Tom looked up again; his eyes were filled with uncertainty and defiance. "We're *not* dead."

Brig shook his head. "Well, you're partly right. I'm not dead, but *you*, my friend... you have assumed room temperature. Best get used to the idea."

Tom clutched his stomach and coughed – just a little raspy cough at first, but before long it escalated into a full-blown hack. He straightened up, and Brig noticed a little roach crawling across the man's cheek. It crept down to his neck, eventually disappearing beneath his shirt collar. Tom reached up and tried to brush it away, but then focused his attention on a second roach, which he succeeded in swatting away.

"Uh, are you alright?" Brig asked.

Tom tried to respond, but for one reason or another, he was unable to find his voice. His cheeks puffed out as if he were about to wail off a Louis Armstrong-style high note on a non-existent trumpet. His cheeks expanded more and more until the skin creaked, having been stretched so far that it appeared paper-thin. Purple veins spider-webbed this way and that over the surface of his face. The vessels disappeared back into his pitted eye sockets, which held large, terrified eyes.

A strange sound came from Tom's mouth – a high pitched, oscillating hum – it reminded Brig of the summer cicadas that always descended on the farm in mid-June, filling the hills with their haunting serenade. The hum grew louder and louder until Brig had to cover his ears, sure that if he didn't, they might start to bleed. Tom opened his mouth wide, and thousands of roaches poured out of it in a raging swarm. They ran in every direction. Some went down the front of his shirt, some down his back, and some even crawled over his upper lip and wiggled into his nose.

He ran in circles like a madman, slapping his head in a futile attempt to rid himself of the six-legged plague. He succeeded in killing a few of them, but overall, his efforts were in vain. The roaches continued to pour out of his mouth, scurrying and gnawing their way over his body until he was covered with shiny, brownish-black insects.

It was shortly after this that Brig got to see something most people never get to see – at least not at the very moment it happens, anyway. Tom stopped running about, and he quit slapping at the roaches. His choked screams settled to silence, and he turned to face Brig. The squishes and crunches of insects unlucky enough to have found their way beneath his feet accompanied his every movement.

Tom wiped the bugs from his face, and Brig could see that panic had been replaced with a sort of stupid joy. Tom started to laugh the cackling laugh of madness, and he danced around, waving his hands in the air like some kind of holy rolling Pentecostal, all the while whooping into the gloomy nighttime sky. He had fallen victim to the horror of The Lower Afterworld. He had given in and lost his mind.

Brig watched his former adversary spin around and around as if he was acting out some surrealistic interpretive dance routine from *The Sound of Music*. But the mountains in this place looked nothing like the Swiss Alps, and Brig doubted Julie Andrews could ever find anything worth singing about here.

Then, Tom tripped on his own feet and went over the cliff, headfirst. He fell into the canyon – the one Brig had heard the sound of screams coming from earlier. The last thing Brig saw of Tom was the dark silhouette of his body against the bright river of lava below – how far below was anyone's guess – but the unnervingly wild laughter only grew louder as he fell.

What if the canyons have no bottom, Brig wondered – a thought which made him shiver all over. He tried to imagine what it would be like for Tom – falling for the balance of all eternity, tumbling through the vacuum of space and time with only the roaches and his own mad laughter to accompany him.

-5-

The bomb's blast shook Erin from her stupor. Before that moment, she had been sound asleep in her recliner with a growing spot of drool soaking into the chair's upholstery beside her head. Her mind was foggy as she sat up to look around the room. Kaitlyn, Brig, and John were all gone. At any other time, she would have been raked with panic, but the high dose of Xanax Brig had given her tamped most of that down. She fell back into the chair and once more drifted off to sleep.

Her next conscious thought came fifteen minutes later when she was jolted awake by the sound of the front door flying open. Kaitlyn ran through it first, followed closely by John. Erin listened with drugged disbelief as Kaitlyn told her what had happened. John confirmed the little girl's story with a nod.

"Oh no," she said, slightly slurring her words. "What are we going to do? Can he get back?"

John had his doubts, but even with those, he did his best to try and comfort her. "I think we can get him back," he said. "We're going to open a portal that only he can pass through. The only problem is that we don't know where he is down there. He has to find the portal, and since none of us have ever been there, we can't guide him. All we can do is open the Gate and hope."

"Hope?"

John lowered his head and said, "Yes, *hope*. I'm afraid that's all we have left."

"And let's suppose he doesn't find the portal. What then?"

There was an uncomfortable silence, and the tension in the room became quite thick. John was wringing his hands as he tried to find a way to gently break the news. There wasn't one. "If he can't make it through, Kaitlyn and I have to go in after him."

"You mean *down there*? Are you *crazy*?"

"I guess I'd have to be, now wouldn't I? Unfortunately, it may be the only way."

Kaitlyn was already well on her way to putting the plan into motion. She stood in front of the fireplace moving her hands in wide circles. The fireplace vanished behind the now-familiar circle of rippling light - only this Gate was outlined with a black rim. Kaitlyn took a step back and touched her temples with her fingers. She tried her best to project a thought to him. [Daddy! Daddy, can you hear me?]

Having just seen Tom dive to his doom, Brig was quickly beginning to appreciate the seriousness of where he was. He suspected that, while horrible, everything he had seen up to this point was nothing more than the shadow of a much larger nightmare.

Kaitlyn's voice came through to him then, but it sounded far away. He had to strain to hear it. Her voice was a soft, soothing breeze - a whisper, a candle in the darkness, and he relished in the comfort it brought to him. She was telling him about a Gate, but some of her words were lost and broken. He tried to respond, but couldn't - the tingle had fled from him.

Kaitlyn repeated herself over and over, and each transmission offered him pieces of information the previous ones hadn't.

A way out! She's giving me a way out! But where? Where is it?

Brig did his best to contact her again, but still no luck. The last two words he heard before her voice fell silent were [Love...daddy.] He made his decision right then not to give up. If there was a way out, he was going to find it. Brig knew he had to survey his surroundings if he was ever going to find a path to take. High ground was the most likely place to do such a thing. He found a solid foothold in the mountainside and gripped a large, knob-shaped protrusion high above his head. The side of the mountain was only a few degrees less than vertical, so he knew that as soon as he started climbing, there would be no time for stopping until he reached the top. He also knew the consequences if he fell.

He reached the peak a while later and sat down on a flat spot to catch his breath. He looked into the purple nighttime sky and saw four moons of different sizes floating high above him. Their light washed the atmosphere clean of any stars whose light might be trying to get through the baleful halo of malignant moonlight. Sparse clouds drifted silently, changing shapes in response to the wind that pushed them along. Brig imagined many things in the murky vapor, and all of them unsettled him.

This all looked so familiar, but despite his efforts, he couldn't remember why. He took his eyes from the sky and looked upon the panorama below. The barren wasteland reminded him of an artistic conception of the surface of Venus he'd seen in science-fiction magazines long ago. Jagged mountain peaks, free of any living vegetation, towered high above the canyons and valleys.

Bright rivers of lava snaked their way down the slopes of several volcanoes, which had been disfigured by eons of such flows. The rivers of fire collected in boiling pools at the bottom. The glow emitted by the lava hung low in the valleys giving the illusion of great cities in the distance. Some of the magma flowed into an ocean of blood whose waves washed over it, sending thick steam into the air.

Brig watched two of the moons disappear below the horizon. He felt himself growing tired. His eyes were heavy and he was losing the battle to stay awake. Seconds later, his body gave in – sitting up required more energy than he had left. As he slipped into unconsciousness, he dreamt of the book he'd read in The Upper Afterworld. Of particular interest to him was the section about the place he was now in. The passage had read:

In that place of fear and dread,
Where shadows are born and nightmares bred,
Flee only when the battles' won,
Run towards the light of the Second Sun.

Brig woke late to a burning heat on the back of his neck. The red sun had risen above the horizon, and it was searing his skin. He flipped up the collar of his polo shirt to try and shield his neck as best he could.

Mouse-like chatters and squeaks were all around him, and it felt like someone was poking his back again and again with the tip of a ballpoint pen. He reached behind himself and grabbed hold of some kind of a creature, which fought valiantly against the giant who had snatched it up. It bit Brig's hand and went into what can only be described as a seizure of ecstasy.

It looked like a little lizard – a gecko, maybe. Its gray nictitating membranes slid up over its eyes and it opened its mouth to reveal a single row of nubby teeth. Brig didn't like the way it squirmed in his hand at all, so he hurled it over the side of the mountain.

It tumbled wildly through the air at first, but managed to straighten itself out. It spread a small pair of wings and took off in flight. Brig became nervous when he saw its wings, because he knew it wasn't just any lizard. It was a baby dragon. He looked around and saw ten or twelve more standing around him. The creatures all rose up on their hind legs and hissed like frightened cats. He supposed that he'd crawled into some sort of nest.

Two of the little beasts clamped their teeth onto the tail of his shirt and pulled as hard as they could. If he didn't know better, he would have sworn they were trying to start up a game of tug-of-war with him. Baby dragons weren't something Brig had a deep knowledge of, but he did know a thing or two about animal behavior. Wherever there were babies, mamma was usually close by – he needed to get out of there and fast.

He swatted the tuggers away. When he did, his shirttail tore. The little dragons rolled backwards; the larger of the two still held a strip of yellow fabric in its mouth. Both of them shook their heads, having been slightly rattled. The smaller one grabbed onto the other end of the cloth strip, and the tug-of-war match was on again.

Brig climbed over the side of the nest and started to make his way down the mountain as quickly as he could. One of the little dragons took interest in the meaty stumps hanging over the side of its nest, and it sank its teeth into one of them. That particular meaty stump just so happened to be Brig's finger. He screamed when the creature's teeth pierced his skin, and he jerked his hand away. The little dragon wanted more; it hopped up onto the edge of the nest and cried out. Brig thumped it under its chin and the creature's cries transformed into a squawk as it scampered back into the nest.

From somewhere below, Brig heard moans and the rattle of falling rocks. He looked down and saw twenty or more people – at least he thought they were people – clawing up the mountain towards him. He looked at the closest one and saw that there was nothing below his waist. Where his legs should have been there hung bloody strips of flesh and a long, noodle-like thing that Brig assumed was an intestine.

It sounded as though they were trying to say something, so Brig listened a little closer. Finally, he heard what it was – they were begging him for forgiveness.

The legless man muscled his way up the mountain, pulling his weight with nothing but his arms. His face was ridden with scabs and sores. His eyes were dark and sunken, his skin slimy and pale. All of their voices came into synch, and their cries took the form of a kind of bizarre chant.

"Forgive us, Lord! Wash us in your blood!"

The legless man seized Brig's ankle. Brig looked down and saw blind hope on the man's face.

"Mercy, Lord! Please have mercy!" they all shouted.

Brig panicked and placed his other shoe against the man's forehead. He pushed and pushed, trying to force him to let go, but with every push the begging got louder and the cries more desperate. Finally, the man's grip failed, and his expression changed from one of hope to one of empty despondence.

Brig watched the torso fall, sure the man would be swallowed by the infinite blackness of the canyon just as Tom had been. But a dragon swooped out of the sky and snatched the man in its talons. It climbed back into the sky, holding the legless body by its intestinal rope. The dragon's wings beat the air, but Brig still heard the man's weeping over the pounding sound:

"Save me, lord! Save me!"

The dragon hovered in midair and sank a hooked talon into the man's chest. Another one soon followed. Then, the body was torn in two. The dragon pitched one half into the nest, and gobbled down the other half itself.

Brig hid inside a deep, crevasse in the cliff face, wanting no part of what was taking place above him. Still, the voices rose to his ears, despite his efforts to shut them out. He screamed with surprise when a woman poked her head into the crack. Half of her face was gone, exposing a bleached, white skull. She reached for him, and he saw her fingers were nothing but bone.

"Just a drop," she pleaded. "A drop on my tongue!"

"I'm not your GOD!" Brig shouted. "Leave me alone!" He kicked her in the chest, and she lost her handholds. When she fell, her head got lodged in a spot where the crack narrowed. The rest of her body tore away from her neck, leaving behind a bloody spinal cord that dangled from her decapitated head like some kind of calcified tail.

She laughed, and Brig saw her lips move again: "C'mon... just a drop! Give mamma *one drop*!" She stuck out her black tongue out and wagged it furiously. It made Brig's stomach turn just to watch. He steadied himself in the crevasse and drew his foot back. He kicked with as much force as he could muster, punting the woman's head across the canyon like a football. She yowled all the way to the other side.

Brig knew better than to try and gauge the passage of time in the other Realities. He had already proven himself somewhat inept at the task. Nonetheless, what seemed like hours had passed, and he'd stayed hidden in the crack as his would-be disciples had been picked off, one at a time, by the dozens of dragons circling overhead like vultures spying the mangled remains of a jackrabbit sizzling beside a hot desert highway.

Once they had all been fed, most of the dragons had flown off to do whatever it is that dragons do when they aren't feasting on lost souls. Brig was happy to see them go; he was even happier that his disciples had been great enough in number as to satiate the beasts' appetites.

When the dragons had arrived, the red sun had just reached its highest point in the sky. The rays had eventually found their way into the crevasse, and although he'd tried to hide, his skin had started to bake again. Dark silhouettes circled high above, and that was probably the only time he'd been grateful for the beasts. Their broad wings and thick bodies brought with them tremendous shadows, which had given Brig respite from the blazing sunlight. Those shadows were gone now. He was thirsty. He needed water soon.

The sun inched towards the horizon, and as Brig watched the wicked star get consumed by the towering peaks in the distance, he wondered if this was how he was going to die – dehydrated and weary, hiding from things he neither saw nor wanted to see. *What a disgraceful way to go*. He knew his father would not have been pleased, but of course, his father wasn't *here*, now was he?

The grim, night sky didn't follow the sunset as Brig had expected it to. Instead, when the red light waned in the east, a smaller, brighter star rose.

The Second Sun!

It climbed in the sky slowly, its rays cool and relieving – a stark divergence from what had been hanging in its place only minutes before. Sighs of sheer relief were heard rising from the valleys below, just as the sun rose in the east.

It occurred to Brig then that the Second Sun, with its façade of grace, was probably the worst torment the inhabitants of The Lower Afterworld would ever know – *the torment of hope*.

Eons and eons of misery had allowed them to arrive at a place in their minds where goodness no longer existed, where hope had been forgotten, and where the cessation of pain was not even conceived of. After all those years – after having been stripped of their humanity so very long ago – along comes the Second Sun with all of its forgotten pleasures falling upon them as soft, golden light.

Pleasures weren't the only thing the sun brought with it. It also brought the unspoken hope of its return – a tale that would be told for eons to come as more and more souls arrived in this place. Every day when the red sun set, all eyes would turn to the east. They would watch, and they would wait. With the dying of the light and the birth of the moons, they would prepare for another day of pain – another day of vain hope. For they had seen the Second Sun once; therefore its existence was without question to them.

The new arrivals into The Lower Afterworld would come to mock them and call them madmen for believing in something that was simply too fantastic to be true. The new ones would call their faith mere superstition, and as the numbers of those who had bathed in the light of the Second Sun dwindled in proportion to those of the new arrivals, they would gradually become the minority. The Second Sun would be reduced to mere superstition and folklore.

But still the believers would wait, and every day at the same time, billions of eyes would look to the east and await a rising that would never come again.

CHAPTER TWENTY-ONE

-1-

The Second Sun rose into the sky and hovered above a cone-shaped mountain, which belched plumes of smoke and ash. Amid the blinding light, Brig saw a familiar shape sitting atop a distant mountain peak. It spread its wings and eclipsed the sun – the light of which surrounded the creature with a halo it did not deserve to wear.

Malocere.

[Are you hiding?] The creature asked. [How long do you really think you can stay in there?]

[What do you care?] Brig was dying of thirst. His body was weak, and he wasn't far from licking the sweat from his arms simply to feel something other than tacky paste on his tongue. It came as no real surprise when a large glass of water mysteriously appeared, floating in midair before him.

[I don't care,] Malocere said. [Stay in there and die if you want to. It makes no real difference to me. I'm just trying to help you.]

Brig licked his lips, which were cracked and dry from the sun, wind, and heat. He wanted the water – wanted it badly – but he knew better than to take it. He wondered if the glass might not be some kind of hallucination. He'd often heard stories of people seeing mirages in the desert, and he wondered if his head wasn't just playing games with him again – some sort of cruel wish-fulfilling fantasy. If the water *wasn't* real and he reached for it, he risked exposing his weakened state. On the other hand, if it *was* real, it was most likely one of Malocere's tricks.

He looked to the creature and said, [Yeah, right. Why would you want to help me? I'm the one that brought you here!]

[I know. There's ill will between us, I won't deny that, but you've shown talent. You're stuck down here anyway. I could use you. What do you say?] While he waited for Brig to answer, Malocere barraged him with subliminal suggestions of thirst in an attempt to get him to accept the water.

Brig took the glass in his hands. It was cold, with small, sweaty beads running down the sides. He didn't know it was Malocere's voice he was hearing inside his head, pleading with him to drink it. Brig had become somewhat delirious over the course of the past few hours. He had been hearing voices and seeing many different things. The dividing line between fantasy and reality had all but vanished.

He looked at the glass again and had his moment of doubt – for a second or two, he was almost willing to sell his soul for the pint of cold liquid. But he resisted and hurled the glass into the canyon where it shattered against the far wall. Malocere laughed, and it made Brig's blood boil.

[You think that's funny?] he asked.

The creature's laughter dropped off. [I just needed to see if you were willing.]

[Willing?]

[Willing to make a deal.] Malocere was well aware of the portal that had been opened, but he wasn't sure if Brig knew about it yet. All attempts to read his mind, which had been clouded with thirst-induced confusion, had failed. Malocere couldn't make sense of the mental jumble. Still, he was intimately acquainted with the dark depths of human desire, and he hoped it would play to his advantage.

[Leave me alone, you bastard!] Brig demanded. [I don't want anything from you.]

[What if I made you an offer you couldn't refuse?] Malocere asked. [Would you listen to what I had to say?]

Brig was getting irritated, but he laughed and said, [Do I have a choice? It doesn't exactly look like I'm going anywhere anytime soon, now does it?]

[What if I was to let you go?]

[You'd never do that,] Brig told him. [Besides, you can't open the Gate.] His mind cleared up for a split second and allowed the creature to see inside. What Malocere found there confirmed his worst fear.

[You know about the portal, don't you?]

Brig nodded that he did. His legs had grown tired, and they were trembling as a result of burning exhaustion. The only thing he wanted, aside from the water, was to get off of the mountain and back on solid ground. He cared nothing of Malocere's offer.

The creature presented the bargain, anyway. [I could give you everything,] he said. [The Earth could be yours to rule.] Another glass appeared - only this time it wasn't filled with water; the glass was filled with blood. Malocere said, [Drink. This is my blood. Drink it as a symbol of your allegiance to me. Do this and you can come down from that mountain. You'll never thirst again.]

Brig was only seconds from falling out. His morals were fading fast, and Malocere's words had begun to make a strange sort of sense. Despite overwhelming fatigue and delirium, Brig understood the deal carried with it a much higher price than his soul. He lifted his eyes to Malocere and asked, [What do you want from me? Why won't you just go away?]

[You'll never make it to the portal alone,] the creature responded. [You're in over your head. You need me. I think you know that now. I'll take you to it, but the deal is that once you're through, you have to open the Gate for my army and me.]

[I *can't* open it,] Brig said. [You *know* that!]

[But the Keeper can.]

[She'll never do it.]

[She will if you tell her to – after all, you're her father.]

[Why would you trust me? Do you really think I'd have her open the Gate once I was through? I'd just leave you here. There's no way I'd let you try and kill my daughter again!]

Malocere explained, [If you agree to my offer, your soul will belong to me. Should you fail to honor the pact, you'll probably live another forty years or so, but one day, you'll die. Your soul will return to me, and my retribution will be unyielding. I can promise you an eternity of more misery than you can possibly imagine. As for your daughter, once the Gate is opened, I won't be the one to kill her – *you will.*]

[What?! You're out of your damn mind!]

[Think about it, you'd be doing her a favor. You'd be sending her to The Upper Afterworld, and you'd be saving yourself as well. Otherwise, you're stuck here. Soon, your legs are going to give out. In fact, I would say you have only seconds to make your decision. What's it going to be?]

Brig knew Malocere was lying, and he sighed, surrendering to his foreordained doom of spending an eternity in The Lower Afterworld. His only other option was one he couldn't choose. He reached out and grabbed the glass of blood. Some of it splashed onto his skin, giving him a tremendous rush.

If only one *drop brings that much pleasure,* he thought, *what might an entire glass do*?

His father's voice screamed, [*It'll drive you* mad!!!]

Brig held the glass over the edge of the cliff and poured it out. As a further gesture of insubordination, he held it up and showed it to Malocere before chucking it over the edge.

[Fool!] The creature shouted.

[I'm no fool,] Brig assured him. [I just understand some things you never will – like love and loyalty. If this is the way it has to be – if sacrificing my life ensures the security of my family's – then so be it.]

[This is no time to be noble,] Malocere spat. [Don't make the mistake of thinking that anyone is going to save you this time. Your god has abandoned you. You're on your own. We're the only one's here right now – just you and I.]

[No one's abandoned me.]

[Then jump,] Malocere said. [If your faith in their allegiance to you is so strong, *jump*. Won't the Agents of the Light tear open the sky and pour in to help you?]

[That's not faith, you idiot. That's arrogance.]

[What other choice do you have?]

Brig decided to make a last-ditch effort to escape. He closed his eyes and pictured the mountaintop Malocere was sitting on was only a half-step away.

S – t – r – e – t – c – h ...

The gulf separating the two points fell away as the topography bowed. Brig hoped he had enough strength left in him to hold the image in his mind's eye.

The Second Sun was well on its way toward its final destination – the distant, western horizon. Brig stepped from the crack and put his foot down upon Malocere's mountain peak.

Snap! Crack!

The creature scanned the mountainside, searching for the man who had been there only seconds before. He heard a noise behind him; it was the sound of Brig clearing his throat. Malocere spun around and then jumped back, falling through the air several feet before spreading his wings and regaining lift. His dorsal fin stiffened.

The sinister veil of night had begun to consume the eastern sky, revealing the scarred and rocky moons above. From below, Brig heard thin screeches and the bony, claw-like clicks of small, nocturnal creatures emerging from their subterranean lairs. These lesser inhabitants of The Lower Realm filled the canyons with vile, echoing cries – cries that were harbingers of torment for the masses in the valleys.

Millions of the creatures surged forth like a torrent of rushing water. The valleys' inhabitants heard the approaching horde and attempted to flee – thousands upon thousands of naked, gray bodies ran just as they had for a million nights before. The Lower Realm had long-since stolen from them their concept of futility; each believed escape was possible.

But alas, such hope was a fallacy. The wave of monsters washed over the panicked mob, using hook-like claws to tear at their victims – ribbons of meat flew into the air giving the appearance of some sort of macabre cloud. Once all flesh and muscle had been consumed, it quickly regenerated, and the feast began again.

The torment would continue until the monsters were chased back into their dark dens by the stabbing rays of merciless, red sunlight. And just as they had every day before, the tortured souls would forget the nighttime horror. When it came again the following evening, the terror would be new, the anguish unfamiliar.

[Is that what you want?] Malocere asked him, perching himself on a nearby ledge. [I can spare you from all of it.]

[I don't want anything from you!] Brig felt power coursing through his body. Up until that point, his abilities had been limited by exhaustion, but his second wind had come. He imagined an arched bridge spanning the chasm between two mountain peaks, and he raced across it as fast as he could.

Malocere watched from the ledge; he was unable to see the bridge, so it looked as if Brig were flying. He was amazed that this man – *this mere human* – was capable of such wondrous feats. He first thought Brig was trying to get away, but he then remembered the Second Sun. He struggled to his feet, spread his wings, and took to the sky. He ascended above the mountains' ridgelines and spotted a tiny figure running westward at tremendous speed. Relativity being what it was, that's the way Brig's space-warp technique appeared to an outside observer. It was quite effective at covering wide spans of unfamiliar terrain in a minimal amount of time.

Malocere folded back his wings and dove from the sky. Brig looked over his shoulder and spotted the winged beast swooping down. He dropped to the ground and rolled away just as Malocere buzzed overhead. A blast of wind followed the creature's passing, generating a cyclone of dust and a wicked roar.

Shrill Morse code sounds rose into the sky. The clicks and wails were practically identical to those that Brig had heard back in the sheriff's station. He thought back to what John had told him many days before:

In his world, he commands many legions. With our forces mobilized, he will be forced to do the same . . .

Oh, no! Brig's mind screamed. *He's rallying his troops!*

Miles off in the distance, a rolling black cloud rushed towards him. In it, he heard what sounded like millions of swarming insects. The unearthly whine validated his earlier suspicions, and he turned to run, but saw another cloud approaching from that direction as well.

They're surrounding me!

The cloud rapidly drew closer, and Brig was now able to make out the shapes of small bodies and the blur of rapidly beating wings, which were what filled the air with the eerie, droning sound. At first, the shapes resembled horseflies, but the closer they came to him, the more he realized that they were much too big to be horseflies. The cloud was composed of millions of the softball creatures. Small, plump bodies stretched to every horizon, forming a massive army, one Brig knew he could never face alone.

Flashes of light pulsed among the army, accompanied by sounds similar to popcorn kernels exploding in a pan of hot oil. One by one, the softball creatures transformed, assuming the more menacing forms of the little goat creatures who hunched over and bared their teeth as they moved towards him, closing the circle.

To Brig's surprise and for no apparent reason, the creatures stopped advancing. They stood still, wringing their hands and softly whispering amongst themselves. A gentle breeze whistled across the barren wasteland; it danced and flirted with the soil. The Second Sun's dying light illuminated the beasts as Brig looked into their vacant eyes and wondered what might dwell behind them – an infinite void or unfathomable evil. He didn't know, nor did he want to find out.

"Lets us kills him, master." One called out. "Yessss." A rumble of conversation began to grow amongst the crowd, hooves stamping the soil with obvious impatience.

"Much too dangerous to let him livz..."

"KILL HIMZ!!!!!!!!!!"

One produced a hammer just as another grabbed hold of it and tried to take it away. "Heez MINE!"

Malocere barked out an order, and dead silence fell, save the foreboding whistle of the wind. Perhaps it was the lustful look in their eyes, but something told Brig an attack was imminent; he could feel it in his bones.

A rigid object pressed against his hip, and he remembered the folding knife John had given him before they'd left the farmhouse. The words John had spoken had been nothing less than prophetic:

This is for all the things I can't *imagine.*

Brig reached into his pocket and removed the knife. It opened easily and locked into place with a sharp *click*. He winced as he dragged the blade over his palm, splitting the skin open, allowing bright-red blood to pour from the wound.

Your blood has power.

The creatures shifted nervously and some licked their lips as he extended his arm and made a 360-degree turn, attempting to create a protective blood perimeter around himself. Once the circle was complete, a few precious beads were still clinging to his fingertips, all of them clotting in the choking air. Partially out of curiosity, but more for the grim fun of it, he flicked his fingers into the face of one of the nearby creatures, peppering it with his blood.

It covered its face and screamed as though it had been hit with acid, instead. It clawed at its face, tearing away sheet after sheet of skin, screaming "BURN! IT BURNS!" A thick, plasma-like fluid oozed from its nasal cavity and eye sockets. It teetered from side to side before falling to the ground where its body burst into thousands of tiny, white maggots, all of which tunneled back into the rocky soil.

Brig looked up in time to see one of the others step forward and assume the position vacated by its fallen comrade. Looking at the multitude around him, he knew he could never take them all down with blood alone – he'd bleed himself dry before he'd even put a dent in this army. He had to think of something else, and he knew he had better come up with it fast.

The Second Sun had already reached the western horizon, and the nocturnal shadows along with millions upon millions of nefarious, chattering life forms, were all creeping closer with every passing second. While he tried his best to hide it, Brig feared the darkness and all the unknown devils lurking within it.

More goat creatures crested over a nearby hill. The sound of their approach was the sound of stampeding cattle. The new horde collided into the existing one, and barks of anger rose from the masses until their discontent was all Brig could hear. Then they began advancing, and he hoped his protective circle would hold.

He pondered how long he could actually stand there in one place. *Minutes? Hours?* However long, he was certain it was far less than Malocere's army was willing to wait. They had all passed through millennia after millennia filled with the promises of the day they would spill righteous blood once more. This was their hour, a day of dark prophecy come to fruition.

Gabe spoke up again: *Reality is nothing more than perception. Picture it the way you want it to be.*

Three-quarters of the Second Sun had now sunken below the horizon. Brig looked at the mob before him and felt a strange anger swelling from deep within. He closed his eyes, and let it grow. His father had told him his role was that of protector – Kaitlyn's fight against Malocere was hers and hers alone. His father said nothing about these pests that surrounded him.

Just when his anger had reached critical mass, he released it. Untold rage manifested itself in the form of a blast wave that parted the herd of beasts and sent them flying left and right through the air. In his head, a voice called out to him – [Daddy!

Hurry! There's not much time! Run, Daddy! Run towards the light!]

Of course, he thought. *The Second Sun isn't a* star *at all – it's a portal – the way back!*

Unless he used the space-warp, Brig would never be able reach the portal before it set. He understood the risks if he were to try to move through solid objects, but it was his only choice. Malocere's army had been pushed back far enough that he decided to give it a shot.

S – t – r – e – t – c – h ...

The portal came within an arm's length. On the other side of it, he saw Erin, Kaitlyn, and John all cheering him on. Erin was holding Kaitlyn close and she hugged the child tightly. John reached out with his hand and telepathically screamed:

[Take it! Take my hand!!]

Brig was relieved. *It's over, he* thought. *It's done.* He stepped forward and plunged his hand through the portal. John took hold of it and pulled.

Kaitlyn shouted, [*DADDY!!!!!*]

From behind, an unseen assailant swept Brig's feet out from under him. His chest slammed into the dirt, instantly knocking the wind out of him. The resulting pain was so intense that it broke his concentration, causing the portal to rocket away.

SNAP! CRACK!

Erin and Kaitlyn screamed in unison as they flew off into the distance. Brig listened as their voices faded and then rolled onto his back where he saw Malocere only a few feet away. A handful of the goat creatures emerged from behind a pile of rocks and inched forward with venom in their eyes. They raised their hands over their heads and protracted sharp claws. The sound of inhuman snarls filled Brig's ears as the aggressors surrounded him.

He looked upon them, taking pity in their malicious nature, for these were truly lesser beings who knew neither pity nor remorse. They had been allied with the Darkness for so very long that their minds no longer knew the mercy of The Light. They only sought to snuff it out.

Brig tried to sit up, but collapsed again in response to the crushing pain in his chest. A whistle-like wheeze in his breathing gave him pause, and his mind shouted: *My ribs! I broke my goddamned ribs!* He looked to his right where Malocere slithered towards him on his belly, dragging his legs behind him.

[Did you really think I'd let you go so easily?] He asked.

Four of the creatures grabbed Brig's ankles and pulled him towards a nearby crater. Brig shut his eyes, unwilling to admit the game was up, but knowing full well his pool of strength was far too shallow to attempt an escape. Sharp rocks tore gashes in his back, which was already throbbing from the slapdash patchwork of puffy brimstone burns.

White lather rolled from the creatures mouths whenever he cried out. Their collective response to his misery unsettled him. He remembered the dream he'd had the morning before leaving Birmingham, and he thought he had a fairly good idea of what was in store for him.

Suddenly, the gathering crowd divided like a zipper comes undone, and a larger male stepped forward. Every head bowed as the figure passed. This one didn't appear like the others. It was hairless and burnt severely. Brig saw no eyes in its head, only dark, cavernous cavities where they should have been. The crowd whispered the figure's name, and Brig detected a mounting atmosphere of restiveness among them:

"Azel! It's Azel! Oh boy, you in for it now, Thunder boy! Dis iz gonna hurt!" Cackles rose immediately as several of the

creatures made bets among each other as to how long it would take Brig to die.

That's when Brig remembered the dream, and in his mind, he saw himself hanging on the cross, silhouetted in the light of the setting moon. Azel clapped his hands and four smaller beings came forth and dragged Brig to the crater's rim where they rolled him over its edge. He tumbled down the steep slope, colliding against a boulder with a meaty pop as another of his ribs snapped away from his sternum.

This is it, he thought. *I'm going to die.*

-2-

Back in the Earthly Realm, Kaitlyn's head hung low as the portal she had opened for her father vanished with a *pop*. She looked up at John and nodded her head, acknowledging that she now understood what needed to be done. Her father's time was short. If they were to save him, Malocere had to be defeated and that meant tremendous risk.

While John had hoped to rescue Brig and avoid apocalyptic prophecy, it appeared as though that was no longer possible. Even if they were able to save him, John feared Brig's injuries would only to make the war exponentially harder to win. It had been preordained that the three of them were to work together as a team. The power of the triad was meant to work as an unyielding force against the powers of Darkness, but Brig's self-serving determination to protect his daughter had broken the triad's back, leaving only John and Kaitlyn to bear the heavy load and a two legged stool cannot stand.

John looked over at Erin, who lay balled up in Brig's recliner, shivering with a crippling mixture of denial and terror. He worried she might be teetering on the verge of a mental break. She had been phenomenally strong up until now, so strong in fact that John had taken her ready willingness to accept the outright implausible as a testament to her mental fortitude. But looking at her now, he didn't know how much more she could take.

Not wanting to give her further reason to panic, he mentally projected his concerns to Kaitlyn, instead of speaking them out loud. The little girl looked back at her mother through empathetic eyes and walked over to her. Erin broke into a round of sobs and hugged her daughter tightly.

The child knelt beside the chair and placed the tips of her fingers on Erin's eyebrows before sliding them down her mother's face, closing her eyelids. John watched the scene unfold from the other side of the room, and he was touched by Kaitlyn's tenderness. She brushed her mother's hair back and planted a soft kiss on her forehead. "You sleep now," she said. "We'll take it from here."

Erin's eyes remained closed and her body stopped shivering as though a blanket of peace had been wrapped around her shoulders. Kaitlyn turned back to John and said, "We need to go now."

"I know," he said. But first you must call to them. Call the Agents. The time for the battle has come."

-3-

Thousands of the goat creatures had surrounded Brig's crater, and they were triumphantly baring ragged teeth and rolling with savage laughter. One picked up a stone and pitched it in. It struck Brig's jaw, but in light of how much he was already suffering, the impact felt like little more than a pinprick. The others quickly joined in the game, and a hailstorm of stones rained down upon Brig's bloodied, broken body.

Malocere appeared at the rim, towering above the pint-sized beings. Acting on their master's command, the army poured into the crater like a herd of antelope fleeing a predator. They surrounded Brig and began chanting in an arcane language he couldn't comprehend.

A few minutes passed, and the crowd split again, forming a sort of aisle up the middle. Brig had picked up on the way the mob-like behavior manifested itself every time a new horror came forth. Just as he'd suspected, two more beings appeared carrying with them a rickety cross made of gnarled and twisted wood. They set it on the ground next to him and hoisted his body onto it, careful to avoid any blood that might remain unclotted.

They went about posing him on the cross, not making the slightest attempt to conceal their passion for the task. They clearly derived some sort of twisted ecstasy from the sound of Brig's moans. Azel lifted his hands again, and the flurry of activity settled to a standstill. All eyes then turned to Malocere, who was wearing a malicious grin.

He said, [Things didn't have to be this way, you know. You really should have considered my offer.]

A tiny blink of light in the west was the Second Sun's final breath. The last ray died, and Brig was consumed by a wave of hopelessness and depression as the curtain of darkness ingested the wasteland with voracious disregard. The other little monsters, all of which had been anxiously awaiting this moment, swarmed into the crater, along with their tittering cries. They shuffled between the goat creatures' legs - some on two legs, others on four, six, and eight.

Azel and his hoard kicked them out of the way as though the little ones were but minor annoyances that had to be tolerated. The tiny miscreations hopped up and down, and they strained their scant voices as they cheered. It wasn't long before the chant caught on, and the goat creatures soon joined in the chorus along with the others, chanting just as Azel and Lamia had that night back in the barn.

"Crucify him! Cross him! Hang him up! Crucify him! Cross him! Hang him up!"

From atop the crater, Malocere bellowed his instructions. No sooner had he done so than Brig felt several hands holding his arms against the horizontal crosspiece. Icy, metal spikes were then positioned over his wrists, and he braced himself for a degree of pain that he was incapable of conceiving. He did the only thing he knew to do; he closed his eyes and he waited.

Azel and Lamia were holding spikes and began tapping them with their hammers – not hard enough to break the skin, but hard enough to send Brig into a colossal panic attack. They leaned in close to his face and sniffed his breath, clearly intoxicated by the aroma of anxiety.

One snickered. "Youz scared, Thunder boy? Youz better be, dis gonna hurt somethin' fierce!"

They brought their hammers down with potent force.

CLANK! CLANK! Brig's lungs practically burst from the force of his screams. The spikes pierced his wrists and bit into the weathered wood beneath. Each spike was then given three more blows and each spike head kinked to the side before the job was deemed complete.

Several others in the crowd scrambled to help raise the cross onto its end while the greater masses cheered with excitement. Some clapped. Others just moaned with delight as the betting among the crowd continued.

Strangely, Brig found himself incapable of anger – his pain was far too great to allow such an all-consuming emotion to compete for center stage. To his horror, a third, much duller spike was driven through his feet, which had been stacked one on top of the another. The spike required an unthinkable eight blows before it fully penetrated both bone and wood. Large, bloody teardrops streamed from Brig's eyes, and he cried out prayers for death.

What he had forgotten was that he was in the one place where the prayers of millions fell upon the ears of none.

The creatures responsible for the crucifixion struggled as they carried the cross over to where they had dug a small posthole. They dropped the vertical section into it and backed away so that they could admire what they had done. The goat creatures joined in with the smaller beings, who had already started chanting: "*Die! Die! Die!*" Brig wanted nothing more than to grant them their wish.

At the foot of the cross, six hooved creatures skipped around it, holding hands and singing, *Ring around the rosie... A pocket full of posies...*

Another round of stoning ensued from a small segment of the crowd, but the rest seemed content to stand idly by and watch him bleed.

Ashes, Ashes...

Brig's breathing became weak and shallow as fluid filled his lungs – every breath was a mixed-blessing of life glazed with a stabbing hunger for death. He focused his attention on his wrists, which were groaning as his bones scraped across the spike shafts. High above, he watched those foreign moons track their way across the sky; the blood in his eyes accentuated their red hue.

Suddenly, three powerful, yet distinct peals of thunder overpowered the heckling. The sky ripped open in broad, jagged slashes. All eyes, large and small, looked toward the anomaly above as blinding, white light raged through the rift.

The taunting turned to terror when an invisible hand peeled back that same section of the sky. Amorphous, white shapes too numerous to count streaked into The Lower

Afterworld. Brig heard galloping horses and the angry roars of thousands of unseen beasts.

The shapes descended in the form of a thick, gelatinous fog, which condensed on a nearby, barren plateau. The shapes began to take on physical form, gradually becoming sharper and more distinct. The first to materialize were enormous stallions with hair so white it was blue. Each was plated in full body armor from head to tail. Angry, red eyes peered out from the holes in their helmets, and steam jetted from their nostrils; the vapor curled as if offended by the hellish atmosphere.

Atop the steeds rode mounted knights in well-polished armor. They were armed with sheathed broadswords and imposing lances. In the armor itself, Brig was able to see white sunlight and powder blue skies as though the metal was some sort of window into the Upper Realm. The mounted knights, as well as those on foot, held shields of burnished bronze; all were adorned with the symbol of the Blood Knights.

Malocere's roars reverberated off the mountains, causing rockslides and seismic tremors. The Dark Agents quickly assembled into well-defined ranks and files, and the two armies faced one another in calculated silence with less than a quarter of a mile separating the two.

A booming voice from the Blood Knight's side sounded off an order. Small figures hurried to the front lines, carrying with them abundantly stocked quivers and far-reaching longbows. The archers wasted no time in taking aim; they pointed their arrows skyward at a 45-degree angle, and waited for their next command.

The Dark Agents obeyed Malocere's orders and advanced. Rusted shields and scythe-like weapons appeared in their previously unarmed hands, conjured from thin air. They all raised the weapons over their heads and cried out with defiance.

The knight's trumpeter relayed an order, instructing the archers to release their arrows. They let them fly, just as the Dark Agents picked up their pace and ran screaming toward the invading army.

Three closely-spaced volleys of arrows streaked from the sky into the advancing mob. A tide of screams overcame the rumble of charging footsteps as the projectiles randomly chose their targets. Each of the three volleys thinned Malocere's forces by a thousand or so at a time. The forces on the front lines fell like waves crashing into a shoreline, and they were trampled by the multitudes rushing up from behind them.

The trumpeter sounded the attack, and the archers stepped aside, allowing the mounted infantry to charge into battle with the foot soldiers closely behind. The ground shook and shuddered as the knights closed the distance. The armor on the huge stallions sparked and clanked with earsplitting percussion as they ran, nostrils flaring and eyes burning with intensity.

The two forces clashed somewhere in the middle of the plateau just south of the towering peak upon which Malocere had perched himself in his efforts to tempt Brig to his side. The carnage multiplied, and what had begun as thin trickles of blood flowing from the battlefield soon swelled into a river. The rocks over which the river flowed drank readily, but the current grew too great even for them to absorb. Soon, the Plateau was ankle-deep in the blood of the fallen.

Five winged creatures crested the eastern horizon soaring in from the direction of The Borderlands – *dragons closing fast.* The knight in charge saw them coming. He used his sword to give the archers a high sign. They responded by aiming into the sky at a lesser degree than before and letting their arrows fly.

Only two hit their intended targets.

Both of the wounded dragons fell from the sky in tight, downward spirals. Undaunted, the remaining three beat their wings harder and harder, eventually achieving mind-numbing speed. A pink sonic cone formed around the leader's head just before he punched through the sound barrier.

The commander raised his shield - as did the knights surrounding him - and the dragons zoomed overhead, bombarding the opposing army with a salvo of fiery breaths, all of which proved ineffective. When the immediate danger had passed, the majority of knights returned to the battle at hand. Six of the taller ones, all captains, kept their faceplates turned towards their commander, awaiting his orders.

The dragons changed course, circling around the mountain peak for another pass over the plateau. The commander twirled his sword above his head, signaling to the others. The six captains nodded, and a pair of jointed wings unfolded from beneath each one's armor. Their wings spread to a height that was nearly twice what the knights were tall. All were covered with feathers made of finely spun gold.

The commander led his captains into the air. All seven ascended with their shields held in front of them and their swords poised behind, ready to strike. The lead dragon belched another burst of fire, which succeeded in knocking one of the seven from the sky.

While the captains battled against two of the remaining dragons, the commander hopped onto the leader's back. The creature reared up and tried its best to shake off the unwelcome rider. The commander wrapped his arm around its neck and dug his heels into its side. He thrust his sword into the dragon's back, driving it in all the way up to the jewel-encrusted hilt.

The beast shrieked and thrashed about, but the commander held on. He unsheathed a dagger from beneath his boot and used it to saw off one of the wings. The dense, porous bone proved no match for the blade, and the appendage came off in one powerful slice. No longer capable of flight, the dragon plummeted to the ground where it crash-landed in a twisted heap.

With the skies clear, the other captains descended to rejoin the battle. However, the commander stayed behind, hovering in midair, surveying the scene. At least a thousand of the goat creatures had converted back to their softball forms and taken flight. They were closing in on the commander from every direction.

Brig lost sight of him in a brilliant ball of golden light, which radiated outward from beneath his armor. The explosion that followed tore the fabric of The Lower Afterworld, creating several deep fault lines. The resulting shockwave dilated outward, peeling the thick clouds back like a scroll and vaporizing everything in its path. Within a matter of seconds, every airborne softball creature had been destroyed.

Despite the aerial victory, the battle was still raging below. Malocere's forces were resisting the invader's onslaught, clearly determined to battle it out to the last. Despite the committed opposition, the Blood army was making considerable progress, but a long fight lie ahead, and the outcome was anything but certain.

CHAPTER TWENTY-TWO

-1-

Brig felt himself slipping away, no longer able to remember what it felt like to breathe without knifelike pain. His body weighed heavily on his wrists as his leg muscles failed him. He felt sure his arms would soon tear from their sockets, but he no longer cared. He looked into the sky a final time, saddened that his last mortal memory would be of The Lower Afterworld's barren moons.

In his peripheral vision, he saw more beating wings approaching from the west. He turned his head towards two white doves descending in his direction. No sooner had he seen them than his body became as light as a feather, and he felt himself floating away. Exhausted, he let his head hang down, convinced he was dying and this was what the endgame felt like.

The doves lighted on a nearby boulder, and were quickly encapsulated in a transformative glow that stretched longer and wider, growing brighter and brighter. Soon, it reached its peak of brilliance and then began to wane. Brig forced himself to blink, so sure his imagination had spawned the figures that now stood before him.

Kaitlyn materialized not as a child, but an older version of herself who appeared to be in her late teens, maybe her early twenties. Her blonde hair hung long and she was clothed all in white. She was thin, but looked strong and ready for battle. In his delirious state, Brig spoke Erin's name as the beautiful young woman before him looked so much like her mother had back in their college days.

Looking up at her father, Kaitlyn covered her face with her hands and turned away, stifling a scream within them. John stood beside her, and his expression bent into one of pained empathy. He stepped forward and looked up at Brig. "We're here to help you," he said. "Hold on and we'll get you down."

Brig tried to speak, but his voice had long-since been stolen by the arid wind. John went back to where Kaitlyn stood and took her hand only to return to the foot of the cross a few seconds later with her in tow. She continued to avert her eyes, unable or perhaps unwilling to look upon her father in such misery.

John told her that she must, for if she didn't, her father would surely die. So reluctantly, Kaitlyn turned her head and brushed her hair from her line of sight as tears pooled in her eyes.

"Daddy..."

"Focus, Kaitlyn!" John said. "Focus on the spikes!"

She closed her eyes, and soon thereafter, the bass-like rumble returned and pulsed around them along with the sound of a mighty wind that howled towards them at tremendous speed. It washed over them, causing Brig's cross to twist and wobble like a street sign whipped about in a hurricane. The weathered wood groaned, and the brittle, fibers popped in response to the inordinate stress and strain.

The upper two-thirds of the cross broke free from its base and spun into the air with blinding velocity. Brig was lost amongst a cyclonic blur of color as the cross spun faster and faster; its initial *humming* sound quickly escalated into an earsplitting whistle. Kaitlyn raised her hands into the air, and the spinning slowed to a stop. The cross hung there, suspended ten feet off the ground. The undercurrent of commotion rising from the distant battlefield fell silent as the small pocket of air surrounding the three of them thickened. Kaitlyn opened her eyes and gritted her teeth; she clenched her hands into tight fists and yanked them backwards, pulling against a tremendous, unseen force.

The spikes that had been driven through Brig's wrists and feet tore out of the cross with the sound of three, simultaneous rifle shots. They zipped through the soupy air and struck the boulder against which Brig had collided after he was shoved into the crater. The massive stone exploded, leaving behind no fragment larger than a pebble. The cross fell away and splintered as it struck the ground.

Brig's body fell forward, but Kaitlyn turned her hands such that her palms faced the sky, halting his descent. His torso floated horizontally, but his arms and legs hung down limp in front of him. Kaitlyn slowly lowered her father's body until it was only a few feet above the ground. She gently rolled him over and stretched him out flat and stiff as a board before laying him down upon the rocky soil. Brig's eyes rolled around in his head. He was in so much pain that he couldn't think, much less speak. His head fell back, and he shut his eyes. From somewhere above him, he heard the fading sound of his daughter crying.

John rushed to Brig's side and Kaitlyn asked him, "Is he okay? Please tell me he's not dead!" She cried out, "Daddy! Wake up!" She fell to her knees and put her hands on his chest, but jerked them away when she felt the jagged bones beneath his skin. Her eyes turned up to John and she said, "He's hurt. He's hurt bad!"

"Can you help him, Kaitlyn?" John asked. "Can you heal him?"

"I don't know," she responded. "I feel funny... *tired.* I don't know if I'm strong enough, but I'll try." She knelt down and placed her hands on her father's chest again. The air around them filled with the sizzling pops of static electricity, but try as she might, nothing happened. It was as though the Lower Afterworld was attempting to smother her power. She cried out, "John! I can't do it! I can't help him! I think he's dying!"

John felt Brig's neck for a pulse. When he couldn't find one, he leaned over and listened for some indication of breathing, instead. "There's no pulse!" He screamed. "He's not breathing, either!"

Kaitlyn sobbed, unable to understand why she couldn't help her father. "Do something!" She cried. "Do something! He's dying!"

"His ribs are broken," John explained. "I can't give him CPR, I might puncture his lungs! I don't know what to do!"

Just then, a sound like ripping fabric surrounded them. A bright, blue slash appeared in midair a few feet away. Another one followed, forming an "X" shape. An armored hand poked through, clutching a polished sword. The hand belonged to the commander, who stepped through the rift and made his way over to where Brig's body lay. He knelt down beside it and removed the cape from his back without saying a word. His helmet's faceplate then opened with a thin, metallic *click*, and he sheathed his sword.

"Can... can you save him?" Kaitlyn asked, "Is he dead?"

The soldier looked into her eyes and smiled an oddly comforting smile. "I'm afraid he is, my dear." He was quick to dry Kaitlyn's tears on the corner of his cape, which he then draped over Brig's body, covering his face with what was now a purple death shroud.

John sat down and buried his face in his hands. Kaitlyn crawled towards her father's body and pulled the heavy fabric back from his face. She kissed him on the forehead and opened her mouth to speak. The words that came out were shaky and broken.

"I love you, daddy," she said after wiping her eyes on the sleeve of her shirt. "I'm sorry I wasn't strong enough to save you." She pulled the cape back over his face as a heartbroken expression settled on her own – it was one of lonesome, abandoned sorrow.

The commander reached out and took her hand. "Don't cry," he said. "If anyone understands that death isn't final, it's you. Your father understood the risks when he came here, but I'm afraid they are far greater than he may have told you. You see... if his soul leaves his body, he'll be trapped in this place. You must find your strength, Kaitlyn. This place is going to do everything it can to quash your power, but you must overcome it.

He took her hand and placed it on Brig's forehead, the other he placed on Brig's chest. "Wish for it," he told her. "Wish for it harder than you've ever wished for anything in your life. *Remember him!* Remember your father's love for you. *Want it!* Believe it will happen! You know how to do this, you've done it before!"

Kaitlyn did as she was told, and a blue bubble formed around them just as it had the day she'd resurrected Buster. The bubble throbbed in synch with her sobs as if it was suffering the same crushing heartbreak right along with her. Unlike before, the ground began to quake. Far in the distance, the mountains shook and boulders tumbled down the slopes.

John shielded his eyes when the calm, blue light bleached to the blinding shade of white. Above them, the clouds hanging in sulphurous sky rolled and churned as lightning flashed within them and howling wind whipped across the plateau. An explosive thunderclap boomed overhead, and from beneath the cape came the sound of violent coughing.

The commander yanked his cape away from Brig's face, and Kaitlyn burst into tears when she saw her father blink his eyes. John shouted, "He's alive! He's alive!"

The commander knelt down on one knee in front of Kaitlyn and said, "I have to go now, but we'll need you soon. I'm afraid time is very short."

Kaitlyn threw her arms around his neck and squeezed him tightly. "Thank you," she said. "Thank you for helping him!"

The commander smiled. "No thanks are necessary. You did it all. I just helped you to remember." He pointed to the distant valley where the battle raged on. "That is no ordinary army," he told her. "Each knight you see down there belongs to the bloodline. We answered your call. We are here for this one purpose. Soon enough you will remember."

With that, he draped two swords across Kaitlyn's back where they crossed with the hilts peeking out over her shoulders. Handing a katana to John, he smiled and said, "For you, my brother," before laying a broadsword beside Brig. Each of the three moons hanging above shone upon the commander's armor as he slid his faceplate closed. He turned toward the clanking metal and pounding footsteps just over the crater's rim and walked towards it, without looking back.

John looked down at Brig and offered him his hand. "Are you strong enough to walk?" he asked. Brig nodded and stood up with a groan. Grit and sand whipped past them, carried along by the stinging breeze. He examined his wrists and found dark, red scars where the spikes had been driven through them. John pointed to the scars and said, "Be proud of those. No medal can ever compare."

Kaitlyn cautiously stepped forward, inching ever closer to her father. Brig saw the uncertainty in her eyes, and he held his arms open, encouraging her to come closer. She finally did, and he squeezed her as hard as he could. He thanked her for what she'd done, before holding her out at arm's length and admiring this more mature version of his daughter.

"You're a beauty," he told her. "You look so much like your mother."

Kaitlyn pointed in the direction the commander had taken and told both her father and John that the time was at hand. Together, the three of them trudged up the crater's steep slope and paused to look down upon the bloody killing fields below.

Hundreds of the knights turned their heads as Kaitlyn appeared, standing high atop the ring of mounded dirt flanked by two men at her side. Behind her, the sky continued to boil as clouds rolled in and thunder rumbled. The wind whipped by them, blowing Kaitlyn's clothes about her as resounding cheers rose from the army, all of which were soon drowned out by trumpet blasts.

The quakes, explosions, and thunder had not gone unnoticed by Malocere. He swept in from a distant mountain perch from which he had been watching the battle rage. He landed in the middle of both armies with a loud thud, crushing some of his own forces. A blast of fire shot from his mouth pushed the knights back.

He took to the air once more and Kaitlyn reached behind her head and unsheathed her two swords. They glimmered with hints of silver and molten metal, but were cool in her hands, light and agile. Her face took on a wise, knowing expression as she moved the swords back and forth through the air before she spun both in a quick flourish. Images flashed in her mind, random but somehow familiar. A feeling came over her almost as though she was remembering another lifetime. She steadied herself in a more defensive posture as Malocere approached.

He stopped and hovered in midair, still a safe distance away, and projected his thoughts to the three standing there. [You never should have come. My forces outnumber yours ten to one. You don't stand a chance.]

Kaitlyn spoke across the chasm with a booming voice, echoing ancient knowledge long-stored in the old soul within her which had now awakened. "Arrogance has always been your weakness! Today, the Light will prevail! Today this ends!"

Malocere beat his wings as he spoke. [Listen well, Keeper. Each day begins in Darkness. Don't over-value the Light.] Again he took off and spoke as he circled the battlefield. [Before, I was in your world, bound by your laws – no more – *now you are in mine.* I think you'll find this battle far more difficult than you might have thought.]

Without another word, Malocere flew off into the distance, shouting out commands as he went before smashing to the ground and folding his wings behind him on the far side of the battlefield. A swarm of his soldiers poured over the hillsides screaming battle cries with their weapons high above their heads. A defiant Malocere glared back at the three on the crater rim and spat out his challenge. [Come if you dare.]

-2-

Kaitlyn bolted for the battlefield and opened a Gate above it allowing thousands of wisps of vapor though it before she slammed it shut again. Each wisp fell and transformed into a separate being, poised with arms out in a perimeter around the knight army. They were all once Keepers and no strangers to battle.

Malocere roared with laughter. "Is this the best you can conjure?" He waved to the legion on his right and commanded them forward. The stamping feet of the soldiers caused several stallions on the opposing side to rear up while their riders held on.

[The first Keeper fought for *three days*, and still I lived.]

[His mission wasn't to kill you. Besides, He told you he would send another – *one stronger* – to defeat you.]

Malocere scoffed. [And that's you? A little girl in a grown up body surrounded by this rag tag bunch of sorcerers and toy soldiers?]

[Today you die.]

[Why won't you say my name?] He hissed.

[I haven't uttered it since you fell. It leaves a bad taste in my mouth.] Kaitlyn crossed her swords in front of her and narrowed her eyes to slits. Something about the way the light glinted off of the sword and shone upon her face allowed Malocere to see past the young girl before him down to the ancient soul beneath.

[Aliel.]

Kaitlyn's lips pulled to the side, pleased to see Malocere display fear for the first time – and with good reason. In the days before the Great War, Malocere and Aliel were commanders in the same legion, more importantly they were brother and sister. His betrayal had hit her hard, but she fought against him, refusing to align with him and his rebellion. In the end, Aliel was the one to throw him from the walls of the Upper Afterworld and watch him plunge.

Malocere barked another order and all of his legions charged. They collided with the Light army in the middle of the plateau as shields and weapons clanged together like bells. The goat creatures proved to be formidable warriors as they pushed forward, hacking and stabbing – all the while screaming "FIGHT!"

The Keepers fought to hold back the advancing mob as best they could, sending power pushes to scatter them while others opted for flame and lightning. Azel pounced towards one of them, bounding from behind using the back of one creature like a springboard. He held a blade back, ready to strike as he flew through the air, chattering his teeth as he called out, "KEEEEEEEEEEEEEEPER!!!!!!!"

The object of his attack spun and sent a jet of fire towards him that missed by a narrow margin, but it was enough to throw him off of his target. Azel struck the ground face first and quickly rose to his feet with a snort and a grunt, swinging his blade left and right with no care whatsoever as to who or what he struck. Finally came the sound of metal on metal.

Azel turned his reptilian eyes to see he had crossed swords with Brig who he had written off as dead on the cross. He bared his teeth. "Wherez you come from, Thunder boy? Thoughts weeez killed you! Once not enough? Huh? Youz wanna die twice?" Without another word, he swung his sword wildly through the air with no form or apparent skill, hoping merely to make contact and cause a fatal wound.

Brig struggled against such random motion in an attempt to block and counter attack, but Azel's blade flew inches from his face like a saw blade. Brig backed away, tripping on a stone before falling onto his back. Azel wasted no time and brought his sword down like an executioner, aiming to cleave Brig's head in two.

The downward stroke was stopped halfway by a gleaming katana that John thrust in its path. Just then, the Keeper who was the initial target of the attack sent forth a blast wave that succeeded in blowing Azel back far enough to allow Brig to get to his feet. Once again the creature charged with sword raised. Brig held firm and only when Azel sprung for the kill, did he drop to his knee and raise his sword, impaling his attacker through the gut. The creature's eyes bulged, and he fell to the ground without so much as a scream. Brig brought his sword down, severing the head which burst into maggots as he'd seen before.

John held out his hand and helped Brig to his feet. Vile creatures of every shape and size crowed all around them. From the corner of his eye, John detected movement, and in one fluid motion, he swung his katana, slicing the head off of one of Malocere's advancing minions. Three more were on him in short time, and he slashed and hacked through them all.

Piercing screams split the sky as Keepers and knights alike found an ever-advancing horde. Keepers were everywhere, casting lightning and conjuring rings of flame. At some point, Malocere had called in another squadron of dragons from the distant Borderlands. They arrived in formation with the sound of fighter jets and bellowing train whistles. Fire poured from their mouths upon the masses below with blatant disregard for whom or what was engulfed by them.

One Keeper yanked a dragon from the sky using an invisible tether and when the creature had struck the ground, she sent forth a tremendous wind full of sand and rock that stripped the flesh from its body as it cried out, screaming for death and release. It came soon enough, and the skeletal remains lay bleached in the dirt.

Brig looked towards Malocere and saw Kaitlyn advancing towards him, slowly, methodically and to his amazement, completely undefended. Her swords were sheathed behind her back and she waded through the crowd as it parted around her like rushing water around a rock.

Above and behind her another dragon dove from the sky. Brig reacted without thinking, going to that place in his gut – the place his father had pointed to – and sent a protective shield her way. It arrived just in time as a spray of flame bounced uselessly off of it.

John trotted up beside him atop a large, white stallion with another in tow. He urged Brig to climb on, which he did. The two bolted toward Kaitlyn, trampling the scurrying masses beneath them.

Brig felt Malocere attempting to burrow into his mind, searching for the memory of the training they had received in the Upper Afterworld in hopes of using that knowledge to his advantage. Brig did his best to wipe his mind clean and shut the intruder out.

Malocere reared up and roared before dropping low to the ground and slithering towards Kaitlyn on his belly. She heard the gallops behind her and she shouted to her father and John. "Back! Get back!!" The two men reared their stallions onto their hind legs in time to see Kaitlyn draw her swords and take down five troll-like things in short order. Each fell with a scream as more advanced and Kaitlyn wove and ducked all around them, slicing their legs out from beneath them and beheading the ones she could.

Now only ten yards away, Malocere lunged. Kaitlyn twirled around and then she was gone. She reappeared behind him, mounted upon his back. She conjured a fiery rope from thin air and lassoed it around his neck with ease. The dragon bucked and howled, but Kaitlyn held on.

Droves of goat creatures were descending on Brig and John – far too many for them to fight, but Keepers materialized around them sending jets, energy and blasts this way and that. One Keeper held a large beast in a chokehold from a distance as a rusty crossbow arrow zipped by his ear with a swish – an inch was all that separated him from certain death. The Keeper cocked his wrist to the side, and the creature's massive neck snapped.

Kaitlyn was soon bucked off of Malocere's back where she landed hard. Back on her feet, she locked eyes with the beast.

The right side of her mouth curled up in a foreboding sneer, and she pulled her hand from behind her back. In it, the fiery rope had become a whip that crackled with heat and flame. She cracked it against the side of Malocere's neck and he jerked his head away to escape the stinging pain. Kaitlyn cracked the whip once more, and he lunged at her, his dagger-like teeth coming within inches of her face.

She thrust her hands out and shoved him away with an incredible force. He rolled over and over several times before finally coming to a stop. Kaitlyn peered off into the distance and was able to make out the shape of galloping horses and her father's features who rode atop one of them.

"Why did you never ask father for mercy," she called out to Malocere. "Were you THAT blinded by hate?"

Malocere hissed back at her. "Mercy is for the weak. Besides no one is listening."

The battle raged around them, but a strange silence fell upon this pocket of the plateau. Brig and John were advancing with two dragons in hot pursuit behind them. Kaitlyn never took her eyes off of Malocere, but the two dragons were suddenly consumed in fire and yanked from the sky with pained screams.

"So you chose to crawl around in this basement on your belly like a snake?" She shouted. "Was it SO bad for you before?"

Malocere stopped and rose up on his hind legs. "Oh Aliel, don't you see? Here I'm not playing second fiddle to that... that pacifist. Here... I'm God."

"Never more than a dim shadow on the wall. That's all you'll ever be. Look at you. Look at what you have become!"

"This? This form... you think this is all I am?" The ground trembled. "You know nothing little sister."

Malocere spread his wings, but before he had a chance to send anything in her direction, Kaitlyn sent an intensely focused, laser-like pulse centered upon his chest. The force was such that it knocked Brig and John from their stallions, and Malocere glowed blue before he vaporized in a blinding flash that drew every eye.

Silence fell. It appeared as though Kaitlyn had vanquished him, but only for the tiniest fraction of time, because a burst of flame erupted in the sky over her head and a booming voice bellowed, "FOOL!"

Kaitlyn summoned a tidal wave of water with a wave of her hand that washed over the fire in the sky, encapsulating it inside a sphere she rotated and sent skyward. Inside, Malocere fought and howled. Never releasing him from the bubble, Kaitlyn sent it crashing down into a spot where corpses littered the ground, marking the spot where the battle's initial clash had taken place.

Meanwhile, the knights had since pushed Malocere's forces a considerable distance back toward the lakes of glowing lava just on the eastern horizon. A handful of Keepers held their ground in the center of a closing circle of trolls and goat creatures as one held the mob at bay with a ring of fire that encircled them. Another lifted his hands to the sky and sent forth a glowing orb that rose to a height of about twenty feet where it hovered like a small star.

The Keeper nodded to the others who withdrew their protections and instead cast their power into the orb. The mob advanced, each cackling beast anxious to be the first to kill a Keeper in this – the Second Great War. In an instant, the orb bloated to ten times its original size and blazed forth a white light that blinded would-be attackers. In the tiniest instant, the bloated orb shrank to a pin-sized singularity and then came the shockwave.

Brig, John, and Kaitlyn all turned to see the blinding flash seconds before the sound of the explosion reached their ears. The blast radiated outward, sending Malocere's forces flying every which way through the air like toys. Wisps of light swirled around the initial column of dust.

The shockwave reached the mountain upon which Malocere had rested while he tried to tempt Brig, the force cracked it in half, sending the cone-shaped portion crumbling down upon the army below as lava ejected into the nighttime sky, cascading over thousands, Dark and Light alike, illuminating them with a hellish orange light.

Brig cast another shield, hoping it would be enough to protect the knights and Keepers while John managed to summon a wave like Kaitlyn had done which succeeded in colliding with the lava as it began to descend, quickly cooling it until it became falling stones. One of the Keepers below sent forth a blast wave from behind Brig's shield that pulverized the lava stones to fine grains of dust which scattered to the wind.

It was a fantastic display of power, enough to distract the three of them from what rose up behind. Malocere had managed to get back to his feet and wasted no time projecting a sort of missile that struck the hillside just beneath the trio's feet. John and Brig were blown to the right. Kaitlyn tumbled down the hill to the left where she came to rest against a boulder, clutching her arm and crying out with pain.

Out of sight, but no doubt nearby, Malocere bellowed with laughter. From a distance of about fifteen feet, John focused healing power towards Kaitlyn in an attempt to mend what he was sure was a broken bone. It worked. Kaitlyn rose to one knee and nodded her thanks, but the energy that particular incantation had required drained him considerably. Brig dragged him behind a boulder for the protection it provided and peeked up over the ridge to assess the situation.

Malocere had been waiting and Brig was hit with a flaming arrow that vanished as soon as it hit, leaving behind the damage it had caused. He fell back and scooted to where John lay. Kaitlyn made a move in his direction – no doubt to heal him, but Brig held up a hand and halted her.

"No," he said. "This is what he wants. He wants to drain us, and you know healing takes just about everything you have. We'll be fine. The time is now, Kaitlyn. Finish this."

Kaitlyn drew her swords as she acknowledged that her father was right. She twirled and was gone.

A booming force caused the ground to tremble. "ALIEL!!!!!!!!!!!!!!!!!! COME FORTH, KEEPER!!!!" Malocere looked this way and that. "I WANT TO LOOK INTO YOUR EYES WHEN I KILL YOU!"

A quick spin of light and Kaitlyn reappeared behind him. "You were always the weaker one," she called out to him, causing him to turn around and gnash his teeth. "Your power lust will be your undoing."

The two circled one another, Kaitlyn with blades at the ready – Malocere lapping the thick air with his forked tongue. John and Brig managed to muscle their way to the crater's rim and peer over. John pried a sword from one of the fallen knight's hands. Brig followed suit.

Malocere launched a flaming jet at Kaitlyn, which she deflected with her sword, but it bought him enough time to spread his wings and vanish in a whirl similar to what she had done earlier. He materialized not as a dragon, but a shapeless mist – black, inky, and practically invisible against the night sky. The only evidence it exited at all was the occasional dark ripple.

The mist condensed and moved about the plateau like a small cyclone.

In the distance, the hacking and slashing rose into the sky as metal collided with metal and the occasional guttural sound that accompanied a kill. Flashes of light blazed against the sky, accompanied by the occasional explosion and crackle of electricity. A bolt of lightning dropped from the sky with the sound of a cannon. Brig and John didn't know what that signified, but the old soul within Kaitlyn did – a fellow Keeper had fallen.

Cries of victory rose from Malocere's army as a disembodied voice spoke to Kaitlyn through the mist – "One down."

Fury raged within her and she sent bolt after bolt of lightning into the mist with no apparent effect. Malocere laughed as she did her best to watch the amorphous shape move about. At times his voice was close enough to whisper in her ear – at others, he was far away, but still she couldn't pin him down. It was then she sheathed her swords and pulled her cloak hood over her head, covering her eyes.

She stretched out with her mind and felt for his aura the same way her father had done the night she was hiding in the fog. Malocere's felt dark, oily, and unclean. It moved about, and without the distraction of her mortal eyes, his location was clear. She felt his intent and sensed him running towards her. In one fluid motion, she drew her swords and brought them forth, colliding with his in a perfectly-timed block. She shoved him back with a swift kick and from her palms blazed a white light that illuminated everything around them and caused Malocere's new figure to stand out plainly. Kaitlyn attacked.

Brig and John were caught by surprise when a small group of the goat creatures crept up behind them. Two seized their legs and dragged them back as several others pelted them with rocks.

John had regained some of his strength, but the two of them were at a decided disadvantage. Malocere kept Kaitlyn occupied as the two battled it out with swords and competing will.

Brig looked up to see hundreds of the softball creatures flying towards him in a swarm. If they were to capture him, they might use him as leverage to get Kaitlyn to surrender. That was something he couldn't allow. He kicked at the creature holding him and sent it toppling to the ground.

"What dat for?" the creature cried out. "Iz ain't even hurts ya yet!"

Just then a column of vapor dropped from the sky. Jacob materialized just as the swarm of creatures popped into their two-legged form. Brig called out to him, but Jacob went right to work casting fire, wind, and water to push the mob back. Hundreds of the creatures soon stood in water ankle deep, shielding their faces from whatever he planned to send their way. Jacob whirled around and with a flick of his index finger sent bolts of lightning into the pool causing the creatures to seize and sizzle as they were electrocuted with a strange chattering sound that escaped clenched jaws. Soon they all fell dead and Jacob turned to face Brig.

"That felt good," he said finally, reaching down to lift his brother up.

Meanwhile, the red fingers of dawn were creeping higher in the eastern sky. Before long, sharp blades of punitive sunlight struck the Dark army, driving the lesser beings scurrying back into the west amid squeals of panic. The knight and Keepers gave chase. Brig, Jacob, and John stood ready – the two mortals with blades drawn.

Behind them, Malocere morphed back into his dragon form and reared up onto his hind legs with a throaty roar. He locked eyes with Kaitlyn, and his forked tongue slid across his upper lip.

He took flight, but soon, Kaitlyn engulfed him in flames and yanked him from the sky in a brilliant streak where he struck the ground in a cloud of dust and rock.

Malocere fought to stand before falling again with a heavy thud. His left wing had been broken in two. The distal half hung by a flap of skin like a child's kite caught on a power line. He emitted a low growl, and the first hint of pain flashed in those dark, bestial eyes. His one good wing flipped about in a frenzy, providing further evidence of his pain.

The knights and Keepers continued their chase, now filled with hot rage once more as they reclaimed the advantage with unmatched fervor. Brig rushed down the steep hillside and charged into the crowd with apparent lack of regard for his own safety. He ducked and bobbed, dodging blades swung at him in all directions. John followed, slashing his own path forward when he saw Brig lean over and pick up a rock.

What he didn't know was that Brig had spotted his other executioner – the one that had taken such glee in hammering the spike into his feet. He whistled loud enough to be heard over the deafening commotion and then shouted its name. "LAMIA!!"

The robed figure standing some thirty yards away turned. Like Azel, Lamia's face was blistered and charred having been set ablaze by Kaitlyn back in the barn before she cast them back into the Lower Afterworld. Lamia recognized this man from her earlier surveillance of the farm and pulled a bloody sword from the belly of a fallen knight as she turned her cavernous eyes in Brig's direction.

Brig hurled the stone through the air with power and accuracy. Lamia no sooner realized what was happening than she was knocked onto her back when the stone stuck her brow with a *whap* sound. Much to John's dismay, Brig brandished his sword and charged. Once he was within striking distance, Lamia rose up onto one knee and held her scythe over her head to shield herself from Brig's downward thrust, which deflected with the scraping sound of metal and a shower of orange sparks.

Brig's momentum propelled him forward several feet beyond his intended target before he was able to stop himself and turn around. Lamia stood and pulled the hood back over her head. Brig bared his teeth and charged again, his blood burning with a maddening desire for revenge.

Lamia stood waiting atop a boulder, scythe poised and ready to strike down this resurrected aggressor. Brig's movements appeared to be blinded by rage and lacking in calculation or forethought. She felt sure the kill would be an easy one.

Ten feet away, Brig raised his sword over his right shoulder, offering every indication of his intentions to wield a mighty deathblow. He swung his sword with all he had in him, lopping off the fiend's head in one powerful blow only to deliver a second, downward stroke, which split her into two halves, each of which fell to either side in distinct, symmetrical halves.

Brig bent down and picked the head up by one horn. He held it high and cried out victoriously before pitching it away. John shouted out to him while pointing toward Malocere with the sword he held in his hand.

"Brig! We have to go back in case Kaitlyn needs our help!" The two men took off running and disappeared over the hilltop. Brig's eyes widened when he peered into the valley. The knights were struggling their way into the ferocious mass of Malocere's forces, battling for every single inch of ground. In the middle of the valley, Kaitlyn was still raging against Malocere.

Despite his broken wing, his moments were quick. For every technique Kaitlyn threw at him, it seemed he had a counter-move. For the time being, the battle seemed evenly matched.

Malocere belched a burst of fire from his mouth, which parted around Kaitlyn who had extended her arm to produce the blue umbrella shield. That was when Kaitlyn was blindsided by a powerful swipe of one of Malocere's arms, sending her tumbling through the air until she collided with a rock wall some distance away.

Malocere seized the advantage and charged, unable to fly due to his broken wing. Once he was within striking distance, he made a leap into the air and snapped at Kaitlyn's throat. He missed and fell to the ground, landing on his side with a *thud*. In a desperate attempt, he swiped at Kaitlyn with razor sharp claws, missing her by a good five feet.

The dangling portion of his wing finally snapped off and was carried away on the breeze until it landed in a fleshy heap some fifty yards away. Kaitlyn summoned a tremendous push and the beast was blasted back enough for her to flourish her sword and sever his other wing. He threw his head back and howled with pain, but quickly whirled and assumed a more human-like form, clothed in black robes with glowing eyes beneath his hood.

Brig and John mounted two nearby steeds and galloped off in Kaitlyn's direction to lend support. As they charged through a particular cluster of knights, one of them held out a lance, offering it to John as he passed. John extended his arm, snagging the lance in his hand as he rode by. He held it high in the air and it blazed with light as the pair approached from the east.

Malocere and Kaitlyn circled one another, neither ready to make the first move – doing so forfeited a certain advantage that neither was willing to concede. Kaitlin twirled her swords in front of her, and Malocere laughed.

[I was always the better swordsman, Aliel.]

She kept her eyes locked on his as a blade slid from the sleeve of his cloak. Behind him, the approaching sounds of thundering hooves grew menacingly closer. John came within striking distance, and he hurled his lance through the air like a javelin. Malocere redirected it midflight without so much as looking at it, casting it into the crowd that had encircled them. The lance impaled a large troll through its back, causing the creature to writhe and frantically grope for it before falling dead and bursting into crackling flame.

The part that was Kaitlyn Bailey knew nothing of the Blood Sword – the ancient soul that was Aliel knew it well for she had been there at the time it was conceived. In his earlier conversations with Erin and Brig, John had simply told them that Kaitlyn would know what to do when the time came. He had been relying on oral history passed down through the ages, but this sword was a topic of great uncertainty, having only been speculated on and reduced to legend.

The bloodline, and as such the history handed down, began after the first Keeper had descended, but as John had professed, all of this was occurring based upon an ancient prophetic timetable. The bloodline never knew about the sword as the information had not been communicated to them. Only a mere mention of it was inked on a scroll, but was enough to bring the legend forth.

The Thunder had three children long before the first war ever took place – there was the First Son, Malocere was the second, and Aliel came along third – the only daughter. Malocere had long been jealous of the First Son and had complained to Aliel on multiple occasions that He was weak and unworthy of the title he bore as the first born.

When the war began, it began as most do – a simple discontent among a group large enough to carry out the deed. In the beginning, Malocere fought alongside Aliel, and their victories were many. But somewhere along the line, the rebellion offered Malocere the thing he wanted most – Kingship. He need only betray The Thunder, his siblings, and lead the rebellion to take the throne.

The Thunder's soul had been split to create the children, and since they were of the same soul and breathed the same divine breath, Malocere was unable to kill them, though he never understood why. It was a colossal miscalculation and a fatal flaw in his plan.

It was this betrayal and the negative energy created by it which led to the fragmentation of Reality and ultimately to Malocere's fall. Only after the First Son had descended as the first Keeper and succeeded in reclaiming the key did He and Aliel conceive of the Blood Sword with the blessing of the Thunder, for it was believed by all that the day would come when Malocere would find a way to retake The Upper Afterworld. The Thunder was forced to concede to killing a portion of its own soul and gave its blessing for the creation of the weapon to be wielded by the last Keeper in the Second Great War.

So with the First Son having stepped up and assumed the role as the first Keeper, Aliel readily accepted the charge of being the last, understanding that when the terrible day came, Reality's only hope was that she would call forth the Blood Sword and strike her brother dead. Malocere never found out about the weapon – never imagined a scenario in which The Thunder would agree to such a thing, and that ignorance would serve Aliel well in her task.

The sword was not a physical object at all, but power and a manifestation of will only capable of being brought forth by the last Keeper through the power of the blood – whatever sword she wielded at the time could become the Blood Sword if she merely called upon it. It could never be taken from her for once she relinquished the blade, it would return to its prior state. The only way to squash its power was to kill the Keeper, and without the sword, Malocere could never do that.

And now they stood facing each other – all those millions of years later – each in another form.

Kaitlyn pleaded with him, "Don't make me do this. I swore I would do it, but there has to be another way. Just ask for forgiveness! Can't you do that??"

Malocere raised his sword. "Salvation isn't really my thing." He whipped his hand through the air and knocked Kaitlyn's legs from beneath her again, sending her to the ground on her back before coming down on her through the air plunging his sword towards her chest.

She rolled to safety and his blade buried itself into the dirt. Kaitlyn charged just as he dislodged the weapon and the two locked in combat, exchanging blows and blasts and pulses with dizzying speed. Both leapt into the air and struck at one another before Malocere gained an advantage and drove them both back down where Kaitlyn lay on her back, blocking blow after blow as he hacked his sword down at her with eyes that glowed red with hate from beneath the hooded cloak.

The part that was Aliel came to accept redemption wasn't possible. A swift kick sent Malocere back. He charged again, but Kaitlyn knelt down and slashed with both blades, cutting his feet from his legs, causing him to fall to his knees. She walked up to him and held one sword to his throat. The other she held behind her head, poised to strike.

"Pull back your hood, brother," she commanded. "Let me see you." Malocere pulled the cloak back and when he did, he transformed into the being Aliel knew – the one with whom she'd shared so much over the course of millennia, and it pained her.

She called forth the power of the blood. Streams of energy jetted from Brig, John, and all the others around her as well as bolts of lightning from the sky as it all was absorbed by the sword which glowed red and emitted a hum. Malocere looked upon it, and in the blade he caught a glimpse into the Upper Afterworld – a sight he had not seen in ages. He saw the throne with his father seated upon it and understood it would never be his.

Defeated, defiant eyes turned back to Kaitlyn. "Do it – *Keeper*."

A tear fell from Kaitlyn's eye as Aliel spoke through her. "I loved you. Father loved you. If I kill you, I kill a part of him – a part of myself – a part of our brother! Damn you for making me do this! Damn you for giving me no choice!"

"You hesitate," Malocere hissed. "That's *your* weakness. I was damned long ago."

Kaitlyn screamed and plunged the Blood Sword into Malocere's chest down to the hilt. It bore him through and poked out the back of his cloak still glowing red. Unable to scream, but in unbearable pain, his eyes bulged and he fell to one side, dead at last.

Placing her foot against his chest, Kaitlyn withdrew the sword and kicked the body away. Booms and peals of thunder roared across the sky with the unyielding frequency as Malocere's forces dropped their weapons and fled into the east amid cries of panic.

John walked up to Malocere and thrust his own sword through the gash in his chest. He sawed back and forth until he was able to pry open the ribcage, after which he plunged his arm into the cavity all the way up to his elbow.

"What the hell are you doing?" Brig asked him. "He's dead!"

John didn't answer, but rather continued on with his task. After a few more minutes of furious sawing, he pulled Malocere's heart from the gaping wound and held it high in the air with both hands for all to see. He dropped it onto the ground where Malocere lie motionless in the dust. A whistle summoned his stallion to him and he mounted it, spearing the heart with the tip of his sword as he did. Without a word, he turned and charged back toward the battlefield, screaming a reverberant war cry while holding the heart high in the air like a banner which proclaimed that the enemy's flag had been captured. The Blood Knights raised their swords and cheered. Others pounded their shields with their battleaxes, creating rhythmic, metallic percussion.

With their leader now slain, and the Dark Agents in full retreat, the knights raged forward with relentless aggression, and what was once a battle became a massacre. The deluge of blood grew steadily deeper, and bloodfalls roared over the towering cliffs, sending droplets of red rain showering into the valleys below where they pooled in a sort of swamp which reeked of carnage and death.

The inhabitants of the valleys cupped their hands to collect whatever liquid they could before the gluttonous sand had the opportunity to slurp it up. The damned opened their mouths and drank the corporeal wine of their fallen tormentors until they were all drunk and dancing with ecstasy.

Brig turned his head and saw that the fire in Kaitlyn's eyes had intensified; he knew right away that her task was not yet complete. With Malocere defeated, there was no need for this third of Reality. Kaitlyn twirled the Blood Sword in her hand and drove it deep into the ground, which split open, forming a jagged crack that raced off toward the battlefield with the sound of ice cracking on a thinly frozen pond.

The knights recognized and reacted to the approaching rumble. They all turned and abandoned the battle. Malocere's forces started to celebrate, mistaken in their assumption that they had somehow repelled the invaders. Their jubilation heightened, and the rising volume of their cheers blinded them as to what horror was headed their way.

It wasn't long before their felicity abated. The ground tore open in front of them and continued on until it disappeared over a distant hilltop. The ground shook and rumbled as the once-narrow fissure widened more and more. A few of the Dark Agents tried to leap across the ravine to the other side, but its rate of expansion was far too great, and they were swallowed in the chasm.

Kaitlyn waved her hands above her head and an arc-shaped rift formed in the hellish morning sky which spread to either horizon in the form of a gigantic rainbow. No sooner had the rift touched the ground than the air filled with the collective sound of a million boards breaking in two.

Malocere's forces were so overcome with terror that their screams rose above every other sound. They now understood what was happening, for it too had been prophesized. Still, they had chosen to ignore the warnings of their own demise, choosing instead to believe that they could somehow dodge the inevitable.

They were wrong.

Just as it had been written, their section of The Lower Afterworld peeled away from the other and tumbled into black, boundless space where it would fall forever – a mere speck in the vacuum of time. Now separated from Reality, the Dark Agents were lost to the great abyss just as Tom had been. Brig strained his ears to listen to their cries. Above them all, he swore he could hear Tom's maniacal laughter.

The four moons as well as the red sun fell along with them. The light from each quickly died out and extinguished to a sorrowful shade of black – its only vestige, the faint retinal halos floating within Brig's field of vision, nothing more than ghosts of what once was.

Brig was now standing at the true lip of reality. He took a few steps back, afraid that he too might tumble off into nothing. He looked back to the battlefield where the Blood army had regrouped into a disorganized collection of battle-weary warriors. Their tattered flags still flew in the whistling breeze, and the entire wasteland glowed with the milky, white light pouring in through the hole in the sky. Never again would the punishing rays of the red sun fall upon a single stone in this place.

All eyes turned skyward in response to a booming voice that spoke in a language unknown to mortals. Every Keeper and knight fell to one knee in reverence. Just then, what looked like a funnel cloud of air and light dropped out of the sky and zigzagged its way across the plateau from the direction of the Borderlands where it had picked up the lost souls who were only there by the trickery of Dark Agents.

To Brig it looked like a tornado as bodies swirled around in side of it. Looking back at the army, he saw the funnel cloud headed straight for them and he cried out, "Why don't they run?

Kaitlyn pressed her finger against her lips and said, "Shhh, just watch."

The mysterious twister consumed the army. When it finally lifted off the ground, every knight and Keeper was gone, both the living and the dead. Brig watched it draw back into the sky and disappear into the claw-shaped rift, which sealed itself over, casting the remaining three of them into maddening darkness.

What John and Brig couldn't see was that Kaitlyn had turned to face the east. She began speaking in the same strange language. Not long thereafter, the darkness was pushed aside by the rising of that soothing Second Sun. The first rays peeked over the eastern horizon and the ground shook and shifted with violent seismic quakes. Kaitlyn turned to her father and shouted, "We have to go – NOW! There's no time left!"

The two stallions that Brig and John had ridden trotted up to them. John mounted his, as did Brig, who then pulled Kaitlyn onto his saddle with him. The horses then galloped off away from the destruction, unaffected by the shifting soil beneath their hooves. Brig looked back over his shoulder and watched as chunk after chunk of The Lower Afterworld crumbled and fell into oblivion.

The stallions charged on, faster and faster. Beneath them, the ground appeared as nothing more than a reddish, brimstone blur. The Second Sun was now above the horizon, floating in the onyx sky like a beaming pearl.

"Are we going to make it?" Brig shouted as the lip of one of the many canyons got closer and closer. Now, ten feet from the edge, he shut his eyes, convinced that they were all about to plunge to their deaths.

The stallions leaped into the air, and wings spread out from their sides. Brig and John were forced to grip their saddle horns to keep from falling off. The wings beat the air with tremendous force, gaining even greater speed.

As they drew nearer to the Second Sun, it grew larger in the sky, shimmering with ripples of silver and white. Brig looked down just in time to see the final chunks of The Lower Afterworld break away and vanish into the lonely gloom.

The stallions' wings continued to propel them through the starless void of eternity. The light raging through Kaitlyn's portal was stronger now and the three of them shielded their eyes from it. The horses' nostril flared as they picked up even more speed. Then they dropped their heads as though they were about to ram into a solid object.

The three riders braced themselves for impact, and John called out, "We're almost there! Hold on!!" His stallion took the lead position with Brig and Kaitlyn's falling in closely behind. The leader leaped into the air, springing with its hind legs off of some non-existent surface and jumped through the portal. From behind, the sight made Brig think of tigers jumping through the hoops of fire at the circus, but before he could finish his thought, his stallion had done the same.

Both winged horses emerged into the Earthly Realm high above Jones Chapel, darting back and forth between baby-blue sky and puffy white clouds. As they descended towards the farm, Brig glanced at Kaitlyn – no longer the version of her older self, she had returned to the five year old who clapped her hands and giggled. She held out her arms, pretending to be an airplane, and the clouds curled around her make-believe wings in misty swirls, which only made her giggling intensify. Brig glanced down as they passed over Hillbilly Hill, and his mind couldn't help but think back to their initial confrontation with Malocere on the front steps of The Haunted House.

The stallions flew on until they touched down on the flat, grassy hayfield somewhere near the family cemetery on the far side of the farm. Their hooves hit the ground galloping at breakneck speed, but gradually slowed to a steady trot. The previous pounding sound reduced to a steady *clop…clop… clop.* When they came to a stop, their enormous wings folded back against their sides and their riders dismounted.

Kaitlyn took off skipping through the wildflowers without a care in the world. She held out her arms and pretended to be an airplane again, twirling about in tight circles until she was so dizzy that she fell over and rolled across the ground again and again. Once she'd tired herself of that, she lay on her back and looked up; one of the stallions was standing directly above her. It dropped its head and touched its nose to hers. The little girl laughed and said, "Horsey!"

Brig shot John a puzzled look. "What's wrong with her?" he asked. "I mean, *look at her*! She's acting goofy! You'd think she was a –"

John took the liberty of finishing his sentence for him, "- a five year old?"

Brig covered his mouth and nodded. "She's forgetting, isn't she?"

"I think so," John agreed. "It's a blessing, really."

"How can you say that? Think about it... all she did for me, *for the world*!"

John took hold of his horse's bridle and led the animal over next to Brig. "These were extraordinary times," he said. "She was given the extraordinary ability to handle it all, but the burden of that knowledge is too great for any human to bear for very long, much less a child. The Thunder has given her a gift. It has given her back her childhood. The soul inside her... Aliel, can now rest."

Brig paused to watch his daughter chase a butterfly, as she so often loved to do. There was a simple peace about her – it shone on her face and in her smile. *Perhaps John's right,* he thought. *Maybe it* is *better this way*. He then recalled all the things his father had taught him, and he asked John: "What about us? Will we forget, too?"

John pursed his lips and nodded, all the while staring at the ground. "In time. All things in time."

Brig and John both stroked the sides of the Pegasus-like stallions. The eyes that peered out from beneath the armor, once fiery red and angry were now peaceful and as black as coal and cool with kindness.

Referring to the stallions, John said, "They can't stay here, you know. This world isn't their own."

In a voice so low that it was almost imperceptible, Brig said, "I know." He looked to John and said, "That's one thing I can't figure out. If they're from the spiritual realm, why are they flesh and blood, standing here with us now? Before, everything from the spirit worlds looked like ghosts."

John smiled. "The nature of Reality is changing, my friend. The distinction between what is spirit and what is flesh no longer exists. I suspect there are many surprises yet in store for us. Don't make the mistake of expecting too much too fast. Reality will follow its own timetable, not ours."

With those words, the stallions reared up on their hind legs and neighed. Both John and Brig let go of their bridles, and the animals set off galloping through the hayfield before turning around and heading back towards them. Twenty feet before they reached the spot where Kaitlyn still lay on the ground, they leaped into the air and spread their wings. After one powerful beat of them, the creatures vanished in a brilliant flash, leaving behind only meandering, feather-like clouds, which were rapidly scattered by the springtime breeze.

A few seconds later, Brig asked, "So, what now? Now that the war is won."

"While Malocere's forces may be defeated, you must understand that evil still dwells within the hearts of men. That's where it has always been, *but goodness dwells there, too*. The two are inseparable; they make us what we are – a dichotomy incarnate."

"Do you think things will change?"

John kept his head down and kicked a rock up from the soil using the toe of his boot. "All things change," he said. "We'll just take it in stride. That's all we can ever do."

The three of them began walking towards the tobacco barn on their way to the gravel drive. Brig was having more and more trouble recalling John's name as the minutes passed. By the time they'd reached the drive, more and more memories had fallen away, but he fought with all he had to hold onto them just a while longer.

"Will I ever see you again?" he asked.

"I'm sure we'll meet again. If not in this life, in the next." John pointed to the little girl with the head full of bright, blonde hair and said, "You take care of that little one." He turned and started to walk towards the highway, but stopped and faced Brig again. "When you get back to your house, Erin is going to think that this has all been a dream – soon, you will too. Just let it be so." With that, he walked away and disappeared around the bend.

Indeed, in the weeks and months to come, there would be nights that Brig would awake, his heart pounding with fear and the acidic sensation that something was there with him. He would sense something hiding somewhere within the dark – something with vacant eyes and an icy touch – a lonely wraith that longed only to feel the warm pulse of a living being. By then, he would have forgotten it all; his three days in The Lower Afterworld would have been reduced to little more than a vivid nightmare. And yet, the residual fear would remain like a light bulb's afterimage once the lamp has been turned off – a psychic brand he would never be rid of.

Despite it all, there would still be times, particularly in the wee hours of the morning, when the voices would speak to him. He would eventually come to accept them as part of his reality, and they would often tell him many things. He would never really question any of it, and although he wouldn't quite remember who it had been, he'd recall something that someone had once told him: *A house can absorb a lot of memories... some good, some bad... and memories are like ghosts – they haunt you.*

Wicklow Weekly Standard

Sunday, May 14, 2000

Tragedy in Jones Chapel

By DAVID DUNCAN

JONES CHAPEL This week has been tragic and eventful in the small town of Jones Chapel, beginning with the disappearance of two local teenage girls, Sammi Pridmore and Sarah Oliver. Authorities and volunteers continue the search, but according to anonymous sources, the case remains a mystery.

The search for the girls is likely to be further affected by an apparent murder-suicide at the County Sherriff Department Headquarters that left three officers and one civilian dead. The alleged shooter is thought to be the civilian, and it is further speculated that one of the deceased officers is none other than longtime Sherriff A.J. Usher. The department has refused to release any details citing an ongoing investigation and notification of next of kin.

Another local man, Harvey Palmer, 65, was the victim of what is being reported as an attempted crucifixion while working at his job on the farm owned until recently by the late Gabriel Bailey. No word yet on potential suspects, though rumor has surfaced that a common assailant is suspected in all three of the above incidents. Last report was that Palmer is in critical, but stable condition at Wicklow Memorial Hospital and is expected to make a full recovery.

On Saturday an apparent earthquake measuring 3.3 on the Richter scale struck Jones Chapel, according to the United States Geological Survey. The epicenter of the quake was reported to be near the amusement park known as Hillbilly Hill. Initial reports include structural damage to the parks Haunted House attraction where the front porch appears to have collapsed in addition to some minor roof damage.

A large fissure has been reported in the adjacent parking lot where recovery crews are attempting to extract a pickup truck that had fallen into the crack. While not confirmed, local sources have told us that the license plate on the vehicle in question is registered to Harvey Palmer, which raises more questions.

A blast was reported near the Bailey farm following the quake. No one was injured, and an investigation is underway. No charges are expected to be filed.

Finally, due to the quake, the National Park Service has notified us that all tours at Mammoth Cave have been cancelled indefinitely as Federal Geologists assess the damage to determine what safety threats, if any, exist to the public. The Weekly Standard will continue to report as these situations develop.

Reuters

Jacob Bailey Murder Case Reopened

By BOB STON

Wicklow Authorities have cited that due to new information, a case long-since closed in Jones Chapel has been reopened for investigation.

The Bailey family was quoted as saying that they are most interested in correcting the death certificate. "For too long, foul play and mis-deeds have been swept under the rug by the sheriff's office," Brig Bailey said. "It's time the truth was brought to light and the people of Kentucky learn what has been going on in this town.

The Standard will report once the case has been resolved.

Shorty's Filling Station Up For Sale

Jones Chapel - After years of declining sales, a local icon is now up for sale.

Shorty's 76 station which Shorty Doyle inherited from his father after his passing ten years ago has been put on the market. Recent rennovations and declining tourism have forced the Jones Chapel native to throw in the towel.

"Bank's been breathin' down my neck for three [explicative deleted] months now," Doyle was reported to say. "can't hold them [explicative deleted] off forever. It's time to call it quits."

Several investors have already looked at the property and the sale should commence soon, according to sources.

www.ingramcontent.com/pod-product-compliance
Lightning Source LLC
Chambersburg PA
CBHW020353310726
48979CB00015B/2573/J